TOMBS

EDITED BY

EDWARD E. KRAMER

AND

PETER CROWTHER

WHITE WOLF
PUBLISHING

DEDICATION

This book is respectfully and affectionately dedicated to Kathleen Crowther and Helen Kramer, two remarkable ladies whose constant good humor, dogged determination and treelike patience are inspirations to anthology editors everywhere.

— Pete and Ed

C O N T E N T S

TOMB SWIFT   AN INTRODUCTION (OF SORTS) BY FORREST J ACKERMAN   1-7

IN TRUST   BEN BOVA   8-24

THE AMBER ROOM   IAN WATSON   25-46

THE BUTTERFLY EFFECT   KATHLEEN ANN GOONAN   47-67

EPISTROPHY   MICHAEL BISHOP   68-73

NO ORDINARY CHRISTIAN   MICHAEL MOORCOCK   74-91

WHITE LADY'S GRAVE   LISA TUTTLE   92-103

BURIAL AT SEA   LARRY BOND AND CHRIS CARLSON   104-129

THE UNCHAINED   KATHE KOJA AND BARRY N. MALZBERG   130-136

THE TIME GARDEN   IAN MCDONALD   137-165

HE ON HONEYDEW   STEWART VON ALLMEN   166-172

CITY DEEP   JEREMY DYSON   173-180

BUT NONE I THINK DO THERE EMBRACE   S.P. SOMTOW   181-194

GINANSIA'S RAVISHMENT   CHRISTOPHER FOWLER   195-209

HEARTFIRES   CHARLES DE LINT   210-220

DROWNING WITH OTHERS   GARY A. BRAUNBECK   221-233

STATION OF THE CROSS   COLIN GREENLAND   234-241

QUEEN OF KNIVES   NEIL GAIMAN   242-250

GOD'S BRIGHT LITTLE ENGINE   STEPHEN GALLAGHER   251-263

THE DARKEST DOCTRINE   BRAD LINAWEAVER   264-280

THE LAND OF THE REFLECTED ONES   NANCY A. COLLINS   281-291

THE TEMPTATION OF WILFRED MALACHEY   WILLIAM F. BUCKLEY, JR.   292-312

BLUE FLAME OF A CANDLE   STORM CONSTANTINE   313-333

FORREST J ACKERMAN

TOMB SWIFT

In responding to a heartfelt (even frenzied, perhaps) request from the very venerable editors that I first-foot this tome of tomes, I feel I must dedicate — with profound apologies (hoping to escape lawsuit) — my introductory scribblings to Ib J. Melchior, world-class authority on the Bard of Avon, trusting that a bard in the hand will be worth…well, you'll get the picture, I'm sure.

This brief tale (and its brevity may well be the only thing for which you will thank me when it's done) amounts to not so much an overview on what will follow, but rather an *underview* on what has gone before. And just what *has* gone before? Why, nothing of course. But, in the pages ahead you will find tales of derring-do (an expression I've never quite fathomed) set in forgotten kingdoms, sunken submarines, and even an abandoned space station. And that's only the beginning….

FJA

'Tis a tale told by a microcephalon, replete with cacophony & ferocity, signifying…nada.

TO SLEEP, perchance to dream. The goosequill pen hesitated, its feathered tip still swaying, almost tickling its scribe's noble nose. Then, dipt anew in the inkpot near the artistic right hand, with one broad stroke it slashed through the five still-wet words upon the parchment, and posterity would never know the original intent of the author.

Instead, William Shockspeare thoughtfully composed:
Morpheus, son of Sleep;
Somnus, god of Dreams;
arcane architects of oracular dramas
that doth engage the stage of mind
in nocturnal reveries,
peopled by players who seek not pay
nor praise, performing only to bemuse, arouse,
perchance to horrify with noxious nightmares the
feckless psyche of the dormant dreamer;
Now, I urge thee,
nay, issue ukase to thy ears:
This All Hallows Eve
create for me
a bevy of birth-bare beauties
submissive to my dark desires,
erotic passions;
puissant pulchrinudes
with offertory milken globes
all lactic laden,
ripe cherry-tipt for avid lips'
sweet succulence,
umbilical indentations
enchaliced for my salivating tongue,
pubic portals crowned by
aromatic curl-twined hair d'amour
inviting entry and reentry
into the pinken fleur
d'extasie.
Once consopite,
forbid my leaden lids to open unto dawnlight
till sated body, perspirant with aftermath of sweat
and spastic from ecstatic surge, hath
drainèd been of Eros' sweet spring of
manhood's saponaceous sap, the ethereal

ichor of the gods sprung from my rampant rod
of masculine identity,
my woman-wanton wand,
my lady-killer,
my prince of penile pleasure,
my fountain of fertility,
the midget god fixt
'twixt my groin
whose magic growth befits a giant's cod.
My coruscating cascade will make miniscule the cost
when postly I must cleanse my merry member
and from my soilèd bedsheet
perforce efface the semen-stained
conspicuosity
of my self-wrought carnal satisfaction.

Shockspeare, as was his wont, hesitated a moment upon completion of that which he had so newly writ, ran a questioning ink-stained finger over each adjective, noun and verb, nodded in satisfaction, then read the prose aloud, envisioning its embodiment in the play of which it was now an integral part,

A MAD SUMMER'S NIGHT SCREAM

Other partially completed manuscripts in his distinctive chirography lay in disarray about the chamber of his auctorial pursuits, for it would be said, four centuries hence, that "a tidy desk is the sign of a sick mind," and Shockspeare would one day by scholars and laymen alike be recognized as a genius for all ages, hence entitled to genius's untidiness.

Let us pause now for a brief respite, for I sense you are hesitant to approach the gruesome climax of this tale; let us tarry for the nonce and cast our glance upon the title pages of several other of his not-yet-completed works.
"The Merchant of Transylvania"
A Bloodcurdling Tale of a Vampire
known as Graf Stokera
"Twelfth Night"
and the sequel certain
to be demanded by his audiences,
"Thirteenth Night"
"The Maiming of the Shrew"

(destined to bring roses to the
nether cheeks of many a blushing
actress laid summarily across the
knees of an angry leading man
for a public thrashing)
"Elyson & Madonna"
(originally to have been
"Romeo & Juliet"*)

At this juncture the pet Dalmatian of Bill (I think we know him well enough by now to call him Bill, and in any event he is in no position to object) — Bill's pet Dalmatian, the world's first mutant Dal (he sported but a single spot) — came roisterously romping into the room, barking raucously, and jet-propelled himself (excusing the anachronism) upon his master's lap, voraciously licking Bill's ink-stained beard. (Evidently the playful dog liked the taste of purple ink.) Annoyed by the boisterous beast's intrusion on his inspired thoughts, and short of temper that it had knocked over the inkpot in the bargain**, Bill roughly pushed the unwelcome canine away and growled, "Out, out, damned
Spot!"

⋇◉⋇

IT IS TIME, now, to introduce Frances Bacon, a pivotal person in this tale of cruelty and revenge. She would have been introduced earlier but, as the wise sage of scientifiction Rae Cummings put it, "Time is what keeps everything from happening at once."

Frances Bacon was a tall titian-haired well-proportioned woman, described by Nell's son, Bond, as "flat where it flattered and curved where it mattered," unfortunately in drunken bouts of temper by bellicose Bill "oft-battered," a state which Frances did not equate with equality, she being a neofeminist, a woman before her time. In a future incarnation she would be Marie Shelley,

---

* A small segment of the original holoscript survives and we include it here for the edification of academicians:
Romeo invited Juliet to dine.
The viands were delicious,
The vintage wine divine.
But crossed of eye
Came our star-crossed lover
When expectantly did the waiter hover,
For the bill forced Romeo into debt
And perforce
Romeo'd for what Juliet.
**Upon recommendation of a veterinarian, Bill had purchased a dog whose cost had lightened his purse by but a few inconsequential coins, for he was advised that "a bargain dog never bites."

who wrote "Frankenstone" — and was chagrined that Frankenstone (a monster, he) did not write back. At a still later date there was conjecture as to whether she might be Marion Room Bradley.

Howsomever, in Shockspeare's time she was Bill's paramour — and more: his unacknowledged collaborator, a silent partner who inspired him when his first love, the Muse, was occupied elsewhere. "MacDonald's," "Teatempestpot" ("Tempest in a Teapot") "Queen Leer," "As You Lick It" (his notorious porno-play), "Henry Took the Fifth" and other well-thought-of works attributed to the Bard were, if truth were known (as it now comes out at last), largely, if not entirely, the pain children of silently suffering Frances.

Long and long did the unappreciated lover brood upon the injustice of her relationship with "his Lordship." More and more frequently she vented her wrath with words upon Bill who, from his own quill, produced such famous quotes concerning her anger as "The Devil's lash hath no sting like that of a churlish woman's scorpion-tongue" and "Hell hath no fury like a woman cornered." From childhood on the object of cruel classmates' ridicule ("Your parents are pigs and you are Bacon!"), now a woman grown, Frances thirsted for revenge that no Coca-Cola, Pepsi, Dr Peeper or Spritz could quench. (This is known as poetic licence, which the author regularly renews.)

To quench that thirst she sought out an apothecary of ill repute and purchased from him a vial of "the Nirvana potion" which came in chloro form and beginning in the year 1757 (according to the Oxford Universal Dictionary) would become known as the powerful anesthetic, "ether." Nightly she would lave the glass-blown vial like her lover's erect penis, relishing the day she would unleash its potent contents on a kerchief and press it savagely upon his arrogant face.

At last that fatal day came. He had commenced to write, "Four score and seven years ago a new notion was born upon this continent, that all men are created criminal" but she had assured him the *hoi polloi* would never be able to calculate by scores of 20 and thus the resultant figure of 87 would be better served by the revision which would be utilized and become world-famous as "Seventeen lustrums and two years agone," the opening of the post-Civil War speech of the great Jewish President Abrahm Lincoln, the man whom the assassin shot in the temple.

When it became evident to Frances that Bill was going to appropriate her "Lustrum" speech and claim it as his own, she barely contained herself till nightfall, then, vial of chloroform in hand, she let herself into his dwelling with her latchkey, stealthily crept on little cat's feet into his bedchamber, held her breath as she soaked a rag with the liquid of Lethe and gloatingly smothered his face with ether.

He came to consciousness only long enough to regard her maniacally distorted face glaring down at him like one of the witches in his bewitched play. Then darkness enveloped him like a robe of night.

Frances, a consummate actress, ran screaming from the house and to the home of the village mortician, conveniently located nearby. Awakened from a deep sleep, he gravely listened with only half an ear (this was before the time of the one-eared Asian painter Go-Gan) and allowed himself to be dragged by the (seemingly) berserk and bereaved woman to the abode of Shockspeare, who indeed appeared to be dead although it was more like a state bordering on narcolepsy, which he might have deduced had he been more fully awake. It was a hot and humid night and the mortician agreed that it would be wise to inter the corpse at once lest something (a line from one of Shockspeare's plays) should "smell to high Heaven" or be "rotten as a cheese in Danesland."

An empty coffin in the conveniently nearby cryptorium served the purpose nicely and…Shockspeare was interred alive in a hastily dug grave! The horror of his situation can only be imagined through the fevered brain of the Martian author Agahr Alien Poh in his classic tale of terror, "The Premature Burying," as the effects of the ether wore off and Shockspeare found himself imprisoned beneath the ground, his heaving chest gasping for breath, his eyes bulging in their bloodshot sockets, his frantic fingers clawing at the lid of the coffin, his cries, stifled beneath six feet of newly planted sod, echoing hollowly in his ears.

✦◉✦

LET US NOW approach (cautiously) the opening decade of the 21st century. (Pelvis Presley discovered to be Whoopy Goldenberger in disguise…Mad Donna putting her clothes back on…Talkshow Winford starring in the 10th remake of "The Phantom of the Oprah"…Farwest Actorman doing his 200th film cameo and confessing that he stole the term "sci-fi" from a man who didn't even write science fiction…Civilization threatening to collapse beneath a reign of pseudo-reality Virtrolas.) A puzzle that has intrigued the minds of children for generations is about to be solved: "Who is buried in Grant's tomb?"

Dignitaries from 7212 countries in the nationally splintered world are assembled; telecams from as many countries, including Los Angeles, Texas, Liechtenstein, Andorra and the newly risen island of Atlantis, are trained on the tomb. Master magician David Cooperfeldt has been chosen to mastermind the ceremonies.

The world holds its breath as the tomb creaks open.

A rotting, time-worn wooden coffin, clots of earth clinging like leprous pustules to its warped and fragile frame, stands revealed. Yoggothian green fungi mottle its sides like Hauwardian worms of the earth.

Reverently Cooperfeldt pries open the receptacle that contains the remains of—?

7212 videocams zoom in for an intimate look.

An upraised clawlike skeletal hand is seen. It seems to be pointing to the top of the interior of the coffin. Cooperfeldt cautiously inserts his head.

A gasp is heard. Cooperfeldt turns toward the expectant throng, his face ashen. "A message from the past...scratched inside!" he chokes. "The body in this casket was buried alive! With a ragged bleeding fingernail — some of the brownish congealed blood is still visible — the occupant wrote":

GRANT that the world may one
day know of the grievous
crime committed upon my
recumbent body by the devil woman
Frances Bacon — may her soul
crisp in the flames of Hell!

The reader is left with many unanswered questions. What became of Frances Bacon? (Rumor has it that she married a scribe named Porcine and together they produced a little Hamlet.) How did the body of William Shockspeare become transported across the Atlantic Ocean and come to reside in Grant's tomb? If Colonel Grant was not buried in the tomb bearing his illustrious name, where is he buried? (This may possibly be the basis of another story — but it is not recommended that the reader, like poor Bill, hold his breath.)

And lastly, how did Forrest J Ackerman have the audacity to perpetrate such a hoax upon an unsuspecting public? What skeletons did he rattle in the closets of the anthologists, what Bribe of Frankenstein did he offer to effect the publication of this insult to the intelligence of a two-year-old?* Ah, there are more things under Heaven and Earth, dear Siegfried Freund, than are dreamt of in your psychology.

*Make that one-year-old. I just resigned — Linotypist

IN TRUST

Trust was not a virtue that came easily to Jason Manning.

He had clawed his way to the top of the multinational corporate ladder mainly by refusing to trust anyone: not his business associates, not his rivals or many enemies, not his so-called friends, not any one of his wives and certainly none of his mistresses.

"Trust nobody," his sainted father had told him since childhood, so often that Jason could never remember when the old man had first said it to him.

Jason followed his father's advice so well that by the time he was forty years old he was one of the twelve wealthiest men in America. He had capped his rise to fortune by deposing his father as CEO of the corporation the old man had founded. Dad had looked deathly surprised when Jason pushed him out of his own company. He had foolishly trusted his own son.

So Jason was in a considerable quandary when it finally sank in on him, almost ten years later, that he was about to die.

He did not trust his personal physician's diagnosis, of course. Pancreatic cancer. He couldn't have pancreatic cancer. That's the kind of terrible retribution that nature plays on you when you haven't taken care of your body properly. Jason had never smoked, drank rarely and then only moderately, and since childhood he had eaten his broccoli and all the other healthful foods his mother had set before him. All his adult life he had followed a strict regimen of high fiber, low fat, and aerobic exercise.

"I want a second opinion!" Jason had snapped at his physician.

"Of course," said the sad-faced doctor. He gave Jason the name of the city's top oncologist.

Jason did not trust that recommendation. He sought his own expert.

"Pancreatic cancer," said the head of the city's most prestigious hospital, dolefully.

Jason snorted angrily and swept out of the woman's office, determined to cancel his generous annual contribution to the hospital's charity drive. He took on an alias, flew alone in coach class across the ocean, and had himself checked over by six other doctors in six other countries, never revealing to any of them who he truly was.

Pancreatic cancer.

"It becomes progressively more painful," one of the diagnosticians told him, his face a somber mask of professional concern.

Another warned, "Toward the end, even our best analgesics become virtually useless." And he burst into tears, being an Italian.

Still another doctor, a kindly Swede, gave Jason the name of a suicide expert. "He can help you to ease your departure," said the doctor.

"I can't do that," Jason muttered, almost embarrassed. "I'm a Catholic."

The Swedish doctor sighed understandingly.

On the long flight back home Jason finally admitted to himself that he was indeed facing death, all that broccoli notwithstanding. *For God's sake*, he realized, *I shouldn't even have trusted Mom!* Her and her, "Eat all of it, Jace. It's good for you."

If there was one person in the entire universe that Jason came close to trusting, it was his brother, the priest. So, after spending the better part of a month making certain rather complicated arrangements, Jason had his chauffeur drive him up to the posh Boston suburb where Monsignor Michael Manning served as pastor of St. Raphael's.

Michael took the news somberly. "I guess that's what I can look forward to, then." Michael was five years younger than Jason, and had faithfully followed all his brother's childhood bouts with chicken pox, measles and mumps. As a teenager he had even broken exactly the same bone in his leg as Jason had, five years after his big brother's accident, in the same way: sliding into third base on the same baseball field.

Jason leaned back in the bottle-green leather armchair and stared into the crackling fireplace, noting as he did every time he visited his brother that Michael's priestly vow of poverty had not prevented him from living quite comfortably. The rectory was a marvelous old house, kept in tip-top condition by teams of devoted parishioners, and generously stocked by the local merchants with viands and all sorts of refreshments. On the coffee table between the two brothers rested a silver tray bearing delicate china cups and a fine English teapot filled with steaming herbal tea.

"There's nothing that can be done?" Michael asked, brotherly concern etched into his face.

"Not now," Jason said.

"How long…?"

"Maybe a hundred years, maybe even more."

Michael blinked with confusion. "A hundred years? What're you talking about, Jace?"

"Freezing."

"Freezing?"

"Freezing," Jason repeated. "I'm going to have myself frozen until medical science figures out how to cure pancreatic cancer. Then I'll have myself thawed out and take up my life again."

Michael sat up straighter in his chair. "You can't have yourself frozen, Jace. Not until you're dead."

"I'm not going to sit still and let the cancer kill me," Jason said, thinking of the pain. "I'm going to get a doctor to fix me an injection."

"But that'd be suicide! A mortal sin!"

"I won't be dead forever. Just until they learn how to cure my cancer."

There was fear in Michael's eyes. "Jace, listen to me. Taking a lethal injection is suicide."

"It's got to be done. They can't freeze me while I'm still alive. Even if they could, that would stop my heart just as completely as the injection would and I'd be dead anyway."

"It's still suicide, Jace," Michael insisted, truly upset. "Holy Mother Church teaches—"

"Holy Mother Church is a couple of centuries behind the times," Jason grumbled. "It's not suicide. It's more like a long-term anesthetic."

"You'll be legally dead."

"But not morally dead," Jason insisted.

"Still…" Michael lapsed into silence, pressing his fingers together prayerfully.

"I'm not committing suicide," Jason tried to explain. "I'm just going to sleep for a while. I won't be committing any sin."

Michael had been his brother's confessor since he had been ordained. He had heard his share of sinning.

"You're treading a very fine line, Jace," the monsignor warned his brother.

"The Church has got to learn to deal with the modern world, Mike."

"Yes, perhaps. But I'm thinking of the legal aspects here. Your doctors will have to declare you legally dead, won't they?"

"It's pretty complicated. I have to give myself the injection, otherwise the state can prosecute them for homicide."

"Your state allows assisted suicides, does it?" Michael asked darkly.

"Yes, even though you think it's a sin."

"It is a sin," Michael snapped. "That's not an opinion, that's a fact."

"The Church will change its stand on that, sooner or later," Jason said.

"Never!"

"It's got to! The Church can't lag behind the modern world forever, Mike. It's got to change."

"You can't change morality, Jace. What was true two thousand years ago is still true today."

Jason rubbed at the bridge of his nose. A headache was starting to throb behind his eyes, the way it always did when he and Michael argued.

"Mike, I didn't come here to fight with you."

The monsignor softened immediately. "I'm sorry, Jace. It's just that...you're running a terrible risk. Suppose you're never awakened? Suppose you finally die while you're frozen? Will God consider that you've committed suicide?"

Jason fell back on the retort that always saved him in arguments with his brother. "God's a lot smarter than either one of us, Mike."

Michael smiled ruefully. "Yes, I suppose He is."

"I'm going to do it, Mike. I'm not going to let myself die in agony if I can avoid it."

His brother conceded the matter with a resigned shrug. But then, suddenly, he sat up ramrod straight again.

"What is it?" Jason asked.

"You'll be legally dead?" Michael asked.

"Yes. I told you—"

"Then your will can go to probate."

"No, I won't be..." Jason stared at his brother. "Oh my God!" he gasped. "My estate! I've got to make sure it's kept intact while I'm frozen."

Michael nodded firmly. "You don't want your money gobbled up while you're in the freezer. You'd wake up penniless."

"My children all have their own lawyers," Jason groaned. "My bankers. My ex-wives!"

Jason ran out of the rectory.

Although the doctors had assured him that it would take months before the pain really got severe, Jason could feel the cancer in his gut, growing and feeding on his healthy cells while he desperately tried to arrange his worldly goods so that no one could steal them while he lay frozen in a vat of liquid nitrogen.

His estate was vast. In his will he had left generous sums for each of his five children and each of his five former wives. Although they hated one another, Jason knew that the instant he was frozen they would unite in their greed to break his will and grab the rest of his fortune.

"I need that money," Jason told himself grimly. "I'm not going to wake up penniless a hundred years or so from now."

His corporate legal staff suggested that they hire a firm of estate specialists. The estate specialists told him they needed the advice of the best constitutional lawyers in Washington.

"This is a matter that will inevitably come up before the Supreme Court," the top constitutional lawyer told him. "I mean, we're talking about the legal definition of death here."

"Maybe I shouldn't have myself frozen until the legal definition of death is settled," Jason told him.

The top constitutional lawyer shrugged his expensively clad shoulders. "Then you'd better be prepared to hang around for another ten years or so. These things take time, you know."

Jason did not have ten months, let alone ten years. He gritted his teeth and went ahead with his plans for freezing, while telling his lawyers he wanted his last will and testament made ironclad, foolproof, unbreakable.

They shook their heads in unison, all eight of them, their faces sad as hounds with toothaches.

"There's no such thing as an unbreakable will," the eldest of the lawyers warned Jason. "If your putative heirs have the time—"

"And the money," said one of the younger attorneys.

"Or the prospect of money," added a still younger one.

"Then they stand a good chance of eventually breaking your will."

Jason growled at them.

Inevitably, the word of his illness and of his plan to freeze himself leaked out beyond the confines of his executive suite. After all, no one could be trusted to keep such momentous news a secret. Rumors began to circulate up and down Wall Street. Reporters began sniffing around.

Jason realized that his secret was out in the open when a delegation of bankers invited him to lunch. They were fat, sleek-headed men, such as sleep of nights, yet they looked clearly worried as Jason sat down with them in the oak-paneled private dining room of their exclusive downtown club.

"Is it true?" blurted the youngest of the group. "Are you dying?"

The others around the circular table all feigned embarrassment but leaned forward eagerly to hear Jason's reply.

He spoke bluntly and truthfully to them.

The oldest of the bankers, a lantern-jawed, white-haired woman of stern visage, was equally blunt. "Your various corporations owe our various banks several billions of dollars, Jason."

"That's business," he replied. "Banks loan billions to corporations all the time. Why are you worried?"

"It's the uncertainty of it all!" blurted the youngest one again. "Are you going to be dead or aren't you?"

"I'll be dead for a while," he answered, "but that will be merely a legal fiction. I'll be back."

"Yes," grumbled one of the older bankers. "But when?"

With a shrug, Jason replied, "That, I can't tell you. I don't know."

"And what happens to your corporations in the meantime?"

"What happens to our outstanding loans?"

Jason saw what was in their eyes. Foreclosure. Demand immediate payment. Take possession of the corporate assets and sell them off. The banks would make a handsome profit and his enemies would gleefully carve up his corporate empire among themselves. His estate — based largely on the value of his holdings in his own corporations — would dwindle to nothing.

Jason went back to his sumptuous office and gulped antacids after his lunch with the bankers. Suddenly a woman burst into his office, her hair hardly mussed from struggling past the cadres of secretaries, executive assistants and office managers who guarded Jason's privacy.

Jason looked up from his bottle of medicine, bleary-eyed, as she stepped in and shut the big double doors behind her, a smile of victory on her pert young face. He did not have to ask who she was or why she was invading his office. He instantly recognized that Internal Revenue Service look about her: cunning, knowing, ruthless, sure of her power.

"Can't a man even die without being hounded by the IRS?" he moaned.

She was good-looking, in a feline, predatory sort of way. Reminded him of his second wife. She prowled slowly across the thickly sumptuous carpeting of Jason's office and curled herself into the hand-carved Danish rocker in front of his desk.

"We understand that you are going to have yourself frozen, Mr. Manning." Her voice was a tawny purr.

"I'm dying," he said.

"You still have to pay your back taxes, dead or alive," she said.

"Take it up with my attorneys. That's what I pay them for."

"This is an unusual situation, Mr. Manning. We've never had to deal with a taxpayer who is planning to have himself frozen." She arched a nicely curved brow at him. "This wouldn't be some elaborate scheme to avoid paying your back taxes, would it?"

"Do you think I gave myself cancer just to avoid paying taxes?"

"We'll have to impound all your holdings as soon as you're frozen."

"What?"

"Impound your holdings. Until we can get a court to rule on whether or not you're deliberately trying to evade your tax responsibilities."

"But that would ruin my corporations!" Jason yelled. "It would drive them into the ground."

"Can't be helped," the IRS agent said, blinking lovely golden-brown eyes at him.

"Why don't you just take out a gun and kill me, right here and now?"

She actually smiled. "It's funny, you know. They used to say that the only two certainties in the world are death and taxes. Well, you may be taking the certainty out of death." Her smile vanished and she finished coldly, "But taxes will always be with us, Mr. Manning. Always!"

And with that, she got up from the chair and swept imperiously out of his office.

Jason grabbed the phone and called his insurance agent.

The man was actually the president of Amalgamated Life Assurance Society, Inc., the largest insurance company in Hartford, a city that still styled itself as The Insurance Capital of the World. He and Jason had been friends — well, acquaintances, actually — for decades. Like Jason, the insurance executive had fought his way to the top of his profession, starting out with practically nothing except his father's modest chain of loan offices and his mother's holdings in AT&T.

"It's the best move you can make," the insurance executive assured Jason. "Life insurance is the safest investment in the world. And the benefits, when we pay off, are not taxable."

That warmed Jason's heart. He smiled at the executive's image in his phone's display screen. The man was handsome, his hair silver, his face tanned, his skin taut from the best cosmetic surgery money could buy.

"The premiums," he added, "will be kind of steep, Jace. After all, you've only got a few months to go."

"But I want my estate protected," Jason said. "What if I dump all my possessions into an insurance policy?"

For just a flash of a moment the executive looked as if an angel had given him personal assurance of eternal bliss. "Your entire estate?" he breathed.

"All my worldly goods."

The man smiled broadly, too broadly, Jason thought. "That would be fine," he said, struggling to control himself. "Just fine. We would take excellent care of your estate. No one would be able to lay a finger on it, believe me."

Jason felt the old warning tingle and heard his father's voice whispering to him.

"My estate will be safe in your hands?"

"Perfectly safe," his erstwhile friend assured him.

"We're talking a long time here," Jason said. "I may stay frozen for years and years. A century or more."

"The insurance industry has been around for centuries, Jace. We're the most stable institution in Western civilization."

Just then the phone screen flickered and went gray. Jason thought that they had been cut off. But before he could do anything about it, a young oriental gentleman's face came on the screen, smiling at him.

"I am the new CEO of Amalgamated Life," he said, in perfectly good American English. "How may I help you?"

"What happened to—"

"Amalgamated has been acquired by Lucky Sun Corporation, a division of Bali Entertainment and Gambling, Limited. We are diversifying into the insurance business. Our new corporate headquarters will be in Las Vegas, Nevada. Now then, how may I be of assistance to you?"

Jason screamed and cut the connection.

Who can I trust? he asked himself, over and over again, as his chauffeur drove him to his palatial home, far out in the countryside. *How can I stash my money away where none of the lawyers or tax people can steal it away from me?*

He thought of Snow White sleeping peacefully while the seven dwarfs faithfully watched over her. *I don't have seven dwarfs,* Jason thought, almost in tears. *I don't have anybody. No one at all.*

The assassination attempt nearly solved his problem for him.

He was alone in his big rambling house, except for the servants. As he often did, Jason stood out on the glassed-in back porch, overlooking the beautifully wooded ravine that gave him a clear view of the sunset. Industrial pollution from the distant city made the sky blaze with brilliant reds and oranges. Jason swirled a badly needed whisky in a heavy crystal glass, trying to overcome his feelings of dread as he watched the sun go down.

He knew that there would be precious few sunsets left for him to see. *Okay, so I won't really be dead,* he told himself. *I'll just be frozen for a while. Like going to sleep. I'll wake up later.*

Oh yeah? a voice in his head challenged. *Who's going to wake you up? What makes you think they'll take care of your frozen body for years, for centuries? What's to stop them from pulling the plug on you? Or selling your body to some medical research lab? Or maybe for meat!*

Jason shuddered. He turned abruptly and headed for the door to the house just as a bullet smashed the curving glass where he had been standing an instant earlier.

Pellets of glass showered him. Jason dropped his glass and staggered through the door into the library.

"A sniper?" he yelped out loud. "Out here?"

No, he thought, with a shake of his head. Snipers do their sniping in the inner city or on college campuses or interstate highways. Not out among the homes of the rich and powerful. He called for his butler.

No answer.

He yelled for any one of his servants.

No reply.

He dashed to the phone on the sherry table by the wing chairs tastefully arranged around the fireplace. The phone was dead. He banged on it, but it remained dead. The fireplace burst into cheery flames, startling him so badly that he nearly fell over the sherry table.

Glancing at his wristwatch, Jason saw that it was precisely seven-thirty. The house's computer was still working, he realized. It started the gas-fed fireplace on time. But the phones are out and the servants aren't answering me. And there's a sniper lurking out in the ravine, taking shots at me.

The door to the library opened slowly. Jason's heart crawled up his throat.

"Wixon, it's you!"

Jason's butler was carrying a silver tray in his gloved hands. "Yes sir," he replied in his usual self-effacing whisper.

"Why didn't you answer me when I called for you? Somebody took a shot at me and—"

"Yes sir, I know. I had to go out to the ravine and deal with the man."

"Deal with him?"

"Yes sir," whispered the butler. "He was a professional assassin, hired by your third wife."

"By Jessica?"

"I believe your former wife wanted you killed before your new will is finalized," said the butler.

"Ohhh." Jason sagged into the wing chair. All the strength seemed to evaporate from him.

"I thought you might like a whisky, sir." The butler bent over him and proffered the silver tray. The crystal of the glass caught the firelight like glittering diamonds. Ice cubes tinkled in the glass reassuringly.

"No thanks," said Jason. "I fixed one for myself when I came in."

"Wouldn't you like another, sir?"

"You know I never have more than one." Jason looked up at the butler's face. Wixon had always looked like a wax dummy, his face expressionless. But at the moment, with the firelight playing across his features, he seemed — intent.

"Shouldn't we phone the police?" Jason asked. "I mean, the man tried to kill me."

"That's all taken care of, sir." Wixon edged the tray closer to Jason. "Your drink, sir."

"I don't want another drink, dammit!"

The butler looked disappointed. "I merely thought, with all the excitement…"

Jason dismissed the butler, who left the drink on the table beside him. Alone in the library, Jason stared into the flames of the gas-fed fireplace. The crystal glass glittered and winked at him alluringly. *Maybe another drink is what I need*, Jason told himself. *It's been a hard day.*

He brought the glass to his lips, then stopped. *Wixon knows I never have more than one drink. Why would he…?*

Poison! Jason threw the glass into the fireplace, leaped up from the chair and dashed for the garage. *They're all out to get me! Five wives, five children, ten sets of lawyers, bankers, the IRS — I'm a hunted man!*

Once down in the dimly lit garage he hesitated only for a moment. They might have rigged a bomb in the Ferrari, he told himself. So, instead, he took the gardener's pickup truck.

As he crunched down the long gravel driveway to the main road, all the library windows blew out in a spectacular gas-fed explosion.

By the time he reached his brother's rectory, it was almost midnight. But Jason felt strangely calm, at peace with himself and the untrustworthy world that he would soon be departing.

Jason pounded on the rectory door until Michael's housekeeper, clutching a houserobe to her skinny frame, reluctantly let him in.

"The monsignor's sound asleep," she insisted, with an angry frown.

"Wake him," Jason insisted even more firmly.

She brought him to the study and told him to wait there. The fireplace was cold and dark. The only light in the room came from the green-shaded lamp on Michael's desk. Jason paced back and forth, too wired to sit still.

As soon as Michael padded into the study, in his bedroom slippers and bathrobe, rubbing sleep from his eyes, Jason started to pour out his soul.

"Give your entire estate to the Church?" Michael sank into one of the leather armchairs.

"Yes!" Jason pulled the other chair close to his brother, and leaned forward eagerly. "With certain provisions, of course."

"Provisions."

Jason ticked off on his fingers, "First, I want the Church to oversee the maintenance of my frozen body. I want the Church to guarantee that nobody's going to pull the plug on me."

Michael nodded warily.

"Second, I want the Church to monitor medical research and decide when I should be revived. And by whom."

Nodding again, Michael said, "Go on."

"That's it."

"Those are the only conditions?"

Jason said, "Yes."

Stirring slightly in his chair, Michael asked, "And what does the Church get out of this?"

"Half my estate."

"Half?" Michael's eyebrows rose.

"I think that's fair, don't you? Half of my estate to the Church, the other half waiting for me when I'm revived."

"Uh…how much is it? I mean, how large is your estate?"

With a shrug, Jason said, "I'm not exactly sure. My personal holdings, real estate, liquid assets — should add up to several billion, I'd guess."

"Billion?" Michael stressed the *b*.

"Billion."

Michael gulped.

Jason leaned back in the bottle-green chair and let out a long breath. "Do that for me and the Church can have half of my estate. You could do a lot of good with a billion and some dollars, Mike."

Michael ran a hand across his stubbly chin. "I'll have to speak to the cardinal," he muttered. Then he broke into a slow smile. "By the saints, I'll probably have to take this all the way to the Vatican!"

When Jason awoke, for a startled instant he thought that something had gone wrong with the freezing. He was still lying on the table in the lab, still surrounded by green-coated doctors and technicians. The air felt chill, and he saw a faint icy mist wafting across his field of view.

But then he realized that the ceiling of the lab had been a blank white, while the ceiling above him now glowed with colors. Blinking, focusing, he saw that the ceiling, the walls, the whole room was decorated with incredible Renaissance paintings of saints and angels in beautiful flowing robes of glowing color.

"Where am I?" he asked, his voice a feeble croak. "What year is this?"

"You are safe," said one of the green-masked persons. "You are cured of your disease. The year is *anno domini* two thousand fifty-nine."

Half a century, Jason said to himself. *I've done it! I've slept more than fifty years and they've awakened me and I'm cured and healthy again!* Jason slipped into the sweetest sleep he had ever known. The fact that the man who spoke to him had a distinct foreign accent did not trouble him in the slightest.

Over the next several days Jason submitted to a dozen physical examinations and endless questions by persons he took to be psychologists. When he tried to find out where he was and what the state of the twenty-first-century world might be, he was told, "Later. There will be plenty of time for that later."

His room was small but very pleasant, his bed comfortable. The room's only window looked out on a flourishing garden, lush trees and bright blossoming flowers in brilliant sunlight. The only time it rained was after dark, and Jason began to wonder if the weather was somehow being controlled deliberately.

Slowly he recovered his strength. The nurses wheeled him down a long corridor, its walls and ceilings totally covered with frescoes. The place did not look like a hospital, nor did it smell like one. After nearly a week, he began to take strolls in the garden by himself. The sunshine felt good, warming. He noticed lots of priests and nuns also strolling in the garden, speaking in foreign languages. Of course, Jason told himself, this place must be run by the Church.

It wasn't until he saw a trio of Swiss Guards in their colorful uniforms that he realized he was in the Vatican.

"Yes, it's true," admitted the youthful woman who was the chief psychologist on his recovery team. "We are in the Vatican." She had a soft voice and spoke English with a faint, charming Italian accent.

"But why—?"

She touched his lips with a cool finger. "His Holiness will explain it all to you."

"His Holiness?"

"*Il Papa.* You are going to see him tomorrow."

The Pope.

They gave Jason a new suit of royal blue to wear for his audience with the Pope. Jason showered, shaved, combed his hair, put on the silky new clothing and then waited impatiently. *I'm going to see the Pope!*

Six Swiss Guardsmen, three black-robed priests and a bishop escorted him through the corridors of the Vatican, out into the private garden, through doors and up staircases. Jason caught a glimpse of long lines of tourists in the distance, but this part of the Vatican was off-limits to them.

At last they ushered him into a small private office. Except for a set of French windows, its walls were covered with frescoes by Raphael. In the center of the marble floor stood an elaborately carved desk. No other furniture in the room. Behind the desk was a small door, hardly noticeable because the paintings masked it almost perfectly. Jason stood up straight in front of the unoccupied desk as the Swiss Guards, priests and bishop arrayed themselves behind him. Then the small door swung open and the Pope, in radiant white robes, entered the room.

It was Michael.

Jason's knees almost buckled when he saw his brother. He was older, but not that much. His hair had gone white, but his face seemed almost the same, just a few more crinkles around the corners of his eyes and mouth. Mike's light-blue eyes were still clear, alert. He stood erect and strong. He looked a hale and vigorous sixty or so, not the ninety-odd years that Jason knew he would have to be.

"Mike?" Jason felt bewildered, staring at this man in the white robes of the Pope. "Mike, is it really you?"

"It's me, Jace."

For a confused moment Jason did not know what to do. He thought he should kneel to the Pope, kiss his ring, show some sign of respect and reverence. But how can it be Mike, how can he be so young if fifty years have gone by?

Then Pope Michael I, beaming at his brother, held out his arms to Jason. And Jason rushed into his brother's arms and let Mike embrace him.

"Please leave us alone," said the Pope to his entourage. The phalanx of priests and guards flowed out of the room, silent except for a faint swishing of black robes.

"Mike? You're the Pope?" Jason could hardly believe it.

"Thanks to you, Jace." Mike's voice was firm and strong, a voice accustomed to authority.

"And you look — how old are you now?"

"Ninety-seven." Michael laughed. "I know I don't look it. There've been a lot of improvements in medicine, thanks to you."

"Me?"

"You started things, Jace. Started me on the road that's led here. You've changed the world, changed it far more than either of us could have guessed back in the old days."

Jason felt weak in the knees. "I don't understand."

Wrapping a strong arm around his brother's shoulders, Pope Michael I led Jason to the French windows. They stepped out onto a small balcony. Jason saw that they were up so high it made him feel a little giddy. The city of Rome lay all around them: magnificent buildings bathed in warm sunshine beaming down from a brilliant clear blue sky. Birds chirped happily from the nearby trees. Church bells rang in the distance.

"Listen," said Michael.

"To what?"

"To what you don't hear."

Jason looked closely at his brother. "Have you gone into Zen or something?"

Michael laughed. "Jace, you don't hear automobile engines, do you? We use electrical cars now, clean and quiet. You don't hear horns or people cursing at each other. Everyone's much more polite, much more respectful. And look at the air! It's clean. No smog or pollution."

Jason nodded numbly. "Things have come a long way since I went under."

"Thanks to you," Michael said again.

"I don't understand."

"You revitalized the Church, Jace. And Holy Mother Church has revitalized Western civilization. We've entered a new age, an age of faith, an age of morality and obedience to the law."

Jason felt overwhelmed. "I revitalized the Church?"

"Your idea of entrusting your estate to the Church. I got to thinking about that. Soon I began spreading the word that the Church was the only institution in the whole world that could be trusted to look after freezees—"

"Freezees?"

"People who've had themselves frozen. That's what they're called now."

"Freezees." It sounded to Jason like an ice-cream treat he had known when he was a kid.

"You hit the right button, Jace," Michael went on, grasping the stone balustrade of the balcony in both hands. "Holy Mother Church has the integrity to look after the freezees while they're helpless, and the endurance to take care of them for centuries, millennia, if necessary."

"But how did that change everything?"

Michael grinned at him. "You, of all people, should be able to figure that out."

"Money," said Jason.

Pope Michael nodded vigorously. "The rich came to us to take care of them while they were frozen. You gave us half your estate; many of the others gave us a lot more. The more desperate they were, the more they offered. We never haggled; we took whatever they were willing to give. Do you have any idea of how much money flowed into the Church? Not just billions, Jace. Trillions! Trillions of dollars."

Jason thought of how much compound interest could accrue in half a century. "How much am I worth now?" he asked.

His brother ignored him. "With all that money came power, Jace. Real power. Power to move politicians. Power to control whole nations. With that power came authority. The Church reasserted itself as the moral leader of the Western world. The people were ready for moral leadership. They needed it and we provided it. The old evil ways are gone, Jace. Banished."

"Yes, but how much—"

"We spent wisely," the Pope continued, his eyes glowing. "We invested in the future. We started to rebuild the world and that gained us the gratitude and loyalty of half the world."

"What should I invest in now?" Jason asked.

Michael turned slightly away from him. "There's a new morality out there, a new world of faith and respect for authority. The world you knew is gone forever, Jace. We've ended hunger. We've stabilized the world's population — *without* artificial birth control."

Jason could not help smiling at his brother. "You're still against contraception."

"Some things don't change. A sin is still a sin."

"You thought temporary suicide was a sin," Jason reminded him.

"It still is," said the Pope, utterly serious.

"But you help people to freeze themselves! You just told me—"

Michael put a hand on Jason's shoulder. "Jace, just because those poor frightened souls entrust their money to Holy Mother Church doesn't mean that they're not committing a mortal sin when they kill themselves."

"But it's not suicide! I'm here, I'm alive again!"

"Legally, you're dead."

"But that—" Jason's breath caught in his throat. He did not like the glitter in Michael's eye.

"Holy Mother Church cannot condone suicide, Jace."

"But you benefit from it!"

"God moves in mysterious ways. We use the money that sinners bestow upon us to help make the world a better place. But they are still sinners."

A terrible realization was beginning to take shape in Jason's frightened mind. "How…how many freezees have you revived?" he asked in a trembling voice.

"You are the first," his brother answered. "And the last."

"But you can't leave them frozen! You promised to revive them!"

Pope Michael shook his head slowly, a look on his face more of pity than sorrow. "We promised to revive you, Jace. We made no such promises to the rest of them. We agreed only to look after them and maintain them until they could be cured of whatever it was that killed them."

"But that means you've got to revive them."

A wintry smile touched the corners of the Pope's lips. "No, it does not. The contract is quite specific. Our best lawyers have honed it to perfection. Many of them are Jesuits, you know. The contract gives the Church the authority to decide when to revive them. We keep them frozen."

Jason could feel his heart thumping against his ribs. "But why would anybody come to you to be frozen when nobody's been revived? Don't they realize—"

"No, they don't realize, Jace. That's the most beautiful part of it. We control the media very thoroughly. And when a person is facing the certainty of death, you would be shocked at how few questions are asked. We offer life after death, just as we always have. They interpret our offer in their own way."

Jason sagged against the stone balustrade. "You mean that even with all the advances in medicine you've made, they still haven't gotten wise?"

"Despite all our medical advances, people still die. And the rich still want to avoid it, if they can. That's when they run to us."

"And you screw them out of their money."

Michael's face hardened. "Jace, the Church has scrupulously kept its end of our bargain with you. We have kept watch over you for more than half a century, and we revived you as soon as your disease became curable, just as I agreed to. But what good does a new life do you when your immortal soul is in danger of damnation?"

"I didn't commit suicide," Jason insisted.

"What you have done — what all the freezees have done — is considered suicide in every court of the Western world."

"The Church controls the courts?"

"All of them," Michael replied. He heaved a sad, patient sigh, then said, "Holy Mother Church's mission is to save souls, not bodies. We're going to save your soul, Jace. Now."

Jason saw that the six Swiss Guards were standing by the French windows, waiting for him.

"You've been through it before, Jace," his brother told him. "You won't feel a thing."

Terrified, Jason shrieked, "You're going to murder me?"

"It isn't murder, Jace. We're simply going to freeze you again. You'll go down into the catacombs with all the others."

"But I'm cured, dammit! I'm all right now!"

"It's for the salvation of your soul, Jace. It's your penance for committing the sin of suicide."

"You're freezing me so you can keep all my money! You're keeping all the others frozen so you can keep their money, too!"

"It's for their own good," said Pope Michael. He nodded to the guards, who stepped onto the balcony and took Jason in their grasp.

"It's like the goddamned Inquisition!" Jason yelled. "Burning people at the stake to save their souls!"

"It's for the best, Jace," Pope Michael I said as the guards dragged Jason away. "It's for the good of the world. It's for the good of the Church, for the good of your immortal soul."

Struggling against the guards, Jason pleaded, "How long will you keep me under? When will you revive me again?"

The Pope shrugged. "Holy Mother Church has lasted more than two thousand years, Jace. But what's a millennium or two when you're waiting for the final trump?"

"Mike!" Jason howled. "For God's sake!"

"God's a lot smarter than both of us," Michael said grimly. "Trust me."

(With special thanks to Michael Bienes.)

THE AMBER ROOM

nd I saw her fall from the sky.
The failed hang glider had begun to spin like a sycamore seed. Then the sail snapped upward at the keel and became a plunging V. At this point she must have pulled the handle of the parachute. The chute failed to separate from her harness. Orange nylon blossomed but was trapped.

I saw Amber fall. That was my intimate name for Isabelle because of the tan of her skin and the beads of her nipples. I watched her plummet to earth.

Afterward I wept for her just as Phaeton's sisters wept for their brother after he was hurled from the sky because he flew the sun-chariot crazily. But my tears were only salt water. They didn't harden into amber. Not as yet…

I must have been eleven when I first began to dream of flying. In my dreams I soared above the ripe cornfields of the English West Country underneath a wing. The wing was smooth, not feathered. I wasn't a bird.

In the sky of my dreams the sun was a golden ball, a rich warm aromatic sphere, the quintessence of harvest. I believed I had identified the true substance of that sun when my grandmother, Gran-Annie, showed me a large bead of amber.

The fields beneath me were imprinted with patterns suggestive of runes or astrological symbols. I honestly can't recall whether "crop circles," so called, had already begun to appear in genuine fields. A memory isn't like a leaf perfectly preserved in amber for all time. We don't remember a past event in itself, but rather our memory of that event. Subsequently we remember the memory of a memory. Thus our mind forever updates itself. Essentially memories are fictions. Each time that we suppose we are remembering, these fictions are being rewritten within ourselves, with ourselves as heroes or victims.

When my dreams began, crop circles were probably already materializing overnight in cornfields. Maybe this had been happening on and off for centuries rather than my dreams being any sort of anticipation of the phenomenon. Later, these circles became a temporary media sensation.

What wild stories there were in the newspapers! The patterns must be enigmatic attempts at communication on the part of some alien intelligence! Or possibly archetypal imagery was being stamped upon patches of plants by some kind of collective planetary mind....

Even to my immature mind I'm sure that speculations of this sort would have seemed nutty. Surely those convolutions in the crops were none other than the wind itself made visible. Eddies and swirls and turbulence. Did not the wind forever comb the hair of corn, gently or roughly? All the air of the world was akin to the skin of a body, ceaselessly rippling and flexing, sweating or shivering. Air is a vast living organ, though a mindless one.

Surely no one could fall from such a dreamy sky? Surely no one could plunge to earth, and die?

In due course I took up hang gliding passionately. Soon I was equipped with a degree in engineering, with a specialty in aerodynamics. Passion became profession. With Max Palmer as partner I founded a fledgling company to design and build new high-performance hang gliders: craft with wider spans and nose angles, with tighter sails and more battens to camber the roached trailing edges of the airfoil (to be technical for a moment).

Maxburn Airfoils combined Max's first name with my surname, suggesting flying feats at the leading edge of possibility. Max Palmer and Peter Burn: two aces. It was financial backing from Max's family that allowed us to set up, thus his name preceded mine. The company fledged and soared. We even carried out some design consultancy work for NASA, honey upon the bread and butter of our regular manufacturing. Usually I wore Gran-Annie's bead as a pendant around my neck in place of a tie.

Surely no one could fall.

Until I fell in love — or in lust — with Max's Isabelle. Until Isabelle — until Amber — fell.

A hang glider pilot aims to see the invisible. He or she watches wind. At first, to do so, he throws dry grasses. He kicks dust. He eyes the flutter of a ribbon, the ripple of treetops, the progress of smoke and clouds. Eventually, for a few of us, an extra perception is born.

As a boy a premonition of this perception showed me the words of wind written upon the fields. In the ghastly wake of Isabelle's death, impassioned perception took me to Kaliningrad on the Baltic coast in search of the lost room of amber — the lost room of Amber herself. I'd begun to dream of finding that room, and my lost love within it.

An entire room wrought of amber!

Gran-Annie first told me the tale. The central luminary of my dreams was a sphere of smoldering amber, so naturally I was enthralled. I concocted various boyish adventure fantasies about finding the room. But it was only after Isabelle died that I began to dream repeatedly of doing so in an airborne context. The room had bizarrely replaced the crop circles. Mountains replaced fields as a setting.

My German grandmother had been dead for five years, but I soon reacquainted myself with all the details of the story.

The creation of the amber room began in the year 1702 in Denmark. There were some disagreements and delays, but by 1713 the amber room was on display in Berlin, either gloriously or partially, when Peter the Great visited Frederick. The ebullient Tsar was so enchanted that Frederick could do no other than make a gift of the whole caboodle to Peter.

Off to the Winter Palace in St. Petersburg went sleighloads of crates containing wall panels, pediments, turned corners, embellishments, rosettes, etc.

In 1755 Empress Elizabeth had the room transferred to the Summer Palace at Tsarskoe Selo. Finishing touches were still being made as late as 1763 — culminating in one of the wonders of the world. Visitors expressed their sense of stepping into a dream or fantasy.

Although constructed by human hands, surely that room did indeed partake of otherness. Such golden luminosity! Such mosaic contrasts of yellows and honey-browns and caramels and clear reds. Such a wealth of carvings: of Roman landscapes allegorizing the human senses, and of flowers and garlands and of tiny figures (as if seen from high in the air) and of trees. Such mirrors, such chandeliers dripping amber lusters. Amazing, the parquet floor. Ravishing, the allegorical ceiling.

In 1941, eight years after Gran-Annie's parents fled with her from Germany, Nazi armies were about to lay siege to Leningrad. Art treasures were being evacuated to vaults in the Urals — but the Germans overran the Summer Palace. They dismantled the amber room and shipped it to Königsberg Castle. There, it was reassembled under the eye of the director of the Prussian Fine Arts Museum, a certain Dr. Alfred Rohde. (It was from seven hundred kilometers farther west, from Hannover, that Gran-Annie's parents had emigrated to England.)

Within a couple of years loot filled Königsberg Castle to the bursting point. But British bombs were raining down. Dismantled once more, the room departed — and so likewise did Rohde. Königsberg Castle was wrecked; Königsberg was overrun, and would soon become Kaliningrad — politically a district of Russia but separated by the three Baltic republics.

Strangely, Dr. Rohde returned to his post. He cooperated freely with the Soviet occupation forces. Yet he disclaimed any knowledge of the whereabouts of this wonder of the world. Soon after Dr. Rohde's return, he and his wife both died suddenly. According to their death certificates the cause was dysentery. These documents were signed by a Dr. Paul Erdman — but when the KGB investigated they could find no trace of any such doctor.

There is such a thing as disinformation....

The Nazis had a fetish about mountains as last redoubts — about Eagle's Nests, and high eyries. Wouldn't the perfect place to hide the amber room be a mountain range, through which aircraft could not easily maneuver and which advancing tanks would avoid? My dreams imposed upon me the conviction that this was so, and that the hiding place could only be found from the air, birdlike, Godlike, in solitary flight. When I contemplated finding that missing room I was a boy again, enraptured.

Thus might Amber's death be exorcised.

Naturally I didn't talk to Max about this method of coping with tragedy. He had his own means of handling grief. Max immersed himself in design work — especially as regards the catastrophic failure of the airfoil which had plunged Isabelle to her death. I was fairly sure that he would search in vain for the cause. His feel for gliders — at the edge of possibility — was less than mine. I'd always been able to reach that little way beyond him. Now I would reach a long way, from England to former East Prussia.

I simply had to visit the last known location of the amber room. Surely I would meet some aficionado of amber who knew more than I could find out in England. Close to Kaliningrad was the seaside town of Yantarny — literally, *Amberville*. That's the source of ninety percent of the world's present-day supply of amber. If you rub amber, it develops a static electric charge. Kaliningrad was drawing me like a magnet.

I told Max that I was going to Germany to revisit my grandmother's roots and to investigate the possibility of exporting hang gliders. I wouldn't try to fool him into thinking that I hoped to sell our products in those lake-strewn, boggy *Baltic* flatlands, where the economies are bumping awkwardly along. Thanks to Gran-Annie I was fluent in German. If English wasn't spoken much in Kaliningrad, German should be a reasonable bet. After the Second World War, most of the German population of Kaliningrad had either been killed, expelled or deported to Siberia, but since the demise of the Soviet Union, Kaliningrad had become a free port, designed to draw prosperity, and the closest source of prosperity was Germany.

With a sail secured on top of the Range Rover, I drove through Germany, then Poland. In Warsaw I was obliged to garage my transport. Whatever its free port status, the Kaliningrad region was militarily sensitive due to being the most westerly redoubt of the rump of Russia. The Polish border wasn't open to ordinary civilian road traffic — and I hardly intended to emulate Matthias Russ, or whatever his name was, by hang gliding my way into the area.

Ach: those Baltic flatlands! The nearest mountains were the Carpathians. A tidy way to the south, they sprawl across a thousand kilometers from Poland to Slovakia and into Romania. The amber room had to be somewhere in the Carpathians. But without some clue to guide him, even a person of special perception could spend ten years searching that range from the air.

I allowed myself two weeks. A longer absence would amount to a betrayal of Max, and of Maxburn Airfoils too.

I had seen Amber fall from the sky.

I flew to Kaliningrad on a newly inaugurated direct flight from Warsaw, and on the way through Immigration I had an encounter that was to prove crucial.

Manning the desk were a fresh-faced young officer and a sallow older colleague whose high cheekbones and absence of epicanthic folds proclaimed Mongol blood in his ancestry

Now, I'd opted for a tourist visa, which meant that I'd been obliged to arrange for my accommodations expensively in advance. Intourist in London had tried to book me in a so-called "floating palace" on the river in the center of the city: a couple of cruise ships were permanently moored to house tourists in lieu of modern luxury hotels. The month of May was an excellent time to stay in one of those, supposedly.

I didn't wish to be cooped up where my comings and goings could be monitored. And what was this business about the month of May? Further questioning of the Intourist lady, who had actually visited Kaliningrad, disclosed that in May the weather wouldn't be scorching, consequently I could keep the porthole of my cabin shut. The river, it seemed, stank somewhat. I opted instead for a hotel on terra firma several kilometers from the city center. The Baltika was very popular with tour companies, I was assured.

The younger immigration officer wanted to see how much money I had with me. This seemed an American sort of question in this city where all hard currencies were legal tender nowadays. Despite having prepaid for my hotel, did I have enough to support myself during my stay? I did have enough, and more. Much more.

He eyed my amber pendant. "Are you here to buy jewelry?" he demanded. "Your passport says you are an engineer."

We were speaking German. The older man interrupted to point out that I seemed to be fluent in German, whereas my passport was British.

"My *Grossmutter* came from Germany," I told him.

"From so-called Northern East Prussia, Herr Burn?" Did I detect a note of nationalist displeasure? "Nördliche Ostpreussen" was how Germans still referred to Kaliningrad Oblast.

"No, she came from Hannover. She fled from the Nazis in '34. She hated Nazis."

The man smiled, then.

"Is an engineer here to buy jewelry?" persisted the junior officer. Why the quiz? Amber is hardly gold or rubies. Who would wish to smuggle it? As I understood it, the bottom had virtually fallen out of the Western market for amber. With the disintegration of the superpower, any wannabee Russian rock group would bring out a haversack full of the stuff to pay their way. Maybe my fellow passengers — principally Poles — weren't as interesting as myself to interrogate. Or maybe obstructiveness still lingered here.

"I'm fascinated by the history of the amber room," I said — a harmless enough admission, not to mention being the truth.

The young man looked blank. "The amber room?" I suppose you might meet a native of London who hasn't the foggiest idea where the Crown Jewels are housed. The other officer spoke rapidly in Russian, enlightening his colleague.

To recover from chagrin, the young officer inquired what sort of engineer I was, and when I specified hang gliders the older man reached for my passport and my hotel confirmation with such an impetuous hand that he actually knocked the documents off the desk. I would have picked these up myself but he stepped swiftly out to do so. As he rose, his lapel bulged and I noticed a badge pinned to the inside where it wouldn't normally be seen. A disc, the size of a small coin, bore a double-headed eagle. The old imperial eagle, emblem of the Tsars... He must be a nationalist — of a far-out eccentric royalist stripe. All sorts of strange creatures had crawled out of the woodwork when the Soviet Union fell apart.

I was irritated by the delay. But also I felt suddenly *possessed*, in that moment, by my dream perception — galvanized and beguiled. The words jerked out of me almost inadvertently:

"Maybe," I burbled, "a hang glider pilot can find the lost amber room, wherever it is!" Then I laughed dismissively.

In fact, the young officer had had my best interests at heart. If I was going to be carrying a lot of money around, it might be sensible to hire a driver, an interpreter, an escort, if I followed his drift. A reliable and discreet man from a private security company. Kaliningrad wasn't awash with crime to the extent, alas, of Moscow or St. Petersburg. Yet even so! A word to the wise. He produced a little printed card with an address and phone number and wrote a name on the back.

"My name. Tell them that I recommended you—"

No doubt for a percentage of the fee which I would be paying…

The older man didn't want me to take the card. He became quite vociferous, in Russian. Maybe he viewed this as an insult to his nation. I think he would have confiscated the card if this had been within his power.

Thus it was that I acquired Pavel as a minder and guide for my stay in Kaliningrad.

The fellow bore quite a resemblance to me — though this was purely coincidental. Both of us were only of medium height, though big-boned. We were both endowed with freckles and curly gingery hair and light blue eyes. Somewhere in Pavel's ancestry there must have been a Viking or two. He could have served as a double for me if he had exchanged his cheap leather jacket for my more fashionable anorak, and had donned the amber pendant. He carried a registered firearm, and was discretion itself as regards my business. Maybe his employers supplied a pamphlet on "How to be a Minder." Rule one: Maintain a bland facade. Of course, to begin with it would have seemed that he was merely minding a tourist with a particular interest in amber.

Next day, he collected me from the Baltika in a dark-green Mercedes with lots of kilometers on the clock. Its bodywork might be green but its exhaust emissions no longer were. Actually, the local petrol was at fault. The streets of this dreary city which had risen upon the ruins of grand old Königsberg were full of fumes. The river was indeed as black and murky as old engine oil. Bleak wastelands punctuated some remarkably ugly Soviet architecture. The old Cathedral was a shell, though some scaffolding hinted at possible restoration. The castle, where Dr. Rohde had stored the room, had been a shell — until it was demolished by dynamite to make way for a House of Soviets which, Pavel remarked, was too ugly for anyone ever to have the gall to complete.

Pavel pointed out a certain pink building beside the North Station, which had been the KGB headquarters. That's where he had worked until he had privatized himself. I suppose this admission exonerated him from being any sort of informer nowadays.

We visited the Amber Museum, which was located in a burly red brick tower. That tower was one of the survivors of war, as were a number of city gates and bastions. Personally I found the museum mediocre, showcasing too much modern jewelry. Through Pavel I quizzed the dumpy lady director, who spoke no German, about the amber room.

She believed the submarine story.

I asked her about Rohde's death. On this topic she had no opinions.

I told her that I was researching a thriller which I had long yearned to write on account of my German grandmother. This cover story had occurred to me after my experience at the airport. I would announce my ambition blatantly — but in the guise of fiction. I aimed to write a story about a hang glider pilot who hunts for, and finds, the lost amber room in a mountainous Nazi hiding place. I assured the lady director that I was interested in any hypothesis, however fantastic.

However, fantasy wasn't her forte. "Herr Burn," she lectured me (via Pavel), "have you not noticed the blinds at all the windows? Have you not seen how thick the glass display cases are? Sunlight degrades amber over a relatively modest time. Amber is chemically a bitumen. Air oxidizes it until it is so brittle that it can disintegrate into a pile of dust. You speak of the amber room being kept in the open somewhere, fully assembled, exposed to wind and sunlight? What stupidity."

Absolutely the room must be out in the open, three-dimensionally, beneath the sky, not packed flat in cases in some cavern! The parquet floor, the great wall panels, the allegorical ceiling dangling its chandeliers: all must be erected and connected, and suffusing and refracting golden light. How else could it conform to my dream? How else could Amber herself be waiting in the room?

"Sheer stupidity."

My interview was at an end.

I went with Pavel to a shop specializing in amber jewelry on Leninsky prospekt, and then to another on prospekt Mira. Despite our proximity to Yantarny — to *Amberville-by-the-sea* — there was a dearth of decent merchandise on display. The proprietor of the first shop became brusque when he grasped that I wasn't interested in buying anything but only in wasting his time with fanciful questions. The manager of the second was eager that I should include the exact address of his premises in my prospective best-seller — which in his opinion ought to be about an attempt to refloat the torpedoed ship, in the style of *Raise the Titanic*, and featuring neo-Nazi conspirators. He urged me to visit the Bunker Museum near the university. That bunker was the command post of Hitler's Reich until the Red Army overran the devastated city. Part of it had been left completely untouched since the day the surrender was signed in it. Such ghosts, Herr Burn, such echoes of the past. Perfect atmosphere for a best-seller.

I wouldn't visit the damned bunker. But Yantarny, yes — I would go there the very next day. At the source of amber I might find some better pointer. Back in the car again, in our cocoon amidst the pollution, Pavel explained that visits to Yantarny were a slightly sensitive matter.

"You see, foreigners can only buy a train ticket to Yantarny if they have a special document...."

My heart sank. "Is it a military zone?"

No, it wasn't. Just along the coast at Baltiysk was a huge naval base. Baltiysk was a restricted area — though nowadays sightseeing visits could even be arranged. For commercial reasons Yantarny was somewhat out of bounds to independent travelers.

"*Somewhat* out of bounds," stressed Pavel. "I could drive you there, but it might be wiser to join a group tour."

He would arrange this. He would accompany me. Even so, at Yantarny I wouldn't be able to visit the workings or the beach. Those were fully out of bounds. I would only be able to gawk at pipelines through which quarried earth and amber were pumped across the town to be separated, and the amber cleaned.

Damnation. Still, did I really need to inspect those workings, like some commercial spy?

I never did get to Yantarny. Back at the Baltika, to my surprise, a message was waiting for me — to telephone a certain number.

Did the proprietor of the amber shop have some new suggestion for my best-seller about sunken treasure? Or, after a change of heart, was it the lady director of the museum who wanted to speak to me?

Not in the least. It proved to be the older immigration officer, who had noted where I was staying. Would I meet him and some friends for a meal and drinks at a restaurant on Leninsky to discuss a matter of mutual interest? But of course. And by the way, had I taken his young colleague's advice regarding a chaperon? Why yes, I had. In that case my minder must remain in the car. This matter was confidential.

The restaurant was very noisy due to the constant loud dance music. This entertainment rendered eavesdropping virtually impossible. It wasn't merely face-to-face but almost nose-to-nose that I met Rylov the immigration officer, and Antonov, and a nameless gentleman, over German beer and fried chicken.

Antonov was of the hefty breed. 58-inch chest and 50-inch waist, with a puce suit to match, crumpled though of decent tailoring. Mongol genes — and tissue courtesy of carbohydrate. He had to be a member of the Kaliningrad mafia. At first I thought that he was here as muscle, a bodyguard for the man with no name. In fact Antonov spoke English well, and was as much a part of this as Rylov or the Enigma. Mr. Mystery was in his seventies: dapper, with close-cropped silvery hair, and of refined features. The heavy, tinted, thick-lensed glasses he wore might have been due to weak eyes but they gave him the appearance of an aristocratic interrogator — though he left the interrogating to Antonov. He gave the appearance of understanding German and English but only spoke, from time to time, in Russian. During our encounter he smoked a dozen of those fragrant cigarettes consisting principally of a cardboard tube.

"So you believe that the pilot of a hang glider can find the lost room?" Antonov said to me.

"Somewhere in the Carpathians," I replied. Mr. Mystery sucked his cigarette, then rapped out something in Russian.

The story which I'd adopted bubbled forth. I was researching a thriller.

Antonov eyed me. "And the room shall appear nakedly out in the open? Without any framework or corset to support it?"

My dream inundated me. "It must. It has to. How else can the flier find it?"

"Ah," said Antonov. "And you are the flier."

"I do fly, that's true."

His next remark amazed me. "Maybe it needs a special perception to find the room."

I must have gaped at him.

Rylov said in halting English, "You not truly *write* novel. To write novel is a lie. You want to find the room." The dance music bawled around me, isolating us in a mad oasis. "*Why* you want to find room, Herr Burn? Because of treasure value?"

"*No!*"

Because Amber fell from the sky. Because she beckoned me from within the golden room. I fingered my talisman.

"It's a personal matter," I said. "An emotional matter." I hesitated before confessing: "I dream. I dream of finding it."

"By magic," said Antonov. I thought he was mocking me. Yet the next minute he began to discourse about the Third Reich and about psychics. For a while I imagined that he might be proposing a new plot for my phantom novel. Now that communism and state atheism had collapsed, was not occultism all the vogue in Russia?

Accompanied by nods from Mr. Mystery, Antonov explained, "The Nazis persecuted most occultists, Mr. Burn, yet some they pampered...."

Seemingly the German navy had financed a major scientific expedition to the Baltic in hopes of determining by radar the concave curvature of the Hollow Earth. The inglorious failure of this demented project did not deter the Naval Research Institute in Berlin from lavishing the finest wines and cigars upon psychics while those visionaries swung pendulums over charts of the Atlantic — this, in response to mounting losses of U-boats. And who knew what had been the upshot of the Nazi-sponsored psychic expedition in Tibet?

The point of all of this was that Antonov and his associates had evidence of a rite being performed within the amber room in Königsberg Castle under the eye of Dr. Alfred Rohde and a high-ranking Nazi — with the aim of concealing the future whereabouts of the room. The otherworldly treasure would be hidden amidst mountains, of course — I was right on that account — but also in some veiled domain adjacent to the mundane world...until someone of vision could rediscover it with suitable aid.

"The name of the doctor who poisoned Rohde and his wife was Erdmann, Mr. Burn. The name means *Earthman*, by contrast with the occult world of spirit." Antonov leered at me, sweating. "And also by contrast with the sky?"

"Why," I asked, "did the Germans take such pains to hide the room?"

"*Why…*" Antonov's tone proclaimed that the answer should be self-evident. Mr. Mystery was fingering the lapel of his own suit. I caught a flash of, yes, a double-headed eagle on a pin. This served as a signal to Antonov to initiate me.

"Because," said the bulky fellow, "the amber room was once the glory of the Tsar's Summer Palace, a symbol of Holy Russia, usurped by the Bolsheviks. Nazis felt hatred for all Russians. The imperial Russian government fought the fathers of those Nazis in the First World War.…" Due to the din of the music he didn't need to lower his voice. "Mr. Burn, the rediscovery of the amber room heralds…the restoration of the Tsars. It will serve as a sure sign."

Rylov nodded. Mr. Mystery exhaled blue smoke. In the logic of loony nationalism perhaps this was true.

"You can help us, Mr. Burn. We will help you fulfill your own private dream! We know where to look, and we have the means to help you see. What we ask is that you buy the means from us, simply to help our funds." He named a figure in Deutschmarks which corresponded with what Rylov already knew I had in my possession.

A scam. This had to be a scam. A confidence trick.

If I tried to walk out on them, would I be detained by a gun held covertly under the table? Would I be robbed while Pavel sat patiently in the car outside? Worse, might the music mask an actual pistol shot?

Ah, but this trio couldn't be sure that the money was on me at the moment.…

"Show me this means of yours," I demanded.

Antonov frowned. "We do not carry it around restaurants. I will come to your hotel tomorrow afternoon. We exchange…with good will."

As Pavel drove me along Moskovsky back toward the Baltika he admitted, "I took a look inside the restaurant, Mr. Burn. I recognized the big man with you. He is a criminal."

I suppose his curiosity was justifiable in view of my mysteriously meeting with strangers within a day of my arrival in Kaliningrad. Did Pavel imagine that I was a criminal too? Or that I was involved in the espionage game? That my interest in amber was merely a front?

"It's all right," I assured him. "Antonov offered to sell me some information about the amber room I've been asking about."

"Antonov is his real name, or at least it's the name he uses."

Ah. Wise Pavel.

"Did you recognize the old man with the glasses?"

My minder shook his head.

"Pavel, tomorrow afternoon Antonov is coming to the hotel to bring me the information. I'm suspicious this might be a *Bauernfängerie*." A "yokel-trap": how picturesque the German word for confidence trick. "I want you to be with me when he visits. There'll be some extra drink-money for you."

We had crossed the ring-road by now, and in the darkness the ten floors of the Baltika loomed on our left.

My room was on the sixth floor. We'd been waiting most of the afternoon. I was eyeing some wasteland through the smog-haze when a white Mercedes came into view, steering erratically at speed. The car barely missed a taxi and a bus before skidding to a halt, narrowly avoiding some German tourists.

A stout figure, unmistakably Antonov, lurched from the car. Clutching his side, he lumbered toward the entrance. Was he injured?

Pavel and I were waiting by the elevator when Antonov spilled out. Luckily the corridor was deserted but for us. We had to heave Antonov along to my room and into a dingy overstuffed armchair. He'd been *shot*. It seemed that this ox of a man was dying, though he wasn't bleeding much at all. Not externally, at least. He'd be bleeding inwardly.

I'd seen Amber bleed inwardly to death, her outward form still fairly unblemished....

Antonov's breath was ragged. "Seeing double," he mumbled in English as he eyed me and Pavel. Pavel said something in Russian, and recognition dawned. "Bodyguard...Rylov said..."

"This is Pavel. Don't worry. He doesn't understand English."

"You met your twin, Mr. Burn....*There are affinities*.... Pavel is Paul, and you are Peter. Both saints attend me." Mysticism was welling up in him along with his lifeblood.

What kind of confidence trick was this, if someone had shot Antonov to try to prevent him from coming to me?

"What happened?" I begged.

Blood bubbled on his lips, consecrating his words.

"Arguing...he who had the *means* in his car...hating foreigners...even if a foreigner does have the vision...." He coughed. "Wasting time...look in the heart of the High Tatras, Mr. Burn."

The High Tatras of Slovakia...

He whispered the name of a town, which I hastened to scribble on a pad. Antonov struggled to reach an inside pocket of his suit, and slid out a spectacle case made of steel. "Look with these...."

I opened the case. The spectacles were so old. The frames, sides, and earrests were of thin tarnished metal. Surely the lenses were of amber, though the amber was so clear and transparent. Apart from their evident age the spectacles looked remarkably like John Lennon glasses.

These were the means to find the amber room?

"Man of the Königsberg Guild made these, Mr. Burn...Christian Proschin...sixteen-nineties...by heating amber gently in..." The English word failed him so he resorted to German. "In *Leinöl*. Blue flower," he mumbled by way of explanation, though I was well aware what *Leinöl* meant, namely linseed. Heat amber in linseed to clarify it — then grind lenses.

"Later on, Mr. Burn, the Nazi magic ceremony, remember..."

A ceremony to enchant the spectacles? To attune them to the amber room! When someone of vision wore these, he would be able to locate the lost room....

Maybe there had been something magical about these glasses even back in the late seventeenth century. Science and magic were still uneasy bedfellows back then. These spectacles had been safeguarded somewhere in the Kaliningrad region throughout the Soviet annexation, in this hard steel case — but not on behalf of covert Nazis. There couldn't have been any Nazis lurking in the vicinity. Nearly all Germans had been killed or deported or sent to Siberia, right? Covert Russian royalists had become the custodians.

It was my luck — no, my destiny — that Rylov was a recruit to this crazy nationalist minority cause and that my quest seemed a godsend to the dotty Tsarists.

Though not to all of them! Many of the newly liberated political animals must be deeply xenophobic. Holy Russia, sacred motherland: safeguard and restore her strength. Let not the West pollute the national soul. There'd been a violent quarrel in the royalist faction. Certain members would have preferred a Rasputin to receive the specs, not a mere visitor from abroad.

Absolutely, this was no yokel-trap, not when it led to murder. Nor could I disbelieve in the spectacles. Too much faith, and death, had been invested in them.

"Blue flowers," repeated Antonov, as if I might find the room in some high meadow full of blooms the hue of the sky itself. This was such an inconsequential detail, communicated with such urgency as thought began to dissipate from the brain. Almost like babbling of green fields.

Finally he slurred something in Russian, and I heard Pavel suck in his breath. Unsurprising that Antonov should revert to his mother tongue in the final moments — as any of us grown-ups might cry out, terminally, to the mother who bore us. Had those last words been a prayer?

He was dead. Those high fatty cheeks slumped a little. Those eyes without any folds to the lids were blank.

I'd imagined that the fall from the sky would kill Isabelle outright, mercifully and abruptly. She should have remained unconscious throughout her dying minutes. Surely she did not once open her eyes and focus upon me!

Pavel was regarding the spectacles in perplexity. The only word of the conversation between myself and Antonov which he could have understood would have been *Leinöl*. Linseed, and a pair of antique glasses. Why should I be willing to spend so much upon old specs? How could those be the motive for a killing?

"Help me get him out of here!" I took out my wallet and removed a couple of hundred-mark bills, which I thrust at Pavel. "He won't be needing money now. Here's an installment on a tip for you." *Ein weniges Trinkgeld.* Oh, quite a lot. "There'll be more to come, at the airport."

After a quick recce, we heaved the body along to a tiny service room. Vacuum cleaner, linen, bars of soap. While I lurked, Pavel summoned the nearby elevator. The corridor remained deserted. The elevator arrived empty. While Pavel delayed the elevator, I dragged the body inside, then I hopped out — as did he, after pressing for the top floor.

"Wir haben Glück, Herr Burn...."

Yes, we'd been lucky, though we still needed to erase scuff marks from the carpet, then wash some spots in my room and rub dirt in to restore their former appearance. Oh, and we reversed the cushions of the armchair. Antonov hadn't bled much at all. Not externally.

The corpse would soon be found. There'd be a bit of a fracas. But in these progressive days no KGB security men routinely haunted the lobby. And Antonov had known my room number in advance.

"By the way," I asked casually, "what did he say in Russian at the very last?"

Pavel grimaced. "It was stupid. 'Long live the Tsar,' he said."

I was hard put to conceal my elation at his final confirmation of Antonov's integrity, nevertheless I agreed that Antonov's last words were completely *Dummkopf*. If Pavel still decided that I was a courier between royalists in Russia and in the West, why, he had more drink-money to look forward to, in return for his discretion!

Oh, I'd seen my love fall from the sky. And now I could find her again.

Where hang gliders are concerned, there's always a thin line between stability and instability; and so it was with Amber too.

A cutting-edge craft which verges on being unstable is going to react wildly when you try some virtuoso maneuver — though equally, a craft which is too stable is an exhausting drag to fly. A bit of instability has its merits. Amber had many merits. She was gorgeous, passionate, adventuresome.

Yet danger excited her rather too much. She courted the frisson. *Not that* she was a dangerous flier. She was too skilled to be dangerous. Skill vetoes silliness. Steering toward a thundercloud wasn't her idea of a good time, but in her regular life she did risk thunder and lightning.

A cuckolded husband is often the last to know that he's being cheated and betrayed; and I was the last of a handful of accomplices in betrayal — the awkward thumb, as it were, since I was the closest to home. The awkward eager thumb.

Isabelle knew how to conduct a liaison, so she protested to me during the early weeks of our own affair. Did Max suspect anything at all about Simon Lee, her previous conquest? Or about Jim Parrish, Lee's predecessor?

Until then, neither had I suspected about Lee or Parrish. Lee was a locally based rally driver and dealer in sports cars. Parrish, it transpired, was a mushroom farmer and membership secretary of some federation of potholers.

Did knowledge of my own predecessors tarnish the craving I felt for her? I suppose I was jealous and at the same time thrillingly flattered to be preferred to other men.

Cuckoldry is such an old-fashioned word for what I was doing to Max, but in view of our close relationship I found the term appropriate. Hitherto Isabelle had cheated — but her lovers weren't as close to Max as I was. Max, whose family's money was our foundation.

Admittedly I had desired Isabelle previously. Yet I wouldn't have dreamed of *doing* anything. You might describe me as inhibited — notwithstanding my soaring dreams! I hadn't become intimate with a woman either at university or subsequently. At a party I might tipsily and jokingly embrace some fellow I knew well — or an older woman acquaintance for whom I felt no frenzy — rather than the girl close by for whom I actually lusted. Displacement, that's the name for it.

When my self-control finally slipped — was stripped away — by Isabelle, I did indeed succumb to erotic frenzy with her to an extent which surprised her, and delighted her. This delight risked being our undoing and the ruin of Maxburn Airfoils. She began to muse about leaving humdrum Max for me. The frisson of flying had hitched her and Max together in the first place (and I assume his future inheritance played a part), but he wasn't fully able to satisfy her, so it seemed. Nor was motherhood an imminent goal. Bloated with child, how might she fly at the edge of possibility?

Pretense in public, frenzy in private!

I remember us relaxing after love-making in the privacy of my cottage, which I'd renamed The Wings. The place was secluded. Woodland, on most sides. A shady lane gave quiet access. The Wings consisted of a south wing and a west wing, with a sheltered, high-hedged wild garden to the rear.

Amber's golden sun-lamp tan left no pale loin-stripe. Blond bloom upon her skin, as on a firm sweet fruit. Those amber aureoles and the succulent beads of her nipples. Freckles on her upper arms and shoulders. Her slim nose, her restless blue eyes framed with challenging violet shadow. She wore her flaxen hair in a long braided rope, baring her brow, offering me a kind of tail to hold.

I was, in our pillow talk, The Thumb. The Thumb would jut stiffly, throbbing to hitch a ride.

"Thumb's up," she would say. "Thumb's up." This was to be her joke — risqué and risky — whenever we were setting out to fly, me and her and Max each with our separate sails.

On this occasion I remember her speculating whether two people could possibly make love aloft, high in the sky, veiled by a cloud, whilst flying tandem side by side together. Would the hang-straps make this totally impossible — unless at least one person unhooked? How wildly would bodily movements pitch the craft? She laughed, she laughed.

"I'd like to go on holiday to Zanzibar," she said. "Nobody else seems to go there. Max isn't interested."

"Well, the two of us can hardly slip away to Zanzibar together."

"I suppose not. I just want to go somewhere where I'm invisible."

"I think you'd be very visible in Zanzibar."

"Somewhere which is my own secret place. And yours."

"We're in it at this moment, aren't we?"

"Jim made love to me in a cave."

I didn't wish to hear about my predecessors.

Isabelle was nominally a silversmith. She had trained thus, indulged by her parents. Courtesy of Max she had a little workshop kitted out with drills and cutters and melting pot, blast burner and drawbench, hammers, burnishers and buffers. She did make some elaborate earrings. She had created perfect little hang gliders to dangle down from one's lobes, sails brushing the wearer's neck like silver insects. She had made life-size slim silver ears to hang underneath one's flesh-and-blood ears. Was this wit or sheer caprice? Expensive toys gave her a pretext to hang out at swanky craft fairs and be admired, and meet such as Simon and Jim.

She began to nag at going away with me.

Going away? Away from my life?

Another time, at The Wings, I told her about the amber room — and immediately there was a place in which we ought to make love. To surprise her, on the next sunny afternoon I pinned golden cellophane over the bedroom window. Was my light-fitting an adequate substitute for a chandelier? Could the carpet become a parquet floor of red and gold and caramel? The only amber was round my neck. And beside me, in bed! Amber's skin hardly needed any tinting by cellophane, though I myself became golden for a couple of hours.

Yes, we trod such a thin line between stability and instability. If Max discovered, what a wreckage of my once-stable life there would be. Did this possibility stimulate Isabelle? Whilst in The Wings, my own self-control evaporated. If the collapse of control were to spread further, involving Maxburn Airfoils in disorder, what then?

Amber said to me, "Of course, if Max had a flying accident I'd feel so wretched and so sad. Worse, you and I could hardly continue loving. If we did, the finger of suspicion would point. Yet how could we stop loving? That's why I'm sure we should go away. Why not to America — where they surf the sky?"

Financially this seemed deeply impractical. Was I to set up shop all over again? Was I to work with designers who might have a veto over me? Isabelle would be deserting her checkbook in the process of deserting Max. Was I to provide her with a new silver smithy?

Horns of a dilemma! Perils of cuckoldry. Terror tiptoed along my spine. Thumbs down.

I had no particular trouble leaving Kaliningrad. The murder had obviously been due to a gangland feud. In spite of the manifest lack of pursuit, the victim must have been trying to hide himself in the hotel — rather than having any special business at the Baltika. The Baltika was certainly not paying any protection money to racketeers. Nyet, nein, absolutely not.

Nor did any xenophobic Tsarists try to hinder me en route to board the Warsaw-bound plane.

Nor was my hang glider stolen by Polish spivs on the road south by way of Kraków.

Guards on the Slovak side of the border with Poland were mainly on the lookout for cheap Polish cigarettes and for migrant Romanians — particularly for gypsy Romanians trying to reach the Shangri-La of Germany. Myself and Range Rover and hang glider passed muster; thus I entered the heart of the High Tatra mountains. I was soon at a certain pleasant resort town crowded with tourists.

Tourists, tourists! Now that snow was thawing on all southerly slopes, the skiing season was over — yet the swelter and thunderstorms of high summer were still a couple of months away. Apart from a lingering chill, this was a fine time to admire towering white peaks and ramble and climb a bit and sup strong Tatra beer. Many Germans were doing so.

Up aloft, the air would be bitter. Even in summer the higher slopes only warmed to a few degrees above zero. Visibility shouldn't be a bother. During full summer the sky would cloud over almost every morning, prelude to thunder and lightning by midday, with clear sky only from late afternoon onward. But not as yet.

I had to visit the nearest flying ground of the Slovak Aeroclub to present my credentials. The amber room might be invisible, but I wouldn't be. I had to demonstrate my sail and my skills, finesse a permit, sign a waiver, take out an expensive insurance bond in case the Mountain Rescue Service needed to be called out. I promised not to drift over the backs of mountains, to flee at the sight of any thundercloud forming, to conduct myself sensibly.

In the hotel where I stayed, vegetables seemed almost entirely absent from meals. Duck with bread dumplings; pork with bacon dumplings. Had these people never heard of a pea or a carrot? Ah, explained a waiter, former Communist mismanagement of agriculture was to blame. I imagined innumerable fields devoted to a monoculture of dumpling bushes.

Isabelle would have liked it here. My Amber was a flesh-eater. She certainly didn't bite or scratch when we quarreled about the idea of her leaving Max. Rather, she hugged and caressed herself, not like some wounded animal, but more as though she were making love to herself before my estranged eyes — becoming almost oblivious to me, inhabiting some domain dominated by her own senses, exhibiting a radical selfishness which chilled and shocked me more than rage would have done. I should feel compelled to reach out and promise anything whatever if only she would return from her self-imposed autistic exile.

How could she, who was usually so outgoing, suddenly go inward thus? I felt that there was a madness in her — not the *mad* of anger, of a whim denied, of desire denied, but the mad of unreason.

This wasn't the Amber whom I had known hitherto. Maybe here was proof that she did truly love me with a consuming passion, a passion which, nonetheless, she had *chosen* to experience for the frisson of it — a passion by which I must in turn fatally be captivated. (And I was, I was; so why was I denying her?)

That afternoon she departed more like a sleepwalker than a woman incensed.

I know that that same night I dreamed forebodingly of driving the several miles to the airfoil shed and doing such-and-such to one of the cutting-edge crafts by torchlight, by dreamlight. In a dream details are elusive. Spurred by trauma, my subconscious mind must have intuited a structural flaw in the newest design. Certainly I woke in my own bed.

Next morning, Isabelle was all smiles. Water under the bridge.

On the low hilltop from which we liked to launch, Max and I both observed her closely as she warmed up and stretched to loosen her body. Kneeling, she strapped in and hooked up. Hang-check, harness check. From the nosewire a thread of red yarn fluttered, reading the breeze. Hands on the uprights of the control bar, she stood up under sail. She stared well ahead, then ran at top speed. She was airborne into the wind rising up the hillside. Perfect.

I was rising over ascending spruce trees. Look: a family of deer down below!

Above, a few patches of cirrocumulus spread wispy fans like lacy bleached corals, tinted faintly by my amber spectacles. I still felt overheated in my thermal underclothes and woolens and gloves and anorak. Well and good! I'd be shivering soon.

Soon enough, spruce was yielding to dwarf pines. As I gained more altitude the pines thinned out. The ground was increasingly jagged and snowy. One never flies the ground, one flies the air. Soon the air was chill, but chill air must still lift over hills, over soaring heights, because of catabatic convection flow. Earlier, occasional poles had marked tracks. No longer, up above the bushline. Earlier, I'd seen dozens of hikers. Now it was as if the whole world had emptied, or as if an alternative world had replaced the previous one. An azure mountain lake on my left. Was some ice still afloat there? I left the lake behind.

A pulse thudded in the pendant tucked above my heart. I found myself looking in vain for blue flowers amidst the snow and cliffs.

In a ravine, through my antique specs, at last I perceived the room — aglow and entire and golden amidst bald boulders with snowy beards and snowy ruffs. Lifting a hand from the control bar, I thrust up my glasses briefly. Of course the room hid itself, chameleon that it was, phenomenon of the realm of amber.

With amber vision I saw it again so clearly. By a shift of perception, through its ceiling I spied the chandeliers hanging downward almost like reflections. No corset sustained the room, nor did any betraying litter of discarded crates lie around — of course not. The room was radiance as much as reality.

Almost, I hesitated. Almost, I fled from the mountains back to the world of a Range Rover and The Wings, the empty Wings, and Max, coping bravely with grief. But my dreams were welling in me, replacing actuality with a more exquisite mode of being.

I began a figure-eight descent, to and fro within the ravine. I intended to alight with a final decisive flare alongside the room. Whether down-gusts buffeted me or the magnetism of so much amber pulled me like a leaf, I found myself swooping down upon the ceiling — surely to shatter it.

Not so, not so. I sprawled upon the amber parquet floor. Above me the allegorical ceiling was intact. I couldn't recall unhooking, yet through a window I saw my sail being borne up and away out of the ravine by wind like a great bird set free.

Scrambling to my feet, I tore off gloves and harness and anorak. It was warm within the room. Within, within! I was inside the treasure room where the Tsars had stood.

Unable to focus upon any single particular, I scanned the wall mosaics and all the intricate carvings of trees and garlands and shells. So many scenes of nature, so many gods and goddesses and other personae. How the faceted amber drops of the chandeliers twinkled. How brightly the clear red plaques shone amidst surrounding yellows and browns. In the giant gilt-framed mirrors at either end of the room I saw myself receding toward infinity. Three windows reached to the floor, their frames richly carved....

Already the ravine had vanished. Dense mist stroked those windows. Condensation trickled. A cloud had nestled down so quickly. Nothing was visible outside.

There were three doors of the folding variety, with ornate frames. I hurried to one but it wouldn't budge. Nor would the next. Nor the third.

Amber. Where was she?

Why, there she was in one of the mirrors — standing alongside one of my more distant reflections! Isabelle was dressed in the same jeans and black polo-neck sweater she had worn on the day she had died. Her flaxen rope of hair hung forward over one shoulder and down her breast, suggestive of a noose not yet knotted. Her expression was weird. She took a step forward.

She did not give rise in the mirror to multiples of herself. She was the one and only. When I glanced back, she wasn't present in the other mirror at all.

She had advanced again. Now she was only four reflections away from me. Could she see me here in the gleaming room?

"Why did you kill me?" she called out, stepping closer. "Why, Peter, why?"

"I dreamed that I did," I admitted. "But how could I have done so? How could I?"

I had strayed closer to the mirror. She was so near to me now. She shook her head at my answer. The flaxen rope swung.

"Look around me," I begged. "It's the amber room." All the decorations to admire! All the allegories to decode!

I was still wearing my antique spectacles, bewitched by some psychic whilst Hitler's empire of death disintegrated. If I snatched the specs off, would she evaporate — and the treasure room too? Would there only be a ravine, and a cold hillside?

Could I embrace her in here, one last forgiving and delirious time? I opened my arms in tentative invitation. She stepped toward me, smiling eerily, the rope of hair slack in her hands. She was intending to loop it around my neck to exact the perfect revenge inside this locked room! The means of death would completely elude any deduction....

Momentarily I shut my eyes so as not to see her accusing eyes upon me.

What I experienced was the perfusion of myself by another being, by the total essence of another, in a way that surely no other lover had ever encountered before. I was Isabelle herself, full of memories other than Peter's.

Yet already this essence was being peeled away, emptying me of her so that only half of myself seemed to remain. I fought in vain to remember a tiny fraction of this ephemeral stupendous event. It had been as though a god, or a goddess, had entered me briefly, granting me a whole extra life filled with incidents and passions. I had not encountered death but its opposite: a doubling of all my days!

Gone from me already, in a robbery absolute, a devastating theft!

Amber wasn't in the room. She was in the other mirror. Her back was to me now. She was pacing away along the line of my reflections.

"Isabelle, come back!" I cried. Vaguer and vaguer she became. Impossible to see her any longer. Only me, and me, and me.

She had never even been in the room with me in physical form. Only her essence had passed through the room, and through me, astonishing me with the fullness of a life I had quenched, then abandoning me utterly. Oh this should be the room where murderers were locked, in so elegant a hell! How I wept for myself, and my reflections wept with me.

When I took off the glasses, the room remained. Those doors wouldn't open. Those windows were blanketed by cloud — nor would they break.

I saw her fall from the sky. The failed hang glider had begun to spin like a sycamore leaf....

I must have been eleven when I first began to dream of flying....

On the way through Immigration an encounter occurred....

Thus it was that I acquired Pavel as my minder....

Neither hunger nor thirst affect me.

I did not notice at first, but after each reliving one of my reflections disappeared from one of the two great mirrors. Initially the queues still looked much the same, but as time repeated itself those queues began visibly shortening.

Now only three reflections remain in one mirror, and two in the other. After five more relivings I shall be on my own.

I live entirely for the brief moment of her passing at the very end of each repetition, of which I always fail to embrace a thousandth part. She wells within me; then the well runs dry.

When my last reflection vanishes, I shall lie down upon the lustrous parquet floor. I shall close my eyes and blindly await, at last, the tangible brush of her rope of hair across my throat. Then I shall truly be joined with her in death.

It can't be that she won't come! It can't be that I shall simply stay here in the room of my dreams with no image of myself to be seen!

Soon another repetition will begin.

All has gone. Only the room remains. I shall lay me down. First I shall strip myself, commencing with the pendant.

But wait!

In Gran-Annie's bead I spy *myself*. I gesture, and the minuscule Peter gestures.

I'm lying on the parquet floor, motionless, tiny, surrounded by amber.

Please pick me up, Isabelle. Please wear me. Wear me in whatever realm you inhabit now.

THE BUTTERFLY EFFECT

eil was trying to get back to his other life when the door creaked behind him.

Anna.

Damn! Always interrupting.

Just on the verge of getting somewhere. He sent half-focused information back into the system and flinched from his wife's hand when she touched his shoulder.

"Aren't you done yet?" she asked. Her voice, as always, was soothing. "Come on, let's go out. It's Sunday. You can't work on neural nets twenty-four hours a day, can you?"

Could she sense that he wanted to use the information he was creating to leave her?

"Of course not," he said. "I need some air." *I need to get home, damn it. Back to my real life. I don't have time to waste.* Time was passing, somewhere, without him. Never mind that he had *wanted* to leave his other life.

"Damn it, Neil," she said, "it's just that you're so preoccupied with this that I never seem to see you anymore."

Why did he feel compunction about something not even real, something made up by a damned fairy, or whatever Mara was?

Because Anna *was* real. This life *was* real. That was the frightening truth.

As he shrugged on his gray tweed overcoat in the foyer, the mirror framed a face still alien to his mind.

Fortyish. Not the younger, dark-haired man he really was. Lines etched by apprehension: *What am I doing here? How did I get here?* A few long strands of blond hair, which he brushed over his widening bald spot, an affectation he used to laugh at in others. He yanked on his black beret.

Anna's pert face was almost hidden beneath an enormous wool hat. Straight blond hair, cut just below her ears, stuck out around the edges. Her wide eyes, brilliant blue, narrowed in fun. "I'm so glad you're getting out," she said. "Let's have a drink and go to a transmit. *The Blue Pacific* got good reviews."

Their eyes locked. Anna loved transmits. He feared them — more evidence of the skewedness of his existence. But he hated how limited her life always seemed to him. He wanted to please her. Sure, the transmits disturbed him. And the odd newspaper article, or a new best-seller. Hell, just about everything, all those vagrant trickles of information which reminded him that everything was different now. Or that he was nuts.

They stepped out onto the concrete stoop and into the cold air. Leafless trees and stately brick townhouses lined the street. A prestigious part of the city. He had always wanted to live in such a place. *At least you did good on that part, Mara.* He had the grudging respect of a few colleagues for his neural net/brain interface research, and all the necessary mental skills and background to pursue his goal of creating ever more sophisticated human-computer interfaces.

But he wanted, he *needed*, to get home.

He was slightly drunk and it was getting dark when they walked into the old Circle Theatre, retooled for transmits. It was crowded, as usual. Neil relaxed into the soft cushions and donned his helmet.

Despite his fear of them, he thought transmits a wonderful idea. Each helmet received information much like a television and translated it into a three-dimensional, all-enveloping experience. Neil usually chose omniscient mode. Being one of the viewpoint characters was much too intense for him. *Keep things at a distance. Don't get drawn in. You never know where it might lead, after all.*

This time he got such an odd tingle when he donned the helmet that he was afraid for a minute that it was defective. He felt like he always had before a thunderstorm, exhilarated, and he heard a high tone which rapidly edged out of his hearing range and left him feeling as if he had somehow changed. He felt light, empty, and free.

He took a deep breath, put it down to nervousness.

And then watched in horror when the transmit began.

The woman he saw sleeping, in an utterly familiar, sunstreaked room, was his former wife, Carolyn. Emily, their six-year-old, flung open the door. But she looked much older. Ten?

The white curtains he had put up when they moved in fluttered. He felt the cool breeze, smelled sweet plumerias.

Felt Emily's fear.

"Mom," she said, "wake *up*. There's something really weird out on the ocean. Some big thing of light. Maybe a bomb. I'm scared."

Helplessness was an explosion in Neil's chest. Why? He wasn't even *there*. *She* wasn't even there....

Neil tore the helmet off and flung it on the seat.

He shoved past the other people to the aisle and hurried out to the lobby, lit a cigarette. The flame of his lighter wavered in his shaking hand. That haunting inscription — "To Neil. Ten Years."

That was the hell of it — he had no way of telling how long he had really been *here*. His referents extended into the past like an avenue down which he could peer only dimly, but the people around him *knew* that past. It was all so clever.

Damn you, Mara.

Rain streamed down the window, and the empty lobby smelled of popcorn. If only he *were* dreaming. But reality, he was forced to conclude, was just a different flavor from dreams — a flavor bitter and unrelenting. Live it out, then die, entirely at the mercy of powerful, unexplained forces. *The transmit is not real. Carolyn and Emily are not in trouble. It's not your fault.*

But he didn't believe it. He wiped his eyes with his rough sleeve.

When he donned his helmet again, the transmit had segued into the life of a family who fled to Maui right after World War II, and how they coped with the Korean occupation — part of the history of *this* world. At least Carolyn and Emily were not in it. If they ever had been, he reminded himself. *Trust nothing in this new place. Nothing.*

✳◉✳

It wasn't chance that he happened upon the transmit. He was looking for it. Apparently his memories, and various extrapolations thereof, were in the public domain.

He found this particular transmit in a theater on Wisconsin Avenue. Flip through the previews and choose.

First go-round through the previews he knew it, and felt sick to his stomach. Then he forced himself to go back to it.

✳◉✳

Constant cafeteria clink of silverware; he sits at a wood plank table left over from WWII. The rustle of palm fronds sweeps through the open window; sweet-scented plumeria petals lie brown outside upon the cracked sidewalk, crushed by the early morning rush of students. An overhead fan pushes the air around. University of Hawaii, 1997.

Stiff with sleeplessness and still-growing rage, Neil, a lowly assistant professor working on neural nets (but no longer now, not after last night, he's through with this, through with everything), looks up from his coffee and sees: black eyes glittering with flirtatious intelligence, a smooth Asian face framed by black hair. She sets her tray down, glances up, pushes her hair back with one hand.

"Hi. Remember me? I'm Mara."

Some damned high-pitched sound. A headache so intense it makes vision waver.

Mara? Must be one of the students who have a crush on him, slip him notes. Something made him quite attractive — he never could figure what. Now that he'd found out about his wife Carolyn and his friend Joel, just last night, he wondered why he'd never taken any of them up on their offers.

He'd spent the night in the lab, after confronting Carolyn, had run across the dark campus to the one place he could find refuge. He donned the prototype helmet with the brain/neural net interface he'd designed, a new way to train the cells in the University's computer. Which was what he was staking his doctorate on. Why did they have to ruin his triumph? Oh, he'd neglected her? What did she expect, Romeo? He was working on a Ph.D., dammit. While she was fooling around with his "friend" and frittering time away with that ad agency of hers. What's that she screamed back at him? At least she was making *money*? More money than he'd ever make? Fifty thousand last year? So *what*?

He ran the pain into the machine — there, take that! As if his neural nets were actually alive and could soothe him, hear him, help him. *Love* him. Someone who'd hacked since he was ten could feel that way. Often did.

He entered his entire thesis, his whole weird program, on top of that, furious, see, I'm *someone*, spurted it into every system he could find, military, University, government systems, the systems of other governments. This is my helmet and I am the world. Here is the information. My life's work.

The hell with everything else.

He fell asleep wearing the helmet, nightmares discharging pain.

And now, while he's drinking wretched coffee, trying to decide what he should do for the rest of his life, some nut *appears*.

"I have the power to grant you one wish." She slides into the chair across from him, peels the lid off her Styrofoam cup with (he distinctly notices through his headache fog) long, thin fingers, and he winces at the screech it makes.

The breeze coming in the window stirs her hair. Beautiful hair, he admits.

She rips open two sugars with brown surfers printed on the package, pours them into the coffee, stirs it with a pen, puts the pen in her mouth briefly, sucks the sugar off.

Smiles. Eyes direct and black.

He tries to say go away. Leave me alone.

"Right," finally comes out. "Well, I sure as hell wish I had another life. One without Carolyn in it. One with a *nice* wife. Someone who loves me."

She nods. Parameters noted.

No problem.

The transmit cut off there.

No problem at all, apparently. That Mara, whoever or whatever the hell she was, could really deliver. In spades.

Neil curled up in his seat in the dark, empty theater for a time. The helmet hurt his head, and he took it off and laid it on the seat next to him.

After a few minutes he put it on again, and tried to find the transmit, run it again, but it was gone.

He left the theater feeling very old. His reflection in the shop windows, that of a prosperous college professor at a prestigious university, was ephemeral, transposed ghostlike on cafés full of people eating, on shop windows where his image merged with mannequins.

At home, Anna met him at the door.

"Where have you been?" she asked. "Dinner's been ready for an hour." Unlike Carolyn, Anna didn't have an outside job. She had nothing to do but take care of him, and seemed to live for just that. *A nice wife. Someone who loves me.*

For once, he didn't mind her constant presence. After all, it was what he'd asked for. He took her in his arms and hugged her.

"Neil, are you all right?"

He turned from her searching eyes and hung up his coat.

He put a stop to the transmit business on a day which smelled of spring, despite the tang of exhaust and the dreary sky, as he walked the few blocks from the Metro to his townhouse. What was wrong with him? This life was a gift. The transmits, when he found them, told him nothing he didn't already know. His former life was not a mystery to him.

He had been absolutely immersed in his work for months before he became aware that Joel and Carolyn were lovers, snapping at Carolyn and Emily whenever they dared to interrupt him. How could he blame Carolyn? He'd begrudged eating and sleeping, couldn't bear to live for a moment away from his precious programs, one of which had passed from self-replicating to self-engendering as he watched, amazed.

He was *still* amazed. Night after wondrous night on the shore of a completely new construct of reality! One which he didn't understand in the least. The formulas it threw at his feet were bizarre; the images it created were worlds unto themselves. He had felt *something* taking shape.

And he had put that *something* into the primitive version of Worldnet in Honolulu. The painstaking work of years. Lost now, whatever it had been, just like his family.

He stopped in front of his steps and lit a cigarette.

He should be ecstatic, considering the vast store of knowledge he'd somehow accumulated. He had been hard at work in this life, and was much older, much smarter, than he had been before. They were worlds ahead in this reality in every field that mattered to him.

And whatever was happening had the undefinable, yet undeniable feel of reality. It had continuity and depth; closure, finality, firm edges, and history. He took a last acrid lungful of smoke, tossed his cigarette onto the sidewalk.

The reputation that he had here, that of an eccentric, was one thing which pleased him immensely. He found that it gave him a degree of freedom he'd never experienced before, and which he accepted gratefully.

But he still hated Mara.

⚒◉⚒

The night he met Kim was several years later.

"Aren't you dressed for the party yet, Neil?"

Anna stood in the doorway. *She* was dressed — in a lovely light blue gown which brought out the color of her eyes. The sounds of cleaning had raged around his office for several hours, giving him a headache. But he'd been so involved with his computer—

"Come on, Neil, these parties are for your own good," she said, mouth turned downward, eyes tinged with anger. "We need to socialize. It really helps you get grants." She gave parties with the same regularity which governed every activity in her life. Three a year for the past four years.

"I know," he said. "I appreciate it. Really."

She retreated. He tried to recapture his mood.

No use. He saved what he had been working on, then browsed among programs downloaded from NIH. They were using transmits to develop positive imaging experiences for cancer and AIDS patients.

The parameters of the third prototype transware program caught his eye. He went back through them. Slowly.

He had written this program. But when?

And hell if he knew where NIH had gotten it.

So many things disoriented him here, even now, despite the time that had passed. How long had he been here, that he was absolutely sure of? Five years? He just tried to stay glued to his computer, the only constant he knew.

Curious and annoyed, he brought up a utility to help him decompile the program.

A jumble of sensors lay on the floor next to him. He ached to put one on, even though transmits still frightened him. Exhilarating as it was to slip into the transmit world, choose alternatives at the speed of thought, and move through simulated worlds which his own research had a hand in creating, he did it only rarely. For him, it was flirting with insanity.

Still, he put a platinum necklace around his neck, then slipped the glovelike sensor helmet over his head. This one, hooked into the inexhaustible store of experiences on Worldnet, called up transmits based on subvocalizations picked up by the necklace. What do you need, what do you desire?

Mostly, he desired, and got, scientific information. Even innocent arcade storyworlds seemed risky, beyond his control. If there was some terrible parallel between the transmits and reality which could control him, he wanted to avoid them. The thought of the world *changing* again, if it ever had, was enough to make him break out in a sweat. Let the kids have their games.

He turned the sensor on and felt the pleasant mild tingle, but didn't put it into Active. There really wasn't time, anyway. He just liked the feel of the helmet on his head, the cool metal against his throat. It helped him think. He kept the eyeflap turned up, velcroed to the forehead of the helmet, so he could see his computer screen.

He stopped scrolling, and after a moment realized that he had stopped breathing too.

His utility revealed the core of the program and he knew, beyond a doubt, that it was exactly what he had been working on just before he found out about Carolyn and Joel.

It *had* been real.

His carefully cultivated doubt about that other life, always so hard to maintain, vanished.

The interlocking chain of thought had an immediacy which glowed on the screen. The reasoning he saw felt to him like a physical thing, a barrier which could also be a window if he just looked at it the right way. It had a viruslike quality about it as well; he could just see it slinking and sliming its way into his computer, flowing through his sensors, flowing into minds that had no idea what they were receiving—

From NIH? The hell it was! How dare they steal his property, this property! What were they doing with it anyway? Visions of a long, nasty lawsuit flashed through his mind.

He sat back.

What good would that do? This was part of the thought of the world, intermingled inextricably with the entire transmit network.

"Honey, aren't you ready yet?" He heard Anna faintly through the door and the helmet. "Someone's at the door."

He felt the energizing tingle which had flowed through him before. His heart beat hard and he forced himself to take a deep breath. The air smelled clean and pure, as if it had come from Arctic icefields, and a high clear tone sounded for a second and then vanished. Everything went dark, then exploded into light.

He yanked the helmet off.

Anna opened the door. "Didn't you hear me? Neil, you're not even ready! John and Sally are here. Hurry up."

Thank God. Everything was the same.

He got up and slipped into the adjoining bedroom to shower and change.

❊

Neil was on his third whisky and feeling jovial — privately celebrating his firm grip on reality, actually — when a young woman walked up to him in the living room.

The house buzzed with conversation, music, clinking glassware, loud laughter. It was packed with people from the University and from the Government. *Thank you, Anna,* he thought.

"Dr. Fisher?"

She was as tall as he and wore a light-green tailored dress. Her complexion was fair, and high eyebrows gave her entire face an engaging expression, one of faint, constant surprise.

"Yes?"

"Oh, good," she said, and held out her hand. "I thought it was you. My name is Kim Sinoose. I'm a friend of Sid Exner. I'm *so* interested in your work."

He soon realized she had read many of his papers. It was pretty nice to meet someone who understood so well what he was doing, and they sat on the couch and talked.

"There are so many possible alternative avenues the brain can take when interpreting reality," he said, "that it's just amazing that everything seems as well put together as it usually does. I mean, reality has folds in it—" He stopped, nervous. He never knew how people would react when he started talking this way.

Kim nodded and took another sip of her whisky tonic. "What do you mean?" she asked.

Neil liked the quiet way her eyes met his, and especially liked the way she found everything he said original and stimulating while at the same time seeming to understand it perfectly. He rattled on about twinning neural nets with the mathematics of chaos, told her about the exciting new collaboration which had sprung up between himself and Sid Exner, their mutual friend who was a mathematician.

"And why shouldn't this kind of information itself affect reality?" His voice broke a little, as it did when he was excited. He cleared his throat. "I mean, *print* changed reality, didn't it? And there's more and more information out there, every day, incredible, powerful new forms of knowledge."

"But isn't it all random?"

"There's an organizing principle, though."

"But that's just the mind. It imposes its own picture on reality based on biology."

"What difference does it make? It's predictable, to some extent, and we call that predictability truth. The more predictable it is, the more useful it becomes. Of course, everyone knows what the butterfly effect is — it's become an archetypal example. But—"

The high, clear tone. Or was it music? "What was that?" he asked and heard panic in his voice. The familiar depression took hold. No control.

She looked around. "What?"

"That sound."

"I didn't hear anything," she said. She opened her purse and made a decisive movement with her hand. Then she pulled out a little compact, squinted into the mirror, and blinked.

"Excuse me, I have something in my eye," she said. She got up and disappeared into the next room.

A moment later, in the confusion of the party, he thought he saw her go into his office and shut the door behind her. He wasn't quite sure it was her, though, because a crowd was clustered there. Laughter rose and fell through the smoky air. He had drunk quite a bit after all, he realized. He took a step toward the door and then Sid was in front of him. "Great party," Sid said, and Neil forgot about Kim until the following day, when he went into his room and shut the door.

Why did he feel that she'd been there, gone through his things?

Yes. The galleys of his new book, *Neural Networks and the Nature of Reality*, lay open to page seventy-nine. A phrase jumped out at him: *It is my opinion that a slight shift in perception would change the very nature of time and reality for humans. This does not contradict (so-called) anthropomorphic cosmological proofs but opens humanity to an entire new realm of experience.*

He turned on his computer and saw a message.

THREE QUESTIONS:

WHAT IS LESS PREDICTABLE THAN LOVE?

WHAT IS MORE REAL THAN LOVE?

WHAT IS LOVE'S MEDIUM?
He never saw her again. When he asked Exner about her he said, "Who?"

❊◉❊

It was raining in Chinatown when Neil emerged from the Metro. Years had passed since the party and Kim Sinoose, but she had become an odd, constant presence in his awareness.

He stood beneath the overhang. Sheets of cold gray rain swept between the buildings. Glancing down, he saw that each floor tile was decorated by a green, stylized dragon, shining wet.

He snapped open his umbrella and stepped out, but it didn't do much good because of the gusting wind. Within a block he was drenched. His thin slacks stuck coldly to his legs as he opened the door of a tiny shop and went inside.

The close air smelled of cloying incense. All around him, interspersed with three-inch holographic statues of Buddhist deities, were the latest models in Chinese transware. The programs that ran them were breathtaking, something entirely new in the evolution of thought. Was there a time when China hadn't led the field? It seemed as if he dimly remembered....

No. He stopped himself from wondering. It did no good.

He looked around the shop. He was lucky to live this close to their only outlet in the U.S., a third-rate country when it came to such technology. His funds, though generous by the University's present standards, which were rapidly going downhill, were far too inadequate to enable him to match the efforts of his Chinese colleagues within the next several years. He couldn't even get a translator for the more obscure journal articles, the ones which might hold the key to taking his line of thought to a higher level. He had the reputation of an unproductive eccentric despite his latest book, which was reviled as obtuse and irrelevant in two recent reviews. He was discouraged.

"Can I help you, sir?" the clerk asked. She was his height, dressed in a Western business suit. Her thick black hair was cut short, and bangs brushed her eyebrows.

He consulted a sodden flyer he pulled from his pocket. The text was in Chinese, but he was anxious to get his hands on anything new, whether or not he knew exactly what it might be. "Yes," he said. "Is this in stock?"

She stood next to him and studied it. He could feel her sidelong glance. "Where did you get this?" she asked.

That simple question set him adrift. He must be getting old. Was this flyer from this world, or something that damned Mara had planted, something to make him look and feel stupid? She did that all the time. Or so it seemed to him. He'd given up wondering why she tortured him, reminded him of his old life and all the damned, perverse holes in reality. He was determined to live as best he could given the conditions, and that was that. It was difficult, though — the doctor had told him that he had a preulcerous condition, and he was jumpy and nervous as he had never been before.

"I got it in the mail," he said resolutely, though he really didn't remember, exactly, where he had gotten it. Even if he had, he wouldn't have trusted the memory. It was all too easy for Mara to fool with that too. For instance, the woman she'd given him as a mother here was absolutely impossible. Dyed blond hair, though she was almost seventy. Loud, harsh cigarette voice, raucous laugh. Easy to see why he'd run away from home when he was sixteen. In this world, he reminded himself. In his own world, his mother was a warm, happy woman, dignified and hard-working. And he had realized a long time ago how utterly unfair he'd been to Carolyn; he hadn't taken her feelings into account at all.

"Sir?" The clerk took the paper and smoothed it out on the counter. The red print ran and gathered in drops of water. "I don't know — let me just think about it. We don't have anything with this particular order number, but perhaps I can figure out what it is from the description."

The shelves were full of boxes of very specialized helmets and probes. Six large, flat screens were set into the wall at intervals, and endlessly replayed the wonders of Chinese transconnects. Programs, optical now, were saved in the form of crystals set in translucent spheres several centimeters in diameter.

So many of the programs were just toys. Create think-art with probes which track brain hormones and translate the information into pictures or music. Stimulate your pleasure centers during dreams via a program which analyzes brainwaves and activates when you enter REM.

But there's more, so much more, Neil thought, with the pain he always felt at having been so far unable to realize the potential. This could solve ancient questions. The naked interface between reality and observer glowed like a will-o-wisp, just out of sight, a dream which lay beneath his every attempt to create a workable metasystem explaining and encompassing reality itself. He was criticized for being too abstract, but as he saw it, the problem was that he wasn't nearly abstract enough. Wouldn't creating an accurate program simply be reality itself? It would be the program of the world. Reality and its apprehension by humans was a compelling puzzle to him, one whose shape kept changing. Even he was beginning to think that he was ridiculous in his conceit, that humans had evolved to understand the astonishing fact that something was *happening*, and to figure out what it was.

As the clerk studied the brochure, rain poured down the front window. The water blurred the yellow stop sign at the corner. A woman hurried by, clad in red and green, as a gust of wind threw rain against the window like a spatter of marbles and Neil thought he heard the *tone* . . . .

But it had been many years. He had even yearned for it at times, but was resigned to thinking it a phantasm. It must have come from one of the cyberconnects which surrounded him.

"Yes," the clerk said, her finger on her chin, new interest in her voice. "I think that we may have this." She looked into his eyes with a straight, clear glance. "It's very new, and you realize, of course, that things are rather backward here. Not a lot of demand. That's why it's unfamiliar. But maybe there is one here — just for you." Her eyes filled with a mischievous glimmer as she turned and went to the back room.

Maybe no one knows what it is, Neil thought, picking up a First Luck headset from the shelf and setting it back down again without examining it. He pulled out his roll of Tums, peeled the wrapper down, and ate two.

After a moment the woman emerged from the back, dusting off a blue cardboard cellophane-wrapped box with her sleeve. "Here," she said, and handed it to him. She sat at a terminal and held her fingers poised over the keys. "Name?"

"Uh — I'll just pay cash," he said.

"We still need your name for our records," she said, and her voice was suddenly melodious, beautiful as the sound of the ocean surging beneath wind-driven clouds. And all around, yes, *unmistakably*, was that high-pitched tone.

"Mara!" he hissed, and slammed open the glass door with his shoulder. He rushed out into the rain, tucking the box inside his coat as he ran. Took the steps on the Metro escalator two at a time and got on the train, which sat on the track with open doors.

He took a seat and began to shake. The train moved into the dark tunnel.

He was nothing but a common thief. And why the heck had he thought that clerk was Mara all of a sudden? He *was* getting to be an absurd old man. Well, not too old. Only fifty-five. But if she were Mara, wouldn't the thing to do be to grab her by the throat and demand that she take him home?

But before even thinking about what was happening he had been terrified that everything would *change* again. And had run. Panicked as a kid who'd broken a window with a baseball.

He sighed. Home. What was it now, what could it be? He'd seen a vagrant transmit, once, of Carolyn slack-faced in a nursing home. One of many which had haunted his entire life. His heart had ached to save her from this awful fate; he had felt as if it was his fault. Absurd! It was all a delusion to think he had had that other life.

He wished there was some way he could *believe* that.

"Where have you been?" asked Anna when he came in the door. "You're soaked! Take off those wet clothes, and—"

"Not now," he said. "I've got this new program to look at."

"Well at least let me make you some hot chocolate," she said. He heard her fill the kettle with water as he closed the door to his study. Wonderful, dependable Anna.

He took out the box and looked at it. It was blank beneath the shiny wet cellophane. He ripped that off and opened the box, hoping to find some documentation.

Again, he was disappointed. Nothing but the crystal. He moved it back and forth, hoping to catch a glimpse of an intensifying hologram, but he didn't see one.

He had no choice but to run it.

He dropped it into the computer.

The first thing he saw on the screen was: YOU NEED A SENSORIAL PLUS HEADSET TO INTERFACE WITH THIS PROGRAM.

He had in his collection free samples of every set which included chunks of his own programming; Sensorial Plus was one of those. He found it, put it on.

Better, whispered the voice inside his head. *Much better.*

Her voice. Mara's.

He reached to switch it off, then — no. Better to meet her now. At last. Head on.

What do you want with me? The anger and frustration of a lifetime welled into his mind.

It's you who want me. I am—

Images cascaded through Neil's mind: Carolyn, looking out the window in the nursing home. He had her viewpoint: a drug-numbed slow-moving distant dream since her stroke.

Then he was Emily, driving somewhere; s/he didn't know where, as the wind blew through the car and open prairie was swept with waves of shimmering light. The prairie began to dissolve, flow upward toward the light, and s/he opened her mouth to say something, just one thing, anything, as s/he lost control of the car. It began to roll, the grasslands flipped to sky; s/he heard the shriek of metal against pavement, saw the dash crumple...

"Here it is, honey," said a voice outside the door.

He wanted, with all his might, to tell her to stay *out*. But he couldn't open his mouth. "No," he finally croaked, but it was too late.

The door opened. Carolyn, young again, held a gin and tonic in each hand.

She stopped when she saw him. "Neil?" she asked. Then she dropped the glasses and ran out the door screaming.

He tore off the headset, and Anna was there. She held hot chocolate, and put her free hand on his forehead. "You got a bad chill. Why don't you take a hot bath?"

When he got out of the tub he didn't even dry himself, just fell onto the bed with water dripping from him.

To his surprise, Anna took her clothes off too. She lay down next to him and gently, with the skill of having done it a thousand times, changed his mood and persuaded him to make love with her.

Afterward she fell asleep and he lay on his back looking at the ceiling. Terrified. He couldn't take it if his life changed again. The hell with neural nets, the hell with research, especially the hell with reality. He was making a good living with royalties. Why probe anymore, why worry? He turned and put his arm around Anna, and she nestled close to him as she slept. This was reality. He held her tighter, then fell asleep.

He was in a complete fog the next morning when he woke up, and the clock said that it was after ten. Why hadn't Anna awakened him? In the darkened room he stared at the clock readout and wondered if it might perhaps be ten at night.

He switched on the light and felt a chill. He forced himself to breathe deeply.

The room was sparse and bare-looking, but the furniture it did contain had a heavy dignity. The vertical lines of the dresser, made of some golden wood he'd never seen before, were a series of intricate insets interspersed with tiny triangles. It had a rectangular mirror to one side.

He got up, looked in it, and saw that he had a young face which was not his.

He opened the door and looked out. Anna was running down the hall toward him, from very far away, and he could not see the end of the hall in either direction. She shouted, "I love you," and the faintness of the shout indicated great distance and frightened him even more than what he saw. "Help me," she shouted, but he couldn't seem to get out of the door and she never came any closer.

He shut the door, and leaned against it. Slowly, he walked back over to the bed and lay down, wished he knew something about praying. He didn't really like this place, beautiful as the woodwork was.

The tone blurred into his mind.

He opened his eyes later and found, to his great relief, that it was morning in his own familiar home.

Just a dream.

He kept telling himself that, over and over, as he shaved his own, familiar face — lined, the face of a man nearing the end of middle age. He took a shower, hot as he could stand, and dressed in clothing which he pulled from the same drawers they'd been stacked in for years.

He went into the kitchen.

"How can I help you?" he asked Anna.

"What are you talking about?" she said. She was standing and buttering toast. The ends of her graying hair brushed the bright green scarf around her neck. She wore a little makeup around her eyes, and simple, heavy gold earrings. "Just get your own breakfast, that's all. I'm running late."

"I thought maybe you haven't been too happy lately," he said.

She looked at him, looked away. "I'm fine," she said. She put the toast down after taking one bite. "Listen, I've got to go. It's been kind of crazy at the office lately." She picked up her keys.

Neil grabbed her shoulders, looked into her eyes. They were a clear, beautiful sky blue, shadowed with pain he now realized he'd caused over the years.

"Anna, I love you," he said. "I'm sorry I've not been all I could have been for you, but I'm going to try now."

"Neil," she said with finality, "I'm late."

"Anna—" He was wrung by anguish so deep that he scarcely knew where it came from. "You can't go. Not right now. We have things to talk about."

Her look became pitying. "Exactly. It's whenever you want to talk about things. Not when *I* want to. Maybe this is as good a time to tell you as any. I've been thinking about this for a long, long time. I'm leaving you. I may be old, but I'm not too old. Not too old to get something out of life." Her voice was strong and sure. "I've already put money down on a house I'm buying on an island in the Caribbean. Remember when I went down there last month?"

He didn't.

"Anna —"

"Neil, I'm very happy." Her face glowed. "I know this is hard for you to understand, but I'm happier than I ever have been in my whole life. I've talked to a lawyer about everything—"

"Anna, I don't remember."

Her voice became flat, angry. "I'm used to that. Don't you see? That's the *problem*."

"Is there someone else?" he asked in as calm a voice as he could muster.

She just stared at him.

"I mean," he stumbled on, "I hope there is, Anna, someone who's *better* for you, someone who appreciates you."

Her voice rose, sharper than he'd ever heard it. "There's only me, *me*, for once in my life instead of you. I thought you'd be angry. But no. You don't care about *anything*. This has been upsetting me for months — years — and it's over in a few seconds. But why should I be surprised? Do you know how hard it is just to talk to you? You act like you're a million miles away. You've locked yourself into some sort of self-imposed tomb and you'll never get out — you don't *want* to. You don't even know that there's a world anymore. You won't mind when I'm gone, will you? Just go back and get busy with your computer." Her mouth twisted in a bitter grimace, and Neil saw tears in her eyes before she slammed the door behind her. Neil opened it to see her jump into her car and screech out of the driveway.

He stood there for a moment. The two boys riding their bikes out on the sidewalk seemed like apparitions from another world, from a pure, intense reality he had never been able to touch, a dimension of life which had always receded from him.

One which he'd always pushed away.

He touched the garage door button, then turned and went inside.

He poured some coffee and sat down at the kitchen table. The whir of the automatic garage door stopped with a whump as it hit the concrete. Then everything was quiet.

He took a few sips of coffee.

Slowly he remembered glimmers. He had been nagging Anna to get a job for years for her own good, not for the money, and she finally had.

Hadn't she? Wasn't that how this had all come about?

Or *was* it?

He felt as if he'd been heavily drugged. Something about that damned program. That much was quite clear to him.

He went back into his office, through Anna's jungle of houseplants which seem to have burgeoned up in the past month or so.

He sat at his computer. It said, WHAT NEXT?

How long had *that* been there?

GOOD QUESTION, he keyed, not daring to put on the helmet. WHY DON'T YOU TELL ME?

REMEMBER CAROLYN AND THE DRINKS?

YES, he wrote, and was filled with an urgency which surprised him. He poised over the keyboard. I WANT TO GO BACK.

REALLY?

The question hung there like fire. Neil stared at it until a drop of sweat splotted onto the keyboard.

"No," he finally muttered, and told it, NO. Not *back*.

The screen went blank.

He made a copy of the crystal from the Chinese transware store. He put the original away.

He started to dissect the copy.

Neural nets were funny things. They operated digitally, inside Worldnet, yet they could learn from experience. They could even teach themselves.

What had they learned?

He decompiled it doggedly, operation by operation. He brought up the utility which would translate code into lines of programming, forced it to yield information which had been compacted and streamlined, unsure of what he would eventually find.

After three hours and many cups of coffee, he found something gorgeous, stunningly elegant.

It clicked, as if Mara whispered the word inside his head.

Mine.

The original chunk of information, the one he'd fed into Worldnet years ago when he'd been an assistant professor at the University of Hawaii.

Self-replicating, self-engendering.

The tiny bit of information that had *changed* everything: the single beat of the butterfly's wing, if you wanted to put it that way.

He'd written the reality metasystem without even knowing it, when he was a young man in another life. A constant feedback loop, changing minutely with each pass of information, *learning about reality*, meshing with the mind of every person who ever hooked into Worldnet, translating image, wish, dream, and desire into itself, giving it back ever more swiftly, pushing back the borders of knowledge and dream with information, relentless and powerful. Hadn't he come across it before? But then he'd forgotten, it had slipped through the mesh of some *change....*

He took the crystal out, held it for a moment, then put it back in. He donned the soft helmet which now, every household had. Just for games.

Just for games.

He rested his fingers on the keys. For a moment, he couldn't bring himself to move them. His stomach was wracked by pain and his hands shook.

This world. He could have Anna back with just a demand, he knew. He could ruin her new happiness and remove her strength in order to have blessed familiarity for himself once again. Wasn't familiarity, solidarity, what he had been searching for so desperately?

Would there even be a seam when he was gone, a ripple? Or would Anna's new life stretch back happily without a memory of him or the pain he had caused her?

He hoped it would.

He keyed the information which would link him in, put it online. Sent it into the Worldnet. Nothing, nothing to lose.

Only something to give. His absence.

He knew there would be something ahead. He just didn't know what. Fear was a precipice over which he fell.

The world was a tone, high and searing, dissolving to pictures, to symbols, to flashing, dense code. His scalp tingled as sensations tumbled atop one another, swift, intense, aching, immense events which he had failed to grasp when within them: Carolyn, stunned by his anger; Anna crying for help; his daughter, lost on a desert and reeling into death.

With all his heart, he poured surcease and light into his visions, knew his subconscious was subvocalizing and that the necklace picked it up. Information held sway, but need and desire were information as well. And love. The blank instant in which he hung suspended was time enough to laugh at the irony of himself, with his paltry understanding of what it was to give to others, serving as a vector for such information.

But that was all he had. An old man now, perhaps he had learned something after all. It was all he could hope for.

✄◉✄

Neil shared the cablecar with a middle-aged woman holding a net bag. He could see that it held three fat red tomatoes, a crusty loaf of bread, a bottle of wine, and something wrapped in white paper. She was reading a book, but he couldn't quite make out the title.

The car jolted to a stop and she smiled at the conductor and stepped onto the cobblestones of the street. The houses in this gentle world looked quite old-fashioned to him, with deep porches and heavily shaded yards. Still, computers had evolved here to a higher form than any he had known before. He knew that they had without even seeing one.

Her name had been in the book — Kim Mara Sinoose.

When he got off the cablecar, he saw that the address was in an old brownstone.

He entered the lobby. The marble floor was scuffed, dulled by years of use. He ran his finger down the directory until he found her name. Suite 515. When he pushed the elevator button nothing happened, so he opened the door to the stairs.

The stairwell smelled of urine and was dark, with broken bottles and trash in the corners. He took the stairs two at a time, then walked down the fifth-floor hallway until he found a smoky-glass window which said Kim Mara Sinoose.

He didn't knock, just opened the door and saw her, a small woman sitting behind a very large desk.

She was absorbed in what she was doing. Her sun-browned face was the same color as her hair, which was shoulder-length and straight; he knew that her eyes would be brown as well. She looked as if she was only nineteen.

He sat down in the wooden chair in front of her desk and watched her work. Her hair stirred slightly in the breeze which came in the open window.

He saw that her keyboard had fewer and larger keys than the ones he had known. They were blank, and she sometimes pressed two or three at a time. The intricacy of the rhythms she used made him feel as if timing had as much to do with the process as which keys she pressed, as if what she was creating had much in common with music.

The window was open and he glimpsed the tops of green trees. This city was quieter than those he was used to; he could hear birdsong in the morning and the air coming in the window was cool and crisp. He felt at ease, felt immense well-being for a moment. If this was a dream, he wished it would never end.

She looked up. "Hello," she said.

"I brought the program," he said. "I changed a few things."

"Ah yes," she said. "It took you long enough."

"All my life." As he handed it to her, he understood that it had been a collaboration between them, although they had never really met before. Not entirely.

She took it. As she stood, he saw that she was medium-tall and lithe, clothed simply in skirt and blouse, with a turquoise sweater thrown over her shoulders. She wore no jewelry. She sat again and held the crystal for a minute.

"Do you understand what has happened?" she asked.

He shook his head. "No. Not really. But I think once you put that sphere in, things will change again. I'm not sure that I'll remember this. I wonder how many folds I've skipped through without remembering. I would really like to know—" he began, then stopped.

"What?" she asked. "What would you like to know?"

"Did I create you or did you create me?"

She laughed, and he felt stung. "I'm not sure that either premise is correct," she said. "Does it matter?"

"It does to me!"

"When I put this in, perhaps we'll find out." She paused for a moment and looked at him. "Or maybe we'll no longer care." She leaned toward the computer and held the crystal above it.

He felt the scarred wood of the old desk beneath his hands as he flattened them against it and hooked his thumbs beneath. "But it's real now, isn't it?" He felt a stab of anxiety.

Her eyes were gentle yet intense, informed by an intelligence he realized was immense.

"No," he whispered. "Don't use it."

She smiled and dropped the sphere in.

She moved long, graceful fingers over the keys in that distinctive, musical cadence and said without looking up, as if she heard his thought, "We don't need helmets here. Our connections are quite direct."

The world gathered into a high, clear tone.

Then it changed.

65

Kim's brown hair went to blond curls, backlit by sun, then was shimmering black, long and straight. Fear tightened Neil's chest.

She looked at him with Anna's compassionate younger face, Carolyn's sharper, more knowing eyes. Above them Dr. Sinoose's lovely eyebrows were raised in question.

Sunlight flashed through the room, but he smelled the scent of water. He looked to his right and saw an open space where the north wall had been; rain pattered gently upon the worn green plastic of an office chair. Small rainbows danced across wallpaper patterned with tiny pink roses. The tall window stretched around some corner he could see no end to, and blossomed with bright, pulsing stars. Mara — was it Mara? — hunched over the keyboard in the starlight, tapping. He couldn't see her face.

He rose, leaned across the desk, touched her shoulder, and a wave of darkness engulfed him. Thoughts beyond his range of comprehension, which reminded him of the impossible geometries of mathematicians, lodged in his body, contorted it almost beyond bearing, while tiny, precise, bright visions flashed ephemerally as lightning bugs, like the glutted accumulations of a million transdreams.

His will had nothing to do with stopping the barrage.

It finally, simply, stopped.

Neil leaned back in his chair, spent, and gazed at his surroundings.

The old desk was there, and the walls of the room were intact once more, though a few drops of water stood on the green plastic seat of the chair in the corner.

He heard the trolley bell ring twice below in the street, and a low rumble as it trundled down the tracks. A gerbera daisy, its face a strong pink sunburst, sat in a jelly jar full of water on the desk, with some tiny white flowers he didn't know the name of. They gave off a strong, sweet scent. The world seemed blessedly the same.

Except that he was alone.

My fault echoed through his limbs like a million one-pound weights.

Who knew what had happened to her, or if he would ever see her again. She had seemed remote, yet he had *known*, for those few moments, that she was really *there*, the organizing principle in the midst of random information. How dear her face had been, and how little he had felt of himself, after she activated the sphere, for the first time in his entire life.

He shouldn't have allowed her to use the program.

Barely able to move for sadness, he went around the desk and stood next to the empty chair, punched the eject and stared at the sphere when it clicked up. What new, strange worlds did it hold? What terrors? What deaths, what pain, because of humankind's unknown whims and its grim, relentless inability to learn from the past? He drew back his arm. Shatter the window with it, pitch it into the street, let it roll into the gutter. Lose this terrible thing forever.

But he paused.

Joy and love were within it too. And what other new knowledge, beyond his ability to conceive of now? Within it was the beauty of the unknown day.

He opened the top drawer of the desk and set the smooth, cool sphere gently in a rice bowl with blue dragons around the rim, in a nest of paper clips and a few rubber bands.

He slid the drawer shut, looked out the window for a moment, then turned from it and left the room.

He trudged down the stairs, pushed the worn brass kickplate with his foot, and stepped onto the sidewalk. He faced the storefronts across the street for a moment, trying to decide. Left or right? What did it matter?

Then a movement down the street caught his eye.

A woman on the next block was walking away from him, headed toward a busy intersection.

She wore a plain skirt. A gust of chilly wind whipped her straight brown hair, and she hugged a turquoise sweater closer as she hopped a curb.

His heart lifted. He turned and followed her.

EPISTROPHY

Julian Wrysodick slumped in harness as I rolled his three-wheeled chair down the beach in a storm of spray and buffeting gusts. His hands posed like crabs on the woolen-clad bones of his thighs. His ungainly gray head lolled in the buffeting gusts. He smelled simultaneously of witch hazel, camphor, and urine, even as his weird fetor carried inland on the buffeting gusts. I wished that my cousin Ferrel, Wrysodick's regular attendant, hadn't taken the flu and called me away from the Seacourt library — that Wrysodick himself had acknowledged his senescence and infirmity and remained indoors, out of the spray and buffeting gusts.

The cold winter twilight flapped around us like unbattened sailcloth.

"Rudy!" Wrysodick barked over one shoulder. "Rudy, why in breezes have you stopped?" His voice? A ratcheting of unoiled gears.

"This is crazy, Mr. J."

"It pains me you think so."

"*Look* at it. We could get caught out, sir. Squall blowing up. Darkness. These buffeting gusts."

"Ferrel wouldn't balk at accompanying me."

What's this accompanying business? I thought: I'm pushing you. Aloud: "No balking to it. I'm simply pointing out the inadvisability."

"You fear a reprimand, or worse, if I croak out here."

"Well, of course."

"Fine. You probably should. Buffeting gusts." He showed me the custard-gray white of one eye and the whiskery corner of a grin.

"So it's all right if I take you back?"

"Ferrel wouldn't. Not old Ferrel. He'd push on." (Yeah. Into the buffeting gusts.)

"Yessir," I said.

"There's something I'd like you to see, Rudy. In fact, there's something *I* want to see. And that…well, that's what counts, isn't it?" He lifted a bony index finger off his leg and wiggled it at a dune-populated cape jutting into the slate-gray chop fifty yards ahead. "Go. Go go go."

I shoved. Wrysodick's chair, designed for a variety of outdoor terrains, including heavy sand, shot forward so quickly that I seemed almost to dogtrot after, rather than to impel, it. Quite a buggy. Why fret the birdshot spray, the menace of falling night, the endlessly buffeting gusts.

After all, the chair had headlamps on each of its otherwise useless armrests, not to mention glowing red running strips on its tires and sides. To a sand crab, we must have looked like a runaway Ferris wheel.

With less hassle than I would have imagined, we negotiated the cape and several shell-studded flats that eventually opened out on a small peninsula of snow-white sand, as if a crew of engineers had poured a concrete base beneath the peninsula's square tip and anchored that platform to the underlying shelf by a method that educated morons like me would never grasp. My chairbound charge gaped into the buffeting gusts.

I rolled Wrysodick toward the spit. From the bottom up, it went like this: concrete subfloor, overfloor of pristine white sand, and, atop this sugary layer, tucked away in an open-faced shelter of cut, intricately fitted, and well-waxed driftwood, the very thing that Wrysodick had wanted to show me and to see again himself. Namely, a jukebox.

By now, the sky had given up all its light, the wind had acquired the droning keen of a dynamo, and Wrysodick had taken on an extra pound or two in the paralyzing soddenness of his woolen clothes. He no longer stank of astringent, camphor, and pee, but of something fleecelike and doggy. When I leaned down to speak directly into his ear, I saw that his ashen bat-fetus face had begun to glow from memory or present-day content. Or possibly both.

In the pink, I thought. Suddenly, the old geezer is in the pink, a sheen of self-satisfied reminiscence.

"Here?" I yelled.

"No, closer. Roll me up. *Roll me up!*"

I would have gladly rolled him up into a bony pellet, like the casts that owls commonly regurgitate, and hurled him into the Atlantic, but reality stayed me. Instead, I rolled the chair. The headlamps on its armrests played like spots on the shimmering formed-plastic tubes and chromium trim of the box, somehow animating all its curves and sponging the night around us with an intangible swirl of emeralds, rubies, sapphires, and flashing lemon drops. The box's console stood five and a half feet tall. Towering over Wrysodick, it throbbed before us like a Titan's heart.

"The Wrysodick 1440, the first model I put into production after the war," Wrysodick said.

Which war? I wondered. And then, cogitating, knew he meant the one that we had ended with atomic bombs, two prodigiously buffeting gusts.

"When material controls ended, I jumped," Wrysodick said. "Back into the game. This beautiful baby was the result."

"You designed jukeboxes?"

"Dreamed. Designed. Crafted. Produced."

"Ferrel said you were a manufacturer of phonographs, stereo equipment, that sort of stuff."

"A jukebox *is* that sort of stuff, Rudy."

A nod at the Wrysodick 1440. "Does it play?"

Even shivering in near-terminal decrepitude, he scoffed at the implied notion that it would not. This unit had its own built-in power source. Wrysodick told me how to activate that power source; how to adjust the volume against the booming of the sea and the wind's shrill vocalizations; how to prime the disc player with a slug that automatically returned itself; and, finally, how to punch out a selection from the twenty-four catalogued in side-by-side rows above the elaborate *Wrysodick* nameplate and the undulant U-shaped tube framing the stained-glass drum of this model's sexy abdomen. I did everything he said, right up to the point of button punching.

"Punch seventeen, Rudy."

"Seventeen?"

"It's been seventeen years since she died."

I punched seventeen: "Misterioso," by Theolonious Monk. With the jukebox's volume on its highest setting, the notes of this oddly syncopated, almost discordant cut banged out at us like the jamming of a quartet of deeply peeved skeletons. The xylophone in it hinted so strongly of smart-aleck bone rattling that I began to shiver even more vehemently than Wrysodick, who grinned like a cadaver. The paired vertical tubes on the front outer edges of the box pulsed in juking rhythm with the music and our chattering teeth.

"Who?" I managed. "Seventeen years?"

"Irene. My wife. My one and only beloved."

"Did she like *that*?" Another nod at the glowing machine.

Wrysodick couldn't see this nod, but had no trouble reading my question. "She liked everything on that baby. It's all jazz, all twenty-four selections." Something flew by overhead: seagull, sandpiper, or scrap of newsprint.

Wrysodick flinched, a self-protective jerk of his massive gray head, as this flimsy UFO fluttered beyond us toward a waste of sea oats and eroded dunes. Then, like a turtle coming back out of its carapace, he recovered:

"Monk on piano. Milt Jackson on vibes. John Simmons on bass. Shadow Wilson on drums."

"Never heard of any of them but what's-his-name," I said. "The lead player, Thelonious."

"They recorded that and a cut called 'Epistrophy' — it's on the box too — in the summer of 1948."

"Nearly twenty years before I was born."

"Really? Well, I was at the height of my powers." A quick involuntary head twist. Another recovery. "The *height*, Rudy."

"Yessir."

"Misterioso" plinked mysteriously to a conclusion. Three minutes plus of cool sardonic playing that Irene Wrysodick had contrived to soar on and that had clearly lifted Julian off the ground too. Even after the mechanical arm inside the console had returned the vinyl disc to its stack, the Wrysodick 1440's sculpted tubes went on geysering. Inside them, in the liquid chemical still boiling there, I could see — or thought I could — tiny floating grains clumping and separating again, dissolving and briefly remanifesting. I left Wrysodick and knelt beside one set of paired tubes.

"What makes them do that?"

"The chemical in there — irenex, I call it — has a really low boiling point." Head loll. Finger twitch. "Small heaters at the bottoms of the tubes." He chortled. He smirked. "*Violà!* Instant Technicolor ebullience."

"It's pretty," I had to admit. It was. A lot prettier, to my way of measuring, than the ivory and bone collisions of "Misterioso." I fingered the console's ever-present slug out of its return slot.

"One more time," Wrysodick said.

"Seventeen?"

"What else? Seventeen."

I stood and pored over the other selections. I would have liked to hit a Sinatra, a Dick Haymes, a Jo Stafford. I would have liked to punch Charlie Parker doing "I Ain't Got Nothin' But the Blues," or Dizzy Gillespie's "Lorraine," or almost anything other than seventeen. Still, I did my duty by Wrysodick, there in the buffeting gusts, and, as they buffeted, dutifully punched seventeen. Thelonious plunked, bubble tubes boiled, waves crashed, and the wind flung shrapnel against the polished backside of the jukebox's driftwood lean-to, tossed the shards in buffeting gusts.

"Irene loved this spot," Wrysodick said. "We put her to rest here."

Behind his chair again, I peered around. "Where?"

"There. Inside my machine. We cremated her. Her bones went into a box, the box into a compartment of the 1440."

"I thought with cremation you got ashes."

"You get *cremains*, Rudy. Lots of ash. Some charred bone fragments. Those we boxed up and stashed in the Wrysodick."

"So what did you do with her ashes?"

"Most we put into the cedar box with the bone fragments. A sprinkle, though, went into each of the bubble tubes."

"The bubble tubes?"

"Sure. Why not? She dances in those things. She inhabits this place."

"Ferrel never told me."

"Good. I'd've fired him if he had. No one has a right to reveal my eccentricities but me."

After a beat or two I said, "Is it legal? Burying someone in a jukebox?"

"My wife. Our property. Our choice. Sure it's legal. If it isn't, nobody's going to tell me so."

Once again, "Misterioso" plinked to an off-key conclusion in the deafening salt air. Meanwhile, Irene Wrysodick, or some gritty part of her, danced in the bebop tubes of her husband's flamboyantly beautiful music box.

✄◉✄

On our way back to his big stucco house, Wrysodick lurched heavily against the straps in his chair.

A heart attack, the coroner said. No autopsy confirmed this assessment. Rather, as stipulated in Wrysodick's will, a cremation was followed by a beachfront memorial service at the site of the enshrined jukebox.

Ferrel got me an invitation by arguing that the person in whose presence the patriarch had died — no one, by the way, ever accused me of either negligence or treachery — had an inviolable right to attend. Who, after all, had last spoken with Julian Wrysodick? Who had beheld his definitive death throe? Who had wiped his mouth of sputum in the buffeting gusts?

At first, I hadn't wanted to go. But Ferrel told me that Emily Singleton, the eldest daughter, had mixed the cremains of her dad with those of her mom and put them all in the cedar box inside the 1440. And some of Wrysodick's ashes had gone into the bubble tubes, there to commingle with those of the beloved mother of his children.

As a result, the ceremony itself, consisting of a text from First Corinthians and seven or eight becoming jukebox numbers, moved me a lot. I began to love Julian Wrysodick and the woman who had predeceased him by seventeen years. I even began to find a happy, if well-hidden, lilt in the Thelonious Monk piece "Misterioso."

After the funeral, Ferrel Kidd — my uncle Garrick's son — and I stopped by the Seacourt Public Library so that I could pick up some work I needed to do at home. We sat down at a table in the community meeting room to talk.

Ferrel is two years younger than I, a card-carrying member of Generation X. At events less solemn than funerals, he wears outsized dungarees, granny glasses, and a Fishbone baseball cap backward. I still hadn't quite adjusted to seeing him in a charcoal chalk-striped suit, even if he had long since shed the jacket and dropped his suspender straps.

"When my time comes," I said, "please find some way to put my mortal remains in a jukebox."

Ferrel raised his grown-together eyebrows. "You realize, cuz, they don't make Wrysodick 1440s anymore? Hell, they don't manufacture Wrysodick boxes at all."

"A comparable competitive model, then."

"What would do? A Seeburg? A Rock-Ola? A Wurlitzer? I don't think any of 'em quite suits."

"I'm snowed, Ferrel. Think of something."

"Tell me what's snowed you."

"The beauty of it. The late Mr. and Mrs. Wrysodick, they jazz each other continually in the rainbow-colored tubes of his namesake machine."

"Yeah."

"Beats going into a cold clayey ground or being randomly scattered at sea."

"I guess," said Ferrel without enthusiasm.

A few months later, Tropical Storm Eliot struck the coast and wreaked havoc. Buffeting and collapsing every building on the Wrysodick estate, this storm built in gusts, soared inland on gusts, and slammed down the jukebox shrine and tomb of the Wrysodicks in a rageful succession of gusts.

Not long after, Ferrel and I threw in together and bought burial plots in a modest Seacourt cemetery. A blue note to end on, but the discordant truth.

NO ORDINARY CHRISTIAN

A TALE OF THE FAR MAGRIB

CHAPTER ONE
VISITORS TO THE CITY

E RODE DOWN *from the Far Atlas with a corpse across his saddle and red hatred in his eyes. He had come out of a desert to reach the mountains. His blonde camel was quite mad, fearing only her rider, the albino aristocrat "Le Loup Blanc," who fought like a Berber and thought like a Jew.*

Even Th'amouent's Caliph, Al Hadj Mou'ini al A' aid, that ogre of self-indulgent cruelty, the shame of Islam, treated Le Loup Blanc with wary respect, and there were orders abroad to let him go freely. For this was no ordinary Christian.

This was one who spoke the purest Arabic of the Mosque, could joke in the coarse, rich Marakshi dialect, converse readily in all the Berber tongues or tell a tale in Egyptian which would make you think him a native of Alexandria or Cairo. Yet he let them call him by no name save his own, though he prayed with every sign of quiet devotion, five times a day.

They must address him in the Christian fashion as Fan Bekh, Al Rique, Bin Basha, but had no idea why anyone would willingly go by such an unholy string of gibberish. Out of respect they called him this to his face, but behind his back they called him Al Rik'h, The Secret One, in the familiar dialect of the Western Rif.

His lips were raw, his eyes dusty as uncut rubies, his white hair caked with the desert's grime. Though he wore the hooded djellaba of the Berberim, it had not protected his strangely unpigmented skin which now flaked like a leper's so it seemed Death himself came riding through the ochre gates of Th'amouent on that May evening, with a crimson sun falling behind the blue mountains and the quarter moon bringing clear light to silver streets and the golden domes of mosques, to blue-tiled towers and time-worn terra-cotta. At that moment the muezzin began to chant. It was like a scene, said Captain Albert Begg, peering from his balcony through dark green palms below, from his favourite Rimsky Korsakov opera, Manfred: or, The Gentleman Houri. Had his visitor seen it in London when he was last there?

"Sadly, the old country's given me my marching orders." Captain Quelch sighed. The hatchet-featured European wore a rather crumpled white dinner jacket and had undone his tie. "So much for non nobis sed omnibus, eh, sport? You said you sold aeroplanes. Any particular type?"

"Well, it's not really aeroplanes," Begg admitted. "It's more general ordnance and that sort of thing."

"Don't be embarrassed, old boy." Quelch brightened up and again helped himself from Begg's decanter. He was making the most of the single malt. His hands were scarcely shaking at all. He winked a bloodshot eye. "I've run a few guns to a few dusky customers in my time. Damned rum chap though, ain't he, that German? Prince what's-his-name? I've seen him before."

"Like a knight of old," said Poppy Begg, taking a poetic sip of her gin. "Like Arthur's paladin upon a quest." She rustled her pretty silk. "He doesn't look happy."

Captain Quelch cleared his throat. "Neither would you, dear, if you'd just come in from the desert with a three-day-old corpse under your nose."

"It could be a dead friend," Poppy offered, anxious to keep the air of romance alive. Boyishly groomed in the very latest London fashion, she was already completely enchanted by the city and its blue-veiled Taurcq, its lively mixture of Arab traders and Berbers, of bustling camels, donkeys and the occasional motor-car. Her uncle had decided to bring her with him on this official trip because it was a better alternative to what she would do if he had left her alone at his Sporting Club Square flat. Poppy felt obliged to be wild. It won her the approval of her peers. Albert Begg had, he believed, never met such an appalling gang of wastrels and scallywags and the thought of even one of them crossing his threshold, especially when he was not there, had been too much to bear.

"He probably has a habit of bringing in every poor little benighted coon who wanders too far away from camp," suggested Captain Quelch. "I wonder what his game is? Is there a reward for that sort of thing?" He frowned and let a small, gentlemanly belch escape his lips. "You must tell me when we meet up again, old soul. I'll be on my way out of here by tomorrow." He patted his jacket. "The sooner I can cash this draft at the Credite Lyonesse in Marrakech, the happier I'll be. He's a bit of an unreliable customer, our Caliph, as I think you know."

"I've still to meet him," said Albert Begg, "but I've had reports." He did not wish Captain Quelch to know that he was here on government business and if his old acquaintance wished to believe he was in the same trade, running guns and tanks into North Africa, it suited him.

Begg's papers introduced him to the Caliph and requested safe passage, but his real purpose here was to meet the man who had just ridden through the Hakhim Gate. So far, an audience with the Caliph, who had a short attention span and a murderous impatience, had not taken place. Begg was confident, however, that his special status as His Majesty's Courier protected both himself and his niece — especially since the Caliph, in one of his most Byzantine schemes, was currently attempting to win British or German support against the French, who were threatening his autonomy. This consideration would last long enough, Begg believed, for him to achieve his mission and return with Poppy to Marrakech, where he would entrain immediately for Casablanca and a navy cruiser waiting in the quarantine harbour to take him home.

"He's my kinsman, I understand," Albert Begg said of von Bek. "The German side of the family was always of a romantic disposition. I put this chap's problems down to reading too much Karl May as a boy. Look what happened to old Lawrence. G.A. Henty as good as murdered him with his bare hands. That kind of fiction isn't healthy for a literal-minded dreamer. Conrad knew. But you can't help feeling that the world's a better place for the likes of our romantic lunatics, wouldn't you say, Quelch?"

"Lock the blighters up and throw away the key, old boy. That's my opinion. They do too much damage. Just think of the chaos Shelley alone has caused in the world! I'm a believer in old-fashioned values when it comes down to particulars. Strict discipline, that's my motto. I was always a good master, you know. The laskars respect a bit of firmness. They loved me, those boys."

"Von Bek's life doesn't make you envy him or want to meet him?"

"I'm sorry, old chap, but I'm rather more fastidious than some, I can't stand fleas. The Kraut's forever in and out of those tents and native hovels. Imagine how infested he must be. No, no, old boy — I'll forego the pleasure until he's had a couple of good carbolic baths."

"Well," said Captain Begg suddenly, "I'm off for my evening stroll. I'll walk you home, captain."

"No need, old soul. I'll just drift down into the bar for a bit. They stay open to residents and I'll give 'em your room number, if you don't mind. Not to worry, my boy. I'll pay cash when it comes to the reckoning."

And with that, Captain Quelch bowed to Poppy, kissed her uncertain hand, and departed. When Captain Begg went down a few minutes later, the old pirate had disappeared.

Captain Begg was not to witness the arrival of Le Loup Blanc at the vividly-painted ornamental gates of the Caliph's palace, and would only hear later how the man he knew as Prince Ulrich von Bek would dismount carefully from his camel and lay the corpse upon the steps, crying out that the God of us all would demand justice for this profoundly wicked murder, and that Al Rik'h of the Forbidden Desert was even now on his way to the mosque to seek guidance and discover if he were to be God's instrument in the matter. If so, the white-faced one promised, he would return in due course to complete his business. It was as though the Lord of Hades himself led his snarling mount back into the gathering darkness of the medina.

When inspected, the corpse was found to be that of a young woman. In death her angelic face was at rest. It was impossible to understand how she could look so seraphic when the rest of her skin had been systematically flayed from her body.

Hearing of the incident, the Caliph ordered the woman's remains to be brought to him. He stared for some time at her, giving her far more attention than he gave most living creatures, particularly women, then eventually shrugged and ordered the corpse disposed of in the usual way. But those who had dared lift their eyes to glance at him noticed that he was disturbed, perhaps even afraid. When, however, his vizier asked if he should increase the guard on the gates, the Caliph was dismissive. "What have I to fear from Al Rik'h? If Allah truly speaks to him, then Allah will advise him of the folly of setting himself against me. I have my soldiers. He has only himself. I am, after all, a true Fathamid, carrying the blood of our Prophet in his veins." This was more a political claim than an exact statement of truth. The Caliph's forefathers, boasting the blood of Fathima, the Prophet's daughter, to be theirs, had seized power in Th'amouent during a period when their predecessors, declaring themselves Sharifians (also of the Prophet's blood) were self-confidently decadent. In such matters, lacking any form of constitutional law, it was usual to make the claims of blood. Yet the Caliph spoke with his usual authority and it was generally supposed that he and the Secret One would go about their affairs without further confrontation, honour having, as it were, been put into the hands of God. There remained, nonetheless, a considerable amount of speculation. Where had Al Rik'h found the body and why had the

N
O

O
R
D
I
N
A
R
Y

C
H
R
I
S
T
I
A
N

discovery so angered him? Why had he assumed the flaying to be the Caliph's work? Why would he, who usually avoided public notoriety, make such a speech for all to hear? Who, anyway, was the dead girl?

And would Le Loup Blanc be back from the mosque to demand entry to the palace and satisfaction from the Caliph? asked a few. It was agreed that not even the Secret One would be the winner in such an encounter.

In all events, having spent the entire night in the mosque, Le Loup Blanc took part in the morning prayer, rolled up his mat and stepped outside to put on his elegant riding boots then mount his camel, who was now rested and not quite as inclined to charge and bite any passer by who caught her disgusted eye. She was a magnificent white camel, worth at least twelve thousand dirhams, and dressed richly enough to rival the most dandified Taureq. Such beasts were rare this side of the Atlas, though bred for their own use by the wild Berberim of the Low Sahara, who had never had a reason to venture this far and no desire to trade their beasts for the trinkets of Th'amouent.

A few loafers followed the camel, asking questions of the owner, which he ignored. They admired it as their European counterparts would admire a Lamborghini and they conferred romance and admiration upon the owner in recognition of his power and his taste. They wondered amongst themselves if Al Rik'h would lead his camel back to the gates of the Caliph's palace. They were denied further excitement, however. The crimson-eyed one took the Sari-al-dhar, where the market stalls were being set up for the day's business, and stabled his camel behind the Restaurant Salaman Rushd', which he entered from the rear to take a glass of mint tea and break his fast. Relaxing in his chair on the verandah he watched Th'amouent go about her business like any local lounger enjoying the pleasure of others' activity, until Captain Albert Begg sat down beside him and ordered a café complait.

"Good morning, captain," said the Secret One softly, in German. "I regret our time together is limited. This new business is a bad one and I must give it all my attention."

Rapidly, Captain Begg extended his government's compliments and relayed its intelligence that Caliph Mou'ini, requiring distractions for a variety of reasons, was planning an expansion of his power into the mountains and beyond. His majesty was anxious to stop such an expansion and sought Prince Ulrich's help.

After some thought, Ulrich von Bek said that the assistance of the British government in this matter would, he believed, be unnecessary. However, he appreciated its concern and assured it that should he ever require help in the region, he would call upon it at the first opportunity.

Amused by this courteous snub, Captain Begg bid his acquaintance good-morning and returned to his hotel. He had decided that the style of his report must be positive, in order to make up for the vagueness of its content.

CHAPTER TWO
THE FORBIDDEN DESERT

THERE WERE A hundred tales told of "Crimson Eyes" across the whole of Europe and most of Africa. The tales added supernatural powers to his undoubted natural gifts, and all were curious as to why he would choose the desert and the wild hills of the Atlas to live. Some scholars believed he might be imitating the Nazarene who, he insisted, was still his master. All were baffled, if this were the case, for in every other respect Al Rik'h appeared a model of Islam.

"There is a pain worse than giving up one's own life," said Th'amouent's local philosopher, the tailor, Al Fezim, as he and Captain Begg sat taking coffee together in the D'Jemaa al Jehudim, the Square of the Jews, "and that is the pain of losing a loved friend or someone of your own blood. That is why I wonder at such a miserable sacrifice on your prophet's part. Nothing, for instance, compared to what Abraham was prepared to do. Certainly, self-sacrifice in pursuit of one's faith can be a noble thing, but the loss of one's first-born is worse."

"And that is what we could be said to imitate," Albert Begg remarked, smiling, "not Christ's act of self-sacrifice, but God's."

"You Christians are as subtle as Jews sometimes," Al Fezim shook his head. "We simple Muslims will never fathom you, I fear."

Those familiar with the tales of Al Rik'h noted that his black companion was not with him. He was said to travel with a giant, Lobangu, who claimed to be an exiled chief of the Zulu and had sworn one day to reclaim his homeland from the Dutch invaders.

Ulrich von Bek, the Secret One, remained in Th'amouent for several more hours, contriving to come unnoticed to Captain Begg's chambers where they discussed certain secret business. Captain Begg was surprised by the visit. He had assumed his interview with Prince von Bek concluded. But the Prince asked a number of pertinent questions concerning British attitudes to the region and seemed satisfied. Then he was introduced to Poppy Begg who was naturally obsessively curious but reluctant to ask questions which would irritate him or cause him to leave. She was anxious for his approval.

When Ulrich von Bek rode his white camel out through the ochre gates of Th'amouent, he still left a city noisy with speculation. He had taken no further action against the Caliph, but had said nothing of future vengeance. He left a tension behind him and a mystery. Ascetic, handsome and alien, he had proved impossibly attractive to Poppy Begg.

For a little while the Caliph considered having Al Rik'h followed, but then thought better of it. Meanwhile Poppy had impulsively hired a fearless boy as her guide and, on horseback, had trailed the albino out of the city and into the hills.

By the evening, when the deep green shrubbery hung upon the limestone, casting rich shadows over the grey-brown rock, and gorgeous orange streamers poured across a dark blue sky, they had entered a narrow gorge which opened into the steep T'Chou Pass and Poppy found herself in utter blackness, the sky obscured by looming shelves of limestone. Unsure whether to camp or to press on, she trusted to her luck and by morning had led herself and the boy to the crest of the pass — where she was rewarded with a distant view of the blonde camel and her magnificent rider moving down toward the near-desert.

It was at this point, however, that the boy discovered an adult prudence, received half his fee, a horse and her good wishes, and headed back for home. With Al Rik'h well in sight, she plunged optimistically in his wake.

On the second night, half-crazed from heat and lack of sleep, she began to panic. She decided to camp. She dismounted and lost her horse immediately. She sat down on a rock and wept. Then she cursed. Then she got up and plunged on into the night, hoping to come upon her horse by chance in that narrow pass.

By morning, she had reached the floor of the desert and saw the tall albino beneath a palm tree, stamping out his fire and saddling his camel. Her horse was nearby, chewing on the rough grass.

Al Rik'h waited, poised in amusement, as she approached.

"Don't be angry," she pleaded. "I know it was awfully rude and deadly bad form to follow you like that, but my curiosity got the better of my manners. All I can do is apologise — and throw myself on your mercy."

Already hooded and veiled in the Taureq fashion, the tall German regarded her from deep-set crimson eyes which were not without irony. "Then I suppose I must forgive you," he said. "But what am I to do with you? I have an urgent appointment. It cannot wait. I suppose I must take you with me. Your horse is refreshed and ready for mounting. I propose you sleep in your saddle as we ride. I will show you how."

With a cord about her waist and pommel, Poppy did in fact sleep through most of the afternoon with the mysterious nobleman relaxing on his own mount and leading hers.

That night he lit a fire and made them comfortable, preparing a soup from ingredients in his saddlebags which would not have been out of place at La Lapine Russe in Paris.

She was entranced by him and begged him to tell her how he had come to this life of hermitage in the far desert.

Prince Ulrich was surprisingly frank. Clearly, he was anything but a misanthrope. His need for isolation had nothing to do with dislike of his fellow creatures. His very openness further made him the object of Poppy's curiosity.

It was an old, familiar story, he said. Even as it was happening, he was aware of its venerable antiquity. Like others of his family, who were Saxons from Bek, he had taken up residence at the family home in Mirenburg, capital of Waldenstein, the loveliest and almost the smallest nation in Middle Europe.

There, the Prince had fallen in love with and married a famous Viennese beauty. Eventually, a few years later, he had fallen in love again, but was still married. There was nothing for it. "I told my wife I was going on a long expedition and left for the desert. I have been here ever since. I do not believe my wife is unhappy with her present status. For her, I think my most attractive feature was my title." And he smiled. "She is fond of sensation. She saw me as an exotic monster and the reality disappointed her. Albinism has been in our family since the Dawn of Time. We carry that stigmata as we carry our motto "Do You The Devil's Work" and defend or pursue the Holy Grail. It is rather easier to follow that motto in the desert.... Certainly less complicated." There was a note of self-mockery in his voice.

Poppy said she thought him brave. Such nobility belonged to an earlier, more romantic century. The wild Berberim of these parts were notorious for their savage treatment of strangers. Even she knew that.

He told her that he had never been troubled by the tribes. He had not sought their approval, he said, or courted them. They understood that he wished to be left to his own devices and seemed to respect that.

"I am not a brave man, Miss Begg. I am a coward, I think. I chose this life because it was the easiest thing I could do. It was a rather selfish choice. I believe it is not uncommon for those of us who seek to escape the emotional complications of the world to become explorers and scientists and such. Believe me, I know that I took the easy way. I have a facility for languages. I was trained to ride and shoot. Nothing I do is very difficult for me. And in my heart I know very well I should have gone back to Mirenburg and faced the consequences — both moral and emotional. Instead, I found a life and a culture which applauded me, respected my love of solitude. My life is not difficult. It's rather simple, in fact, most of the time. With a couple of good camels and enough water, I had no other problems. For years, if I was not happy, at least I was pleasantly distracted. I swear that I did not expect to remain as long as I did. But I found my perfect home and I stayed. I am taking you to that home now. You could be only the third living European to see it."

He glanced away. She wondered if he expected her to die in the desert. Maybe he planned to kill her? He spoke so openly of his past. Or was he merely willing to trust her own sense of honour? She hoped it was the latter.

They travelled for two more days. She had taken to dozing in her saddle in the afternoons and was only vaguely aware that they pushed farther and farther into the gray-brown semidesert, what the Far Atlas Berberim called the *rach*, while in the distance lay only the rolling dunes of the unmapped Sahara. It was in the red early evening, with the sun settling in the west, that she opened her eyes to discover they were still on the stony *rach*, but were descending into a shallow valley filling with pink sand, at the end of which were mounds of wind-worn rock. She believed that she deceived herself into catching glimpses of green, but she saw no water.

Poppy Begg knew that she had reached that mysterious corner of the Sahara uncrossed by caravans or tribes but shunned as the home of ifrits and djinns. Ahead lay an horizon without apparent end and, lost in a haze of shimmering silver blue, was the cluster of rocks, looking positively welcoming. "My home," said Al Rik'h, pointing. "They know it as the lost oasis of Kufar'dh. You can see how anyone would believe this area barren." And he laughed.

As they descended further down the valley, Poppy began to notice the corroded remains of bones, some of them almost certainly human; of metal tools, weapons, armour, horse furniture and other artefacts — as if all the armies of history had marched here to die.

At last von Bek explained:

"A legend — it was only ever that — concerning the gold of Carthage was always attached to Kufar'dh and brought adventurers here. It still brings one or two. But Kufar'dh has no gold, as far as I know. Though once she must have had it."

"Only the Grail," she said, and had the pleasure of seeing the faintest flicker of confusion on his features. Then he laughed, as if she had joked.

"I grew to resent my responsibilities, you know. Perhaps falling in love was a distraction, deliberately engineered? I was, for a while, a gambler. Not at the French tables — at least, not much — but in Mirenburg, for the Game of Time. It was too complex, I suppose. I still remember my duty to the Grail, but I perform it in the old places, the places of that holy cup's genesis, Miss Begg. They say we are the descendants of angels, yet I see no evidence for it, do you?"

His handsome camel reared her head, sniffing and growling. "She knows we are close to home," said von Bek. "You think me a hermit, don't you? Perhaps a little mad? Well, I have a great deal of company here, most of it dead. You see the remains of those who visited here. All the tribes and races of mankind from Zanzibar to Zamarra have come here and will no doubt continue to come while folk tell stories. And will no doubt always be disappointed. I am perhaps the only one not to be. But I did not come looking for the gold of Carthage. I have known this place for twenty years. I have lived here for ten. I found it by accident."

The rocks rose steeply overhead, taller than they had appeared from a distance, and Poppy could smell water suddenly. Sweet water. She smelled it long before she saw, protected by a huge tongue of cool limestone hanging over it, a large, clear pool. Foliage, shrubbery, desert flowers, palms, were all reflected in the water. But her attention was immediately drawn to the dominant reflection, of glittering blues and geometric yellows and scarlets and dusty browns, and she gasped. She was looking at the tall, ornamental columns of an Egyptian temple! The building was in an astonishing state of preservation. It was like nothing she had seen even at Luxor or Abu Simbal. The temple might have been built that very day.

The vivid hieroglyphs were in the familiar styles, but protected by a clear glaze, evidently of the same period, which here and there had begun to flake. Like the lake that surrounded it, the building was completely invisible either from the air or the surrounding ground. The temple was of local stone. Deep within the rocky overhang, it drew all its light from the water's reflection.

At first only surprised by the state of preservation, Poppy was quick to realize how significant an architectural find this must be. Egypt was three thousand miles away across unrelenting desert! She could not speak for the questions crowding her mind.

Understanding, Ulrich von Bek smiled. "There's no particular mystery to it, Miss Begg. It is the temple and living quarters of the worshippers of Atun. They believed in a single deity, whom they symbolized by the sun. He bore rather a lot of characteristics in common with our Judaeo-Christian interpretations. This shocking heresy was, they believed, stamped out in Egypt. Clearly it lived on here, with some ups and downs, for centuries. Then, little by little, the inhabitants left or died and only their architecture remains of their civilized and disciplined way of life. There is some evidence that the last of them, all ancient, died in defence of their home when the first band of Benin warriors came through."

Dismounting, they let their animals drink and graze. A wooden bridge stretched from the shore to the little island on which the hidden temple was built. At length, he led her across this. She paused at the first pillar, running slender fingers over the bright paintings. "All because they disagreed with a religious orthodoxy. They walked three thousand miles until they were sure they were safe. They walked all that way in order to practice their faith!"

"Ironically, they went through a series of apostasies over the centuries. There are records inside. It's clear a pantheon was worshipped here, at least for a while. Maybe they invoked the old gods, and the old gods punished them for their desertion of Egypt. Aha!" He paused, his voice becoming gentler. "Here's a visitor I'm hoping will survive: He was not in a good way when I left!"

On the broad stone apron of the temple, propped against an inner pillar, just outside the huge main door, Poppy saw a young man. He had black hair, dark eyes and an almost feminine mouth. Clearly he was not in his right mind. He gasped and murmured feverishly, unable to focus on them even as they approached.

Prince Ulrich hurried to fetch the boy some water and herbs, which he mixed and presented in a small bowl, doing what he could to make the boy comfortable. He did not seem injured. He wore the uniform of the Spanish

NO ORDINARY CHRISTIAN

Foreign Legion, but with golden eagle wings, showing him to be an air auxiliary. "A pilot," she said. "You found him in the desert?"

"His plane crashed about five miles away." Von Bek had seen it go down.

"Is she here?" said the boy suddenly in Spanish. "Is she here?"

Prince von Bek tried to calm him, but the young pilot would have none of it. He clawed at the albino's burnoose and veil. "You must tell me the truth. Believe me, I'm strong. It is the wondering which is weakening me. Please, my dear fellow, tell me the truth!"

Prince von Bek nodded. He knew that he owed the boy that degree of respect. "She is not alive," he said.

"Oh, my God!" The boy almost shrieked his horror. Yet the herbs had restored him. He turned away, then spoke. "You got to the place. It was the right place? She was there? You were too late." Another, long pause, then: "How did she die?"

Von Bek's compassion took hold of him.

"By her own hand," he said, and rose to his feet.

He and Poppy Begg walked to the far end of the apron, staring into the perfect waters of the oasis, listening, with as much self-control as they could muster, to the boy's appalling weeping.

A little later, when the boy slept, von Bek lit an enormous Byzantine candelabra and by its guttering flames displayed the interior of the temple, the massive public rooms decorated with images of Ra and Atun, before which bowed, in homage, the old beast-headed gods of Egypt — the cow, the panther, the goat, the ram and the jackal, the hawk and the lion. This strange pantheon, depicted as all-powerful in so many Egyptian paintings, were here the subjects of Atun. In the smaller chambers other stories were told, other beliefs depicted. He showed her the chambers of the priests and their families, their kitchens, their meeting rooms, their sarcophagi. In the kitchen, using methods older than time, he made her a delicious couscous, which she ate with considerable relish, enthusing on his virtues until he was driven to go and see how the Spanish boy was doing.

"He's weak," reported von Bek. Making sure that she had eaten and drunk all she needed, he led her to a small, comfortably furnished chamber which appeared to have something of a woman's touch to it, with brocaded shawls and richly woven carpets festooned over an ottoman and a massive brass bed. He was pleased by her surprise. "I have had time to come by most of the comforts of Europe," he said. "This is your room. It was originally intended for a mourning chamber or a tomb. You may use my home in any way you please. All that I ask is that you remain with the boy if I am gone for any reason." He hesitated, then said: "I had occasion to take his service revolver. You will find it behind the main altar in the central temple. It has four rounds. I cannot see that you will need it, but it is as well to know."

Before she could question him further, the albino had disappeared back into the passages and chambers of his strange, adopted home.

Before she went to sleep, she explored the room, smoking one of the slim, brown cigarettes he had given her, a local kind. Soon she became drowsy and a sense of extraordinary well-being filled her, in spite of the image of the weeping boy still occupying her thoughts. With a sigh, she prepared for rest, changing into the old-fashioned white cotton and lace nightgown provided for her, then climbed into the high bed, to sink into a feather mattress and huge, down pillows. She barely had time to reflect on the peculiar paradox of such luxury, in the middle of a region known as the Forbidden Desert, before she fell into a profound sleep.

Anubis was the first to visit her. The jackal-headed god, wise and compassionate, was dressed in a suit of dark silk, his linen brilliant, almost incandescent. He held a deck of cards in his slender hands and offered to teach her to play. *I will teach you to play with the gods themselves*, he said. *I am your master. I am your friend.* And he grew to twice his original size, until his head touched the dark ceiling of her chamber and he glared down at her and he smiled. *Lord Anubis*, he said, and the words were a growl of deep satisfaction with his condition and his power. *Lord Anubis.*

I have no words, she said, *for addressing a god. Nor for parleying with the dead. I am not of your people.*

I will make you mine. It takes nothing for that. I promise. I shall neither smite nor devour thee. Sweet slave. I am your kind master. You have no power save that which I bestow upon thee.

But after Anubis came Set and Horus and Osiris, with the heads of snakes and birds and mammals, and all had the stink of the beast, the foetid stench of animal power, the terrible stench of inevitable death. And she recoiled and she wept and begged for their mercy and they granted it, they said. All she had to do was accept their rule, their arrogant existence, and she would live without pain. Then came Atun, striding into the already crowded room, his face a blinding ball of fire, his voice the rich roll of thunder, his hands ablaze with lightings, his body boiling with a strange, multi-coloured dust. Atun-Ra the all-powerful, all-seeing. Atun-Ra, tasting the boyhood of a jubilant monotheism, conscious that he somehow carried with him a power greater than all these combined, yet still a barbarian god, still bearing the unmistakeable hint of the beast.

She expected him to save her. To dismiss these others. But instead he smiled upon them all as a master might smile upon his favorite pets at play and he vanished. It occurred to her that, as yet, he was unwilling or afraid to test his strength.

Anubis took her up. His eyes were without malice and his white fangs gleamed in a grin of kindness. And they flew across all the magnificent cities of the world, in all their ages and conditions, and then she returned. She lay in her bed watching as the races and nations of mankind marched across the room.

And then they were gone and there was a silence.

She became aware of movement, in corners, beneath furniture, inside draperies and against walls. Small, flickering movements at first, and tiny sounds, almost laughter, perhaps weeping. She strained to hear and then, as the sounds grew louder, tried to block them, gasping and shouting against the insinuating horror of the greedy dead. Out of the walls and the quilts and the pillows they came; out of the carpets and the brocades, the cupboards and the chests, barely seen at first. The greedy dead. All those restless ghouls who had sought gold at the Temple of Atun and had found only painful, prolonged death. Now it was not gold they yearned for, but a little warm blood, a taste of human life, of living flesh and a vibrant soul. They were so hungry, they said. We are forbidden the Afterlife.

She felt the weight of the wraiths upon her body. She sensed that they sought some means of sucking the lifestuff from her. To keep themselves alive — if this were life — for a few more pointless years.

Then she grew even more terrified. What if it were only she? What if it were some specific chemistry of her own that attracted these phantoms?

She began to scream. But door upon door had been closed, all the way to the far exterior, and nothing could hear her, unless it wanted to.

And then Anubis had returned, dismissing the wraiths with familiar contempt, his muzzle curling back over his teeth in a grin of disgust. Within seconds they were all gone. He knelt beside her bed and took her hand. His snout was soft against her skin, his breath warm and moist. *This is our final tomb. So little sustains us now. I am the beast and the beast is your enemy. But it is you I would have live.*

The boy, she said. *The boy is weak. He has no will to live. He has no belief left. Help him with the strength he needs.*

I will go to him soon and I promise you I will guide him safely into the Land of Death, for this tomb is the gateway to that land.

No, she said. *It is life which must be asserted now. Help him, I beg you. You bring us death. I offer you life.*

There is more than you know, said Anubis. *For every death there is new life. For every tomb a cradle.* He gestured and she stared into the blackness of the ether, into the blossoming stars, into the broad rays of multi-coloured light which radiated everywhere and made paths. Down these moonbeam roads strode all the old gods of Egypt, the beast-headed immortals of Assyria and Babylon, and of Carthage. To stand before her, as if in gratitude. She lowered her eyes against their alien brilliance, averted her head from their heavy stink, and for a moment they regarded her gravely before seeming to make a decision amongst themselves. There was a chorus of shrieks and bellowings: their language. When she looked back, the moonbeams were fading and she saw the last of the old gods disappearing into the great, rich darkness of the ether; and soon there were only stars. Then she saw only the walls of the tomb, her chamber, and she was again alone.

Anubis was gone. Anubis, and with him all the rest of the pantheon. She closed her eyes tight against any further visions and slept dreamlessly until morning.

When she found the Spanish boy, he was much stronger. He spoke of having seen a jackal come to the pool and drink in the moonlight. The jackal had remained, sitting and watching him, all night. Only at dawn had the creature risen and loped off into the desert. The boy believed that the jackal carried the spirit of his dead girl. "She lives in the desert now, where she was always happiest, where she was free."

"That is my consolation."

She went to find Al Rik'h, but his camel was gone. The boy reported that the albino had left early, riding off in the same direction as the jackal.

"He went into the lands of the Beni Rabi'. He told me he had a duty to perform. I am familiar with those warlike Taureqs. They allow none but their own blood kin to ride with them, yet he is welcome among them."

Von Bek had not told the young airman when he would return.

Poppy Begg was still lost in the memory of her vivid dreams. She had never experienced such complex illusions. She could even recall the smell of those creatures: that stink of ancient vitality. She remembered the kindness of Anubis and she knew that he had answered her prayer. He had brought some comfort, at least, to the Spanish airman.

She wondered for a moment if Prince Ulrich von Bek had deliberately exposed her to whatever old magic still soaked the stones of the tomb he had turned into a bed-chamber. One day she would ask him.

Meanwhile, she thought often of the jackal. When she returned to her bed that night, he came to her again.

To claim, he reminded her gently, his price.

CHAPTER THREE
HOW VENGEANCE CAME TO TH' AMOUENT

POPPY BEGG BUSIED herself all that week, tending to the young airman and watching him grow stronger and sadder by the hour. Her clear, grey eyes were full of sympathy for him. At length he asked her if he might tell her his story. She had been too discreet to propose it. She said that he must not weaken himself. She would let him talk, but if he grew too tired, she would stop him. He was like a child now, almost wholly obedient to her tender will.

He told her at once who the young woman had been.

"She was my wife," he said. "I had not seen her for three years." He had met her in Casablanca and they had fallen in love. Against the wishes of her father and his own parents, they had married. Life in the army had been difficult. He took an extended leave and they went to live in Madrid, then in Paris.

Poppy suggested there had been problems involving race, but the young lieutenant shook his head. "She was Caucasian, with that clear, pale skin and aquiline beauty of the Western Berber. She looked, to European eyes, every inch an aristocrat of an old family. Most people assumed her to be Viennese. Our problems had to do with her restlessness. I should never have taken her away from the desert. Like you, she sought exotic romance, but unlike you she did not live to learn a lesson. She disappeared one night, near Les Halles. I became frantic and began searching for her. I searched for a year without success, without a single clue, and eventually I was forced to rejoin my regiment. I prayed that I might find her back in the Magrib. Here, at least, there were rumours, a fragment of hope."

"You heard of her?"

"She heard of me. She learned that I was stationed in Tangier and she got word to me. She had been sold to the Caliph of Th'amouent and was a prisoner in his cruel household. She begged me to help her escape. There were people to bribe, others to cajole or to blackmail, and so on. It took me six months. I raised all the money I could, paid whoever might require a bribe, and I was successful. My wife was freed with the help of a high-ranking servant of the Caliph. She was given a map, a compass and a horse. She was also given instructions for reaching the Wadi-al-Hara, the River of Stones. There, I might safely land my aeroplane. The rest is everything you might have guessed. My plane crashed here. I had engine trouble. I was tormented with the vision of my wife waiting alone by the Wadi-al-Hara, expecting me at any moment — and so vulnerable, so horribly vulnerable, to the Caliph's forces, who would track her as a matter of principle as soon as it was discovered that she was gone. She had already let me know the fate of any woman who sought to escape his harem. If they caught her, they would be allowed to determine how she would be punished, whether to finish her by stoning or flaying, and what to do with her in the meantime. Then, because the Caliph is a cautious man, anxious not to upset the sensibilities of his foreign investors, they would dismember and butcher the corpse beyond recognition...."

At this the young Spaniard broke down. He rapidly took control of himself, but could not speak for a while.

Later Poppy learned how Al Rik'h had found the young man in the wrecked plane. He was already feverish, babbling of his wife's danger and pleading with the crimson-eyed aristocrat to take him to her, to save her.

Instead the Secret One had made him comfortable and had gone rapidly in search of the woman.

Poppy assumed that this was all he knew of the story, but now he revealed that Al Rik'h had spoken long into the night. According to the albino, his wife had stabbed herself when she saw the Caliph's men riding down on her and no sign of the aeroplane, but was still alive when they reached her. It was then that Al Rik'h had arrived at the Wadi-al-Har and disposed rapidly of the ruffians before they could touch the woman. She was still alive when he had dealt with the Caliph's riders, but only barely. She had whispered her desperate request into her saviour's ear — that he tell her father, Sheikh Aron ben Sid', that she loved him and had never meant to shame him and to tell her husband that she had never willingly betrayed him.

"And where has he gone now?" Poppy's lovely face was full of pity and concern. She brushed her brown hair back from her cheeks and turned her head away, so that he might not see the tears. She was not puzzled by the discrepancy in the story. Clearly Al Rik'h had wanted to spare the young flyer's feelings.

"I think he intends to deliver the other part of her message," said the lieutenant. "He has gone out there" — he indicated the depths of the far Sahara — "to seek Sheikh Aron, who is the great patriarch of the Beni Rabi' and counts Le Loup Blanc as his son. Von Bek will be welcome. My wife, you see, was Sheikh Aron's daughter. I think that for once the Caliph of Th'amouent has misjudged his enemy."

Together they prepared to wait for the return of the Secret One. On some nights, Poppy Begg did not visit her chamber, but tended to the young airman, cradling his head on her breast as he slept and murmured and wept in his dreams.

They were not to see Al Rik'h again for another five days, when he brought them fresh horses and provisions and instructed them on how they might reach Th'amouent. He seemed distant and thoughtful and would tell them nothing of what had taken place between himself and the Ben Rabi'.

"I think you will swiftly come to know the end of this particular tale," he assured them.

When they arrived at last in Th'amouent, Poppy found the character of the city subtly changed. She was thankful that her uncle had waited for her. He already knew that she was safe.

"There is a new master of the city," he told her. "A new Caliph. Th'amouent has only just finished celebrating the end of tyranny."

He had seen the whole affair from his rooms, he said, when one morning, without warning, the veiled warriors of the Beni Rabi' had ridden their magnificent horses and camels through the Hakhim Gate and streamed through Th'amouent's narrow streets to surround the palace of the Caliph, their blue cloaks rising and falling in the wind like a vengeful tide. Then, at a word from their white-faced leader, they had engulfed the palace. And by evening the city was informed that the Caliph, his kin and all his favourite servants were dead or in the process of dying and that Th'amouent was now under the protection of Allah and his faithful servant the Sheikh Aron ben Salim of the Beni Rabi'. The flayed corpses were displayed in the D'Jemaa-al-Jehudim, the glaring heads preserved in salt. It was what the populace expected and demanded of their new Caliph.

But Poppy Begg remained all the more in love with the crimson-eyed albino, who had returned to his forbidden desert, to his strange, god-haunted home.

Poppy Begg stayed for many months in Th'amouent and was treated with extravagant and courteous hospitality by the new Caliph, who readily assumed his responsibilities and seemed willing to treat her as the daughter he had lost. But Al Rik'h, his Zulu companion Lobangu and their snow-white camels were reported as having been seen in the mountains of Abyssinia, helping the people against the Italian invaders.

Poppy yearned for the aristocratic albino and prayed for him to come to her. Though she asked after him often, she kept her word to him. She never told of the lost oasis, of the hidden temple or of the visions she had experienced there. She showed a certain interest in images of Anubis, and read much of Egyptian antiquity. And she did not offer the Spanish airman the true story he would never hear, once he was gone from the region, of his wife's death.

The Spaniard was ordered one day to Marrakech, to take the army train to Tangier. There was news of an uprising amongst the Rif, of a charismatic leader who threatened to drive all Christians into the sea and seemed able to keep his word. The young airman would die in an early expedition against Abd'-al-Krim, brought down by the long guns of the Berber sharpshooters.

At last Sir Albert Begg came out to find her. It was early 1939 and the volatile politics of Europe had drawn attention away from expansionist dreams in Africa, at least for the moment.

Sir Albert persuaded his niece to return with him to England. He could not otherwise vouch for her safety. Soon the power of the British Empire would be stretched to the full and there would be parts of the world where it would not stretch at all....

Until the Blitz of 1940, in which she acquitted herself with some heroism, Poppy Begg was more bored in London than ever before, dreaming each night of an Egyptian temple, preserved almost as new, hidden in a lost oasis, deep within the forbidden Sahara. She dreamed, too, of a white rider on a white camel, a rider whose deep-set crimson eyes looked with affection into hers and whose kiss drew the soul from her body. She dreamed of Anubis the Jackal God, who would come to make love to her, to carry her away into the depths of the ancient Sahara, where all our histories were written in the dust which blew perpetually across the dunes in that deep, unmapped wilderness that is the world beyond the West. She dreamed of prehistoric lusts, of supernatural satisfactions, of the great, bestial intelligences whose law still threatened the living. She dreamed, again and again, everything she had dreamed before, in that hidden temple, where time and even entropy were forgotten. And all the while the bombs fell around her and her city blazed.

One day, after the end of the Second World War, but just before the Egyptian Revolution, which ejected Farouk and the British, she went to live in Egypt, a famous recluse. She has a homestead of sorts there still, above Aswan, looking down upon the great white rocks of the first and second cataracts, still busy with the traffic of centuries.

They say she worships the old gods, that she is a witch, but a benign one. She is almost a mascot to the local people. There was never any trouble here, up on the Nubian border. Not the sort they had in Cairo. They say she goes into the deepest desert, where the ancients built a tomb for Atun, their dead god, and that at night the old pantheon visits her, disporting with her and telling her all the secrets of Time.

Sometimes, in the afternoons, she will lay out her tea service and entertain her friend, the Wesleyan chaplain of the Cataract Hotel, favoured chiefly these days by German tourists of the old school. He rarely removes his dark glasses. He has the face of a Jesuit and some believe him miraculously recovered from leprosy. He is in fact a pure albino, of uncertain age.

The old couple are enjoying their last years. They sit in Miss Begg's wicker chairs, below the slow, lazy fans, and tell stories, one after another, until the sun goes down over the Nile.

And, perhaps occasionally, on a warm, Spring evening, the chaplain will inquire politely if it would be convenient for him to stay the night.

And, politely, she will assure him of his welcome.

WHITE LADY'S GRAVE

I thought, when I moved to Scotland, that I was leaving romance behind, but here I am, in it over my head.

Men have called me beautiful, called me princess, wooed me, sometimes left other women, even their wives, for me. Usually in the end I found it was not me they loved but a fantasy-figure, something from their own imaginations. Their love was a private world I couldn't enter. But I kept hoping, kept trying to get in, to make them see me, to make the happy-ever-after dream come true. All through my teens and twenties I fell in and out of love, recovered, went on to the next man, bruised but still believing. In my thirties my enthusiasm soured. I began to question the truth of this story which had been my life.

Then I met Angus, a stocky, red-headed Scotsman, and although he wasn't my physical type, he won me over with his gentleness, his warmth, his sense of humor, and his practical attitude toward life. I didn't have to pretend with him; I didn't feel I was risking his disappointment every time I opened my mouth to say what I really thought.

Angus wasn't a dreamer, he was a doer. He had a proposal which appealed to me: We would run a fish farm in Scotland, perhaps doing a bit of bed-and-breakfast on the side, in the season. It would be a wholesome, outdoor, rural life, particularly good for children.

I liked the idea of having children, and I longed to get out of London, which had become murky with memory and the failure of desire. By going away with Angus I thought I could escape my own history and the doomed inevitability of repeating it.

Before, when I'd gone away with a man, whether for a weekend or a life together, there had always been the sense that I was being swept away, that I was only acceding to a force greater than myself. But when I married Angus it was an act of will.

I willed myself to be happy, and I was. We both were. Our new life together was different and satisfying, and even though, after three years, there was no sign of a child and I was nearly forty, I was determined we would be happy ever after.

So I felt no intimations of danger when I noticed the stranger in the bar of our local hotel that August evening, even though he was looking at me. I thought marriage, contentment, and age all protected me from romance. There were lines on my face, gray in my hair, and my body had thickened with the passage of years. So I looked back at the stranger, feeling quite safe, and accepted his offer of a drink. Angus was just the other side of the room, playing billiards. I was friendly in the way you can be when you expect everyone to know you're married.

He was handsome: gray eyes in a lean, clean-shaven face; fair hair pulled back into a ponytail; a long, strong-looking body. He had the sort of self-confidence that expects, and gets, a warm welcome wherever it goes, and he must have been at least ten years younger than me. I was flattered by his attention, no longer the young woman who would have taken it as her due.

I can't remember the first thing he said to me, how we got started, but before very long he was telling me a story. There was a lilt to his voice, the trace of an accent which made me think he might have grown up speaking Gaelic, and it was as much a pleasure to listen as to look at him.

"Long ago," he said, "and far away, in the land of the ever-young, a great prince by the name of Midhir fell in love with a woman so beautiful, so fair to look upon, that she was known always as The Fair Woman. But when he took her back to his palace to be his wife there was another woman there who was jealous and turned The Fair Woman into a butterfly and summoned up a magical wind which blew her about the land for seven times seven years, never allowing her a moment's rest. It blew her finally out of the land of the ever-young, into the world of mortal men, and then across the sea, and then at last into the garden of a house where a woman sat in company, eating and drinking beneath the trees. The butterfly was blown into the woman's cup and the woman saw this but was unable to stop herself from swallowing it with her drink. Some months later this woman, whose name was Rona, gave birth to a daughter and named her Elaine. And Elaine grew up to be as fair as The Fair Woman, yet never knowing her true origins — except as she might glimpse them in dreams — and with no idea that her husband, Midhir, loved and searched for her still."

The man stopped speaking and watched me. I was confused and upset and didn't like to show it. Anyone could have told him — although I hadn't

— that my name was Elaine, but only Angus, in this company, knew my mother's name. And not even Angus knew my mother's story — one of the embarrassments of my childhood — about swallowing a butterfly in a glass of beer and then imagining, when she felt my first movements in her womb that same day, that it was the butterfly trapped inside her. I looked into my wine, smiling vaguely. "Nice story. Did you make it up?"

"Of course not. It's true." His eyes met mine and I felt a warm, intimate tingle accompanying the certainty that we really did know one another, were already lovers on some other level, in some other time and place.... Uh-oh. I knew what *that* meant, although I hadn't felt it in years. That unexpected, unwilled response made me nervous, and I was gracelessly abrupt.

"I'm married."

"You're married here. In the land of the ever-young you were married to me."

"Ah, but that was in another country, and, besides, The Fair Woman is dead."

"Not dead. In that country no one ever dies; everyone is young and strong, without blemish, sin, or guilt. Fair Woman, will you come with me there to reign beside me as my queen?"

If he was crazy, it was a most attractive madness. But if this was his usual pickup line, surely he could see I was too old for fairy tales. I wondered what he'd do if I said yes. Take me up to his room? Row me out to his yacht, at anchor in the harbor? A little devil inside urged me to accept, just to see what excuse he'd come up with for not being able to take me to his magical country this instant. But I knew too well how affairs got started, and how they always ended. Flirtation with this man was too risky. I knew I wouldn't be tempted if I wasn't seriously attracted. I couldn't even think up a teasing refusal, just shook my head and repeated, "I'm married."

"Would your husband give you to me?"

I nearly choked on my wine. "We're not that sort of people!"

"If he sold you, would you leave him?"

"He wouldn't. He couldn't. Women aren't bought and sold here — I don't know what it's like in your country."

"My country is your country. There is no buying or selling there, no thine or mine. Please, won't you come with me there?" I felt such yearning for him as he spoke — for his fantasy or for his body was something I couldn't distinguish — that I could only cope by walking away.

"Sorry," I said, brusquely, getting up. "I'm flattered, of course, but you've mistaken me for someone else."

I couldn't get Midhir or his story out of my head. I remembered my mother's story of how she became aware that she was pregnant with me after swallowing a butterfly, and I wondered if she'd read the same book Midhir had plundered for his chatup line. I went to our little local library the next day and told Maire Mackenzie the story that the stranger had told me.

"'The Wooing of Etain,'" the librarian said. "It's an old Irish story."

"I'd like to read it."

I expected her to fill out a card — most books I'd expressed interest in had to be requested from other libraries — but she went straight to the shelves. "Here's a version for children, and it's quoted in a couple of the local guidebooks."

"Local? You said it was Irish."

"So were the Dalriadan kings. We share a common culture, and we're close enough for there to have been lots of sea-crossings in the old days. When Dierdre had to get away, it was to the west coast of Scotland that she came. Do you know how Sliabh Gaoil got its name?"

"I don't even know what it is."

"Of course you do; your house is in its shadow. *Sliabh* is the Gaelic for mountain. 'Sliabh Gaoil' means 'the lovers' mountain,' and the lovers who are remembered in that name might well have been Etain and Midhir. Ah." She pulled a shabby green volume from the collection of books about the area. "Etain and Midhir are connected, by local tradition, with a chambered cairn in the Achaglachgach Forest."

My stomach constricted with surprise. Angus and I lived in the Achaglachgach Forest. "Is that the cairn called the White Lady's Grave?"

Maire wrinkled her nose. "Who calls it that?"

"One of our neighbors. She's lived on the edge of that forest forever. Angus and I noticed there was a chambered cairn marked on the map, and wondered if we'd be able to find it, and she said there was a stone sticking out the side of it that the locals called the door, and supposedly if you rapped on it after moonrise on a night of the full moon the King of the Fairies would open and give you your heart's desire. Anyway, Angus and I walked up there one afternoon. It's quite an easy walk. But except for the standing stone there's nothing much to see. If I hadn't known what it was I would have thought it was just a hillock."

"You wouldn't have recognized it as an entrance to Fairyland?"

"Is it? Gosh, imagine having it so close!"

"Oh, it's not unique. They all are, all the old tumuli. That's why the fairies were called the *sidh* or the people of the mounds — the mounds themselves are *sidh*. That term isn't as common here as in Ireland, but your cairn is called Sidh Ban Finn. Is there something wrong?"

Her calling it "your cairn" had made me shiver, but I shrugged it off. "Goose on my grave. What does 'shee baan finn' mean?"

"Well, it doesn't mean 'white lady.' It's the *sidh* of The Fair Woman."

WHITE LADYS GRAVE

Midhir, according to the children's book, is the King of the Fairies. After losing his wife, he finds her dwelling, reborn as a mortal woman, wife of the High King Eochy. She refuses to go away with the stranger unless her husband gives her to him. Midhir challenges Eochy to a game of chess and, losing, performs a number of magical tasks for the king until, finally, Midhir wins a game, and asks as his reward a kiss from Etain. Although unwilling, Eochy can see no honorable way out and so agrees. As soon as Midhir has his arms around Etain the two rise into the air and become a pair of swans flying away.

The children's story ended there, but one of the guidebooks gave more of it, complete with variant endings.

Eochy now searched everywhere for his wife, just as Midhir once had done, and eventually learned from a druid that she was being held in Midhir's royal palace, which appeared to human eyes as the Sidh Ban Finn. Eochy took his men and they began to dig it up, but whatever they dug up one day would be filled in again the next, so they made no progress. Yet the battle took its toll upon Midhir, too, and after nine years he appeared and offered to give up Etain. He then sent his wife, with fifty handmaidens, back to the king, magically making them all look exactly alike. In one version, Eochy was able to recognize his wife because she gave him a sign; in another, he mistakenly chose his own daughter, and made her pregnant before he learned the truth.

It was all more complicated than the simple love story the stranger had told me. It was not exactly a huge shock to discover that the jealous woman at the fairy court who cast the first spell was actually Midhir's first wife.

Now I knew more about the story, but nothing about the stranger, or why he'd told it to me. Could it be that he'd thought I'd recognize it? It wasn't impossible that someone might have told him where I lived, recommending us for B&B, and a glance at the map would have shown how close we were to the Sidh Ban Finn. Tourists always expected locals to know everything about the area, not realizing we had other things to do than read guidebooks and explore ancient monuments. Maybe he'd expected me to correct him, and was waiting for me to say, "But I'm Elaine, not Etain," so he could put out his hand saying, "And I'm Mather, not Midhir; Peter Mather, from Donegal."

It could be that he wasn't even attracted to me at all, that he was just one of those attractive young men who flirts, as a matter of course, with anything female. That thought gave me a terrible, hollow sensation, and I knew I must not see him again.

When Angus next suggested going out for a drink I had too much to do in the house, or there was something on television I particularly wanted to see. He stayed home with me the first two times, but on the third night he went out alone, and came home looking both puzzled and pleased with himself. He told me the story:

A stranger had challenged him to a game of pool, winner to declare the stakes. Angus, when he won, tried to laugh it off, saying he never played for money.

"Nor I," said the stranger. "But ask me for something, anything I can give you. Surely there must be some task you want done?"

"He wouldn't be put off," Angus told me. "When I tried, you'd have thought I was insulting him. We were that close to a fight. So I said there was something I could use a hand with, if he really meant it — our garage needs a roof. Well, you know we could wait half the year before Duncan gets around to helping me with it, whereas this Mither, or whatever his name is, will be here tomorrow. So what's the harm? It might turn out he'll let me pay him something in the end, or I could find some other jobs that want doing, and pay him for those. Could be he's really looking for work."

"Could be he's looking for something else," I said.

"What do you mean? He seemed honest to me."

Seeming honest was the con man's stock in trade, of course. Away from the city, how quickly we'd forgotten. But a man who presented himself as a prince from another world was not someone to be trusted. I said nothing of my own emotions, but now I told Angus the story he had told me.

"So you're saying it was all a ploy on his part to get another look at my wife? It would serve him right if you stayed in the house all day and never showed your face...or, better yet, went away to Glasgow shopping."

The little, internal lurch of disappointment I felt at the thought of doing that told me how much I wanted to see Midhir again. It was a warning I disregarded. "No, I'm not saying that. Why would he tell me that story? He couldn't expect me to believe it."

Angus shrugged. "He's Irish. The gift of the blarney, and there's something fey about him...maybe he believes it's true. He's young...."

"At least ten years younger than me, maybe more. That's my point. Why chat *me* up?"

My husband put an arm around me. "You were the most beautiful woman in the bar that night, as you are every night. Ten years from now you'll still be inspiring young poets like him to flights of fancy. And I hope you'll still be mine."

"Of course." I thought I could will it to be true.

The first glance from Midhir's gray eyes when I opened the door to him next morning pierced me with sweet pain and I began to smile. My hands and feet felt very far away. I was full of bubbles, lighter than air. Angus came through and took Midhir out to show him what wanted doing to the garage, and I said, "I'll make the tea," and grinned and grinned like an idiot in the empty kitchen.

I felt wonderful. I realized that before I met Midhir, I had scarcely been alive, just surviving. All day, I kept singing to myself as I started one task and then abandoned it for another, unable to concentrate, unable to care, not worried about a thing. Life was grand. All day I scarcely saw him, but was aware of him, the way you're aware of a warm fire in the corner of a room, or the sun in the sky. He was there, the most important thing in my world.

I managed to cook a meal — not one of my better efforts — and served it in the evening, and as the wine flowed, so did my feelings, overflowing into the looks I could not stop exchanging with him. I wanted to touch him but could not, not with Angus there between us. At first his mere presence was enough, but as the evening wore on I began to feel restless, wanting more.

After we'd eaten, Midhir challenged my husband to a game of chess.

"I suppose the stakes are the same as before?" asked Angus. "Winner to name the forfeit?"

"If you agree," said Midhir.

"Oh, aye. There's lots of odd jobs that want doing around here. I'd be happy to pay to have them done."

"Some things can't be bought or sold, they can only be won or lost."

"As you wish," said Angus, and went to get his chess set.

I said nothing while he was gone, and Midhir gazed at the tabletop and not at me. We were in suspense. The air was heavy with anticipation. As if we were listening to a story, there was nothing we could do to hurry it along or change the eventual outcome.

Rather to my surprise — although I knew he had played competitively when younger — Angus won the game.

"Name the stake," said Midhir.

Angus frowned in thought. I wondered if I should remind him that we'd been meaning to put a new ceiling in the kitchen, or suggest repainting the entire house. I wanted a job that would bring Midhir back here day after day — and surely the young man wanted the same. But then Angus said that the spare room's light fitting needed replacing.

"I'll do it now," said the young man.

I gave a cry of disappointment, and when they both looked at me had to fumble for a reason. "You can't — not now. You shouldn't fool around with electricity; not when you've both been drinking."

"For goodness' sake, woman, it's only a light fitting," said Angus. "I'm not asking him to rewire the house."

He was done in a quarter of an hour. I had the brandy bottle and three glasses out by then.

"Another game?" said Angus.

"Stakes to be decided as before."

"Aye."

I drank two glasses of brandy and then heard Midhir say, "Checkmate." And suddenly suspected that in spite of my husband's skill at chess Midhir could have won the first game as easily as this one, if he'd wanted to. Looking at him, I could see Angus thinking the same thing. The room was very quiet as we waited to hear the forfeit.

"I want your wife in my arms and a kiss from her lips. This is all I ask."

"That's not fair! I mean, you can't ask me for something that isn't mine to give."

"Then I ask you to give her permission to give herself to me."

I felt a fluttering deep inside, as if it were the butterfly my mother had swallowed. I didn't dare look at Midhir, afraid my desire for him would be too blatant.

"Elaine doesn't need my permission. She's not my property; she's a free woman. Ask me for something else."

"There's nothing else I want."

"Then it's Elaine you should have challenged, not me."

Both men were watching me. I felt a childish fury at Angus for making this so difficult, yet knowing I would have been even more furious had he dared to treat me as his property. And much greater than any anger, discomfort or embarrassment was the powerful longing I felt to give Midhir the kiss he wanted, to be held in his arms, to be his, however briefly.

I went to him and he put his arms around me. As we kissed, I became aware of a sound like a great beating of wings around us, and I felt myself begin to rise.

And then I was standing on the floor of the sitting room, looking at Midhir, who was backing away from me. He looked confused; for a moment I thought he was going to stumble, but he recovered himself and sketched a brief, courtly bow to Angus.

"Thank you for your hospitality. I must go now."

"I'll show you out," said Angus. I saw by the careful way he held himself and didn't look at me that he was hurt but wouldn't make an issue of it. Least said, soonest mended. That was one of his sensible mottoes, and his dislike of emotional postmortems had been very attractive to me after involvements with men who'd insisted on analyzing every disagreement or hurt feeling throughout our affairs. Yes, I thought, you're hurt now but you'll soon get over it; we'll both recover and our marriage will go on as before. After all, it was only a kiss.

When Angus came back we began to clear away the dishes and the empty bottles and he said, "We had a lot to drink."

"Too much," I agreed. Then, impulsively, "Angus, I'm sorry—"

"Don't," he said swiftly. "It's all right."

I was on the point of reassuring him but then couldn't as I understood that I had already left him. I had ended our marriage when I walked into Midhir's arms.

But as quickly as that insight came it left me. Common sense bustled up importantly. What nonsense. Of course our marriage wasn't over; of course I hadn't left Angus. Here we were in our home, about to do the washing-up together, like any other night. Brandy on top of wine and sexual intoxication had made me silly. A kiss was just a kiss, not a binding promise, not an irrevocable step, not the destruction of a marriage, not unless you wanted it to be.

But I did want it to be.

Common sense lay down and died. Love had me in its grip. I'd tried to pretend I didn't believe in it, that it was just an illusion, that peace and contentment and all sorts of other things were more important, but I'd only managed to stave it off for a few years: this desire, this disease I had in me.

Angus was a good man, and he had been good to me. I didn't wish him any sorrow. But even if Midhir was mad or a liar, he was the one I wanted, he was the man I'd already gone after in my heart.

I left Angus while he was washing the dishes. He thought I was going to the bathroom, but I went out of the house by the front door, saying nothing, taking nothing with me, not even my handbag or a cardigan against the chill. I didn't say good-bye or leave a note because I knew this was madness, what I was doing, and if Midhir wasn't nearby, waiting for me, I would have to go back. Then I could say I'd just been out looking at the moon. I could go on being the wife of Angus and try to forget I'd ever wanted anything else.

I wonder what Etain really wanted, which man she really loved? Perhaps neither. In the story she's simply dutiful, giving her loyalty to the one who owns her, simply an object, like Helen of Troy, for men to fight over. But what about the real woman, if there ever was one? What about me?

The moon was full and the night clear, so I had no trouble seeing my way. As I reached the bottom of our drive I saw a man waiting on the old stone bridge where the forestry track leading into the hills splits off from the paved road, and my heart and stomach clenched in a way more like fear than joy. I ran to him anyway, as if I had no choice.

We kissed, and I shivered with passion and fear in his arms.

"I thought you'd forgotten me," he said. "When the magic didn't work, I thought I'd lost you forever, that you'd been blown too far out of our world ever to return."

I understood what he meant, because I'd felt it, too. When we'd kissed, it should have happened then: The roof should have opened, and we should have flown away together then, like in the story. But that kind of magic didn't work in this world.

"Your magic did work," I said. "Look, here I am."

"You'll live with me forever," he said. "We'll never grow old. Come."

"Where are we going?" I looked up and down the dark, empty, tree-lined road. "Where's your car?"

"We're going to my palace. Come, it's not very far." Holding my hand warmly and tightly in his he led me up the forestry track, deeper into the forest on the side of Sliabh Gaoil, the lovers' hill.

What did I think, as I went with him?

I thought maybe he'd parked his car out of sight of the house, a little way into the forest. I thought maybe he was taking me to some isolated spot where we could make love —I was eager enough, abandoned enough, to have done it with him right away, in the wet grass, anywhere. I thought maybe he was a fairy prince whose palace looked to ordinary mortal eyes like nothing but a grassy hillock, and when we reached the Sidh Ban Finn it would be transformed — that with my hand in his I would be able to walk through a newly opened door into another world of unimaginable splendor.

I thought that no matter what happened at least I would be with him, and that would be magic enough.

Lord, what fools these mortals be!

Before long we left the road. I remembered a short, stiffish climb from my daytime visit to the mound with Angus; at night, the bracken, brambles and uneven ground were all far more treacherous, as threatening and mindless as a bad dream. I clung to Midhir, who more than half-carried me over the roughest ground.

Then we stopped. We were on a hillside, in a treeless space where the bracken grew as high as my head. No lights showed in any direction, although I knew we must be less than a mile, as the crow flies, from my own house. I felt my orientation shift until I had no idea where we were, no notion how one bit of this wilderness fit with any other. I looked at the man beside me and knew him even less than I knew this moonlit territory. For a moment I recognized my own insanity in allowing him to take me here, and then I embraced the madness. This was what I wanted, this crazy love, this stranger. I shivered and leaned against him.

"You see it," he said softly.

I frowned into the darkness, wanting to please him. "What...?"

"My sidh. The entrance to my world."

A particular massive darkness detached itself from the general gloom, and I realized it was a standing stone. "This is the Sidh Ban Finn."

"You can see!" He sounded so joyful I didn't have the heart to confess I had only guessed. "Oh, my darling, I thought perhaps you'd been away so long, and come so far, I might never get you back. Magic hardly ever works in this dreadful world."

"I never believed in magic before I met you."

"Come, let's not linger out here, while the gates to my country are open."

I let him lead me forward, his arm around my waist. "Tell me where we're going…describe it to me. I can't see very much in the dark."

"It won't be dark for long, my love — surely you see the light ahead?"

Did I see a light at the end of a dark tunnel, or was it only imagination, fueled by the desperate need to see something? I decided it didn't matter. The will to believe would be enough.

I went with my love into the darkness, eyes fixed on the dim light I'd willed into existence. We went into the side of the mound. *That* I didn't imagine: there was an opening, an entrance of some kind that had not been there when I'd seen it in daylight with Angus. A door opened for us, and we went through.

For a brief moment I knew I was in another country. I could feel warmer air moving against my face, a spring breeze, scented with apple blossom; and above me an open, starry sky — or were those torches?

I paused to look up and I stumbled — or he did — and his hand slipped away from my waist, and suddenly I was in pitch darkness and alone. Everything changed in an instant. The air was still, close, stale and damp, and smelled strongly of earth. There was not even the hint of a light anywhere, and my lover had gone.

"Midhir —where are you?"

My own voice came back to me, loud and flat, words spoken too loudly in a small enclosure, and as I stretched out my arms to reach for him my fingers touched cold, damp stone.

Where was he? Where was I? Why couldn't I see? Where was the moon?

Panic threatened and I struggled for control, exploring my surroundings by touch. It didn't take long. Stone walls perhaps six feet apart on either side, extending maybe ten or twelve in length; a stone ceiling a few inches above my head. I was inside a rectangular chambered cairn, inside the Sidh Ban Finn.

There had been a way in, so there must be a way out. But no matter how I pressed, pulled and prodded at the stone slabs, I couldn't find it.

And where was Midhir, who had been beside me until a moment ago?

He had gone into that other country — close at hand, yet closed to me. He must still be beside me, pleading with me to open my eyes and see, casting his useless magical spells.

It was so dark that it made no difference whether my eyes were open or shut, so I shut them and tried to convince myself that Midhir was standing beside me, that I could feel his lips on mine, and that when I opened my eyes I would see him smiling at me, his handsome face illuminated by the thousand fairy-lights decorating his palace. I had believed enough to come this far; I must be able to push myself further. I concentrated on Midhir and opened my eyes.

Nothing. Blackness, stale air, the approach of a lonely death. The will to believe was not enough. I could not believe in Fairyland, not even to save my own life.

To Midhir this was a fairy palace and the entrance to another world. To me it is a grave. It was always my grave, and now I am in it.

BURIAL AT SEA

USS *Lafayette* moved quietly through the Atlantic Ocean at a stately eight knots, her black cigar shape blending in with the dark-green water surrounding her. Even though she was four hundred and twenty-five feet long and displaced over eight thousand tons, she seemed to move effortlessly through the water. While able to go nearly three times as fast as she was now, she almost never did. In submarine warfare, speed is noise, and noise helps the enemy find you. And ballistic missile submarines don't like to be found.

Instead, like the rest of her kind, she "transited" at ten to twelve knots from her base to a patrol area where she slowed and became quieter still: waiting for the launch order that no one wanted to hear.

Now, her job was over. Newer, even better subs and a changing world had made her obsolete.

She was in no rush to get to Washington state, where a shipyard indifferently awaited her arrival. She would be just another nuclear sub lying about until it was time to chop her into small cubes and sell them as scrap metal. At the age of twenty-seven, which is old for a submarine, she was ready for retirement. But while on her way to the scrapyard, *Lafayette* was going to be allowed one last fling.

CONTROL ROOM

"Officer of the deck." Lieutenant Pat Coppens looked up from the BQR-21 sonar display to see his captain, Commander Alex Wadsworth, walk into the control room.

"Yes, sir?"

"What's our status?"

As the officer of the deck, Coppens was responsible for knowing the ship's exact situation at all times. He stepped down from the periscope stand to meet Wadsworth at the quartermaster's plotting table.

"Well, captain, our present position is right about here," he said, pointing to a chart spread out over the small table.

"We're a little more than 50 miles northeast of the entrance to the Northeast Providence Channel. At present speed we should rendezvous with the *City of Corpus Christi* in about six hours. We have ten sonar contacts; four are classified as merchants and the rest are probably fishing trawlers. None are very close."

"Good; we should be right on time for the combat system trials with *Miami*. Then, 'Comrade Lieutenant,' we will put on our Smurf suits and pit ourselves against those American imperialists!" Wadsworth chuckled as he referred to the electric blue color of the Russian submariner's at-sea work uniform.

Commander Wadsworth, like most of the crew, wore the standard American submariner's uniform while submerged — a dark-blue coverall, along with brightly colored, nonregulation running shoes. Coppens too wore running shoes, but he also wore a brightly colored tie-dyed T-shirt, made by his six-year-old daughter, underneath his coverall. Each crewman, within limits, was allowed to personalize his attire. The stern planesman, who was from west Texas, had added a Western belt and a bolo tie.

Navy uniform regulations were relaxed on board a submerged sub, both for need and for morale. Sneakers were quieter than hard-soled leather shoes, and on a long patrol, isolated from the rest of the world, a little color and individuality were welcome.

Coppens was looking forward to the upcoming exercise, even if it meant being a target for USS *Miami*'s test of her new BSY-1 integrated sonar and combat system. Referred to as BuSY-1, it greatly increased sonar detection range and tracking ability. This was good if you had the system, not good if you were its target.

Still, the exercise would be a lot more fun than boring holes in the ocean, which was the normal lot of a boomer. Oddly, though, they were going to play the role of a Russian boomer — a DELTA IV-class ballistic missile sub. And for this exercise they were also going to have a simulated AKULA-class attack submarine escort, played by USS *City of Corpus Christi*. The Russians routinely escorted their boomers, something the U.S. Navy never did.

"Da, captain. But methinks we will get our buttskis kicked by the *Miami* with her fancy new sonar and combat system."

"Patrick," said Wadsworth with mock sternness. "You need to have more faith in our abilities and those of C-Cubed. We have to make the *Miami* work for her win; otherwise the Navy won't be able to accurately judge the effectiveness of the BSY-1 system. But if it will make you feel any better, I promise your widow will receive your posthumous Hero of the Soviet Union medal or whatever the Russian equivalent is when we lose."

"Thank you, sir, I think," Coppens replied sarcastically. Both men were in a lighthearted mood. It had been a long haul from Holy Loch, Scotland, to Charleston, South Carolina, where the Poseidon ballistic missiles were removed and concrete ballast canisters loaded, and the crew was tired. Everyone on board was eagerly looking forward to spending some time in the sunny Bahamas, where the U.S. Atlantic Fleet's acoustic test range was located.

As Coppens headed back to the periscope stand, he paused and turned back toward his CO. "Ah, captain? Request permission to shoot an XBT from the after signal ejector. We're close enough to the rendezvous point now that the sound velocity profile it will provide should be good enough for us to do our sonar search planning for tomorrow's test runs."

Wadsworth looked briefly at the chart again and nodded. "Good idea, Pat. Might as well get that evolution over and done with. Permission granted. Load an XBT in the after signal ejector and call me when you're ready to shoot."

"Load an XBT in the after signal ejector and call you when we are ready to shoot, aye, aye sir," repeated Coppens with typical submariner precision.

Coppens then quickly climbed up and crossed the periscope stand, deftly dodging the two periscopes right in the middle, and came to rest on the railing that faced the ship control party. Here, the helmsman, stern planesman, chief of the watch, and diving officer of the watch all worked together to keep *Lafayette* on the right course and at the right depth.

"Chief of the watch," said Coppens. "Would you please have your messenger locate Petty Officer Gates and have him report to Control."

REACTOR COMPARTMENT TUNNEL

The watertight door between Auxiliary Machinery Room Number One and the reactor compartment (RC) was opened effortlessly by a pair of huge hands belonging to Torpedoman's Mate Second Class George "Georgie" Simons. The rest of Simons' massive bulk squeezed through the narrow opening, followed closely by the much smaller Fire Control Technician Second Class Mark Gates. To see the two of them together one would be reminded of Arnold Schwarzenegger and Danny DeVito in the movie *Twins*. But the comparison didn't end with the physical disparity between the two men. Simons was an incredibly bright and easygoing fellow, despite the traditional label of "Trained Monkey" that went along with the TM rating. Gates was like the DeVito character in that he was feisty and outspoken, but he wasn't caustic or self-centered. The two were definitely an odd-looking pair, but this didn't bother either of them, and they were the closest of friends.

"I tell you, Georgie, Andros Island is not the best of liberty ports. There is very little to do there," complained Gates. "No bars, no casinos, no nothin'! Why couldn't we pull into St. Thomas instead?"

"Mark," Simons responded with an audible sigh, "there is more to life than just getting drunk or pouring your money into a casino's vault. The water in the Bahamas is beautiful and makes for great swimming and diving. Tell you what: After we are through here with the *Miami* I'll get us some tanks and we'll do some spear fishing."

"Great. With my luck I'll probably just wing a barracuda and make it mad."

Both men quickly traversed the dome-shaped reactor compartment tunnel, a heavily shielded passageway between *Lafayette's* main engineering spaces and the missile compartment. The tunnel is the only part of the reactor compartment that is safe for human beings when the reactor is critical, because of the intense radiation that accompanies nuclear fission.

Walking down a short three-stepped ladder, Gates stopped just short of the watertight door to Auxiliary Machinery Room Number Two (AMR 2). Simons looked at his friend, knowing exactly what he was going to say next; some things never seem to change.

"You know, Georgie, I hate going back here," remarked Gates. Simons tried very hard not to snicker and settled for a mental "I knew it."

"Every time it's the same thing — 'Hey Coner, you lost?' I wish the nukes would get a decent sense of humor or at least a new joke book."

The title "Coner" is a derogatory term used by the nuclear-trained personnel on board submarines to designate those individuals who work with the weapon systems, particularly torpedoes. This was all part of the friendly rivalry that the engineers back aft and the operators up forward had, but Gates didn't quite see how "friendly" fit into the scheme of things. He hated the title and the inferiority it implied.

"They can't help it, Mark," said Simons with feigned sincerity. "It's the radiation. It affects the brain in such a way as to render them incapable of understanding higher forms of humor. But we aren't going to accomplish very much by standing here and complaining, so let's get to the task at hand."

Resigned to his fate, Gates opened the door and stepped into AMR 2. Immediately upon entering, Gates could hear the noise of steam flowing through the large pipes just above his head. Simons followed his friend and, once clear, shut the door. Remembering a recent and unpleasant trip to AMR 2, Simons kept crouched over as he descended another small ladder so as not to hit his head against the huge valve wheels of the main steam stops.

As they proceeded down the narrow passageway between numerous cabinets housing the nuclear instruments and safety circuits, Simons couldn't help but be impressed by all the complex equipment required to keep a nuclear

B
U
R
I
A
L

A
T

S
E
A

reactor operating safely. Gates, however, was more in awe of the main electrical switchboards just aft of the nuclear systems cabinets. Here, several megawatts of power, produced by the ship's service turbine generators (SSTGs), were routed throughout the boat. If someone were to short out one of the massive circuit breakers, the resulting arc would leave nothing but a pair of smoking tennis shoes. The mere thought of this sent shivers up Gates' spine, even though he knew it was almost impossible for this to occur by just walking by. A few feet farther aft of the switchboards was the watertight door to the engine room, where the after signal ejector was located.

ENGINE ROOM

Stepping through the watertight door, Gates almost collided with Machinist Mate First Class Bob Gordon.

"Hey Coner, are you lost or just passing through?" asked Gordon sarcastically.

Gates moaned inwardly while silently mouthing Gordon's words. "Gordon," Gates finally replied in an exasperated tone, "trust me, I don't come back here for your rather limited inventory of nuke jokes. As it so happens to be, Petty Officer Simons and I are here to shoot an XBT. So if you will kindly get the hell out of our way, we'll do our job and leave."

"Don't mind him, Bob," said Simons as he pushed his way into the engine room. "He's all pissed off because he can't go carousing on Andros."

"That's OK, Georgie. Mark is always pissed off when he's aft of the RC."

Gates realized that there was no way to win this one and trudged off to Maneuvering to report to the engineering officer of the watch (EOOW). Simons paused only to shrug his shoulders at the grinning machinist mate before following his now-irate friend.

On a *Lafayette*-class SSBN, the engine room is the third-largest compartment and contains everything needed to take the steam generated by the reactor and convert it to movement and electricity. Occupying the center of the engine room were the SSTGs, main engines, reduction gear, lube oil and seawater pumps, and many other pieces of auxiliary equipment. The surrounding area housed the hydraulic system, high-pressure air compressors, electrical switchboards, and numerous storage tanks. Very little room was wasted on such amenities as storage lockers, work benches, or the ever-needed coffee mess.

To anyone but a submariner, the space was a rat's nest of white piping, gray boxes, and larger gray shapes that provided no clue to their function. Black label plates such as "MAIN SWBD 2S" provided only limited clues. A submariner not only knew what each item was and how it worked, but how it affected other pieces of equipment, and how to get along without it, if possible.

"Engineering officer of the watch, permission to enter Maneuvering," asked Gates.

"Enter Maneuvering," answered Lieutenant David Stewart.

Being only a little larger than a walk-in closet, Maneuvering was the nerve center for the submarine's propulsion plant. Here, three highly trained enlisted personnel and one officer monitored and controlled all the major pieces of equipment that gave *Lafayette* the ability to move and carry out her mission.

Gates, as short and thin as he was, had to squeeze behind the throttleman and the reactor operator to enter Maneuvering. Being far larger, Simons patiently waited outside.

"Mr. Stewart, Petty Officer Simons and I have been ordered to prepare an XBT for firing. I will be manning the phones to Control while Petty Officer Simons performs the evolution. We'll report back to you when we are done so that you can verify that the after signal ejector has been properly rigged for dive." Gates' request was carefully worded and formally spoken. On a nuclear sub, everything is done by the numbers. The words "sloppy" and "dead" in the submarine community are almost synonymous.

"Very well. Proceed with the evolution," responded Stewart unemotionally.

Gates squirmed his way out of Maneuvering, nodded to Simons and headed aft. The two only went a few steps before Gates motioned for Simons to bend forward.

"That man is the perfect nuke. Cold as a dead fish," whispered Gates .

"That may be true, Mark, but I've seen him out on the beach. He is one mean party animal — a regular Dr. Jekyll and Mr. Hyde. C'mon, we've got a job to do."

Lafayette's after signal ejector was located in the back third of the engine room, on the port side just outboard of the reduction gear. A set of narrow walkways between the SSTGs and the main propulsion turbines and around the reduction gear led to the signal ejector and the accompanying pyrotechnics locker. Of necessity, Simons and Gates proceeded down the walkways in single file.

As quiet as *Lafayette* was in the water, it sure was loud in here, thought Gates. Warm too. The two men rounded the reduction gear, jumped down a two-stepped ladder and finally ended up at the after signal ejector.

Simons took a key from his pocket, unlocked the large, dark-gray padlock on the pyrotechnics locker and opened it. Meanwhile, Gates pulled out a set of sound-powered phones from a storage box, plugged them into a nearby special internal communications socket and hooked the breastplate holding the mike around his neck. After adjusting the plate and placing the headphones over his ears, Gates was ready.

"Control, Engine Room Upper Level (ERUL). ERUL on line." Gates spoke slowly and carefully into the sound-powered mike. The microphone picked up the vibrations of his voice and converted it to an electrical signal using only sound energy, hence the name "sound-powered." The ability to work without the need for electrical power made sound-powered mikes very useful in emergency situations.

"ERUL, Control. Control on line."

While Gates was establishing communications with Control, Simons pulled out an XBT, or expendable bathythermograph probe, from the locker, laid it on the deck, and opened the signal ejector manual to the proper procedure. After finding the correct page, Simons looked at Gates and nodded that he was ready.

In sharp contrast to the technological complexity of most submarine systems, an XBT is a very simple device. Essentially, it consists of a spin-stabilized, precision-weighted probe body that contains a very accurate thermometer and a spool of wire. The design of the probe body ensures a very predictable rate of descent, which is necessary if depth is to be determined accurately. A second spool of wire outside the probe's body compensates for the ship's movement. All of this is contained in a plastic shell just over eighteen inches long and three inches in diameter. As the probe sinks, it sends back to the submarine, via the wire, a temperature profile of the water. This temperature profile is important in predicting sonar detection ranges and is essential if a good sonar search plan is to be derived.

"Control, ERUL. Ready to load an XBT in the aft signal ejector," reported Gates. The response came as anticipated.

"ERUL, Control. Load an XBT in the aft signal ejector."

"Load an XBT in the aft signal ejector. ERUL aye." By repeating the order back to Control, Gates was confirming that he had heard it correctly. Even though he had performed this operation many times before, it was standard procedure in the Navy to repeat back orders in order to minimize errors in communication. Such errors had proved to be deadly.

"All right, Georgie, read off step number one," said Gates.

Simons began reading the methodical step-by-step procedure that checked all the valves to ensure that they were in the proper position and that the signal ejector was indeed empty. Once that had been completed, Simons opened the breech door.

A signal ejector is nothing more than a miniature torpedo tube about four and a half feet long and three inches in diameter. Built out of the same high-strength steel as the pressure hull it penetrates, the signal ejector is designed to withstand the pressure of deep water and the stress of the firing sequence. A large ball-shaped external muzzle valve keeps the ocean at bay while a hinged door and locking ring arrangement provides the internal watertight boundary. Both the muzzle valve and the breech door are connected to a mechanical interlock system that prevents both from being open at the same time.

The signal ejector launching system operates on the same principles as the much larger air-water ram impulse system used to push one-and-a-half-ton torpedoes out of the tube. But instead of launching torpedoes, the signal ejector is used to launch acoustic countermeasures, smoke markers and flares, and the bathythermograph probes to record the ocean's temperature at various depths.

"Hand me the flashlight, will you Mark?" asked Simons as he made a careful visual inspection of the tube and the muzzle valve at the other end. The muzzle valve was, at that moment, holding back water that was pressing on it with over a ton of force, but it had been designed to take much more. Shining his light into the opening, all Simons could see was an empty steel tube.

"Everything looks good here," said Simons. "I'll load the XBT while you hook up the wire connector." The wire would feed the temperature data to the sonar team as the probe dove into the depths.

Simons and Gates worked well as a team. They moved around each other quickly and easily in the confined area, despite Simons' large size. In short order, the XBT was loaded and hooked up. Simons then shut and dogged the breech door while Gates reported their progress to Control.

"Control, ERUL. XBT loaded and breech door secured. Request permission to flood down and equalize signal ejector to sea pressure and open the muzzle valve."

"ERUL, Control. Aye wait."

CONTROL ROOM

"Officer of the whole deck," called Quartermaster First Class Fred Price playfully. "ERUL reports the XBT is loaded, the breech door is secured, and requests permission to flood down, equalize and open the muzzle valve."

Price recited his request from memory, again part of the carefully crafted and scrupulously followed procedure. Launching an XBT would involve, if only for the shortest moment, opening a hole in *Lafayette*'s pressure hull. The risks in that were obvious and frightening. Both the design of the signal ejector and the procedures to operate it were as precise as the launch of a space shuttle.

"Very well, chief of the watch," responded Coppens as he picked up the phone to the wardroom and hit the buzzer.

"Captain," came the curt reply over the phone.

"Captain, sir, officer of the deck. The XBT has been loaded, the breech door is secured; request permission to flood the signal ejector, open the muzzle valve and shoot the XBT."

"Permission granted; open the muzzle valve and shoot the XBT. Report to me when the evolution is completed," said Wadsworth.

Coppens, as before, repeated his captain's orders and placed the phone back into its holder. He then turned and ordered the chief of the watch to relay to Gates that they could proceed with the next step.

"Flood down, equalize and open the muzzle valve. ERUL aye," acknowledged Gates. "OK, Georgie, flood the signal ejector and equalize to sea pressure."

Simons, out of sheer habit, repeated his friend's order as he opened the valve to let seawater into the signal ejector. Once the valve was cracked open, Simons heard the unmistakable hiss of water flowing under high pressure.

"Hey Georgie, how's it going?" asked Gordon as he came around the corner of the reduction gear.

"Not too shabby," replied Simons. "We should be done here in about fifteen or twenty minutes."

"Well, don't rush it on my account," said Gordon. "That's a three-inch hole with a straight line to the whole Atlantic Ocean and I have no desire for it to move in here with us."

"All right, knock it off, nuke," growled Gates in an icy tone. "Are you ready to open the muzzle valve, Georgie?"

"Ahh, yeah — the signal ejector is pressurized to sea pressure. Opening the muzzle valve now." Simons pulled the hydraulic operating lever for the muzzle valve from the shut to open position. This allowed high-pressure hydraulic oil to drive a rack and pinion which slowly rotated the muzzle valve. Since the ball valve was designed to hold back the pressure of seawater down to *Lafayette*'s collapse depth, it had to be a big piece of metal and it required considerable force to move it, even with the pressure equalized.

But, weakened by twenty-seven years of use, the connecting rod between the pinion gear and the ball-shaped muzzle valve began to twist on itself. As it twisted, the metal became stiffer and the connecting rod started to fracture. By the time the muzzle valve was completely open, only a small strand of stretched metal connected the rod to the muzzle valve.

"Control, ERUL. The muzzle valve is open. Request permission to shoot the XBT," asked Gates.

"ERUL, Control. Shoot the XBT," came the response.

"Shoot the XBT. ERUL aye."

"Shoot that bad boy, Georgie," Gates ordered.

With a big grin, like a kid with an air gun, Simons pulled on the firing valve, which released high-pressure air from a special storage bottle into the lower part of the impulse cylinder. There, the air rapidly moved a piston that pushed a slug of high-speed water into the bottom of the signal ejector and quickly expelled the XBT.

This time, however, part of the plastic casing that held the XBT probe and external wire spool shattered when the water slug hit it. This sent dozens of small plastic shards whirling around the inside of the signal ejector, and also ripped the wire. Untethered and now useless, the XBT left *Lafayette*, pitched over and sank like a rock. Several pieces of the broken plastic housing were also ejected from the submarine, but not all of them.

CONTROL ROOM

"Conn, Sonar. Negative temperature trace. Believe we have a bad XBT," reported the sonar watch supervisor.

"Sonar, Conn. Aye," said Coppens. "Chief of the watch, inform ERUL that the XBT failed and have them prepare another one." Coppens then reached for the phone to inform the captain.

ENGINE ROOM

"Damn it!" Gates swore. "Control says that the XBT was bad and that we have to try again."

"Chill out, Mark!" Simons snapped back. "This isn't the first time we've had a bad XBT and it certainly won't be the last, so let's get ready to shoot another one. Closing the muzzle valve now." Simons pushed the muzzle valve lever to the shut position. But this time, instead of the valve body rotating shut, the connecting rod twisted on itself and finally separated from the valve body.

No one noticed that the mechanical position indicator moved a little faster than normal toward the end of the closing sequence. Nor was anyone able to see, or know, that the mechanical interlock that prevented both the muzzle valve and breach door from opening simultaneously was now disabled. Because the connecting rod had rotated, the mechanical linkages associated with the interlock also rotated. And thus, as far as the interlock was concerned, the muzzle valve was closed.

"Muzzle valve is shut," reported Simons to Gates. "I'll have the signal ejector drained momentarily."

"Say Georgie, does this happen often?" asked Gordon with sincerity.

"I honestly can't give you a percent occurrence, I know that's what you nukes like, but I've had a number of these things go Tango Uniform on me," replied Simons.

"The closest I could say was maybe one in four fail on launch," Gates added in a more hospitable tone. He liked it when the nukes asked him questions about his gear.

Simons got down on one knee and cracked open the drain valve. Almost immediately there was a rush of water from the drain line into the engine room bilge below. Under normal circumstances, Simons or Gates would have realized that something was wrong, since there would have been a continuous flow of water at high pressure with the muzzle valve open. But as the water started flowing out of the signal ejector, a couple of pieces of the broken plastic

XBT casing were sucked into the drain line and wedged up against the pipe walls. This slowed the flow of water into the bilge and also increased the pressure on the pieces, wedging them tighter and tighter. Soon the pieces were packed so tightly that the drain line was completely blocked.

The flow slowed to a trickle, then stopped altogether. "The signal ejector is drained," said Simons as he closed the drain valve.

"Gotcha, Georgie," responded Gates. "I've got the next XBT broken out and all ready to be loaded."

"Understood. I'm opening the breech door," said Simons. He pulled on the release. Funny, he thought, but the breech door seemed a little harder to open than usual.

"Mark, this door is sticking just a bit. I think we'd better check the..."

Simons never got the chance to finish his sentence. The breech door snapped open and water began gushing into the engine room.

At a depth of 800 feet, the high hydrostatic pressure pushed the water through the signal ejector at a speed of more than 120 miles per hour. Simons, who was looking right at the breach door, was hit by a jet of water with a force equivalent to a compact car traveling at freeway speeds. The hapless sailor's head was ripped right off his torso and bounced along the deck.

Gates, who had just seen his friend quickly decapitated, was hit by part of the water stream as it bounced off the deck. The force of the impact threw Gates six feet into the air. Unable to control his fall, he crashed onto the astern throttle elements of the port main engine. Gates died instantly, his spinal column severed in several places as the engine's steel rods were driven through it.

Gordon was luckier than either Simons or Gates. He too was hit by the water jet as it ricocheted off the deck, but was only propelled down the narrow walkway. His battered and unconscious body came to rest just forward of the port SSTG.

In Maneuvering, Lieutenant Stewart jumped out of his chair when he heard the incredible roar coming from behind him. Moving quickly to the doorway, Stewart looked aft and saw the growing cloud of mist filling the engine room. The salty taste of the air told him the worst — seawater was flooding into the engine room.

"Oh my God...flooding in the engine room! Flooding in the engine room!" Stewart shouted. Scrambling back to his small desk and the alarm switches, all Stewart could numbly think was, "This is not good, this is definitely not good." Almost falling, Stewart fumbled for the red-colored Collision/Flooding Alarm and pulled the handle.

Throughout *Lafayette* a loud whining siren blared.

Stewart then grabbed the 1MC, the main announcing circuit mike, and yelled:

"Flooding in the engine room! Flooding in the engine room!" Stewart repeated the warning a second time. But because of the tremendous roar generated by the flooding, he couldn't hear himself yelling and doubted whether anyone else could either.

TORPEDO ROOM

Torpedoman's Mate Third Class Russ Giesecke practically flew off the torpedo storage skid when the alarm pierced the evening quiet. The Torpedoman's 2 & 3 manual he had been studying tumbled uncontrollably out of his lap as he raced for the watertight door. In a quick and well-practiced manner, Giesecke closed and dogged shut the door and sealed off the compartment from the sub's ventilation system. The torpedo room was now watertight.

Unlike most nuclear-powered submarines in the U.S. Navy, *Lafayette* and her sisters had bow-mounted torpedo tubes. This made for a small torpedo room as the pressure hull diameter tapered down into the smooth hemispherical bow. The four torpedo tubes, pneumatic discharge ram, and numerous valves and operating levers occupied most of the forward part of the torpedo room. Storage for another eight torpedoes took up the majority of the remaining space. What little room was left was split among a small storage closet, a three-man bunk room, and the forward signal ejector and its accompanying pyrotechnics locker.

Giesecke was looking forward to transferring off *Lafayette* when they reached Washington state. It wasn't that he didn't like the old girl, but he wanted to be on a fast attack boat where the torpedo was the main weapon. *Lafayette* carried only twelve torpedoes, half as many as an SSN, and these were for self-defense purposes. The submarine-launched ballistic missile was the main reason for a boomer's existence, and even the *Ohio* class, with its fancy torpedo room, wouldn't change that. Still, Giesecke was glad that he had served on *Lafayette*. Being a third-generation torpedoman, Giesecke appreciated how his father and grandfather before him had loaded torpedoes with rope and a block and tackle because that was how torpedoes were loaded on *Lafayette*. And even though he had never met his grandpa, who had been lost aboard USS *Seawolf* during World War II, Giesecke knew that Gramps would have been proud of his grandson.

Fumbling for the sound-powered phones, Giesecke muttered to himself that the executive officer (XO) was being particularly cruel to run a flooding drill during the movie. But before he could don the headset, Giesecke heard what sounded like loud static coming from the announcing system speaker.

"What's going on?" asked Giesecke aloud. The XO had never used special effects in the ship's drills before, he thought. Bewildered, Giesecke finished putting on the sound-powered phones and reported the torpedo room's status to Control.

"Control, torpedo room. Torpedo room rigged for flooding."

"Torpedo room, Control. Aye," came the response from the chief of the watch.

As Giesecke listened to the other compartments make their reports, he started to get worried. The operations, missile, and reactor compartments all made their reports with the usual calm that one expected during a drill. The report from AMR2, however, was barely understandable, as the man on the phones was clearly terrified and was shouting into the phones. All Giesecke was able to make out was "Flooding in the engine room…no drill…no drill!"

CONTROL ROOM

"Diving officer!" shouted Coppens. "What's your trim look like?"

"She's looking heavy aft, sir," replied Chief Electronics Technician Bill Fitzgerald. "I'd say that this is for real, Mr. Coppens."

"Officer of the deck," called Commander Wadsworth as he and the executive officer, Lieutenant Commander Tom Johnston, ran into Control. "What the devil is happening?"

"Sir, I have multiple indications of some sort of flooding in the engine room. Request permission to conduct an emergency surface."

"You think it's that bad, Patrick?" asked Wadsworth.

"Yes sir, I do," responded Coppens with forced calmness.

"All right, lieutenant, put her on the roof — emergency surface," ordered Wadsworth. He had come to trust his officers' judgment and now was not the time to question it. Coppens quickly repeated the order.

"XO," said Wadsworth, turning toward his executive officer. "Get your butt back aft and find out what's going on. I need an accurate assessment of the casualty."

"Understood, captain!" replied Johnston as he started running down the narrow passageway.

"Diving officer," said Coppens. "Emergency blow all main ballast tanks. Chief of the watch, over the 1MC, emergency surface." Both men repeated their orders and immediately began to carry them out.

"Fairwater and stern planes on full rise!" ordered Chief Fitzgerald. "Helmsman, ring up all ahead full. Stern planesman, give me a positive 25-degree angle on the boat."

The helmsman pulled back hard on the control yoke for the fairwater planes while simultaneously reaching down and turning the selection arrow on the engine order telegraph to ahead full. Almost immediately, the second arrow moved to ahead full, indicating that Maneuvering acknowledged the order to increase the submarine's speed.

"Diving officer," reported the helmsman. "Fairwater planes are on full rise and Maneuvering answers all ahead full."

T
O
M
B
S

The stern planesman also pulled back on his control yoke. As the stern planes moved to the rise position, the back end of *Lafayette* started to move downward, which placed a positive angle on the submarine as a whole. By doing this, the hull of the submarine acted like a big flap on an aircraft's wing, pushing the submarine upward.

"Diving officer," reported the stern planesman in a deep Texan drawl and with a hint of fear. "Stern planes are on full rise. Angle on the boat is coming up to a positive 25 degrees."

"Very well," responded Fitzgerald to both reports.

By now, Price had made the announcement over the 1MC and had hit the diving alarm three times. This informed all hands that the boat was executing an emergency surface in response to the flooding casualty. Satisfied that all the other parts of the casualty procedure were being met, Fitzgerald grabbed the two large, silver, air-actuated switches and pushed them upward.

ENGINE ROOM

The salty mist spewing fourth from the signal ejector now filled the entire engine room, making it difficult to see objects or people farther than four or five feet away. At a depth of 800 feet, seawater was flooding into *Lafayette* at rate of about one ton every second. With that much seawater coming in so quickly, the after engine room bilge was already full and the lube oil bay deck plates were under an inch of water.

After sounding the alarm, Lieutenant Stewart reached up and started switching the emergency flood control levers above his chair to the "shut" position. By doing so, Stewart was remotely shutting all the large hull and backup valves associated with the main and auxiliary seawater systems. If the flooding was from one of these, it would stop immediately once the hull and backup valves were shut hydraulically. Even though Stewart was working very quickly, it seemed to take an eternity to shut the twelve emergency flood control levers. Once done, Stewart looked at his watch and thought, *No more than five seconds; then we'll know where we stand.*

The incredible roar continued unabated — the flooding hadn't stopped.

"Damn!" Stewart swore to himself. The fact that the flooding didn't stop was a case of good news/bad news. Good news because the flooding was from one of the smaller pressure hull penetrations, which meant that they had a good chance of surviving the casualty — provided they could get to the surface. It was bad news in that it wasn't one of the larger holes that would be plugged right now! Realizing that they would need the main engines to get to the surface, Stewart started repositioning the flood control levers for the main seawater hull and backup valves. He wanted to get cooling water flowing through the condensers again before the steam pressure could build up and cause the main engines to shut down.

Unfortunately, the haze prevented Stewart from seeing that the engine order telegraph had just jumped to ahead full. This was as fast as *Lafayette* could go without shifting the reactor coolant pumps to a higher speed, something not done during a casualty because of the higher possibility of losing a pump and thus causing a reactor SCRAM or emergency shutdown — which would result in a loss of all propulsion and probably the boat as well. The throttleman quickly acknowledged the order to increase speed and, without looking to see what the EOOW was doing, started to open the throttle controls, thus allowing more steam to flow to the main engines. With the increased steam flow and little or no cooling water flowing through the condensers, the pressure rose quickly and exceeded the safety setpoint. Automatically, the main steam supply valves tripped shut and cut off all steam flow to the main engines and the SSTGs.

It was the electrical operator who, because he was closer to the EOOW, got Stewart's attention and motioned that something was wrong. Stewart moved closer to the panel and saw that both the SSTGs' RPM had dropped considerably and that the battery was being discharged.

"The SSTGs have tripped on low frequency!" yelled the electrical operator. "We've lost steam flow."

Stewart quickly moved over to the steam plant control panel and saw the two blinking red condenser overpressure alarm lights. The throttleman hadn't seen the condenser lights yet; there were already a large number of alarms showing and no one could hear the hideous alarm buzzer over the din of the flooding. Shaking the throttleman to get his attention, Stewart pointed to the alarm lights and motioned for him to close the throttles. Just at that moment, the engineering watch supervisor, Chief Machinist Mate Paul Robinson, ran into Maneuvering. Stewart pulled Robinson over to the steam plant control panel and pointed to the condenser alarms.

"Chief, we need to reset the supply valves for the main engines!" yelled Stewart as loud as he could. "We'll need propulsion if we're gonna get to the surface!"

"I'm on it, lieutenant!" screamed Robinson. And with a quick pseudo-salute he dashed out of Maneuvering and headed aft to the main engines.

Stewart moved back behind the reactor control panel so that he could see everyone in Maneuvering. In so doing, he noticed that the boat was starting to develop an up angle. A waving hand on his right side caught his attention. Looking over, he saw that the electrical operator had finished his electric plant lineup change and had put on a set of sound-powered phones. Moving closer, Stewart yelled reports to the electrical operator for him to pass to Control.

TORPEDO ROOM

"Emergency Surface, Emergency Surface." ARUUGA, ARUUGA, ARUUGA. "Emergency Surface, Emergency Surface," came the announcement over the 1MC. Giesecke, knowing what was going to happen next, moved forward as fast as his sound-powered phone leash would permit. Suddenly, he heard two loud pops, followed immediately by an incredible roaring noise.

The pops were the rapid opening of the emergency main ballast tank blow valves; the roar was the sound made by high-pressure air being dumped from the air banks directly into the main ballast tanks. Wincing, Giesecke looked to verify that both valves were indeed open. This was easier to do than one might think; the valve bodies began to ice up as the rapidly moving air lowered their temperature below freezing. As he started walking back toward the after section of the torpedo room, Giesecke thought he was walking between two jet engines running at full power. Going around the corner of the storage closet and hugging the door, Giesecke was able to shield himself from the noise. There he made his report to Control.

"Control, torpedo room. Both emergency main ballast tank blow valves are open."

"Torpedo room, Control. Say again your last," said the chief of the watch.

"Control, torpedo room. Both emergency main ballast tank blow valves are open!" shouted Giesecke.

"Torpedo room, Control. Understand both emergency main ballast tank blow valves are open, Control aye."

Making that report was the last item on the torpedo room flooding casualty checklist. It was only then that Giesecke realized that the entire procedure had been completed in a little over a minute. All those drills had really paid off. Now all Giesecke could do was sit, wait, and listen to what was happening back aft in the engine room. The reports were frightening.

The XO called in and reported that the engine room was completely obscured by a mist. He requested the captain's permission to open the watertight door and enter the engine room. The "Old Man" then got on the line and told the XO that he could enter the engine room and that he was to report on the source of the flooding ASAP. And then, finally, Maneuvering reported in. It was difficult to make out the words with all the background noise, but Giesecke managed to hear that not only had the sub begun flooding uncontrollably, but that both main engines had shut down as well.

CONTROL ROOM

"Passing 750 feet," reported Chief Fitzgerald. "Officer of the deck, we're slowing down!"

"You sure about that, chief?" asked a bewildered Coppens.

"Yes sir! There is no doubt about it. We had our speed up to ten knots and now it's dropped back down to eight."

"Captain...captain!" shouted Coppens in a voice that showed he was beginning to losing his composure.

"Steady, Patrick. That's better. Now tell me, what else has gone wrong?" asked Wadsworth in a firm tone. Wadsworth had fallen a bit behind on the rapidly changing situation during his short discussion with his XO, and he needed good reports to catch up, not the babblings of a scared sailor.

"Sir, we are not gaining speed. In fact, we've lost two knots," reported Coppens. Before Wadsworth could ask any questions, the chief of the watch motioned for him and Coppens to move closer.

"Maneuvering, Control. Understand you have uncontrollable flooding. Both main engines tripped on overpressure. Engineering watch supervisor resetting. Control aye." Price finished repeating the report, looked up at the anxious faces of the two officers and said, "We are in deep kimchee, captain."

ENGINE ROOM

Chief Robinson stumbled back to the main engines as the walkway was becoming slick with seawater. The up angle that *Lafayette* was developing didn't help either, but he wasn't going to complain too loudly about it. Blinded by the dense mist, Robinson felt his way to the main engines. The mist stung his eyes as it whirled about, but the unbelievable noise was the really painful sensation. The only other time he had heard such a roar was at Niagara Falls when he and his wife had celebrated their tenth wedding anniversary. *Now*, he thought, *I'm walking into a waterfall*. Suddenly, Robinson lost his footing and almost fell, but he managed to grab hold of the walkway railing.

Mumbling a few traditional Navy obscenities, Robinson pulled himself back to his feet and looked around for the hydraulic operator for the starboard steam supply valve. Almost instinctively, he homed in on it immediately and pushed the "open" plunger. A quick look at the mechanical indicator satisfied him that the valve was indeed open.

The submarine's angle was becoming more of a hazard now that the deck was covered by a small stream of water, so Robinson turned himself about slowly and kept a firm grip on the railing. Once he was set, he reached out with his right hand until he felt the railing on the other side of the walkway. Grabbing hold, Robinson quickly pulled himself over to the port main engine and found himself staring into Gates' contorted face. It was all that Robinson could do just to hold on, and for a few seconds he simply looked at the shattered body while fighting the urge to throw up. Regaining his senses, Robinson moved Gates' body aside and hit the "open" plunger for the port steam supply valve. Again he verified that the valve was open by checking the mechanical indicator. Before starting his climb back to Maneuvering, Robinson turned and looked at Gates' body.

"It was nice working with you, shipmate," said Robinson with great sincerity.

In Maneuvering, Stewart was trying to inform Johnston as to the probable cause of the flooding when the throttleman excitedly pointed out that the supply valves had been opened.

"Well done, chief!" thought Stewart, who then proceeded to make a twirling motion with his hand. The throttleman understood exactly what his EOOW meant and started to open the throttles on the main engines. Reaching up to the engine order telegraph, the throttleman moved the indicator arrow to ahead full.

TORPEDO ROOM

Giesecke sat wondering just how long this ungodly noise was going to last. It was extremely frustrating trying to make out the reports over the sound-powered phones with a howling banshee in the same room. Then came a report from Maneuvering. Crouching over to cover the headphones with his body, Giesecke hoped to screen out some of the noise so that he could hear what was going on.

Report from the XO...main engines running...probable cause of flooding the after signal ejector. With these last words Giesecke went numb.

Georgie was back there, he thought, and Mark too. *Dear God, I hope they're OK.* But somewhere in the back of his mind, a nagging thought said, "dream on." Suddenly, Giesecke started sliding toward the bulkhead. Quickly, he uncurled himself and stuck his feet out against the steel wall to stop his fall. The boat's up angle was getting pretty steep, steeper than he could ever remember it getting during routine sea trials, where the XO did his best to shake things loose with his large up and down angles.

CONTROL ROOM

"Passing 650 feet, angle on the boat plus 20 degrees," reported Fitzgerald.

"Very well: dive," answered Coppens.

Fitzgerald then leaned over to his stern planesman and said, "Ease off on the stern planes, Texas. Remember: Hold the bubble at plus 25 degrees."

Before Fitzgerald could get the normal repeat back of the order, he noticed that the engine order telegraph had changed from all stop to ahead full.

"Officer of the deck!" yelled Fitzgerald. "Maneuvering is answering all ahead full!"

"Outstanding, chief!" exclaimed Coppens. "That's the best news I've heard in the last two minutes." Wadsworth merely smiled as he watched his crew respond to the casualty in an exemplary manner.

The crew is really holding up well, he thought to himself.

At that moment, Price held up his hand to indicate another report from Maneuvering. Both Coppens and Wadsworth crowded around the chief of the watch as he repeated the report.

"Maneuvering, Control. Understand main engines are back on line. Probable source of flooding is the after signal ejector. The XO is in charge at the scene. Control, aye."

"The after signal ejector?" questioned Coppens. "That's can't be right. The interlock system is virtually foolproof!"

"It's also irrelevant at the moment, lieutenant," said Wadsworth sternly. "If that's the XO's best estimate, then we'll work with it. We'll figure out the details after we have the ship in a safe and stable condition. For now, I think we'd better…" Wadsworth stopped in midsentence as he glanced at the ship control panel and saw that the angle on the ship had just gone by a positive 30 degrees.

"Diving officer!" shouted Wadsworth. "The bubble!"

Chief Fitzgerald, who had been listening in on the report from Maneuvering, spun around and saw that the stern planesman had frozen with the stern planes at full rise. Reaching over the terrified young man, Fitzgerald ripped the control yoke out of his hands and shoved it forward as far as it would go.

"Damn it, Texas!" yelled Fitzgerald. "Snap out of it!"

The stern planesman didn't even blink. He just stared at the ship control panel, his hands still trying to pull on the control yoke that was no longer there.

"Passing 580 feet, angle on the boat plus 33 degrees and increasing," said Fitzgerald. "Captain, I think we've literally lost the bubble."

"Me too, chief," said Wadsworth gravely.

Lafayette was now out of control. The effect of the prolonged use of stern planes on full rise, in addition to over seventy-five tons of seawater in the engine room, was causing the submarine's stern to pitch downward at a rapid rate. Chief Fitzgerald's belated action of slamming the stern planes on full dive had little effect on the increasing angle as inertia was now the dominating factor. *Lafayette* was acting just like a clock pendulum on a downward swing. As the angle on the submarine exceeded 45 degrees, air started gurgling out of the bottom of the main ballast tanks through the flood grates — air that would be needed to keep *Lafayette* on the surface once she got there.

ENGINE ROOM

Robinson didn't need to see a gauge to know that *Lafayette*'s up angle was a lot larger than it should be. He could feel the trip back to Maneuvering getting harder with each step. When a coffee cup fell out of its storage rack and went whizzing by his head, he was sure that something was drastically wrong. Climbing up on the port side of the walkway, Robinson pulled himself alongside one of the air-conditioning units. There he stopped momentarily to rest and to get his bearings. He could barely see the doorway to Maneuvering in the haze but he knew that he would have to cross over to the other side of the walkway to get there. Reaching across, he felt for and found the other railing. But before he could get a good grip he slipped on the treacherously slick deck and started to slide back toward the main engines. With all that water on the walkway, it acted just like a water slide at an amusement park — only there wasn't a nice pool of water to catch Robinson at the end of the ride. Instead, he slid past the main engines and collided with the small stepladder that led to the auxiliary throttle controls in front of the reduction gear. Hitting headfirst, Robinson flew up and over the stepladder and came to rest in a bloody, unconscious jumble against the auxiliary throttle wheel.

Directly below Robinson's battered body was the lube oil bay, where the main and auxiliary shaft lube oil pumps were located. These pumps provided a constant flow of lubricating oil to the shaft journal bearings, thrust bearing, and reduction gear. Without these pumps, parts of the shaft would quickly come into contact with the metal bearings — with disastrous results. Driven by the excessive up angle, all the seawater that had flooded into the engine room now began to rush down and collect in the lube oil bay. As the moving water collided with the standing pool, waves began to form. These waves got larger and larger as more water was added. Soon the waves were tall enough to engulf the shaft lube oil pumps. Although designed to operate in a wet environment, the pumps would not work when submerged. Thus, when a wave placed the main pump underwater, it quickly shorted out and stopped. The pressure sensors in the shaft lube oil system detected the sudden drop in output pressure when the main pump died and, true to their design, started the auxiliary pump in an attempt to restore system pressure to its proper level. The resulting electrical arc from the starting surge blew the waterlogged auxiliary pump right off its mount.

In Maneuvering, Stewart and Johnston stared in horror as, one by one, the shaft journal bearings, thrust bearing, and reduction gear low-shaft lube oil pressure alarms lit up.

TORPEDO ROOM

Giesecke struggled to keep from falling off his perch by the storage closet door, but the large up angle was making it very difficult. The loud roar of rushing air from the emergency main ballast tank blow system had finally stopped. Checking the pressure gauge on the bulkhead above him, Giesecke saw that the forward high-pressure air banks had been completely depleted. Taking off the sound-powered phone headset, Giesecke shook his head to try to get the ringing in his ears to stop. After about ten seconds the ringing started to go away. Or did it? Concentrating, Giesecke couldn't quite place the sound he was hearing now. It was a vague rumbling noise — like someone blowing bubbles through a straw in a water glass. Giesecke turned pale when he finally realized what he was hearing. Air was bubbling out of the forward ballast tanks.

CONTROL ROOM

"Passing 450 feet, angle on the boat plus 45 degrees," reported Fitzgerald in a strangely calm voice.

"Are the stern planes having any effect on the bubble, Chief?" asked Wadsworth.

"Negative, captain! Passing 400 feet, angle on the boat is plus 46 degrees and still increasing," answered Fitzgerald.

"Captain!" shouted Price. "The torpedo room watch reports that he hears air leaking from the forward main ballast tanks."

"Officer of the deck, request permission to open the vents on main ballast tank number one," said Fitzgerald without hesitation.

"What!?!" screamed Coppens. "Chief, are you insane?"

"No, Lieutenant," injected Wadsworth. "We're losing air as it is, but the chief's idea may help get the boat's angle down so that we can stay up once we do surface." Wadsworth looked intensely at Pat Coppens and saw that he wasn't following his captain's explanation; he was too scared and couldn't think straight.

"The captain has the deck and the conn," announced Wadsworth. Turning to Price, Wadsworth gave the risky order which might or might not save them.

"Chief of the watch, open the vents on Main Ballast Tank Number One for fifteen seconds."

"Open the vents on Main Ballast Tank Number One for fifteen seconds. Chief of the watch, aye," responded Price nervously. He then reached up to the main ballast tank section of the ballast control panel and put the vent switch for Main Ballast Tank Number One in the open position. Just above the switch, the indicator changed from a red dash to a green circle, which meant that the vent valves had opened.

By opening the most forward main ballast tank, Chief Fitzgerald was attempting to develop a counterbalancing weight to the water in the engine room. Hopefully, this would pull *Lafayette*'s nose down and reduce the up angle without seriously jeopardizing the boat's buoyancy. Fitzgerald knew, as did the captain, that the weight of water in the engine room wasn't enough to kill them. The excessive angle it was generating probably would, though, if it wasn't reduced.

"Passing 300 feet, angle on the boat plus 48 degrees," reported Fitzgerald.

"Very well, chief," responded Wadsworth.

"Captain!" yelled a very excited Price. "The XO reports that both shaft lube oil pumps are gone! We have maybe thirty seconds before all propulsion is lost."

Wadsworth acknowledged the disheartening report with a simple nod of his head. If they didn't stay up after they broke the surface, they were doomed. There wouldn't be anything left for a second try.

"Passing 200 feet, angle on the boat plus 50 degrees," said Fitzgerald.

"Very well, chief. Any indication that the venting of Main Ballast Tank Number One is having any effect?" asked Wadsworth.

"Yes sir! She's starting to come down now," exclaimed Fitzgerald. "Passing

150 feet, angle on the boat is plus 49 degrees. Come on baby, get your nose down!"

"Closing the vents on Main Ballast Tank Number One," said Price.

"Very well, chief of the watch," responded Wadsworth.

"Passing 100 feet, angle on the boat plus 47 degrees!" shouted Fitzgerald. "Passing 50 feet. It's going to be close, captain!"

"I hear you, chief," said Wadsworth. "Hang on everyone, it's going to get bumpy!"

Lafayette leapt out of the water like a breaching whale. Given the speed and angle of her ascent, almost half of the submarine cleared the water before she fell back down with a tremendous impact. Inside *Lafayette*, people and loose objects were helplessly thrown about. The shock from the impact caused many of the sub's systems to fail, including the lighting system, which plunged most of the submarine's interior into darkness. What little light there was came from a few emergency battle lanterns that turned on automatically. In the engine room, the shock caused the shaft to bounce on its journal bearings. Without the protection of the oil layer, the shaft and the bearings came into direct contact and started to grind away at each other. To make matters worse, the shaft bowed a little under the uneven loading, which put an excessive torque on the reduction gear. Built with higher tolerances than the best Swiss watch, the reduction gear couldn't handle the strain and proceeded to shred itself violently. Within seconds the shaft came to a screeching halt.

Lafayette bobbed up and down several times but only once did she ever clear the surface. She wallowed a bit near the surface, but the large up angle made staying up unmanageable. By the time the oscillations had stopped, she was already at 100 feet and sinking fast. Groggily, Wadsworth pulled himself up and tried to clear his vision. A grinding, stabbing pain when he tried to move his left arm told him that it was broken. Looking at the back of the periscope stand, he saw an unconscious Coppens lying on the deck with a huge gash in his head. Wadsworth surveyed the rest of Control as best he could in the dim light and found only he and Chief Fitzgerald were moving. Fred Price was still strapped into his chair at the ballast control panel, but his head hung at an unnatural angle.

Slowly, Wadsworth climbed down from the periscope stand. It was an extremely difficult trip, given the submarine's steep up angle and his broken arm. Pulling himself over to the ballast control panel, Wadsworth looked at Price's face. The vacant eyes told Wadsworth that his best quartermaster was dead — his neck had been snapped like a dry stick. Wadsworth closed Price's eyes and worked his way toward the ship control panel. He had to find out what was happening to his submarine. All the digital indicators on the panel were blank. He had to maneuver himself around to the mechanical depth and inclination gauges, another painful trip. There, his worst fears were

BURIAL

AT

SEA

confirmed. *Lafayette* was at a depth of 300 feet and sinking rapidly. The angle on the boat was plus 50 degrees and increasing slowly. Defeated, Wadsworth hung his head let out an exasperated sigh.

"How bad is it, captain?" asked Fitzgerald in a shaky voice.

"We're not going to make it, chief," said Wadsworth gravely.

"Well, at least we gave it a damn good try sir. Nothing to be ashamed of in that," answered Fitzgerald consolingly.

"You're right, chief," said Wadsworth with a faint smile. "It was a damn good try. I'm just sorry for the crew that it wasn't good enough."

With that, Fitzgerald and Wadsworth sat silently, waiting for the great depths to crush the hull like an empty beer can.

TORPEDO ROOM

Giesecke picked himself slowly off the deck. Although battered and bruised from the wild ride, he was otherwise not badly hurt. Leaning against the after torpedo room bulkhead for support, Giesecke waited for his head to stop spinning and the rumbling in his ears to die down. It was while he stood there that he noticed that the main lighting was out. The two battle lanterns at the ends of the compartment were working, but they didn't provide enough light to see what was going on.

"I'd better get a flashlight," said Giesecke to himself sluggishly. But as he was making his way over to the damage control locker, Giesecke remembered that he still had the sound-powered phones on. As fast as his bruised body would let him, he adjusted the breastplate and put the headphones back on and listened. There was only silence.

"Control, torpedo room. Can you hear me?" asked Giesecke.

There was no answer to his call.

"Control, torpedo room. Chief of the watch, can you hear me?"

Again there was no answer.

"Any station, torpedo room. Can anybody hear me?" begged Giesecke.

Frustrated and scared by the lack of a response, Giesecke removed the sound-powered phones and threw them on the deck. Suddenly, Giesecke realized that the rumbling in his ears wasn't from being tossed around like a ping-pong ball, but rather from the ballast tanks, which were still losing air. Moving as quickly as he could, Giesecke went to the damage control locker, grabbed a flashlight and put it in one of the front pockets of his coverall. He then started climbing up the torpedo stowage racks, making his way to the forward end of the torpedo room, where he would find a depth gauge. As he scaled the stowage racks, Giesecke was afraid that the large up angle would cause one of the pickle-green Mk 48 torpedoes to break free from its restraining straps, roll over, and squish him like a bug. The climb was a difficult one, but Giesecke soon found himself at the forward end of the compartment, right by the torpedo tubes. With his back resting on the forward bulkhead of the storage closet, Giesecke pulled the flashlight from his pocket, turned it on, and pointed it at the depth gauge. What he saw almost made him drop it. The depth gauge read 800 feet and the dial was steadily moving toward lower depths.

Stunned, Giesecke froze in place; he simply couldn't believe his eyes. As he continued to stare at the depth gauge, the dial went past 900 feet, then 1,000 feet before the reality of what was happening finally struck him. Near panic, Giesecke tried in vain to look for a way out. He couldn't use the escape chamber because he was far too deep to make a free ascent. His lungs would be crushed as soon as he left the boat. He couldn't open the torpedo room watertight door. The angle on the boat meant he would have to lift the massive door. There was no way he could do that. Besides, it wouldn't save him from the horrible death that awaited. In a hopeless gesture, Giesecke crawled up between the torpedo tubes as far forward as he could and braced himself against the manual firing levers of the lower torpedo tubes.

Faced with certain death, Giesecke stood there alone. There was little he could do except wait for everyone else to die before his own life was snuffed out by an unrelenting sea. The prospect of being the last to die pushed the young torpedoman to the brink of insanity.

"I don't want to die alone!!" he screamed.

With the fear that had been building up finally released, Giesecke began to sob uncontrollably. The angle of the submarine became steeper. He sensed that the end was near.

"Lord help me," was the only prayer Giesecke was capable of offering. Then came the haunting metallic groaning sounds which Giesecke knew were *Lafayette*'s cries of agony. The ocean was slowly crushing her, killing her, as well as every man on board. The groaning sounds grew in intensity and pitch until they became a shriek. Like the sound of a nail on a blackboard, the scream tortured Giesecke's already frayed nerves. He wanted so much to cover his ears and hide from the noise, but his arms would not let go of the torpedo tube linkages. They were frozen in place.

The thunderclap that followed rattled the hull so badly that Giesecke almost lost his grip. Then the groaning started all over again. The engine room compartment had collapsed. *Lafayette* was dying in the slowest and most excruciating manner: inch by inch, compartment by compartment. Auxiliary Machinery Room Number Two went next, followed shortly thereafter by the reactor compartment. The two jolts associated with the collapse of these compartments broke the stems of several forward main ballast tank vent valves and the ocean began to spray into the torpedo room, accompanied by a high-pitched whistle.

Suddenly, everything seemed to go into slow motion for Giesecke. The leaking vent valves looked more like fountains and the noise was no longer hideous or terrifying. In the back of the torpedo room, Giesecke thought he saw something move. Yes, there was something back there. He tried to identify whatever it was, but the collapse of the missile compartment shook the submarine so violently that it was all Giesecke could do just to hang on. When he was able to take another look, Giesecke saw a wispy, whitish, manlike form. The apparition was walking slowly toward him, but paused for a moment to inspect one of the Mk 48 torpedoes. A ghostly hand seemed to feel the torpedo's smooth hull while the rest of the creature moved around the weapon with an air of experience. The look on its face spoke of being impressed with the torpedo.

Is this an angel? thought Giesecke. No, it couldn't be. Not unless angels wore white Navy jumpers instead of gowns.

"Who are you?" inquired Giesecke when his curiosity had finally won out over his fear. The ghostly figure looked toward the young torpedoman and raised a single finger to its lips, motioning him to be silent.

Another jolt rocked *Lafayette* as the operations compartment collapsed. Giesecke was now the only member of the crew still alive. All 128 shipmates were now gone. Deep sorrow temporarily eclipsed Giesecke's fear. A wall of water from the breached compartment slammed into the already battered watertight door. Unable to take the strain any longer, the door bent in a little at the seam, and seawater started to spray in around the imperfect seal.

The apparition was now only four or five feet away when Giesecke saw the rating badge on its uniform — a torpedoman's mate. Awestruck, Giesecke looked closely at the face of his supernatural shipmate and found it to be very familiar.

"Grandpa," asked Giesecke in a timid voice. "Is it really you?"

The ghostly torpedoman smiled and nodded its head. It then held out its arms for the young man.

"Grandpa, I'm afraid to die," said Giesecke.

The ghost had a compassionate and understanding look on its face and it motioned with its arms for Giesecke to come to it. Adjusting his stance slightly, Giesecke reached out with one hand for the ghost of his grandfather. He felt something solid and this encouraged him to let go with the other hand. Falling into his grandfather's embrace, Giesecke felt a strange serenity possess him. So complete was this feeling of calm and peace that Giesecke never even noticed the torpedo room collapsing in on him.

Lafayette's crushed and mangled hull took five more minutes to travel the remainder of the 8,000 feet to the ocean floor. As she skidded to her and her crew's final resting place, it was ironic to note that she had evaded the shipyard's cutting torch after all. Her destiny was no longer to be found in a scrap heap. Instead, she had joined the ranks of those submarines on eternal patrol.

BURIAL AT SEA

KATHE KOJA

BARRY N MALZBERG

THE UNCHAINED

Ah, Lazarus. The crumble of his features, the sad expanse of bone, dense template of the skull slowly reaching for the sun, for the light like a growing plant, crops in the field, a flower: the stink we will not even discuss. Here in this high and dreadful noon his scent is that of offal, graves, the fine constancy of the finger of death as with the delicate insistence of fact it traces his features and his flesh. His face in my hands now, he is the world to me: death expands at the point of release; he may as well be the world and what lies beyond it.

Oh, Lazarus: I can raise you from the dead — having placed you there, along with so many others, it becomes the least effortful if largest of blessings to restore you — but having done so, having accomplished this cold and posthumous miracle within this stone enclosure, turning you to walk among us once more, trudging stride, grateful smile and all the rest...if I do this, what next? Raise the dead, heal the dead, strike fires into the collected and yielding souls of all the departed as I may — as I can — how will I approach the more central mysteries? How will I *know*?

Shall I speculate, here in this cathedral, rock and bone and the crowd outside; what shall I ask, what will I say?

And to whom?

"Well, he's steadier anyway," the night nurse said, checking vitals, stethoscope swing and hear that faint wheeze beneath the hospital blankets, twig-twitch of arms and legs; faint wheeze of her own breath and he had caught her again in the nursing home parking lot, half-hidden, half-turned into the right angle of dead brick and dying brush, sneaking a smoke. Gloomy defiance with a Kool in her hand, she smoked like a chimney, smelled like an ashtray, Davis would have loved her. *Would have*: stop that. Familiar burning in his belly, an ulcer, something small and red and evil like the end of the end of the world: it hurts? Too bad.

"Steadier than what?" See the tendons in the neck, turkey-wattle, scrawny arms entubed and purple; blond hair combed back, combed away from the dreadful face, the face beloved; *I will love you forever. Anything*, that was what Davis had said to him, mouth to his ear, heart to his heart: lying together, warm together, safe in a way he had never been with anyone else: *I would do anything for you.*

Again his own voice, not loud but loud in here: "Steadier than *what*," and she came to him, crossed the small and crowded room to squeeze his arm; crying again, he was crying. Amazing how one could cry without even knowing it. "Steadier than you," her voice dry and professionally tender; she was a good nurse, Davis was lucky. *He* was lucky: she let him come and go as he liked, tried to warn him when others — the family — were present, tried to shield him (did she?) from the worst sights and "Why don't you get out for a little, get some fresh air? You been out at all tonight?"

He shook his head. "It's a beautiful night," she said.

"For who?" and ashamed at once in the speaking, none of this was her fault or doing, no one's doing and "No," he said, tears on his face, "no, you're right, it's a good idea. I'll walk around the building or something, stretch my legs."

"Sure," the night nurse said. "He's going to sleep awhile anyway, but if anything, you know—"

"Sure," he said, looking past her to Davis lying like a prince on the bed, beautiful, ugly, dying. Sleeping Beauty. Death and the maiden. "Sure," and once in motion stayed in motion, leave the room, walk the hall, press the crashbar on the door and like a prayer answered, like a granted wish the air, the darkness, the stretch of the night outside as blank and calm as a sheet of paper on which he might write anything, anything at all.

Well, it is hardly mine to speculate; the ordering and penetration of detail were never after all my specialty. What I do is what must be done: capsulize what is possible and leave the eschatology to observers who might —will — have something to say, long after the occasion, to render matters proportionate. Render to Caesar what is Caesar's.

And for now, this day, this hour in the tomb my task is to hold the body, the corpse and breathe: bellows, exhortation of air deep within his lungs, say what must be said and wait for him to inflate, ever so slowly, seizing life even as life can be said to have been extracted from him; the dead returning to life, I have noted many times already, might as well be the living become dead, the traversal in either case is toward a kind of elemental stasis as if caught in pause, poised on the edge of knowledge and no-knowledge, between yes and the eternal where the decision made once is made forever; in its own way it is simple, very simple after all.

There: breathe now. Uneven whoop of lungs and the slow steam, gaining rhythms of his recovery: the beauty of it, the grave sad grasp of the tissue upon life itself. Beauty; and yet for me always that inner distance, even here, even now; sow the seed, raise the dead, heal the sick, perform small astonishments for the ones who will never believe and all of it to postpone — does it? — the larger, unabating circumstances, the questions without answers, the answers without mercy or pity or cease.

The sullen landscape of rock upon rock, cold-hewn; faint cry as he tastes of his body's own stink, the air of the land of the living. Breathe now.

Outside the sound of crickets, whisper of cars on the highway some blocks away; dead cigarette butts, hundreds of cigarette butts, a broken liquor bottle, a dried-out rubber. Remember, kids: the best sex is safe sex! or, for the truly dedicated, God's sweet paranoids, how about no sex at all? Just ask me, Mr. Play-It-Safe, the sole survivor: ask me what it feels like, ask me how I am. Go ahead, ask me.

He's dying; he's going to die tonight.

Stop it — said from self to self, terror and the inanition of great pain, of despair like a stone on the brain to crush it stupid and juiceless, a bug left to dry in a jar: stop it, you don't know what's going to happen, where you'll be in a day, two days, two weeks: here, this grass quadrangle, cigarette butts and night air? Inside, at the bedside? a funeral home, where? Shaking hands with people you don't know, relatives, business associates — but no, to do that you must first be acknowledged, recognized as *one of the family*, a human being and by whom? His teenage daughters, his bewildered just-married son? Or how about his ex-wife Dolores, who, outlaw herself, hates you still and more than ever? "Longtime companion," "partner." *He is my life*, you could say that but would it be true? His arms around you in the midnights, after parties, drinking the brandy he loved, dark taste sweet and bitter and who dies, inside there, you or he? who lies on the bed, sarcophagus stare, who wears the tubes, the scars, the lesions, the spots? Not you: your skin is blameless, your body functions; your life appears to be going on.

More tears: go ahead, cry. Cry yourself stupid, it won't do any good, it won't bring him back, will not restore him as he was and though you say, and mean it too, *I would die for him* still you don't, you can't: build the tomb and furnish it, weep yourself dry at its closure but still he enters alone.

And you outside stand breathing. Whether you want to or not.

He breathes on his own now, with attendant conviction and determination, alive, alive and there, at an open distance, past the rock and the blur of stink waits the crowd itself, a mixture of the credulous and the dumb, the observant and the doubtful, the vicarious participants and those who would deny the rising of the breath, the insect-flutter of the legs, even as it all occurs: they know what they know, they believe what the pain inside, the terror, the mean and greedy breath instructs as worthy; they are what they are, no change is possible.

Even the sisters, those good women: Mary is Mary, the enchanted, the enthralled and Martha — ah, Martha, shrewd in her terror, her weakness, her pain: *she* believes what she sees, smells, tastes in the mouth, grasps in the hand and "If you had been here," her voice harsh now, parched by weeping, "my brother would never have died." From Mary it is faith, the simplicity of a child; from her sister it is the accusation but I know how to answer Martha, I know that for her, as for the crowd, only deeds will serve: and so this deed, this final action itself reversing another perceived as the most final of all.

And oh, hear their slow, astonished murmurs as, dressed in his rags, his graveclothes he rises: apprehend now the real dimensions of their terror, the tenor of doubt become dread as the inescapable evidence of Lazarus in motion becomes more real to them with every step he takes: *he has come back*, they say, *from the dead he has come back!* and now I see, I understand that those past amazements, those signs and miracles have only worked the road toward greater terrors and as Lazarus in his stink and wonder begins to approach me, approach those who stand behind — those fluttering wrists, that unfolding consciousness — I can hear as well in the gasps and prayers of the crowd intimations of belief more dangerous than doubt: never a favorite, followed as a mountebank is followed, the clown pursued for the tricks to come still I am now in greater peril for this act of resurrection; in destroying their conviction — *dead is dead* — I have opened them to the phantasms of a world in which all is possible.

If one cannot trust death—?

The clutch and waver of the fingers, the bony hands; he had been so ill, so ill, returning life has given him no vitality, no flush of health or strength. Heaped like shed skin the graveclothes, the stinking wraps and bindings and someone screams, a woman, Mary, screams like an angel before the Ark, before the face of the Father Himself and beside her Martha white to the lips, bleached by terror and gripping her sister's arm as if to prevent that reunion, that kiss bestowed by living lips to flesh so recently putrid, so formally and evidently dead.

And in my gaze the sun, heat and light, sweat to proclaim for all to see my own mortality as: *Lazarus*, my cry, call, invocation, *Lazarus, come forth*.

Inside the smells more pungent, more unhealthy for the dose of cleaner air; the night nurse gone from her station, out for a smoke? but no, the floor seemed empty, cold with silence untoward and inside the simple command, shout from flesh to brain bewildered, urged by clues the conscious mind could not bestow: *go* and he went, *hurry* and he ran, down the hall, down the hall, pushing into the tomb of a room past what might be a doctor, an intern, somebody and there she was, Miss Night Nurse, Miss Sense and Sensibility and

Davis

was blue, cyanotic, breath thick as blood in his chest and "I was coming for you," she said, "I was coming —" but hearing he did not answer, moving he could not reach and stumbling, balance lost he fell: fell across the bed, atop that body, precious corpus whose eyes beneath their sluggish lids did not appear to move, morphine and Demerol, all dreams extinguished and "Davis," his own voice, that face: blond hair, closed eyes, that body, his body: *I love you, I love you* and "We can resuscitate," the night nurse urgent, "we can try if you want to, if you—"

"—family says?" from someone else, that other presence in the room: nurse or intern or the avatar of painful death, wanton death in medical drag and "He *is* the family," impatiently and to him: "Quick," staring at him, poised to move. "Hurry, decide."

Blue mouth: blond hair. Drowning sounds.

Lying back on the pallet from which he had been carried to his grave, he looks at me, this resurrected angel, this hostage from the home of the dead: tears in his eyes, he is crying. The sisters beside him weep as well, weep for the joy of restoration, the lost who now is found, *praise be the name of the Lord* but down his cheeks like blood, like oil those tears which tell me only of the journey, tell me of where he has been, where all must go: even I. Even I.

"You are whole," Martha half-laughing, feeling with those strong and living hands his arms, forearms, shoulders, wrists, working the joints, folding the flaccid grip into fists as sweet as a baby's, "you are *whole*," and he speaks to me, softly, softly, as if his voice must call past deeps and terrible mountains, must reach like thunder to announce the neverending storm: "Rabbi," he says. "Rabbi."

The crowd at the windows, the doors: staring, breathing, murmuring one to another, calling his name: *Lazarus, Lazarus* as if he now has what all must desire, that knowledge, oh what those empty, empty eyes have seen and "Rabbi," again and most urgently, most poignantly to me as I bend to him, reach for him, lower myself to his touch through what seem to me to be whole tunnels of altered sensibility and misdirection to a place whose name I do not know but whose possessions and accouterments seem inevitable: past the crowds, past the sisters, past the grip of life itself and the stare of death: but who are the dead? Does he know now, is this what he must tell me, speak, communicate to one who will need that knowledge soon? Or is it something simpler, deeper which he seeks and seeks to give me, advice from one who has crossed but in no chariot of fire, no prophet's coach, borne only by the body lost in the bridging instant, life's home now forcibly discarded, left at last like life itself behind?

His breath in my face; his hands on mine. Oh, the smell.

"No code."

Davis in extremis; the nurse at his side and "Are you sure?" she said. "Are you absolutely—"

His heart now broken, good; good. "No code."

Who are the dead? It is this question which vaults me to my own tomb, which sends me past those sisters, those watchers, that crowd parting now in superstitious awe to make a fresher tunnel for my passing: and my followers behind, praising and mumbling, whispering one to another as we pass the open rock, cheated mouth still empty, graveclothes scattered flat upon the earth.

Shall the dead praise thee? and for what?

"He's gone," said the night nurse. "I'm so sorry. I'm so sorry."

The room cold, so cold around him and that stricken face like a bas-relief, wax and bone, pure silence now past those parted lips: *I would do anything for you.* "Call his wife," he said, standing over the bed, the body. "His ex-wife, her number's on the card—"

"Go outside," said the night nurse, touching him on the shoulder. "Go on. There are things I have to do now, for him — here," handing him something, a package, pack of cigarettes. "Go have a cigarette. I'll call you when I'm done."

"All right," he said and pushed again at the door, the crashbar, back again into the night to stand like a child in the corner, right angle of wall to wall, broken glass and torn rubbers, his own body as empty as death would ever leave it; good. Night air on his face; he smoked a cigarette inexpertly, smoked two, waited. The sound of the cars on the highway; the sound his shoe made as he scraped it back and forth, back and forth against the pavement, scattering the cigarette butts, sending dust shin-high into the close, ungiving air. The shadows above him slowly coalescing, turning to the sliding and shimmering light and upon him then the shroud, the tendrils of a tallis grazing him ever so delicately in the space between the darkness and his eyes, before him then the floating and final face and to the lips a question: *Yes? Yes, then?* And in that perfect and formless darkness he stands arched to that question, his answer a shout, contained and uncontained within the cracked-open vessel of his sensibility.

"No," he says, finally, "not that, not that at all."

Light taken is at last unbroken.

THE TIME GARDEN

A FAERY STORY

t really wasn't a castle at all.

That was the second disappointment. The first had been Ma's announcement that they would all be going away to Killynether Castle while she catalogued its antiquities for the Historic Houses Trust of Ireland, and that they would be there all summer. Ewan had settled deeper in his chair and pulled his cap down so you could just see his eyes over the top of the Game Boy and know from them that his cool had been monumentally affronted. At sixteen, cool is more than life itself. Thirteen-year-old Emer had planned a summer of hitching with friends and shopping, but under no circumstances in a one-room crossroads grocer's with turf and bottled gas stacked behind the door and a shopkeeper who doubled as taxi driver and television repairman, and could be guaranteed to stock only Daniel O'Donnell cassettes and T-shirts for New Kids on the Block, or even, dear Jesus, Jason Donovan. She would die. She would have to lock herself in her room and die, that was all. Da was not happy about going either, but he had not been happy about anything since he got the sack from the College of Music and Ma had been forced to put her long-dormant History of Art M.A. to work. The Trust had given him something to do around the gardens which were Killynether Castle's fame and glory, but everyone knew that it was just to keep him busy. The real work was Ma's, verifying and indexing the castle's contents before the Trust put in a coffeeshop and a souvenir stall and opened the place to the paying public.

"Well, we're going," Ma said in the teeth of sullen protest. "It's not as if we can pick and choose work these days."

Only Aoife had been happy with the idea, but when you are nine a summer in a castle in Donegal is just the most romantic thing you can imagine.

And then at the end of the long loughside drive at the end of the longer and interminably boring drive from Dublin, the big white Volvo had swung through the dark rhododendrons into the gravel carriage park and even that hope of redemption had gone into the ashtray with the candy wrappers and bits of hardened chewing gum — because it wasn't even a castle at all.

What it was was a square Georgian country house, such as the minor gentry or the major clergy might have built for themselves. It was big enough to be grand and small enough to be intimate. Its plaster rendering had been painted the strong terra-cotta the Georgians loved, which had faded over two centuries to a warm russet that in the July afternoon sun seemed to glow with its own light. It was a house that welcomed whatever the season, whatever the weather. The panes of the latticed windows were white so that the rooms would be bright and airy with reflected light. The portico was guarded by stone lions, much belichened; the double doors had a wide fanlight above them. The door knocker was the laurel-wreathed head of some female bit player in the Classical pantheon. In its every part Killynether harmonized the balance and grace of the Palladian with the Georgian love of the sensual and physical.

"No satellite dish," Ewan complained. "I bet they haven't even got terrestrial TV. I'm out of this place."

"But it's not a castle," Aoife said as they staggered up the worn stone steps to deposit bags, boxes and suitcases on the porch.

"I've told you, the original Killynether Castle was burned down at the time of the Flight of the Earls," Ma said, sliding a box of breakfast cereals and defrosted burgers out of the Volvo's long boot. "This one was built in 1785 by the Pusey family, who made a lot of money shipping port from Lisbon and came back to Ireland after the end of the penal era and wanted somewhere to live. Puseys lived in it until 1989, when the last one died and left it to the Historic Houses Trust."

"Didn't a whole lot of them disappear mysteriously in eighteen-something?" Emer asked, thirteen being the age of mysteries and miracles, the greatest of which are the swelling buds on your chest and the dark twitch in your belly. "Vanished into thin air and never were found."

"Who gives a flying one?" Ewan growled. He kicked the pink gravel of the carriage drive into mounds, which Emer wished he would not do because she reckoned he could be an almost decent person were he not so occupied with the politics of cool. "Is there anything to eat? I'm starving."

"Once we get sorted," Ma said.

"Can we have a barbecue?" Aoife asked brightly.

Any room you like, Ma had said. Except the ones marked *Restoration*

Completed, or the master bedroom at the front with the view of the lake, because that's ours. Which still left six bedrooms to choose from. Three were at the back overlooking the stable block; one smelled like something had died in there and not been found after two and a bit centuries; and the blue one with the four-poster Aoife had bagged; and the one Emer really wanted on the east side looking down the lough Ewan wanted as well, so they had tossed for it and he'd cheated but she could never prove it. So she took the yellow room on the west side which, when she looked at it with the afternoon sun streaming through the grimy window, lighting up the faded gold wall damasks woven with fauns and Pans and Bacchuses and the big high bed you could do serious damage to yourself if you rolled off with the eight pillows and the honey-colored wooden furniture that felt smooth like skin feels smooth, and the ceiling with its huge central rose picked out in yellow and burnt umber, was probably even better. In fact, because hers was the only room that overlooked the gardens, definitely the very best. It smelled a bit, but they all did. The whole house smelled, not quite of dead things as she had feared it would, but of time: much-used time, well-used time. And light, as if light, like candles, could be used up, and leave behind a residue of itself like smoke.

It took her several minutes to work out how to open the sash window, and even then she did not trust it not to fall as she was leaning out and chop her head clean off. To the right she could see the lawns going down in big gentle steps to the loughside. Across the water were the hills of Donegal. Before and to the left of her were the gardens. Near the house they were formal affairs, laid out in beds and hedges with box and privet and yew, some of which had been clipped into the shapes of chesspieces and dogs and Irish harps and deer with twig antlers. Statues of Classical figures reposed in hedged niches; gravel pathways led the eye to fountains and stone cockleshells and tritons with horns clogged up with green algae, and Manikin Pises with the same complaint in a worse place. Farther from the house the gardens became larger and less orderly, so that Emer could not tell where one ended and another began. Hedges grew into rows of trees which became walls of rhododendron or laurel; through the foliage, roofs and turrets of little follies and summer houses could be glimpsed, and — was it her imagination? — no, those sharp-edged lines of yew could only be a maze. Beyond the informal gardens rose the tall trees of the arboretum, and beyond the tall trees rose the high hills at the head of the lough, and the blue sky above and beyond them all.

It had to be a barbecue after all, because the Historic Houses Trust had forgotten to switch the electricity on.

"I knew it, no television," Ewan moaned.

"You could always read a book," Da said. "There's an entire library full."

Ewan pulled in his chin and stuck out his top lip in the way he had seen teenagers do in American sitcoms that is supposed to mean, *I would sooner eat my own shit.*

"More importantly, how am I going to run my laptop?" Ma said.

"You've got a solar charger; weather looks set fair for a few days." Da flipped the burgers with an eighteenth-century carving set. The Georgian stone birdbath on the west terrace made an improvised barbecue, a kitchen cake rack a satisfactory grill. "Who needs electricity?"

"Your father likes to think he's the eternal Boy Scout," Ma said to Emer. "Just wait until he can't boil a kettle for his tea in the morning. He'll be at that fusebox quickly enough."

"Anyone for a burger?" Da flourished the triumph of his skill on the end of the sterling silver fork. "Aoife, haul the Coke cans from the fishpond, would you? Meanwhile, Mrs. Blennerhasset, a glass of the blushing grape I liberated from the cellars." He clinked the bottle of red in his left hand against the two glasses in his right.

"Have a care, man!" Ma exclaimed. "Those are 1850 acid-etched Bohemian crystal, each worth more than I make in a month. And the wine is technically Trust property."

"What are they going to do with it, sell it in the coffeeshop? You're the one taking the inventory; no one will miss a bottle or two that never gets recorded." He raised a full glass. "To summer, kids!"

"Ma!" Ewan's voice. "Ma, my Game Boy's banjaxed. I can't get the screen to light up."

The last time Emer had gone to bed by candlelight had been on the night of the big storm when the power lines came down and she had had to take a run past the bogeyman behind the bathroom door. No more. When you are thirteen you have no fear of the monsters of the mind, not even in a house as full of time and the departed as Killynether Castle.

No one can ever sleep the first night in a strange bed. Especially when that bed is high and hard and heaped with heavy quilts on a night too warm for anything more than just a sheet. No point even trying. Too hot, and too silent. In Dublin there had never been silence like this. Always somewhere there had been the slush and swish of traffic, or the high drone of an aeroplane. In Dublin you never heard your parents' voices as they sat below your window drinking the very good wine from the cellars, talking just for the sake of talking, and laughing. In Dublin, she had not heard them laugh for as long as she could remember.

Knuckles quietly rapped paneling, the bedroom door opened. Aoife stood on the threshold in her Barney Dog nightie, hair brushed straight out, carrying a lighted candle in a silver stick.

"You be careful with that, punk," Emer warned. "You can't set this on fire, it isn't ours. Can't sleep either?"

Her sister nodded and knelt beside Emer on the Ottoman by the window. "It's too hot."

"It's all right, though," Emer said.

"It's not like I thought it would be." Aoife set the candlestick on the sill. "It's different. Better, I think. It feels like a magic place."

On the sunset side of the house there was still a little light above the western hills. The gardens seemed huge and strange in the twilight, as if the two girls knelt on the lighted fo'csle of a ship anchored off a newly discovered continent that lured with its mysterious jungles and half-hidden ruins and exotic perfumes but upon which they could not set foot until morning.

Loud laughter drifted up from below. Figures moved on the parterre: a man extending a hand to a woman. Joined, they entered the house through the French windows. The silence closed in behind them, comfortable and peaceful and welcoming. A glissando of piano notes sounded in the music room beneath. Emer recognized the piece: a Debussey Arabesque. Her father had not laid fingers to keys since he had lost his job in the School of Music. The piano in Heytesbury Street had gathered dust, coffee rings and the post with cellophane windows that her parents had put to one side and pretended had never arrived. The notes tumbled through the open French windows into the warm night air; Emer imagined them like birds, flocking, tumbling, finding places to roost in the trees of the arboretum. It seemed to her that the gardens pressed closer to the house, as if listening.

The Debussy ended. There was a burst of solo applause from downstairs, then a closing of windows and doors and the sound of two pairs of feet on the hanging staircase.

"They never go to bed together in Heytesbury Street," Emer said.

"Do you think they'll have sex?" Aoife whispered. If so, this must be a magic place indeed.

"Go to bed, punk," Emer said, handing her sister her light. "You need to sleep. We've exploring to do in the morning."

She did not know when the silence woke her but it was sometime in the darkness before dawn. There was a sliver of moon; its radiance through the window threw rectangles of silver light onto the carpet with its threadbare dryads and hamadryads. The silence was so loud she wondered if she had gone deaf. Room, house, gardens, world seemed to hold their breaths. Emer leaned out of the window, trying to discover if whatever it was that had awakened her was out in the gardens. For something had awakened her. Not an absence. An indisputable presence.

The lawns were a dewy silver; the topiary creatures threw eerie moon-shadows across the terraces and parterres. Some of the shadows were moving.

Emer held her breath with the room, and the house, and the gardens, and the world. The heat, the stillness were intense. The perfume of the night-blooming flowers in the gardens was overpowering.

Dark shapes flittered across the gravel paths of the Italian garden and darted to cover behind urns and plinths: small, low shapes, long-snouted, prick-eared. Foxes, perhaps. Animals, certainly, but what was that ungainly, two-legged waddling thing, like a goose, but squatter and fatter, with that downturn to its beak? And what was that she had glimpsed among the shadows of the Triton Garden, that looked to have the feet and legs of a goat? And among the trees of the arboretum, way beyond the maze, was that a roof like one of those funny Russian churches catching the moonlight — and what shone so brightly on the top of it? She did not remember having seen such a thing that afternoon.

Then she heard it. It came from so far away that it was no more than a breath, but in the great silence she could distinguish every note. It had something of the sound of a flute, though more breathy, more earthy; it had something of the panpipes, but more refined, more unearthly. The tune it played obeyed no rule of music Emer had ever learned from her father. But it cohered. It made you listen with every pore. It suspended time and space and took you to places beyond human rules where music could be as wild and free as it wished.

As she began to understand, it left her and faded into a silence deeper and more perfect than before. Not a leaf stirred, not a shadow moved on the terrace or across the lawns. Moon and stars seemed frozen in the sky and Emer knew that, like her, they were waiting to hear if the music would come back. Time hung suspended from the terminal note, then broke as, from every tree and shrub, birds sang out in the dawn chorus.

Da had got up before any of them and fixed the electricity so there was hot water in the kettle and cold milk for cereals in the fridge. Ma was looking very smug, Emer thought as she watched the Cocopops turn her milk brown. She never wore her cotton kimono that loosely at home.

After breakfast Ma took herself, laptop and a cafetiere of coffee into the library, which meant she was not to be disturbed until lunchtime. Da was already at work outside, so Emer and Aoife went exploring. Ewan had discovered an old black-and-white portable the restorers had left behind and was in bed eating toast and watching *The Big Breakfast*. The girls did not miss him. He would only have complained. He complained about everything. Nothing was ever right for him, even leaving him alone. Emer was glad she was a girl. Girls could pretend they could be got round by being bought things.

They discovered the first wonder almost immediately. The rolling doors of one of the stable blocks opened to reveal an ice yacht within. Born under the shadow of global warming, the girls had never seen such a thing, but they knew a beautiful artifact when they saw one; and from its mast and sail, reefed to the boom with brass buckles, and the long lean lines that terminated in still-sharp silver skates, they could deduce its purpose. A name was painted on either side of the nose: *Erehwesle.*

"Errewail," Emer decided, picking the most romantic possible pronunciation.

"'Elsewhere' backward," said pragmatic Aoife. "The whole lough must have frozen over, once upon a time."

"It would never get that cold for long enough now," Emer said, imagining the sleek, lacquered thing sliding across the frozen lake, faster than the wind, crewed by well-whiskered, better-muffled Victorians.

The ice yacht was indeed a marvelous thing, but only a memory of a wonder, whose wonderful purpose would never be again. The gardens were wonders present and incarnate. By the Laurel Way the girls chased through the raw rocks of the Alpine Garden, thence under the overgrown trellises of the Rose Walk to the first of three green gardens — green gravel, dwarf evergreens clipped within an inch of the ground, green privet, the green cornucopias of shade-loving hostas — that together formed the trefoil of the shamrock. They lingered awhile in the Shamrock Garden, then went by way of the Long Water — planted in the formal rectilinear Dutch style along the sides of a straight, narrow pond — to the Doo'cot Garden, with its cylindrical clay pigeon lofts balanced on slender Doric pillars; and so to the Stone Garden, which extended the view of the west parterre from the dining and music rooms to the tall screen of cypresses that marked the boundary of the inner gardens with the outer. Hidden here was genuine magic.

The builders had been clever, concealing them in nooks and crevices in foliage or walls so you could walk right past them without knowing they were looking at you — but when you glimpsed one, it became a game between you and the builders to see how many you could find. In the space of time it took the sun to come over the clock tower on the stables and pour full over the west face of the house, the girls discovered dozens of the little statues. Animals, mostly, in appropriate habitats: an owl hiding on the roof of the gazebo; a toad crouching among cobbles at the edge of the pond; a heron fishing in ornamental bulrushes; a lizard clinging upside-down to a wall; a wren on a balustrade; a hare, hidden in long grass, watching with round stone eyes. An entire bestiary, but also beasts from legend and history: a griffon masquerading as one leg of a stone bench; a dodo nesting in a collection of stone jars; a wolf scowling deep in the shadows under the ornamental currants; a dragon coiled around the pillar of a bird table, jaws open at the rim to snap up unwary feeders. And things that were not beasts, but not humans either: half-and-half things, a big man with lots of muscles who had the head of a ram, crouching in the bamboo.

"He's got a very big thing," Aoife giggled.

But beautiful eyes, Emer thought.

Freshwater mermaids and merboys languished in the pool; a willowy girl with twigs for fingers and moss for hair seemed to have been caught in the act of stepping out of a sessile oak. And in a little niche in the cypress hedge that you could only see when you were right in front of it was a statue of a teenage boy with the horns and legs of a goat. The sculptor had chiseled the curly wool of his legs and short beard very well. His eyes were stone but they were smiling. Emer could not rid herself of the sensation that behind the stone eyes were flesh eyes and that it was the smile of those she could see.

"Come on, we're almost at the maze!" Aoife shouted.

It was a very old, very good maze; of that dense, dark yew hedging from which all the best mazes are grown. The restorers had cleared and clipped it and kept the passages in good order but had left no instructions or guides to the maze's secrets. Rushing with Aoife through a new gap in the yew to come on the same blind alley for the third time, Emer began to wonder if they would be out of it by lunchtime. She had read somewhere that mazes are either left-handed or right-handed and that if you make all your turns accordingly, it will either lead you in or lead you out.

The builders of this maze had not read those books. In five turns Emer was no longer certain which direction was in or which was out. It had not yet come to standing on one of the occasional stone benches to peer over the hedges, but it might soon. It was still a grand game to Aoife so she need not worry yet about her sister becoming claustrophobic and panicky.

The problem with mazes is the problem of most puzzles and mysteries: The payoff is seldom worth the investment. Emer had been certain they had come through the door before, but Aoife insisted they had not, and it took them into a curving walk that without warning opened into the center of the maze. This was a grassy circle some ten paces across, spaced equally around which, like the hours on a clock, were twelve short stone pillars bearing sundials. They were not even very good sundials, because no two of them cast the same shadow. In the center of the lawn was an ornamental construction that looked a bit like a tree and a bit like a fountain and seemed to have no other purpose than to mark the center of the maze. At the top of the long central stalk, from which water would have jetted had it been a fountain, was a sheared-off brass bolt. Emer prodded around in the ankle-length grass for whatever might have fallen off the top of the stalk but found only the restorers' beer cans and cigarette ends.

"What's that?"

Emer followed her sister's shout and pointing finger to the object that had aroused her interest. Something caught the light among the big trees of the arboretum, where a breeze that did not blow down in the hot, still gardens moved the topmost branches. Emer glimpsed the onion dome of the garden folly she had seen the night before.

"I don't know, some kind of summer house, I suppose."

"I want to go there next," Aoife said decisively.

"We'll not have time before lunch; remember how long it took us to find our way in?"

"No problem. I remembered the way we came in."

Aoife had. Every twist and turn and double-back of it, and all the wrong ways to be avoided as well.

From the south entrance of the maze the glittering thing vanished into the tree canopy. Emer led her sister along the northern edge of the Walled Garden through the Scented Garden and the Butterfly Garden to a wisteria walk that should have brought them right to the gates of the arboretum, except that they ended up in an informal water garden with the tall trees and the reflecting dome of the summer house well to their left. They left the water garden by the stream path into a Japanese temple garden and from there into a small woodland grotto with a statue group of St. Francis preaching to the birds. Trees and summer house, which should have been directly in front of them were now over to the right.

"Let me," said Aoife. "You've no sense of direction. You could get lost in the jax."

Aoife led Emer along a woodland track past a stone hermitage with bell and chain and an abandoned icehouse through a gate in a wall of rhododendrons into a small heather glen through which a burn tumbled by bouldered pools to Lough Gorisk.

"Where is it?" Aoife demanded.

"Right behind you, sense-of-direction," Emer said. The trees were so close she could see the big spatulate leaves on the branches; however, the onion dome and pepperpot walls of the folly, which had looked to be in the middle of them, now seemed to be a considerable distance behind them. Aoife struck off straight for the trees but the rhododendrons forced her into a way that wound by shadowy, cool bamboo paths back to the Butterfly Garden, from which she ran down the west path around the Walled Garden to an iron gate which should have brought her under the shade of the branches but instead left them back in the Topiary Garden with the trees farther to the left than ever and the summer house so distant as to be almost invisible.

"It's turning us around," Aoife panted. Frustration made her only more determined. "It doesn't want us to find it."

"It's lunchtime anyway," said Emer. "We can try again this afternoon."

But lunch was big and filling and the afternoon was very hot and sleepy and the waters of the lough cool and much more inviting than chasing along dusty garden paths, so Emer and Aoife decided to put it off — for today at least.

Inspired by his triumph over the electricity, Da hauled Ewan down from his room to help move the wicker conservatory furniture down to the landing stage on the lough side for dinner *alfresco*.

"While we have the weather and the environment in which to do it, we might as well live the lifestyle," he declared, handing round a dish of salad.

"Those plates are Meissen, I hope you know," Ma said, pouring a wine that was older than Ewan into a Bohemian glass than was older than all of them put together. Mayflies waltzed across the still surface of the lough. Every so often a fish would gulp one down with a glop of water and a spreading halo of ripples. "You girls have got the sun today. Calamine lotion for the pair of you."

Over dinner Aoife told the story about the maze with the sundials and the summer house in the woods that wouldn't let itself be found. Ewan laughed in the back of his throat in that snorting way he had learned from *Beavis and Butt-head* that is supposed to sound withering but is more like an unpleasant adenoid infection, and said he was glad that everyone thought it was so fine and lovely and that this was the life and so sorry that he was bored out of his skull and he wouldn't upset anyone's enjoyment any longer, and went back across the lawns and up to his room to watch the portable without asking if he might leave the table.

Ma saw that Ewan had upset Aoife and whispered to her, "If you come into the library, I've found something that might help you find what you're looking for."

It was a plan of the gardens, drawn in sepia ink on a thin, crisp paper that had been so long folded it had forgotten how to lie flat. Ma had laid it carefully out on one of the two leather-topped mahogany reading tables and weighed the corners down with volumes of parish history. They all drew close into the pool of light from the desk lamp and leaned over the map. Emer could just decipher the date 1868 in the corner.

"I found it in a slip-sleeve inside the year's volume of household records," Ma explained. "I believe it's the original sketch hand-drawn by Dr. Marius Pusey from which the landscapers took their blueprints. The gardens were not an original feature here: Robert Constant Pusey, the port tycoon, who built the current house in 1785, had the gardens laid out according to the principles of Capability Brown and the landscapers — sweeping vistas, lakes, parklands — that were very much the vogue then. Marius Pusey, his great-grandson, inherited Killynether in 1862 after his father accidentally drowned in a vat of whiskey while visiting the old Coleraine Distillery in which he was hoping to buy an interest."

"Threw himself back in three times," Da joked.

"Marius Pusey had traveled widely in Europe, Asia and America and developed a great interest in esoteric learning," Ma went on.

"What's esoteric?" Aoife asked.

"Profound. Mystical. Secret," Emer said.

"It's all in the year lists. Fascinating stuff; I was reading it all afternoon, which is why I hardly got started on the furniture. He evolved a very individual, eccentric theory of horticulture and garden design that drew something from the formal gardens of Japan and China and the paradise gardens of ancient Persia. Instead of making gardens look like idealized landscapes, he argued, a garden should not be one thing but many things, reflecting the many moods and facets of nature by its layout, shape, the color and types and scents of the plantings and architecture, or even no plantings at all. Taking the idea further, he theorized that gardens could not just reflect, but create these different moods. He called this type of garden "The Garden of the Mind," through which you would pass and experience all manner of emotions and feelings and thoughts and ideas. Like many people of that time, he believed that there was a great but uncontrolled creative power in nature, and that a garden was a place where that power — that magic, we would call it — met the civilizing influences of ordered thought symbolized by the country house and, in so doing, was channeled into many different powers and forms so that you would never be quite sure what you would meet out in the gardens. His ideas became quite fashionable — the gardens at Kiladress in Tipperary, and at Rowallane and Mount Stewart in County Down draw on Marius Pusey's writings in the *Journals of the Irish Horticultural Fellowship*. Killynether is the original, though, and the best."

"How long did they take to build?" Emer asked, poring over the map, following the faded brown-on-brown lines, contours and crosshatchings of then-imaginary plantings, trying to fathom the spidery copper-plate Latin taxonomy.

"There are bills of lading and copies of handling instructions to stevedores at Derry and Letterkenny about imported specimen trees from the Botanical Gardens at Glasnevin and also direct from the Far East. The last dates I found were in the summer of 1872."

"Dr. Marius Pusey. Wasn't he the one that disappeared, and all his family with him?" At that moment the power supply decided to fail.

"Nice sense of the theatrical," Da said, finding candlesticks and setting them on the reading table. "I'm not going to poke around in that antique fusebox this time of night."

"They disappeared in 1880." Ma smoothly picked up the thread of her story. "The gardens would have been quite well established by then. It seems odd that they should up and leave everything that they had worked for so painstakingly over so many years."

"What happened to them?" Aoife asked.

"They disappeared without a trace and no one ever heard of them again," Emer said in her best pajama-party ghost-story voice, moving her face over a candle flame so that it cast sinister shadows upward.

"The records do end abruptly, and local legend has it that the estate workers found all the clothes laid out on the beds and the crockery on the table for dinner and the roast burned to a crisp in the oven and books and sewing and games left where they had been laid down, as if they had been called away for a moment," Ma said mysteriously, entering into the spirit of the thing.

"And never came back," Da whispered in that way he could that sounded like his voice was coming from somewhere else. Aoife's eyes were wide in the candlelight.

"Now let's see if we can find this mysterious summer house that hid itself from you," Ma said, knowing when enough was enough. "Where did you say you saw it?"

They ran their fingers through Elysian fields and Arcadian dells and Temples of Flora and Fauna and Druid Oak groves and hilltop belvederes and shady gazebos, but they found no summer house with an onion dome and a shiny thing that caught the sun among the trees of the arboretum.

"Must have been a later addition," Ma said. "I'll have a look through the accounts after the disappearance, when the house passed to the cousins."

Emer had run her finger into the margin of the sheet, where designs had been scribbled in pencil.

"I knew there was something missing," she said. The sketches were of the ornament at the center of the maze, inked and delicately shaded with artist's pencils. All differed slightly except in one vital respect: The central stalk of each was crowned by a multifaceted globe about eight inches in diameter. The artist's shading hinted at transparency: Sideways up the margin were scribbled the words *pure and perfect crystal*.

"You certainly would have noticed this if it was still in the maze," Da said.

"It may still turn up somewhere in the house," Ma said.

"If it hasn't been sold out of the county," Da warned. Emer peered at the drawing of the maze, with its sundials and central decoration in position. Beneath them, in letters so tiny she could not imagine any pen could have written them, were the words *The Time Garden*.

A door slammed. Feet hammered along the landing, down the stairs, across the hall. Everyone looked at everyone else, imagining a vanished Pusey returned. The library door creaked open. Aoife gave a little squeak. Ewan rushed in. His face was white, his chest heaved, his eyes were wide but he was valiantly trying to recover cool.

"There's something in my room."

Five pairs of footsteps thundered back across the hall, up the hanging staircase and along the east landing. Da thrust a candelabra into the bedroom. A winged something swooped at him from the ceiling. Everyone jumped back.

"It's just a bat," he said.

It is never just a bat, Emer thought.

Da pushed up the bedroom window as high as it would go, set down his candelabra and waved his arms in an attempt to shoo the silly thing into the gardens. It flittered and fluttered around him as if enjoying the sport. It was rather large for a bat, Emer thought. And rather pale. *Luminous* almost. It threw a fast orbit around the ceiling rose, dived at the family cowering in the doorway and shot straight out the window. It seemed to Emer that it left a faintly phosphorescent trail behind it that settled like dust onto the drive. And when it swooped that final time, that face had been more like a person's than a bat's. A tiny, furry, winged person. By the expressions on her family's faces, Emer knew they thought so too.

It woke her again that night, the music at once near and farther than anything could be far. She went again to the window. Down on the parterre the shadows of animals were abroad again, darting through the moonlight. She knew what they were now. They were the statues of the creatures worldly and otherworldly from the Stone Gardens.

The music faded with the lightening of the sky over the eastern end of the lough. Emer slept then and did not wake until morning.

Ma had been up early and, thanks to Da's handiwork, had been able to brew her beloved Bewley's and was therefore full of grand schemes and energy. By the time Emer wandered downstairs she had been through the records as far as the turn of the century and had been unable to find any reference to the building of a summer house in the arboretum, or anywhere else. While she tackled the twentieth-century archives, Emer and Aoife were sent out with the Polaroid to capture images of this elusive artifact.

"And if you find Ewan, tell him lunch will be around one."

"Isn't he in his room watching TV?" Emer asked.

"Amazingly, he was up before me, large as life in his shorts and T-shirt and saying he was going to the woods around the head of the lough."

Amazingly, indeed.

Aoife wanted to hunt for the summer house at once, but Emer persuaded her to detour via the maze and search the Time Garden for the globe of pure and perfect crystal. They tripped over Da on the herb terrace. Weeding abandoned, he was lying on a stone bench in only his swimming trunks, a battered fishing hat and his work boots, sunning himself and humming tunelessly to Ewan's Walkman.

"With weather like this you imagine it can never end," he said loudly, as people listening to Walkmans do. Aoife snapped him with the Polaroid. "Show that to your mother and your pocket money's stopped forever," he said, genial and sun-warmed.

Either Aoife's memory was not so good as she thought or the maze had rearranged itself in the night, for within five turns of her remembered path the sisters were lost.

"Maybe instead of trying to find our own way though the maze, we should let it guide us," Emer suggested. Anything sounds good when you are lost in thick Irish yew. "Walk the way we feel the maze wants us to walk."

Which they did, and found openings and shortcuts and hidden alleys that brought them spiraling round to the Time Garden in a few tens of footsteps.

"I'm sure it's still here," Emer said, sweeping around in the grass with her fingertips. "I think we just missed it yesterday."

"Did we miss that yesterday?" Aoife asked. On a plinth between the six and seven o'clock sundials stood a statue of a goat-horned, goat-legged youth, smiling. They had not missed it yesterday. Neither he nor his plinth had been there yesterday. Where they had been yesterday was an alcove of the cypress walk by the Stone Garden.

"Do you think Da put it there?" Aoife asked.

"Da? It's much too heavy for him."

"Then how did it get here?" Aoife saw the only answer to her own question, and avoided it. "Do you think we should tell someone about this?"

"Would they believe us?" Emer said.

They searched the green for half an hour, the grinning satyr watching, but found not even a shard of pure and perfect crystal. The summer house in the arboretum had lost none of its coyness, sending them hither, thither, now to the left, now to the right, now behind them. Aoife took some shaky Polaroids of what the viewfinder could glimpse through the leaves; Emer managed details of the dome and the finial, which was in the shape of the puff-cheeked winged head of a cherub.

"One of the Four Winds," Ma said, studying the photographs spread out on the wicker table in front of her. She had moved notebooks, discs and laptop onto the north terrace overlooking the lough. "Too hot and stuffy in the library," she had explained. She was dressed in pink shorts, a floral halter top and a huge floppy straw hat, none of which Emer had ever seen on her before. She had traced the history of Killynether through the days of patriots and crinolines and the terrible foreign war, and the war of independence and the civil war that always follows wars of independence and the birth of a nation and the years when it hid from the shadow of the mushroom cloud in its valley deep among the hills and had found no record anywhere of a summer house with a cherubic Wind on top of it. "I've to go shopping in Dunnes in Letterkenny on Thursday; I'll call at the Area Management Board to see if they're archiving any documents from here. Summer houses do not spring from the ground."

Neither do statues walk in the night, Emer thought. Except she had seen them, and so maybe summer houses could. Anything could, at Killynether Castle.

"Oh, by the way, salad for lunch I'm afraid. The power went off about eleven o'clock and there's neither hide nor hair of your father to fix it."

Ewan was back from the woods in good time for dinner by the waterside.

"There are deer up there," he told them as they sat around the table, basking in the evening warmth, listening to the slow lap of water against stone and a Mozart piano concerto on an aged wind-up gramophone Ma had unearthed in her cataloguing, along with a grand collection of 78s from the thirties. "I got real close to them, I could have touched them. They weren't afraid of me in the least. It's amazing country up there."

Emer had not heard him excited by mere things since he started leaving pubic hairs in the bathroom.

Da played the piano again that night, improvising around a dancing, jigging tune that Emer did not know but which reminded her of something. Afterward, she heard her parents laugh and talk in low soft voices in which you could only hear the feeling. On the edge of sleep she remembered what it had been about the piano tune. It was the music of the piper beyond the edge of the world.

That night when it woke her she did not go to the window, but crept quietly along the landing and down the stairs and through the music-room French windows that were always left open because of the heat and out onto the west terrace. The flagstones were still warm under her bare feet. She had never smelled anything so sweet as the scent of the night-blooming flowers in the Midnight Garden. A movement on a stone bench startled her: a figure. Ewan, in just his underpants.

"You hear it too?" he asked.

Emer nodded. "How long have you been hearing it?"

"Since we came here. It scared me a bit at first — I didn't know what it was — but not anymore."

"Do you know what it is now?"

Ewan smiled in a way that said he might know, but would not tell.

"There's something strong and strange about this place, but I don't want to leave it. Not now. I thought I'd hate it, now I don't ever want to go back. It feels like — I don't know — like it's always summer here."

"I wish we could stay here always," Emer said. A bank of ornamental grasses rustled. A little fox-mask peeped out at them for just the moment it took them to recognize what it was, then disappeared. "I think the statues move around at night.'"

"They do. And more," Ewan said.

Emer knew he would not expand on this comment either.

"Ewan, what do you think happened to the people who built the gardens? The Puseys? Do you really think they disappeared?"

Ewan looked out across the silver and shadow of the Long Vista to the screening cypresses of the Provincial Garden.

"You won't think I'm mad, will you?"

Emer shook her head.

"I think they're still here. I think they went into their gardens one day and forgot to come back. Went so far into them that they couldn't get back."

"Yes," Emer said, swinging her bare legs. "And do you ever think that maybe they want others to come and join them?"

It was Da who made the discovery. His weeding had taken him along the Wisteria Walk into the maze, and, responding to the weeder's state of Zen mindlessness, the maze had opened itself before him and brought him into the Time Garden at its heart. As he worked his way around the central ornament he uncovered it beneath a wad of couch grass roots. When he saw what it was, he quickly uncovered the remainder of it and fetched the Polaroid. At dinner he laid the photographs down like a riverboat gambler laying down a flush.

The photographs were of small square slabs of stone inscribed with words.

"They run round in a circle," he said. "That's why I had to get them all before they made any sense."

All Time Shall Be One Time When Shines the Leo Moon, said the stones.

"What does it mean?" Emer asked.

Da poured himself and Ma another glass of wine. With high summer showing no sign of ending, his hat, boots and swimming trunks had become a uniform, as had Aoife and Emer's oversize T-shirts and cycle shorts, Ewan's surf cutoffs and Ma's pink hotpants and halter top. *We are becoming a tribe of naked pagans*, Emer thought. Like Presbyterians shipwrecked on a desert island, far from civilization. It was a thought at once comfortable and disturbing, as was the realization that her parents were flesh, and body, and could relish in their own physicality as much as their children.

"What it *means* is that we've been totally wrong about the Time Garden. They aren't sundials spaced around it. They're moondials. That crystal globe in the sketches: I've been thinking for some time that it's obviously meant to reflect light onto the dials so that they all show the same time."

"'All Time Shall Be One Time,'" Ma said.

"Exactly. What I hadn't figured until I found the inscription is that it's the light of the full moon. The full August moon, in fact, which is the moon of Leo. Twenty-first of the month. Ten days from now."

"What happens then?" Ma asked.

"I don't know," Da said.

"I do," Aoife piped up. "Something wonderful."

That night was the hottest yet. All around, distant thunder grumbled, but never in the valley among the hills where it was always summer. Even in just her knickers with no covers, Emer could not sleep. She went down to the kitchen to help herself to milk before it went off and took the glass out onto the north terrace to drink it, but it was no cooler out than in tonight. An edge of light lingered along the hills at the head of the valley. The stars were very high and sharp; the moon was in its first quarter, but so bright that Emer could clearly see the figure on the lawn, silhouetted against the silver of Lough Gorisk.

"Ewan?" She kept her voice low. She did not want to wake her parents from their postcoital slumber in the room above. The figure turned and moved away from her. Emer followed it down the grass banks. "Ewan?" The silhouette sat down at the dining table by the water's edge, back toward her, contemplating the lough. "Ewan? Da?" She touched the figure on the shoulder. It rose and turned simultaneously.

A cry rose in Emer's throat and died there as she realized that she had no reason to be afraid of that thing before her; that she could not be afraid of it; that she had no wish to; that fear was not a thing it understood, only mystery, and moonlit awe.

"Your father is asleep, and your brother is not here," the satyr said. "He is occupied elsewhere." He was taller in the flesh than stone; his skin and hair and hooves were a dark, glowing bronze, which surprised Emer, for she had never thought of mythological creatures as being any particular color. His torso was wide and heavily muscled, but his face was gentle beneath the deceptively treacherous-looking goatee. His voice was deeper and darker and more liquid than all the water in deep Lough Gorisk. "But it is good you have come at last. I have been such a time waiting."

"Is it you who plays the music?"

"Another calls; I merely wait, and meet, and guide you."

"Ewan hears the music. Are you waiting for him too?"

"You all hear it, in your own ways. You will all meet us, in your own ways."

The satyr crooked an arm, an invitation to link and walk with him along by the waterside. He cocked a pointed ear, listening to the song of a bird trilling in the deep twilight. The different jointing of the satyr's leg made him difficult to walk beside; this simple anatomical observation more readily convinced Emer of his reality than anything he might have said.

"There is a place beyond this world," he said. "An Other world, where all the things that have ever been dreamed and ever will be dreamed live, all at once, outside time. But sometimes, very rare and special sometimes, they cross into this world."

"You are my dream?"

"No, I am part of another's dream, that still goes on, beyond."

"The ones who disappeared?"

"My father's gardens focused the power of the Other place, channeling it, directing and shaping it, and it drew us from this world into that Other he desired more than life itself."

"Who are you?" Emer was suddenly afraid, knowing he was no dream, but historical fact, written down in the leather-bound books in the library.

"Once I was Jasper Aurelius Pusey. Now I am what I desired to be, and the name of the desire is Logrus. Come, there are things you must see to understand." He leaped away and in two bounds crossed the lawn to the gate of the Garden of Sleep.

"Logrus! Wait, I can't keep up with you!"

In an instant the satyr was by her side, grinning a goatish grin in which there was still an echo of the lost Victorian boy.

"You think not? I think different. Behold."

She followed the downward sweep of his hand, and beheld. Breasts. She had *breasts*. Firm, upturned breasts with proud nipples like ripe berries. She felt them with her fingertips, reeling with pleasure and astonishment. Eyes and fingers explored downward. Her belly was hard and firm with muscle; between her long, strong thighs was a triangle of dark, dense pubic hair. But her legs, her feet... From the knee down her calves were covered in long, silky chestnut hair that parted above two elegant, polished, pointed hooves.

"What have you done?" she cried.

"I have done nothing," Logrus said. "You are only the you you have the potential to be. You are your own dreaming, by your own power and the power flowing through these gardens tonight. Look again." He showed her her reflection in the smooth water of the Lough. She saw hair, glossy and straight and hanging to her bottom, as a girl condemned to a lifetime of straight bobs dreams her hair might hang. She saw a face she hardly recognized: The features were her own, but the years of experience and wisdom and laughter and maturity that made them into beauty came from another life entirely.

"Oh," she said simply. "Oh, I'm beautiful."

"You will be always so, in the gardens of the night," Logrus said gently, then commanded imperiously, "Come!" and together they sprang across the lawn, hooves barely touching the grass. The gate opened before them and they raced side by side down gravel paths, through arbors and bowers, past fountains and pools where fish jumped languidly in air as thick and still as water, past the Walled Garden and the Physic Garden dense with the complex perfumes of herbs, and by the stone oratory to the Bluebell Glade and the woodland gardens beyond. Cool mist lay trapped under the canopy of leaves; the earth was still moist with last autumn's leaf-litter. Rare moonbeams shone between the leaves; by their light Emer glimpsed the figures lying together beneath the stalks of giant hemlock, watched over by a priapic statue of a Roman god.

"Quiet," the satyr said. He whistled gently, no more than a breath, but something heard, and came to his call: A veil of glowing vapor stirred out of the mist and gathered over the entwined bodies. By its light Emer saw that the woman had the head and dappled hide of a deer, but her body and limbs were indisputably human. She was curled against the side of the other, which Emer saw shared with her some aspects of the deer: the short, dappled fur, a pair of branching, many-tined antlers. But the face was human. Emer parted the bracken fronds for a closer look.

Ewan's. The face was Ewan's, but Ewan as a man, deeper and stronger and weathered by time and visions, but with the softness of forever-sixteen mellowing it. The muscles of his chest and shoulders were heavy and moved slowly, powerfully, as he breathed deep in sleep.

"Logrus—"

The satyr touched finger to lips. A wave of his hand dispelled the cloud of light and, hand in hand, they stole away. When they were a safe distance from the grove, Logrus said, "He wants to be careful. Cernunnos is jealous of his hinds — he caught just such a demi-cerv with one of his brides, shackled him hand to foot with unbreakable iron and had him sealed within the earth in a faery hill for ten thousand years. Or is that yet to come? Time runs in strange directions in this between-place. Do not worry for your brother; what has happened to him is only what is happening to you, to all of you. In the night you are becoming the shapes of your dreams, for the night is the place where human dreams live."

"All of us?"

The satyr made no answer, only grinned and sped away through the woods. Emer followed, her mane of chestnut hair streaming out behind her as she chased him through the gardens beneath the ascendant moon of Leo. In the Chinese Garden she caught up with Logrus and he seized her, pulled her into a small tiled pavilion and kissed her. The kiss was like every wild thing she had ever dreamed of. It seemed the culminating moment of her life so far. Then, hand in hand, they ran onward. In the Beehive Garden Emer stopped, hearing unexpected laughter. It led her a subtle, stealthy path through the Knot Garden, along the Magnolia Way, across the Chamomile Lawn and the Doo'cot Garden. She gingerly parted the beech hedging around the Triton Garden and peeped through. Two voices were laughing, a man's and a woman's. The man was chasing the woman around and around the lawn about the Triton Pond. She was shrieking, he was laughing and making pretend horns. Both were naked. The naked man picked up the naked, squealing, laughing woman, pretended to throw her into the Triton Fountain and fell in with her. They surfaced embracing each other, and sank down until only their shoulders showed.

"Ma? Da?" Emer whispered. Those horns that Da was still making: Were they pretend, or were they real?

It was raining in Letterkenny. It had not been raining at Killynether, but by the time they got to Letterkenny it had that set-for-the-day look. Emer felt miserable in apricot Lycra shorts and cagoule. Especially after having been a beautiful, swift, proud horse-woman from a legend. That was the thing that seemed real, Letterkenny the drab dream from which could always wake yourself.

Ma had a battle with a yob with a Barry McGuigan mustache who swung his Ford Fiesta into her parking space at Dunnes while she struggled with the lumbering Volvo. Drenched, they shoveled plastic carrier bags of food into the back. *Care for your environment,* said the bags. *Please dispose of this carrier thoughtfully.* Emer had no great desire to wait flicking through old copies of *Phoenix* and *Irish Field* in reception at the Historic Houses Trust while Ma searched the archives for the elusive summer house, so she arranged to meet in a halfway decent coffeeshop (in that it did not expect its clients to sit on plastic patio furniture) and in the meantime wandered up and down Letterkenny's wet, diesel-y streets windowshopping. The clothes shops were as bad as she had imagined back in Dublin. The music shops were worse. The souvenir shops exceeded both in atrociousness. The candle-and-hand-carved-by-Filipino-children ethnic woodwork shops smelled of potpourri and played New Age harp and synthesizer music.

The antique shop stopped her dead, oblivious even to the gutter dripping on her hood. She looked long to make sure what she saw was no illusion and went straight back to the Trust offices. When Ma learned what she had seen in the window, coffee, shopping, even the frustrations of Trust bureaucracy were forgotten.

"How much do you want for the crystal ball in the window?"

"Says forty pounds, but I'll take twenty-five," said the woman behind the counter in the raggy cardigan that smelled faintly of cat piss.

"Do you know anything about it? Where it came from?" Ma wrote out the check.

"That's Tir-Nan-Og Antiques, dear. I got it in a job lot from a house clearance a year or so ago. Laborer's cottage, up by the Killynether demesne. I think it's rock crystal, but as to what it's for, I haven't the faintest idea. There's a screw mount on the bottom, so it's likely it was attached to some kind of base. Gypsy crystal ball, as like as not."

She wrote the card number on the back of the check, checked signatures, wrapped the globe in several sheets of Irish *Times* and popped it in a crinkly white plastic bag.

"Oh yes, I almost forgot. This comes with it, apparently."

She slid a cracked document wallet tied up with yellowed string over the table.

"'It is to us as the sea is to the land, in that they share a common globe, yet are separate and hostile to each other, and one may not easily pass from one to another, except by certain places which are to it as the shore is to ocean and land. For a man who enters the sea by leaping from a high cliff brings destruction to himself, whereas the man who wades carefully from the shore does so without harm, and may return again to the land, and from it may then launch out craft to embark upon longer voyages."'

Ma took off her reading glasses and let them hang from the cord around her neck. The Blennerhasset family sat around their table by the water's edge under the darkening sky. Late swifts dipped and flitted, early bats darted silently after insects. By the light of two many-branched candelabra, parents and children read from the papers they had spread from the document wallet across the tabletop. The air was so still the candle flames rose without a flicker, like ascending spirits. The crystal globe which formed their centerpiece caught the candlelight and threw it in a hundred different directions.

"'The gardens are a point of embarkation,'" Da read in that storytelling voice Emer remembered so surprisingly vividly. "'When I conceived them, it was as a place where the primal forces of nature and the civilizing power of man might meet and be reconciled. I had never considered them becoming the literal embodiment of that abstract theory: a place between this world and the other.'"

"'Tir-nan-og; Otherworld; Paradise; Elysium; Olympus; Arcadia; Eden: We have many names for it, but it has no name for itself, for it is the place from which all names come; how, then, can such a place succumb to permitting itself to be named and mastered?'" Ma read, holding the right leg of her glasses.

"'It is always summer there,'" Aoife read out. "'Except when it is winter, but when it is what it is, it is for always.'"

"'As the mill race channels the brook to turn the mighty wheel and do useful work for the good and profit of many, so the gardens channel the power that runs from the Other place into this, that we call imagination and creation,'" Ewan read. Candlelight cast shadows on his face that made him look older, wiser, wilder, the face of the Ewan Emer had spied on in the hemlock glade. "'But, as the tides run with the moon, so the flow of power turns with the phases of our celestial companion. I believe that when the configuration of the heavens is correct, the tides will reverse and ebb from this world into the Other. At that time those who have the courage and craft may ride the flow into the place beyond.'"

"Is this all written by Dr. Pusey?" Da asked.

"Mine looks like a little girl's handwriting," Aoife said.

"Mine was written by Mrs. Pusey," Emer said. "Listen. 'There is no age there, and no dying, no want and no hunger. There is joy, there is hurt, there is sorrow, yes, these things, for without these life is less than living. It is the reflection of all that is rich in our humanity, but no sorrow endures forever, no thing can harm you, for these are things of time and it is as beyond time as it is beyond our measurements of space. It is all, and always!'"

Wind gusted across the lough. The waxy leaves of the rhododendrons rattled, the candle flames wavered. The moon rose over the eastern end of the lake, high and bright in its third quarter.

She had run all the dark of the night with the satyr, through gardens wilder and more beautiful than any she had seen before. As the moon of Leo waxed, the gardens of the earthly side encroached more and more closely on the gardens of the other side. Emer's hooves carried her tirelessly through glen and glade and valley, past temples to unknown gods and oratories of unspoken wisdom, and she no longer knew or cared through which world she ran.

In midgallop, it stopped her. The music: louder, clearer than she had ever heard it before. Nearer.

"Who is it that plays that music?" she asked.

"The time has come for you to see," said Logrus, leading Emer through moon-shadowed thickets to arrive abruptly at the place on the south walk of the Walled Garden where a statue of the infant Samuel guarded a privet arch to the arboretum. They passed through and Emer found herself in a clearing among the tall trees at the foot of a cylindrical building ten times her height, topped with an elegant onion dome and a golden cherub.

"The summer house," she breathed.

The satyr guided Emer by the hand through the open fan-lighted door and up a spiral staircase to a wooden-floored circular room. There were four tall lattice windows at each cardinal point; the walls between were covered in white plaster flutes and pipes from which the music flowed.

It is like being inside a church organ, Emer thought. *But in a church to a wild and generous and laughing God.*

"The Temple of the Winds," Logrus announced. "Hail Aeolus and Ventus!"

The pipes replied with a sudden, stentorian, strident discord and fell silent.

"The winds blow through the vents beneath the dome and down through the pipes and so the Temple sings." The satyr cupped his hands to his mouth and softly sang, "Hello..."

Wind blew up the spiral staircase and across the parquet floor. The pipes hummed and creaked and then a voice so hushed that Emer could not be certain it was not a trick of the wind whispered, *Good night, my son.*

"A good night to my father. You see, she came."

She was called; she could do no other, the pipes hummed. New harmonies entered, like two dissimilar voices speaking in unison. *You are most welcome, child, after so many years when no one had ears to hear, much less the power to call us back to the edge of this world. It lives in a very few, this power, all female, and only expresses itself at the threshold of womanhood: like yourself, Emer.*

"You know my name? You know about — all that?"

I know all that goes abroad beneath the four winds. And I have seen it blossom before, the power to touch the place beyond, and call it into this world. I have seen it in my own daughter.

"Your own daughter — you are Dr. Marius Pusey?" Emer asked.

I was. Now I alone remain in the place between to summon and to light the way to beyond. But this is only my physical body; my spirit flies with the four winds.

"What is beyond? We want to know, but we are afraid to trust what we cannot see."

The place of heart's desiring. The land of always-summer. The country of dreams, where the legends live. Wonder and beauties and horrors, joys and tragedies: It is the very stuff of these things. The farther you go into it, the bigger it becomes. Another place. A better place, perhaps. A different place, certainly. Go, look from the north window.

Her hooves clattered in the marquetry inlay that mirrored the ceiling. Moonlight filled the Temple of the Winds, threw a net of shadow over Emer's new body. The window from which she looked had raised itself above the tops of the trees and she could see over them and across the shining water to the far side of the lough. The rock and heather hillsides were dark with many trees, among which the moonlight illuminated the white stone temples and statues and pavilions. Yellow lights shone from some, tiny but welcoming. Emer craned to her right for a glimpse of the reassuring architectural presence of Killynether Castle among the unfamiliarity. She saw only gardens, gardens upon gardens within gardens among gardens, endless gardens under the moon. She rushed to the east window. The Georgian house stood square and comfortable behind its reef of hedging and topiary. Looking left, the hills of Donegal were once again rock and grass and moonlit heather.

From this place, it was as easy to go on as back. Neither held any fear for her now, for she understood that there fear was conquered, as were age, grief, time, death. The human part of her flew out from the Temple of the Winds across the green counties to Dublin, and the house in Heytesbury Street, and the building society who had almost taken it away from them, and Da sitting all day in his jogging suit watching daytime television because he could no longer find the energy to apply for jobs, and Ewan hiding in his room because he envied and was afraid of others his own age who seemed to have everything he did not, and she thought about school and about exams and about university, and work, and money, and marrying, and mortgages, and every day having to do things you did not much want to but which were forced on you against your bidding, and the ugliness of the world that was getting uglier and older and sicker every day, as did the lives of the people who tried to live with it; and then she thought of a land where summer never ended and sadness was not the end of every story and the beautiful was the thing that endured. More than anything, she wanted to go down into that other land, but she

159

restrained herself.

"We must all go together."

Of course, said the voice of the four winds. *But will they come?*

"Yes," she said, certain now. "Yes, they will."

The Temple of the Winds sighed in all its pipes and flutes and tubes and a sudden gust of air swirled the dust in the upper room and whirled down the spiral staircase and fled into the night.

It was Da's idea that they turn it into a little ritual. Aoife went first carrying the three-branch candlestick, then Da with the toolbox, then Ma with the crystal on a little satin cushion, then Ewan with the wind-up gramophone — the power had failed terminally two days ago—and last of all Emer with the five-branch candelabra. The maze smiled at their merry solemnity and opened its arches and alleys to them. In the Time Garden the lightbearers stood on either side of the central ornament while Ewan played appropriately stirring 78s and Da tried to screw the crystal globe onto the mount, decided time had burred it too heavily to be trustworthy, and produced a tube of Super-Glue.

"Stick anything," he said confidently. "Including crystal globes." When it was on they all stood back and waited for something magical to happen. The evening deepened, bats began to hunt and glide, that was all.

"My back's itchy," said Aoife unexpectedly.

"Actually, now you mention it, my head's a bit sore," said Da, rubbing his forehead.

"Mine too," said Ewan.

"It's my feet that ache," Emer complained. They all looked at Ma.

"Actually, I'm just dandy," she said happily.

The moon rose above the yew hedges, huge and blue and seeming so close you could pick it from the sky like fruit.

"When is it full?" Aoife asked.

"The moon of Leo is the night after tomorrow," Da answered.

"I hope it won't be cloudy. I want to see it."

"I don't think it will be cloudy," Ma said.

"What happens then?"

"Why, we go," Ma said, as if she knew that everyone would know what she meant, though it was the first time any of them had mentioned the Other place, beyond the gardens.

"There?" Ewan asked.

"What is there to stay here for?" Da said.

"Will we be back in time for school?" Aoife asked.

No one answered that one, but instead rubbed their sore heads or flexed their sore feet or scratched their itchy backs or, if they were neither itchy nor sore, watched the moon.

That night no music woke the people of Killynether House to call them into the gardens along the edge of Otherworld. They slept, they woke, they washed, they came down for breakfast outside.

"Emer, why are you wearing knee socks on a beautiful day like this?" Ma asked.

"Ewan, you must be boiled in that thick sweatshirt and jeans," Emer said.

"Ma, my back is still really itchy," Aoife said. Da, in his boots, trunks and fisherman's hat, grinned sheepishly.

"Actually, I have a confession to make." He doffed his hat and swept his hair away from his temples. On each side, just above the eyes, two tiny nibs of horn pushed from his skin.

"Actually, so have I," said Emer and took off her long socks to reveal that from the knees down her legs sprouted chestnut stubble.

Ewan winced self-consciously.

"Me too." He took off his jeans and sweatshirt and everyone saw how his body was covered in thick, glossy brown hair mottled with pale spots.

"Aoife?" Ma asked.

The nine-year-old rolled up the back of her T-shirt all the way to her neck. Just below each shoulder blade was an angry red swelling, oval-shaped, about eight inches long.

"Don't look at me," Ma said. "I'm no less perfectly all right than last night."

"It's starting, isn't it?" Aoife asked.

"It started the moment we turned into the drive," Ma said.

Again that night the music did not speak from the Temple of the Winds and the house slept peacefully, but for sudden wracking pains that woke the sleepers and then passed so suddenly they were asleep before they could ask themselves what had roused them.

Emer woke early — hot, sweaty, bleary. She climbed out of the big high bed. Her feet made an odd noise on the floor.

She looked.

Two gleaming, pert hooves stood on the bedside rug. Long, silky chestnut hair covered ankles and calves.

She leaped from her bed to the full-length mirror and cried aloud.

She was tall.

She had firm, uptilted breasts.

She had long, glossy hair that hung to her bottom.

She was old.

She was beautiful.

She was the she into which the gardens changed her in the night. She was the she of her dreaming.

She looked away and looked back. She was still the same she. And would remain so for as long as she dreamed she could be.

She could dream that dream for always.

She pirouetted in front of the mirror, stamped her hooves. Her hair flew around her like a thick red veil.

They could not go back now. The world would not receive them anymore. They had been trapped the moment the house heard their wish never to leave again, and slowly shaped them for the place beyond that was the only place they could go now — out, through the gardens into the land that got bigger the farther you went into it, until, at the heart, it reached forever. She had been reluctant to leave her bedroom for what the others might think, but now that all other ways had been closed to her, she was proud of what she had become. Hers was a strong dreaming. She flung open the bedroom door and strode onto the landing. At the same moment a door opened across the stairs. A spreading pair of antlers cautiously negotiated a way out.

"Ewan?"

"Emer?"

He was the young stag now: the hunting, rutting one of the wildwoods. Muscles moved easily under his gorgeous mottled pelt. He had grown ten inches, in every direction Emer noted. The door seemed barely wide enough to admit his chest, let along the ten-point tines that spread from his temples. Rags of velvet clung to them; the topmost points scraped the ceiling.

"Aoife?"

They banged on their sister's door but there was no reply, only a low-pitched humming.

"Hallo the house!" a voice boomed from the north lawns. "A grand and glorious morning, thanks be to God!"

From the window at the end of the landing Emer and Ewan beheld the widest man either of them had ever seen, standing on the gravel path beneath the first flight of steps. His shoulders and chest were as wide as a span of oxen, his legs as massive as the trunks of holy oaks. His skin was smooth and tanned a dark leather. He had a mane of black curly hair and a tight curly beard and twinkling blue eyes. It was by the eyes that Emer recognized the creature. Not even the heavy, double-curved ram horns could disguise the light of her father's eyes.

"Da!" They banged the glass. He saw them, pointed and laughed like a small hurricane. He stroked his horns.

"Suit me much better than that stupid paddy hat!" he bellowed.

A golden something darted past Emer. A second blur of light looped over Ewan and vanished into the swags and tails around the window. Georgian fabric tore, there was a sound of rapid fluttering, as if a bird had become entangled in the drapes. The whole curtain lifted off the wall and passed over their heads. As it did Emer glimpsed the means of levitation. Holding it aloft were two golden cherubs, each no bigger than her hand, wings humming furiously, faces puffed with exertion as they struggled the weight of fabric into the empty space above the stairwell.

A golden glow lit the ceiling and swept down the walls as the source of illumination rose upward. The banister rods cast long, prison-bar shadows on the walls; the busts of eminent Victorians in their niches passed from malevolence to beneficence as the changing light played games with their features.

A woman rose into the space above in the middle of the hanging staircase. She had the old-young timeless beauty of goddesses in Renaissance allegorical paintings, but rather than their characteristic bovine docility, she brimmed with an inner energy that shone from her in a golden aura. The cherubs dipped and hovered and clothed her nakedness in swathes of curtain material.

"Hi, kids," Ma said. "What shall we do today, then?"

For fun they tried the Volvo but Ewan's antlers wouldn't fit into it, Emer's hooves couldn't manage the pedals, one of Ma's cherubs got caught under the clutch and emitted a fearful squeal and after all that it didn't start anyway — which did not surprise them, for they had reckoned before they began that it had gone the way of the electrical system. So they all went to swim and splash in the lough and play softball and dance to 78s of Charlestons and Black Bottoms while the cherubs obligingly cranked the gramophone.

"Anyone seen Aoife?" Da asked.

"She'll be here," Ma said and everyone knew she was speaking the certain truth because her aura shone so bright it could be seen even in the afternoon sun.

As the shadows began to lengthen they carried the conservatory furniture up from the water steps to the west terrace. Da bore the big table on his back. His eyes glittered in the shade beneath. Ewan and Emer took chairs; Ma's cherubs busied themselves with cruets and cutlery while Ma carefully packed the Meissen and Bohemian crystal.

"When's Aoife coming?" Ewan asked.

"When she's ready," Ma assured them.

"Finest of wines!" Pa brought two fistfuls of bottles dusty and cobwebby from the cellars. He filled four glasses. "Might as well get the taste for it now, kids. It'll be nothing but the juice of Bacchus, *there*." They drank down their wine and talked about what they thought they would find, *there*....

"Something wonderful, as Aoife says," Emer said.

"Everything wonderful," Ma said knowingly.

Da glanced at his watch, which he had had to open to the last notch to fit around his transformed wrist.

"Moonrise in forty minutes." He opened another bottle of vintage. The light faded from the sky, the birds fell silent. The world turned violet and purple and warm and incredibly still.

"I wish it could always be like this," Emer said, curling her hooves up beside her on the wicker chair.

"It will," Da said. "That's why."

The darkness deepened. The gramophone cranked out dance tunes from the glory days of the Big Bands. Da lit candles. The terrace sparkled with dozens of tiny flames. A silver light fell on the gardens and the lough: The moon had risen, though the west side of the house still threw its dark shadow across the gardens. A line of light appeared over the parapet. A corner of moon appeared.

"'The moon of Leo!" Da proclaimed. "To the Time Garden!"

They ran, they galloped, they flew to beat the rising moon. They passed through the twists and turns of the maze as if they were not there — for in a sense, they were not, having no purpose anymore — and came to the central green. White fire sparkled on the heart of the crystal Super-Glued to the little monument. The moon sailed up the sky, through the trees of the arboretum. It cleared the topmost branches. The moon of Leo shone full into the Time Garden, and the globe of pure and perfect crystal blazed with light. The witnesses fell back as twelve shafts of silver beamed from the facets of the crystal, each perfectly aligned with its moondial. The gnomons and cut-cube faces burned. Emer cantered from dial to dial, reading the time.

"All the same," she shouted. "All the same time!"

"What time?" Ma asked.

"Every time and no time!"

Da lifted his shaggy, horned head, smiling.

"Listen, it's beginning. Come on!"

He led the race back through gardens now ablaze with light. Silver radiance poured from the Time Garden, streaked around the twinings of the maze and along paths and walks, clung to the outlines of the beds and plantings, dripped from the statues and fountains and floral arches. Emer leaped over a torrent of light cascading down the Azalea Path. Every leaf, every flower and bud burned with the light from the other place.

"The tide is ebbing; we must catch it before it flows out altogether!" Da shouted as they arrived on the west terrace.

"But how?" Ewan demanded. "How do we ride it?"

"Here's how," said Ma in a voice that made everyone turn to look at her.

They followed her pointing finger. It came slowly, gracefully across the lawns and parterres, silver runners ablaze with moonfire: the ice yacht *Erehwesle*.

"Come on, come on, no time to lose!" Da said as the ice yacht drew up beside their table and came to a halt. They needed no bidding. Ma took the forward seat, her cherubs lifting the bridle lines for her to steer the front skates. Da sat behind, back against the mast, his wife folded in his arms. Ewan stood on the left runner, Emer on the right, clinging to the mast.

"Where's Aoife? We can't leave her."

"Here she comes!" Emer cried. "Here she comes!"

At first she had thought it was a shooting star; then she had thought it was a ball of wild magic escaped from the gardens; last of all, as the glowing object with its wake of sprinkled silver drew close, she saw that it was a woman: a tiny, perfect woman no longer than her forearm, flying on wings of sheer gossamer. A tiny winged woman with the face of her sister. Aoife swooped around the mast in an arc of glitterdust and settled on the prow of the ice yacht.

A wind from Elsewhere filled the sail with a crack and snuffed the candles into glowing red wicks. Dark shapes poured up the terrace steps and through the open French windows into the house: the bestiary of the Stone Gardens, reclaiming their inheritance. Very slowly the ice yacht moved across the west terrace, all the time gathering speed as it caught the tide to another place. Onto the north terrace, faster now; down the stepped grass, its crew shrieking with laughter and clinging to whatever was clingable. Faster: across the lawns, sail billowing, filled with silver light, to the water steps, and out over the moonlit waters of the lough, toward the hills beyond where a thousand lights were shining and the land went up and up for always, into places more wonderful than human words could tell.

HE ON HONEYDEW

And all should cry, Beware! Beware!
His flashing eyes, his floating hair!
Weave a circle round him thrice,
And close your eyes with holy dread,
for he on honey-dew hath fed,
And drunk the milk of Paradise.

— Samuel Taylor Coleridge, "Kubla Khan"

 legend told in a practiced voice to the children of the people many ages hence:

Secrets of the past, hints of our forgotten dreams for the future, and knowledge to live contentedly in the present all drift with the dark waves below us. Yet we may only stand on the cliffs over the tumultuous ocean, awaiting discovery or insight. Somewhere within the depths of the bubbling, saline water below are the answers to all the questions we pose — if only we could reach them. This knowledge is too bitter for us, but the whales drink of it freely.

Even so, there are some secrets, if only a pitiful handful, we still possess. Some mysteries we can explain. Some things are too intimate to be stripped from our memories. So here, before the green plasmic sea, I'll reveal the fate of the one person who humbled us all to our present lowly station. And though it's the last days in the life of the diabolical fiend of our debauched past that usurped us from our throne on Earth, I will regretfully remind you that it was the wanton and slovenly ways of generations of your ancestors before that monstrous man, the Destroyer, that sowed the fields of rotten grain he so casually raped and reaped.

Yes, you know much of this man already, and many of you justly twist your faces in disgust and anguish at his mention. The Destroyer was the sickness from which blossomed fields of fungi. A blight more heinous than a hundred or thousandfold what he did to the planet and to the people. A horror so unbelievably, so irredeemably, corrupted and villainous that his like had never been known in the thousands of wars and millions of skirmishes in the times before him. No dictator ever was so unrelentingly oppressive. No warrior ever was so hideously cruel! Not one of the people since before we were people, since before we were savages before we were people, was so evil.

I cannot reveal more about the man than his actions tell you, but listen, for even such a powerful man may be brought down. I will tell you of his demise....

It was long ago, but it was still after the end of the world, and the whales already shared their wisdom only through song. Without the words they once spoke, though, and even without sound at all, the aquatic behemoths yet communicate a soulful message. Those not already choking under the weight of their indifference and vapidity of vision could still translate this golden music to priceless wisdom.

But the Destroyer was not content to hear the music. He wanted the voice. Even if he was tone-deaf, he sought to sing.

That's what must have compelled him to venture so far from the safety of dry, unmoving, unprovoking land. He gave up the rational region he'd conquered for the spiritual waters yet unclaimed. He must have intended to plumb the depths for more answers. Maybe he thought he would gain all the answers when the world fell before him. But even the greatest banks of memory among men were marred by gaps and holes.

From where he stood on the prow of his boat — more properly a ship, for his was not like the hand-propelled ones we use today, it was an enormous vessel of metal grander even than the one commanded by the wealthiest of the Admiralty and larger even than the God Ear when it's unfolded and rotating and listening for whispers from Heaven — he surveyed things I can only guess.

So soon after the apocalypse which brought about the end of the world — for the Destruction was not long since past, at least not long enough for the grossest poisons to evaporate and dissipate from the Earth as they never will from the memory of people — he must have seen things that cause me to shudder. If sights of oceans frothing with glow and red from the miasma that hung to the surface like leeches clinging desperately for each faint sparkling peek of the sun; or a sky littered not with the sprinkling of spindles of white puff on deepest turquoise that have since returned but instead clogged by a hideous tangle of swirling masses of taint and pollution; or the fading land on the horizon which still burped a charred and ruinous cargo to the surface where it ran in streams of putrescent brown ooze and black sludge to every hidden community of people…if these sights could not alone grant him understanding or perspective, then I wonder what he hoped to find in the contaminated grottos deep in the ocean where only the enormous custodians of wisdom could survive by straining the sickness from the bits of healthy matter with their porous mouths.

But he was the Destroyer — tall and proud and fresh from a victory over everything that yet inched and huddled on land. There was no force to challenge him and no will to oppose him, so he continued to pursue his own ambitions. But he was no longer simply conquering the world.

The conqueror's boat was not unlike the ghost cities spread across our continent. It was the size of one hundred of our villages, and had enough room to house every inhabitant of nearby New Bay, but not another living thing accompanied the man aboard his boat. However, he was not alone. Men of metal and the disincarnate voices he caged in metal houses were his only companions. None of them possessed souls any longer. If they had, and had they too the courage, then they might have dissuaded the Destroyer from his outrageous quest to steal the wealth of the sea.

He was still a relatively young man. Fit and powerful, this warrior had already proved himself capable of surmounting any physical challenge. His erect and commanding posture stood out sharply against the wasted, vaguely luminous sky. He wore clothing that protected him from any lingering toxins that could harm a person, and which also served to make him indistinguishable from the people made completely of metal who were always near, but there can be no questioning the vigorous man whose relentless ambition demanded homage from even the sewage-strewn waters of the ocean.

The doomed man knew generally where he needed to go, though once there he knew specifically what had to be done. The feats possible by the complex tools on his boat would not be believed if I even knew enough to tell you of them. But there are other legends — perhaps you've heard them — of the terrible weapons of fire and smoke the boat carried. These were monstrous devices capable of razing our entire village in an instant.

Massive but delicately sensitive probes, like the long sticks we use to determine the depth of the waterholes, plunged deep into the water. Examining, testing, inspecting. Every little bit of information gleaned by these probes was carried into the heart of the boat, where those same complicated devices quartered, dismembered, dissected and completely analyzed them.

Submersible boats dove into the water as well. These, like the probes, needed no people at the oars or helm. More complicated devices directed their movements. Instructions from their master somehow penetrated the greasy slime that carpeted the surface of the water. More probes were attached to the outsides of these boats, which snaked and wound their way to the center of those hidden grottos. Hopelessly inadequate details of the aquatic mysteries that these probes encountered were transmitted wordlessly through the quicksilver froth of the ocean back to their master. He did not question the information he received.

This was the wisdom he sought to rape from the ocean. It was a search without self-discovery. Without a landscape surrounding the goal, the discovery loses its context. Plying the waves in his floating fortress, safe from the ochre he drudged for truth, this misguided man foolishly placed himself above that which was beyond him.

No one knows how long he persisted in his tireless search. Though unwilling to give of his spirit and join the waves, the Destroyer did give of his inexhaustible energy and ambition. Finally, a hint of the goal was espied and he pursued his quarry of knowledge with the vigor of a desiccated man harried by dreams of the purest spring water. One of the submersible boats, navigating the mazy madness of a hidden hollow, signaled success. The Destroyer hopped from his perch at the prow, radiating a desire more intense than the invisible waves that struck men down a little time before. He had found it. This is what would make him master of both the known and unknown. He demanded his own submersible boat be prepared, for it was of such a size that a man could fit within and safely roam beneath the water for hours or even days at a time. Like a decadent king's pleasure garden, the forces inside the ship responded and soon a gleaming boat of metal was ready for the master's descent. How, though, do you oppose the man who brought not just one human, not simply a group, not merely a nation or continent, but an entire world and its great culture down before him? Or with him.

There was a seat like a chair inside the boat, though the occupant was forced to recline almost prone. Surrounding the seat was a vast array of complex devices, but since he commanded the operation of a boat the size of New Bay, one so small posed no problem.

Secured within the belly of the submersible, the Destroyer was deposited over the side of the larger boat. The metallic capsule dropped into the ocean, dolloping through the dark and fetid waters like a stone, sinking until the pilot adroitly activated the controls and powerful forces buoyed the submersible boat. So, like the unmanned ones that searched before it, the boat rose and fell and rotated within the water.

The Destroyer did not penetrate the depths alone. An armada of unmanned submersible boats accompanied him. He and they all followed the probe as it retraced its steps to the site of the discovery that caused him such anxiety. He needed this assistance, for even when so close he was incapable of finding the cavern. The landscape was foreign to his perspective. Only in the context of an entire journey through the sea can a person find this place.

Only if the currents and the will are right. The man's perverted will was enough to thwart the currents.

Mountains of stone and darkness loomed above the Destroyer as he dove deeper and deeper in pursuit of his ephemeral guide. He was undaunted by the solitude and heedless of the warnings. At one point the submersed boat became wedged to the walls of the winding ways to the chamber, for the chamber ahead was not meant to be entered thus — not by a man encased in metal. And he would have been lost to the unknowable oceans if the unmanned boats had proved incapable of scraping and gouging the walls to force the villain's passage through the conglomerate tunnel.

The foolish man ignored his single warning and glided deeper still into the opaque waters. He pushed on. Until it was revealed to him. It was that which he sought — the Behemoth's Chamber, the lair of the greatest, most ancient whale.

The chamber was rounded and enormous. Even the feeble light of the hazy sun that managed to penetrate into the water did not reach here. The only light was the sickly purple luminescence of the growths feeding on the walls. Only where these spots of light were obscured was it possible to gain the impression of the mammoth inhabitant of the chamber, for the blackness of the mighty whale within was such that it was nearly invisible.

It was a huge and ancient and powerful creature. It hung motionless in the water of the stone chamber somewhere in the seas of the world. Around the whale were perhaps a hundred such tunnels as the one the intruding boats exploited. From each of the tunnels blew a ripple of water.

Hibernating, as the Destroyer knew it should be, the whale was unaware of being examined. The man in the submersed boat therefore calmly powered his way around the monolithic mammal. The other submersible boats dispersed in a scattering storm to swarm around the noble beast. They prodded toward it with their extended probes, but they did not touch.

Floating at the base of the whale's skull, the intruder examined where to lance it through the rear of the head. It was here that he must drive the probe that would draw the wisdom of the whale to be wordlessly transmitted to the boat. The whale head is so large because it constantly bathes in the wisdom of the deep waters for its entire life; and this whale, trapped in the chamber because no passages existed that could accommodate its bulk, bathed in the waters richest in knowledge — for all the waters of the world, swallowed from the heights of the oldest mountains and dredged from the deepest mines, passed through this chamber. Feeding on all this knowledge, the whale grew and grew until finally the whale's bulk was such that it rivaled the floating fortress still clinging safely to the surface of the shadowy water, which was beneath the whale, for the creature rested upside down. At least to the intruder's enlightened understanding of gravity.

The villain saw that the whale did not breathe, though as a warm-blooded animal, like people, it must. The depth of its meditation was such that it could not be concerned with such trivialities. Likewise, the man's meditations on the state of the whale consumed him and made him careless. Overconfident and careless. When the intruder strayed too close to the mouth of the great whale, the large creature awoke.

The submersed boat was capable of great speeds, but what use is speed when you seek to outrun the infinite?

Without hesitation, without need to shake the cobwebs which might clog the mind of one sleeping so long, the massive whale hinged open its gargantuan jaws. But a shrug and its awesome head gained the reach needed to net the buzzing waterbug that exhausted itself in a futile escape.

The inky darkness grew a shade deeper as the whale's mouth folded shut over the struggling boat. Massive teeth pounded together to imprison the powerful man. Then the whale showed its first real sense of what it had done, for its entire body shuddered as it swallowed this distasteful load.

But moments from fancies of ultimate knowledge, the Destroyer was trapped forever, entombed in the belly of the greatest whale.

The whale began to settle back into its sleep, a sleep that would be less troubled because the cause of many of the concerns carried to it by the currents was now at the center of the currents. In its stomach. The unmanned submersible boats, however, would not allow a relaxing slumber. Though insignificant, they darted about the bulk of the whale and annoyed it. So the whale loosed some of the currents that ran calmly through its home. A great whipping and splashing sounded and water rocketed in whirlpools and spouts and flushed the small boats from the chamber.

The great whale knew then that peace would not be regained. The man in his stomach was still alive and could yet be rescued by way of a terrific effort. When a last remaining unmanned submersible began to chirp and whirl and communicate with the large boat above, the great whale knew such an effort would be made for the one he'd swallowed. And for this man there could be no return. Others, in ages past, and surely in ages to come, would be vomited out and returned to their homes by the invisible currents at the disposal of the mighty creature, but the indomitable warrior dove deeper than he could swim and would not be allowed to return.

So the whale fled its home. For the first time since the end of the world it uncurled its massive tail. The whale rocked uneasily in a housing too small for ambitions of motion, but it unleashed its powerful pectoral fin on the surrounding rock and by dint of enormous strength pulverized it in a short time. With long, thunderous strokes, it shot through the gaping hole for even deeper oceans, beyond the reach of even more who might seek him, but fewer now were worthy of the great prize of wisdom it could grant anyway, so that mattered little to it.

Above, for the whale swam upright now, the huge boat miraculously mirrored the movements of the whale, due, no doubt, to the wordless instructions transmitted from inside the belly of the whale. Both whale and boat bore through the thickened goop that was once more liquid, but the debris of the apocalypse were deep in the water and slowed the great whale more than boat.

But as the whale swam the oceans round the world were rerouted. The apocalypse that beset the Earth at the hands of the one now in the belly of the whale demanded that the currents be redistributed anyway, so with each stroke of its vigorous tail, the mighty whale set patterns into effect that altered the flow worldwide. It ensured that the currents would always follow it and would always deposit all knowledge, from the least scrap to the grandest banquet, in the new chamber it would choose.

Even with the impetus gained from countless currents nourishing its speed, the whale could not outpace the large boat above. Powered by fuels unknown to us now, the boat surged in time to the whale.

Escape by flight seemingly impossible, the great whale resorted to another tactic. It rose rapidly to pummel the boat as it had the mountain which until recently had contained it, but the boat responded first. Unlike the slow-moving probes that earlier poked into the depths, the boat loosed bolts of metal that careened down through a sloppy mess to strike the great whale. The dreary waters argued their passage, but the lances swam true and penetrated the tremendous body of the whale.

The blows, however, were insignificant and the whale surfaced for the first time in millennia. It blew a great blast of moisture and gas from its blowhole and the heavens rumbled in retort. Already rampaging because its sleep was disturbed, its home ruined, and its flanks wounded, the whale saw for itself that what it already knew of the surface world was true. But like emotions that cannot be gauged until heartfelt, the nightmares of the whale only now took full form. With a single, resounding blow the precariously floating fortress was upended.

The whale did not pause to mourn the dying city. It traveled the breadth of the waters of the world to confirm that what it knew was indeed truth.

And so the foul burden buried in the belly of the whale toured the world less a lord than before.

And so, children, well after the end of the world, and long since the whales ceased to speak and would only sing their wisdom to us, the currents began to flow again.

Now go to bed. It is late. Next time you will learn something of what the God Ear hears, but for now consider the Destroyer in his grave amidst the wisdom he sought to conquer.

T
O
M
B
S

CITY DEEP

Foster hated the Tube. He hated it because he feared it. His fears were grounded in a combination of claustrophobia and pessimism. The intolerant crushing crowd, the confined carriages, the tight tunnels that pressed in around the trains, the sense of weight above: concrete, basements, roads. All these factors were at the front of Foster's mind when he reluctantly rode the lines that wormed their way through London's depths.

Perhaps his fears might have been reined in if he had more faith in the management and working procedures of the London Underground — but the constant fire scares, the stifling delays and the ubiquitous evidence of incompetence merely fed his phobias and made them more real. At any time it seemed the train he was riding might collide with another. Some terrible bomb left by a vengeful terrorist might explode, bringing London crashing down to crush his carriage. Perhaps a fireball belched from the Victorian bowels of the archaic system might roar down the tunnel, engulfing the coaches, baking their screaming occupants alive. These terrors, while Foster acknowledged their improbability, were all plausible enough to keep him from using the Tube whenever he could.

His work, thank God, did not necessitate much travel. His position as a sales coordinator for a small building publication kept him safely within an office off Tottenham Court Road. His flat in Hammersmith could be reached as easily, if not as quickly, by the Number 9 bus as by the Piccadilly Line. And so, over the years, he had reached a tolerable enough compromise. He had to leave half an hour earlier in the mornings and accept less time at home in the evenings, but it was a small price to pay for his peace of mind. Without even noticing it, his life had been shaped by his fears. Friends who did not live on the bus routes were neglected, venues not easily visited overground remained unvisited, and large areas of the capital city had become, albeit subconsciously, out of bounds. Perhaps if Foster had bought a car — for he could drive — his social life would have been more eventful, but it was an action that had been postponed once too often for it to become a reality.

If Foster had voiced his dread more frequently, maybe it would have become manageable, but fear of ridicule had kept it internalized so that it had become ingrained within his psyche and remained there like a dark stain. On the few occasions he had been forced to venture underground (an appointment at St. Bartholomew's Hospital, a nightmarish trip to Heathrow), he had spent each journey in a state of abject terror, perched on the edge of his seat, reacting frantically to every tortured scream of the rolling stock as if it hailed an imminent destruction.

And yet, despite all this antipathy, Foster now seriously considered descending the steps at Piccadilly Circus. It was pouring with rain. Worse than pouring. Great sheets of water tumbled from above, dispersing in the freezing wind. It was six-thirty. Every other bus but his had been past five times. He was becoming increasingly annoyed as Number 14s paraded round the corner of Haymarket in groups of two or sometimes three, even though nobody wanted to board them. Similarly, clutches of 19s made their way empty to Clapham Junction, as did every other bus but his that stopped at the top of Piccadilly. What looked teasingly like a figure nine as it trundled through the downpour would become a twenty-one as the vehicle drew closer.

Foster was cold enough and wet enough to think about entering the warmer and considerably drier environment of the Tube. After all, it was only ten or fifteen minutes at the most. He had the *Standard* to read and then he would be home. The rush hour was in its closing minutes, the weather having discouraged people from lingering in the West End. He could at least be sure of getting a seat. It was decided. Purposefully he looked at his watch, tutted loudly so that observers might understand his behavior, and marched toward the pelican crossing.

The rain became noticeably heavier, balls of water falling from the skies bouncing off the flooded pavements. Eros cursed the heavens with his bow as Foster entered the station.

People stood dripping in the golden glow of the renovated concourse. Most seemed to be sheltering from the rain. Suddenly Foster was seized with an urge to join them, to wait for the storm to pass and return to the bus stop. However, with a great effort of will, he walked resolutely toward the ticket machine and paid for his journey. This would do him good. It would prove that he was still able to overcome his fear in the face of necessity and therefore that it was founded in common sense, not neurosis.

The entrance gate swallowed his ticket, ejecting it as he passed through. The escalators yawned ahead of him, waiting to take him to the station's belly. He stepped on and looked down at his distant destination. Strange to experience vertigo underground. Hamburgers and pizzas slipped slowly past, marking his descent. Once the length of these moving staircases had filled him with awe. They were monuments to their creator's ingenuity, carrying endless lines of passengers elegantly up and down. Now their extension was daunting, merely reminding Foster how far he was actually slipping beneath the surface of the city. And their age made him nervous, bringing to mind the decrepitude of the whole system.

He watched the faces rising toward him, all of them raised in anticipation of surfacing, or so it seemed. Did they share his fears? Were they relieved to reach fresh air? Or was he alone in his anxiety?

The tinny sound of a busker drifted closer as the steps flattened out, depositing Foster on the walkway. An impatient businessman pushed past him, rushing hopelessly toward a distantly departing train. Foster mentally congratulated himself on his calmness and strode casually around the corner to the second escalator, the one that would carry him to the Piccadilly Line platform.

The light seemed brighter down here, the air drier, removed as he was from the stormy conditions of the streets. In fact, it occurred to him that this was one of the advantages of an underground transportation system: the consistency of the atmosphere. Passengers could wait for trains without being frozen or soaked. There was a certain sense of shelter in depth. Which was why Foster found it strange to see puddles on the floor when he reached the bottom.

"It's been dripping all day," the morose-looking busker informed him, putting down his guitar. "Whole bloody place is falling to pieces." Foster tried to smile in agreement, as if the decayed state of the station was something that amused him. He threw a couple of coins into the busker's empty cap and passed through the arch down the tunnel towards the trains.

How appropriate a vernacular "the Tube" was, thought Foster, on this last leg of his voyage to the Piccadilly Line platform, for it referred not just to the tunnels through which the trains passed, but to the shape of the pedestrian passages as well.

A rush of air met his face, heralding the imminent arrival of his train. He ran the last few yards, panting as he reached the platform — which seemed astonishingly empty. The gray carriages poured screaming out of the black mouth of the tunnel, and, as they came to a halt, the doors snapped open. Foster jumped onboard, wiping away the water that had dripped onto him from the roof above.

The doors slid shut as he found a seat in the sparsely populated carriage. Its few occupants were hidden behind newspapers. He waited for the train to move. The platform remained immobile. He read an advertisement for Kelly Girls written in the style of a diary entry. Whatever a Kelly Girl was, she led a very drab life. The outside world juddered once and became still again. Foster suppressed a flash of panic. He had been doing well, but this pause in his motion had allowed his usual fears to begin their slow ascent. What if the train remains stuck here? What if the doors won't open? What if there's a fire? What if there's a bomb? What if? What if? What if? These negative hypotheses spiraled upward together, taking his heartbeat with them.

"Stop it," he said firmly to himself, trying to regain reality before it slipped away altogether.

"It's the rain," said the man opposite, which didn't help matters. Unless things had changed since he'd last journeyed on the Tube, it was not the done thing to converse with one's fellow passengers. "I said, it's the rain." It was no good. Foster had been singled out to join this unusually talkative commuter in conversation, whether he liked it or not. "It does things to the rails when it gets in. Shorts them out." Foster wasn't sure he wanted to hear any of this. He had enough difficulty dealing with his own imaginary fears; he did not wish to share anybody else's. "I used to work the tunnels, see."

"Really?" Foster responded dutifully. However, he found his curiosity was sparked, despite himself, as people are often intrigued by things which they morbidly fear.

"Yeah. Before I was a driver. Started just after they opened Leicester Square station." Foster looked incredulous. The few strands of his fellow traveler's gray hair suggested age, but his soft pink skin made him look no older than sixty. "1935. I can remember it like it were yesterday. Fifteen I was." A few *Standards* rustled further down the carriage, wielded defensively against this all-too-public autobiography. He continued unabated. "There was a flood in one of the Northern Line tunnels then, even though it was May. They had to divert some steam engines from up the line to keep it going."

"They had steam engines...down here?" Foster had assumed the Tube had always been electric.

"Oh yeah, right up until the sixties." Quite suddenly, the train shuddered into life and swept off toward Green Park.

"I thought we were never going to leave. You sometimes think the whole place is going to fall down on your head."

"Oh, there's no danger of that, mate. They knew how to build things in those days. The electrics might go occasionally, but these tunnels are built to last. Even the ones they don't use anymore are still in good nick."

"What do you mean 'the ones they don't use anymore'?"

"There's a load, extra lines built at the start of the war. Bet you didn't know about the one between Whitehall and the Palace."

"No, I didn't."

"Then of course there's the Coronation Line." There was a hint of conspiratorial pride in the man's voice, as if he was imparting some treasured secret.

"The Coronation Line? Which one's that?"

"It was an extension of the old Metropolitan line which used to run between Paddington and Farringdon at the end of the last century. It went right through Shepherd's Bush, Kensington, Hyde Park Corner, up through the West End and back to Farringdon via Holborn. In fact, we're in a bit of it now."

"Really?" Foster was genuinely intrigued.

"Yeah. This stretch of the Piccadilly Line between Holborn and Green Park was part of it. 'Course it had a load of stations of its own which they don't use anymore: Sussex Square, Craven Hill, Moscow Road. They built over 'em but they're still there."

"Why don't they use it anymore? London could do with another line, I would have thought."

"They couldn't use it now, not without knocking down half the new office blocks in London to reopen the stations." He stared out of the window into the strobing blackness beyond. "Anyway they're still probably 'prohibited'."

Green Park arrived to halt the man's discourse. Foster was too fascinated to tolerate a pause. "What do you mean 'prohibited'?"

The man looked at him as if he was weighing Foster up, deciding whether or not he was a worthy recipient of this information. He must have reached a positive conclusion, for he leaned forward and lowered his voice:

"Well, it hadn't been in use as a line since the turn of the century. The company that owned it went bust. The Piccadilly Line was opened in 1906, and the Coronation had been closed at least a couple of years before that. But in '37, just after I started working, they were getting ready for the war — that's how I knew there was going to be a war — and they were talking of using the Underground for air-raid shelters. Well, they was going to reopen the whole of the Coronation Line and put beds down there, a sort of massive dormitory. Some of my mates started on the cleaning-up, but then the Army took over. They must have changed their minds 'cos they never used it for civilians."

"You mean the Army used it for themselves."

"That's what we reckoned. You see, the Coronation Line ran deeper than just about anything else in London. The Army decided it was perfect for testing — there was s'posed to be all sorts of secret weapons on the go — and the whole thing remained off-limits right through the war." Green Park slipped backward, replaced once more by the conspiratorial blackness of the tunnel. "They kept it sealed off, though. All sorts of rumors went flying. We 'eard that they'd found things."

He paused slightly. Foster couldn't resist the urge for clarification. "What do you mean 'found things'? What sort of 'things'?"

His companion leaned even closer, lowering his voice yet again.

"Strange things," he whispered. "Tunnels that weren't man-made and that went down." He made an appropriate gesture with his finger. "Old things like you get in a museum: pots, flints, spears."

"Spears!"

"Bones, skulls, all sorts."

"Are you suggesting there was a prehistoric community *down here?*"

"I ain't suggesting anything. I'm telling you what I heard. Anyway, it wasn't just what they found. We heard some soldiers had disappeared. Went investigating one of the tunnels and never came back."

"I don't understand. Where could they have possibly gone to?"

The man shrugged his shoulders theatrically. "Who knows? I will say this though: It never surprised me. Every driver's got his own story. Things he's seen on the late runs. There was even a story about how they lost a train once, complete with all its passengers."

"I don't believe it."

"Oh, I do. There's old things down here. Things best left undisturbed. I can remember when I was cleaning tunnels — we had to defluff them every night, the tracks get clogged up with hair. I used to hear things, chitterings and scratchings, like monkeys at the zoo."

Suddenly the train shuddered to a halt, although Hyde Park Corner was still some distance away. Foster tensed in his seat, gripping the upholstery with fear-stiffened fingers. This was what he hated the most; when the motion ceased in between stations, he suddenly became aware of his location, hundreds of feet beneath the city, frozen in concrete. His alarm must have been noticeable, for his companion tried to comfort him. "'Ere, there's nothing to worry about. It's just a logjam. One train gets delayed at a station, the one behind has to stay where it is. You're a nervy devil, aren't you?" Foster started playing with his hair and pulling at the skin of his neck as he always did when agitated. The other passengers still steadfastly shielded themselves with their evening papers, some of which were being shaken with more than usual vigor as the pages were turned.

"I...I get claustrophobic sometimes," he proffered, aware how foolish his fear must seem to this hardened subterranean.

"Just relax. We won't stop for long. No matter what the problem is, the priority's always to keep things moving." The lights dimmed and flickered, and for one terrible moment Foster thought that they would be abandoned to the darkness altogether, but they soon returned to their usual intensity. There was an enormous creaking and screeching of metal as movement was resumed. "Told you!" the man declared triumphantly.

Foster relaxed a little. He tried to remember what it was he was going to ask, but the sharp fear had driven the questions from his mind.

"You see, we're quite safe down here," his companion continued. "Quite safe. I've spent me whole life down 'ere, and no 'arm's ever come to me."

The train began to slow in anticipation of the next station. Foster had to admit he was tempted to get out. The rain must have eased off a little by now, and he could catch a Number 10 as well as a Number 9 from Hyde Park Corner. He could have a cigarette while he waited. Reaching for his briefcase, he eased himself out of the seat, ready to get out when the doors opened.

"You getting off 'ere, then?" the man smiled at him.

"Yes, yes. Thank you for the history lesson. It was most interesting."

The train slowed to a stop. Foster peered through the glass, waiting for the doors to open. The sign on the wall read CUMBERLAND GATE, clearly illuminated by the gas lights above it. The doors slid open, revealing the silent platform beyond. There were no people, although Foster noticed that green filing cabinets somewhat absurdly lined one of the walls, partly obscuring a large Ovaltine poster.

"I must have lost track of the stations," he said to the man, who was still smiling. Before he could decide whether to step down to the concrete, the doors had closed once again and the train had resumed its journey. Unsure quite what to do, Foster returned to his seat. None of the other passengers seemed concerned about the disappearance of Hyde Park Corner. They remained resolutely hidden behind their papers. Only their hands were visible, fat and pink, all without fingernails.

"When they retired me, I couldn't cope with life up there. After all, I wasn't used to it." The man had resumed his autobiography, somewhat inappropriately Foster thought, feeling the embers of his panic rekindling themselves. "I kept coming back down 'ere, on me own. Did a bit of exploring. Couldn't believe what I found. I was made welcome, so I decided to stay. It's much safer down here."

As if on cue, the papers were lowered. Strangely, it was only then that Foster noticed that they all carried different headlines, all referring to long-gone events.

"We do like to get dressed up and go for a ride every so often, though. See what we can find."

Foster was reminded of fairground chimps wearing human clothes. Except these mockeries of mankind were completely hairless, their eyes huge and white, their lips slack and wet. The lights went out before he could study them more closely.

"And they've taught me so many things." Even in the darkness, Foster could sense they were traveling downward at an alarming rate, and he would have screamed were it not for the soft fingers that filled his mouth. "You won't believe what's down 'ere!" the man reiterated gleefully as the train shrieked onward through London's ancient bowels.

BUT NONE I THINK DO THERE EMBRACE

I don't move well in constricting costumes, and as I lay on the floor of my final resting place, trying to get enough air into my lungs so that my diaphragm could properly support those floated top A's in O *terra addio*, I was making a mental note to myself to try to get that git of a production designer sacked.

In fact, I was rehearsing my speech to the *Opernhaus* director in my mind, this sort of thing: "I mean, the nerve of it! You just don't do *Aïda* in a bikini and veils, love. Okay, I'm supposed to be the dusky, sensual, oversexed Ethiopian princess, but aren't we a couple of thousand years too early for the Big Famine? You know my tits are too big for that iron Maidenform your cocksucking costumier's ah, 'created' for me. That's it, I'm walking. And I'm not returning the fee. Either he goes or I go. Or should I say she? Yes, yes, I'll bleeding well wait for you to get your dick out of his Khyber. Just make sure you wipe it."

I'm good at temperament. Bloody well ought to be at my age. It is rumored that I once made Rudolf Bing vomit up a beluga-covered toast point with my demand for a 5% bonus over the salary of any tenor who dared brave my dueling tonsils. Got it, too. It's been a long way from Tooting Bec to the world's great opera houses, don't I know it, love, but I still know a thing or two. They don't call me The Big One for nothing. (Behind my back, that is. I answer only to Dorothea…or Miss Masters.)

Hate that bloody art director, Damien Diavolo. Particularly, I hate his silly hat. It's the sort of hat that chemo patients wear to hide their baldness, but you see a fringe of hair, so that's not it, exactly. It's a hat that exists purely to annoy me. It's even worse than his lack of talent.

Take this tomb set, for example. As I lay concealed behind a gargantuan papier-mâché statue of Horus, waiting for my cue, I couldn't help realizing just how vulgar it was. The lighting was in the nineteenth-century New Orleans-whorehouse style; the flats were busy with haphazard hieroglyphs and dizzy dancing girls; and the foreground had so many scarabs, idols, sarcophagi and Tutankhamen masks that it looked more like some Cairo tourist trap than a princess's tomb.

Thank God that I was supposed to be weak, worn out and dying from lack of oxygen in the tomb scene. I don't think I could have actually *acted*. I could imagine impaling myself on the Eye of Horus in mid-aria, or waving my arms about and punching through the Sphinx.

Dutifully, I waited for my beloved, the righteously rotund Hector Fortinbras. Hector is *huge*, but they had dressed him sensibly: The flowing-robes approach is always good for the heroic tenor, and Hector's shopworn body certainly needed the drapes.

And he was singing up a storm. I mean, for a prince who had lost his beloved, his generalship, his country, and was being sealed up alive in a tomb in punishment for one brief moment of weakness, and who was rapidly running out of air, he certainly wasn't giving much thought to conserving oxygen. But that's the beauty of grand opera, isn't it then?

God, he was gorgeous as he thudded through the set. Oh, haggard, assuredly, and past his prime, and all that. The voice was a little off-color, too, but he could certainly belt out those top A's, B's and C's, and you could hear the audience gasping at every stratospheric one of them, including several that weren't in the score. But Verdi wouldn't have minded, poor love. He doesn't half make that tenor carry on; bit of a wanker, really. *The fatal stone has closed above me...never shall I see the light of day...nor see Aïda...*oops, fluffed it a bit there, didn't you? *Heavens...Aïda!* Time for me to emerge. "'Tis I..." then, at the top of his lungs: *"Tu! in questa tomba!"* Strewth! Splendid stuff.

We sang our guts out for the next twenty minutes. *Farewell, O Earth! Farewell, O vale of tears!* I was weeping real tears as I fell into Hector's all-embracing embrace, and it seemed to me that Hector, too, was doing a lot better than average...in fact, he seemed to be the best Radamès I had ever sung with...which seemed improbable; after all, I did my first *Aïda* subbing for Renata opposite Jussi Bjoerling, for God's sake; I've done Corelli and Domingo, and my last one was with Carreras, though admittedly it was only because Mirella canceled at the last minute.

Yet this second-string, bloated blancmange was outsinging them all. What on earth had got into him? Was it his much-made-fun-of sojourn at the fat farm in Miami, or his visit to the Dalai Lama? I couldn't wait to ask him after the curtain calls. We were obviously going to have many.

We had a really good time at the end of the love-death duet. It was sort of "any high note you can sing pianissimo, I can sing more pianissimo," and you could have heard a pin drop in that forsaken *Opernhaus*, because we made those top A's *hum*, made the rafters tremble with a sympathetic vibration, the sort of thing you can only do if you hit the note dead on to within a cent of its true pitch, not an easy thing to do with a foghorn soprano like me and a has-been like Hector.

As I sank, dying, into my lover's arms, I was aware that I had sung the finest *Aïda* of my vicissitudinous career. And as the curtain fell over the languid orchestral closing chords, I was also becoming aware that the audience was too stunned to applaud. That incredible moment when they're just too dumbfounded even to clap their hands is a very special thing, and you only hear it once or twice in your life. I knew there was going to be a tumultuous ovation. I puffed up, put on an expression of divalike hauteur, and prepared to receive it.

It never came.

The curtain didn't rise.

In fact, there was a deathly, mausoleumlike hush after those lush chords died away. When the curtain didn't budge for a few minutes (I was dead, of course, but I peeked now and then to make sure I could get up for my curtsy in time) I fished around in my gold-lamé bra thing for my glasses. But it always takes a while to get used to seeing again, so everything was swimming. I've never been able to perform in contacts; I keep thinking they'll pop out if I have to belt out a sustained B flat.

Hector had stood up and was peering at a Styrofoam sarcophagus which stood upright between two papier-mâché Diavolo Anubises. He rapped at the coffin with his knuckles. It sounded remarkably metallic.

"Hector, love," I said, "what's going on then?"

He turned to me with a look of distraction. "Dorothea! I did not realize that you, too, would be caught up in this horror…if only I had known…."

"This horror? What horror?" I said.

He strode over to me, knelt over me (I was still struggling to raise my fifteen-stone carcass from the floor) and shook me. He had one of those violent, crazed serial killer expressions that you see in video nasties.

"Can't you see it, you cow?" he screamed. "It's really happened. We've been sealed up in this tomb for all eternity."

His voice echoed as though the place were really made of marble. And come to think of it, the wooden stage floor was bloody freezing. I rubbed it with one hand. It was cold. As my vision became clearer, I saw that it was white with pink veins. Italian, it looked like.

"Get a grip on yourself, love," I said, for Hector was obviously going stark staring bonkers. I knew that he'd done a lot of weird stuff on his last tour of America. "Really, Hector, this cult-of-the-month thing has got to stop. I'm not talking about fat farms — we opera singers of the old school can always lose weight — but really, the Dalai Lama. I heard you've done other stuff too:

dianetics, est, Sedona, even dabbled with that born-again Christian crowd. It's not good for you, Hector. I know you're still worried about your two divorces and the palimony payments to that bimbo in Shepherd's Bush, but you really must come down to earth sometime, darling."

Although to tell the truth, I was getting very nervous indeed. You see, I had just noticed that there was no curtain. Where the curtain should have been, there was a wall. It too was marble, and all very monumental, covered with a frantic frieze of nymphs, fauns, pharaohs, birdheaded deities, and harp-playing bunnies. It fit right in with the rest of Damien Diavolo's nonsense.

"You don't understand," said Hector fretfully, "it's more than est. I've had a little bout with the Big One since we last met."

"You are bonkers. The last time we had it off was ten years ago — don't you remember? It was the night you bombed in *Otello*. You were very depressed."

"No, no, I don't mean you, Dorothea dear, I mean the *other* Big One: you know, the Goat, the Lord of the Flies, the Prince of Darkness."

"Luciano Pavarotti?"

"Oh, don't be tiresome, Dorothea. I'm telling you I've signed a pact with the devil."

❄◉❄

"I see," I said. I was trapped in the Twilight Zone with a madman, so I thought I'd better humor him. "You mean Satan?"

Hector must have thought it was beneath him to respond to such an obvious question. Well, I may sound uneducated, but I'm not. I know how these things work as well as the next diva — I've done *Faust* often enough, silly little piece of fluff, really. There had to have been something Hector really wanted...and a price he was willing to pay.

"This may seem odd, coming from me," he said, "but I'm really a very bad heroic tenor."

"Truth or dare, is it?" I said.

"Oh, don't be flippant, Dorothea dear. You wouldn't understand. You always had such a head for business, and when the voice gave out you could still muddle through on nostalgia and hard-nosed contracts. But me, well, you know what Anna Russell said about tenors: 'They have resonance where their brains ought to be.'"

"Who said my voice has given out?" I said. I was starting to get just the slightest bit pissed off.

"It's common knowledge," said Hector Fortinbras. He pounded on Anubis once again, and it was now ominously clear that *something* untoward was going on.

"Common bleeding knowledge?" I screamed, although he was only repeating something the *Gramophone* critic had opined just last month. Then I stopped myself for just a moment. After all, beyond that wall, which was surely an illusion, the audience was probably still sitting. Watching the whole spectacle, no doubt. Laughing its collective head off. *That* was a chilling thought. I dropped my voice. "Didn't you experience the same night at the opera as I did? That was a bloody fine performance I gave tonight. Couldn't have bettered it in my heyday. Those final high pianissimos were like handkerchiefs fluttering down from heaven. Those '*mai più*' in the third act were so damned plangent I could hear hearts cracking in the second tier. The conductor was weeping up a storm. If anyone's past their prime, it's you," I added. He really had touched a nerve. Every soprano knows there will come a day when she'll end up doing Gilbert and Sullivan in Blackpool.

"I *did* experience the same night as you, my dear," said Hector. "I am fully aware that tonight I was more lyrical than Bjoerling, more powerful than Corelli, and more intelligent than Windgassen. But unlike you, I know the reason for it. It was, you see, my pact with Satan. I'm afraid I asked for one perfect performance of *Aïda*, at which point he was welcome to my soul."

"You didn't happen to throw *my* soul into the bargain, did you?"

"Well, that's the part I don't quite understand. I was fully expecting, after this performance, to be the subject of a negative assumption — a privilege only accorded, in the past, to Faust and Don Juan — but I hardly thought I'd be trapped in a *faux* Egyptian tomb with a superannuated tart from Tooting."

"So are we dead?" This was all too fantastical to be true, yet it had the sort of *ring* of truth to it. Being stuck in a small room full of vulgar furniture, with no exit and a bald fat tenor calling you names, was extremely close to my personal vision of hell. I scanned the tomb again. There were no exits.

What had I done to deserve this? I wondered. I had really led a very ordinary life. Childhood had been a perpetual teatime of the living dead; adolescence a rampant rutting which still haunted me from time to time, when some ex-yob from the past would come bursting into my dressing room calling for Dolly, Doll, Lolly, Lolita, or Dot — all childhood nicknames I detest. The Guildhall had been an escape from it all, although I never lived down my accent until I discovered that I could sing in Italian, German and French without sounding the least bit Cockney. Then, touring at the Dallas opera, I discovered something even stranger…that the Yanks can't tell the difference between Oxbridge and Hounslow…it all sounds equally la-di-da to them.

Then the usual five marriages, condo in Miami, summer home in Nice, that sort of thing…I don't suppose I set my sights on heaven as such, but hell really did seem like a bit much for the likes of me. Like hanging someone for shoplifting. And it wasn't even my hell.

"I'm getting out of here," I said. "Maybe you did make your deal with the devil — but I haven't signed anything."

"But Dorothea, Dorothea — you can't just *leave* me!"

I certainly could, and I attempted to do so by pummeling my fists on the solid limestone blocks of what had once been the blue velvet drapery of the *Opernhaus*.

I banged and banged. My fists had become red and raw by the time I realized it was going to be no bloody use. At that point, something very strange happened. At first I thought I must have conked my head against the rock, because I was seeing double…the little ridges and clefts in the limestone were twanging back and forth like harpstrings. Then the stone seemed to acquire a certain translucence, and through it I could see vague shapes…human shapes…well, sort of human, anyway…they weren't much different from a matinee at the Met, you know, dinner-jacketed socialites rubbing shoulders with music students in grunge…but they were rather more bulbous…with round, green heads and snail-like antennae. I squinted. A face came right up to my face, and it was something straight out of *Close Encounters*.

"We're not in hell at all," I said. "We've been abducted by aliens."

⊰◉⊱

I thought about the last time Hector and I had been thrown together. Yes, he had bombed in *Otello*. He was in such bad voice that in the last act he took to sort of shouting instead of singing, hoping that the missed notes and weird intonation would be interpreted as histrionic brilliance. We all do that sometimes when we're a bit off, fudging a high note into a shriek of passion and what have you, but by the end of the opera, by the time he was supposed to strangle me, he had been reduced to squawking. Since he had never been able to act, his attempts to sound like a brilliant actor were less than convincing; and he bungled his suicide scene, tripping over the Venetian nuncio, banging his head against a bust of Zeus, and landing on me in such a way that I had to wriggle free or suffocate, which wasn't very convenient as I was already supposed to have been suffocated.

I ended up with one his plates of meat sticking in my mouth.

Un bacio, he sighed. *Ancora un bacio…un altro ba…*but before he could expire, a little sachet of Max Factor theatrical blood slid out of his robes and bounced about on the floor.

Needless to say, the *Times* was not generous. I was, however. I did him in the back seat of his agent's Rolls.

Afterwards, he wept and carried on (his agent was in some pub meanwhile, clinching a deal with another tenor) and kept repeating, "I'm a failure, I'm a terrible singer, I'll have to go back to being a bank clerk."

I adjusted my bra. "Don't worry, love — opera's pretty much done for anyway; we're all going to be on the dole soon enough."

"Fuck you!" he screamed, though I really didn't feel like a second helping. "Can't you see that I'm in agony, that I'm tormented by inner demons, that I should probably be on Prozac? I sang my heart out on that stage, but my heart has diarrhea. I'd give anything for just one absolutely brilliant performance. Music is my life, for God's sake! I gave up a promising career at Barclays so that I could become a sacred vessel through which the inspirations of Verdi, Puccini, Mozart and Rossini could pour out…and instead I'm here, trysting with a tub of lard in another man's Silver Shadow. I'd give anything, I tell you…maybe even my own soul."

Outside the Rolls, it was beginning to rain. It was an extremely mythic moment. The agent's cellular phone began to ring.

"Do you think I should pick it up?" said Hector.

"Up to you," I said.

"But what if it's Luciano or José…or one of my agent's other 'A list' friends? They'll already have heard about the debacle."

It went on ringing. And ringing. And ringing.

"Well," I said, "I'm not going to do it. It's your agent, ducks, not mine."

It rang and rang and rang.

"Look," I said at last. "Are you going to pick it up or not? I'm not going to sit around forever, waiting for you to rectify that premature ejaculation."

He let out a hideous wail of self-pity and gingerly picked up the phone. "Hello," he said. "Who is this? Is this some kind of joke?"

He never did rectify that premature ejaculation, and I took a taxi home, unsatisfied.

I was always unsatisfied.

Wasn't that the truth.

>◎<

"Abducted by aliens? Oh, fiddlesticks," said Hector Fortinbras.

"Come and look for yourself," I said, and he sidled up beside me to peer through the wall of limestone, which was wavering back and forth between cloudiness and lucidity.

"My goodness," he said. "It seems that we do have an audience after all. Just look at them! But they're walking about, jabbing their fingers against the wall. Rude little things."

One of them was leering at me. "I wonder if they mean to perform scientific experiments on us and rape us," I said. "I read about something like that in the tabloids."

"Rape you, Dorothea! I think you flatter yourself."

We stared through the wall for a long time, but presently the images began to fade. The aliens appeared to be departing. Perhaps it was closing time at the zoo, I reflected, as I attempted to recall the details of the *Twilight Zone* episode that most resembled this tableau.

It did all seem remarkably like some sci-fi television drama…or one of those things you read about in The Sun. And now that the images were fading, I began to wonder whether they had merely been manufactured by my mind. You know, to explain away the incomprehensible.

"It's getting darker and darker out there," said Hector. The limestone was losing its transparency. In a moment it would be completely opaque. Hector and I would be alone together once more.

"If we *are* dead, then one has to assume that we are now our immortal souls, and that we can't die again," I said. "You're hardly the person I would have picked to spend eternity with."

"Which goes to prove my point," said Hector. "This is hell."

"But the flames — the torture?"

"Oh, you are silly. What relevance can those medieval metaphors have to this palpable, *living* hell that now engulfs us?"

"Cor," I said.

We stared at each other for about an hour.

"This is just like *Waiting for Godot*," said Hector.

"What's that?"

"Illiterate as well, are we?" he said. "This is grand. I can see I'm really going to love spending eternity with you."

We stared at each other for about an hour.

We stared at each other for about an hour.

We stared at each other for about an hour.

><◉><

I used the time to reflect on the horror of my situation. I should have known something like this would happen. Music is always magical, when you do it right. The first time I found that out was when I did *Rosenkavalier* at the Met, and met my first husband. He was standing outside my dressing room with a silver rose in his hand and that musky leather jacket of his and no shirt, and he told me that my top B in the third-act trio had changed his life.

A year later, after I muffed the climactic B flat of *Un bel dì* in *Butterfly* at a matinee in Seattle, we got a divorce.

By the next season, my top was back in shape again (I even shattered a goblet for a Memorex commercial) and I remarried, this time a Jewish cowboy with a ranch in Montana and a condo in Tel Aviv — Delbert Horowitz. That lasted several years. I had several abortions in between tours. The other husbands are not really worth remarking on.

Sitting here, staring alternately at Hector and the wall, I reached a painful conclusion.

I've never had a life.

There had to be something I could do about it.

At length, Hector began to speak, more to himself than to me. "I've been considering the question of where we are," he said, "very carefully. It's really quite profound. Obviously, in terms of space, we have gone nowhere at all. Everything around us is still the same. In a manner of speaking. The ancients located the physical hell at the center of the earth, but geologically speaking we know that's out of the question. In *Doctor Faustus*, on the other hand, Marlowe implies very strongly that hell is a state of mind, or at least can have a sort of parallel existence right next to our own reality. Then there's the existential hell of Jean-Paul Sartre's *Huis Clos*, in which hell is a state where three people torture each other for all eternity with their sheer presence…and don't have the will to leave even when the door is deliberately left open. The hell we're in now, I guess, leans in the existential direction…after all, this is the twentieth century, I suppose, and hell's got to keep up with the times as much as anything else…but one must admire the elegant simplicity of this mise-en-scène. I mean, there we were, stuck in the middle of a world of canvas and papier-mâché — a territory of illusions — and the way this hell has sprung into being was by *actualizing* the illusion, you see. And making the real world false. Reverse-polarizing reality, as it were. Of course, he's the father of lies, so I suppose this sort of thing is just up his alley. Dorothea, dear, the devil is devilishly clever!"

"What did he look like?" I asked him.

"Oh, you know. Horns, cloven hooves, the usual sort of thing. You know, you would think someone like that would be really hard to get to — secretaries, appointment books, double bookings — but I only had to wait a week to get a meeting with him. I got to pick the restaurant, too."

"Where did you go?"

"Fortnum and Mason," he said. "Well, I was doing *Siegfried* at the Coliseum that week. The *Times* said that I sounded like a piledriver with tuberculosis."

"You met Satan at Fortnum and Mason? What did all the American tourists think, for God's sake?"

"He wore a hat," said Hector. "I saw the horns when we went to the lavatory. Saw more than the horns, actually. To seal the deal, I was forced to kiss the Satanic arse, you see. Thank God I didn't have to suck his dick! Linda Lovelace couldn't have swallowed that thing."

"He wore a hat?" I said.

"Yes, one of those stretchy, woolen hats—"

"Like a cancer patient?"

"Yes, why?"

Damien Diavolo. I should have known. It had to have been him. He designed the set...and he must have built in its innate ability to change from the illusion of a tomb to a real tomb...triggered by the magical power of our perfect performance. "I know who the devil is," I said. "It was the production designer."

"Are you sure?"

"You only flew in this afternoon, didn't you? You're doing *Radamès* in ten cities, not bothering yourself with the ins and outs of each production, relying on your ability to belt your way through the score without paying any attention to the nuances of staging and character and the finer points of the different conductors' interpretations—"

"Well now, that's hardly my fault," he said. "I'm a star."

"Well," I said, "I'm telling you — the man who put me into this strapless Valkyrie brassiere and you into those silly robes, who erected these ridiculous statues, who painted these garish murals, and who minced about muttering nasty asides about my girth all weekend — that's your man. Just imagine! In between acts tonight, I was practicing the fit of temperament I was going to use to get him the sack."

There was no need for me to practice now. I was already working myself up into a frenzy of soprano fury. I shrieked. I stubbed my toe on a stone Anubis. I flung a gold statuette of Osiris at the wall. "I don't even bloody believe in you," I screamed at Damien Diavolo, who suddenly seemed omnipresent even though we couldn't see him. "I'm not going to stand for it. If I get out of here, I'll see that you never get another job in production design. Unless it's cleaning up after the elephants in that *Aïda* in Verona..."

"I just thought of something, Dorothea dear...and it gives me hope. There must be a way out. Here we are, in this tomb in what is presumably the subterranean depths of the earth. There's no electricity. There's not even a torch on the wall. Where's the light coming from?"

Suddenly, the limestone partition that had once been the stage curtain began to go all translucent again. Once more we could see glimpses of another world. But there were no aliens this time. Instead, there were flames. Pools of burning lava. You could almost smell the sulfur. And as we gazed, noses to the limestone, transfixed by the vision, we could see naked people writhing in torment, just like in the illustrated edition of *Inferno* that my fifth husband kept on the mantelpiece. Demons with pitchforks were jabbing at them, and they hopped from crag to crag above the churning brimstone.

"God," said Hector, "oh, God," as though the reality of what he had done were sinking in for the first time.

"That evening in the Rolls, years back," I said to Hector Fortinbras. "That was the devil, wasn't it?"

"Well, I didn't believe it at first. But he kept calling. Always seemed to know where I was. Even called the Intercontinental in the Azores once. After a few years I finally agreed to meet him at Fortnum's, and the rest is history."

"Ah, but it needn't be," I said. Because, strangely enough, a plan was actually crystallizing in my brain. I knew that there had to be a fatal flaw in this entombment. After all, I wasn't part of the bargain, and if I had not been part of the devil's design, and I was here anyway, it only stood to reason that Some Other Power must have placed me here. But *what* power? I stopped believing in God the day my father drowned himself in the Thames after being arrested for exposing himself in the lavatory of the Picadilly Circus tube station. Satan was a slightly more credible figure — after all, the world is a very unsavory place, and might well belong to an unsavory god. But frankly, the whole "battle between good and evil" thing seemed to me to be a load of codswallop. *There's got to be something bigger than all this*, I thought, *something huge enough to contain all of heaven, earth, and hell*. But what mystery could possibly be so vast?

"What if," I said to Hector, "you hadn't come in your pants?"

"What are you talking about, Dorothea dear? I *never* come in my pants. In the red-light districts of Hamburg and Amsterdam, they call me the Rock of Gibraltar."

"Oh, nonsense, you bloated balloon of a male ego, you. *Think!* Just before that phone call. Something happened."

"I bombed as Otello. Never done the role since."

"Then something else."

"Dejected, I allowed my agent to suggest that he take you and me out to a postopera dinner. He had to run off to meet a client at a pub. We were stuck in the back seat of the Rolls by ourselves; it was a brilliant night, and we had a glorious fuck. It made me feel much, much better, and I've always been grateful to you for it."

"I'm afraid not, Hector. Listen to that muse of memory…I mean, listen really hard. What actually happened?"

I decided to leave him alone for a few moments while he confronted his own sexual inadequacies…and I strolled about the set-*cum*-tomb, which had grown much darker since our little vision of Inferno.

Shafts of red light emanated from the eyes of the Anubises, and a pale blue glow radiated from the crack beneath the lid of the sarcophagus. The little Sphinxes, too, had eyes that glittered. They were all watching us. I thought I could detect a glint of intelligence behind their stony features. Even the harpists in the murals seemed to glare maleficently with phosphorescent eyes, and a great Eye of Horus, which overlooked the painted scene, was an expanse of glowering red.

Was it blinking? Butterflies in my stomach now. I could hear my own blood racing. My god, I thought, I'm actually feeling things…I'm actually getting a life...now, when it's probably too late. My heart pounded like the drumstrokes in the last movement of Mahler's Tenth. My teeth chattered like the xylophone runs in the Danse Macabre. Whatever they were — aliens, demons, the opera-going public — I suppose it doesn't really matter what they were since they were all metaphors anyway — they had moved from beyond the limestone curtain. Now they were sharing the stage with us. Everything was closing in on us. I knew then that I was on the right track. There *was* a deeper magic than this God and Satan thing, and somehow I held the key to it.

"Oh, my God," Hector exclaimed. "I remember it now. Oh, God." He was weeping.

"Then," I said, "you see the solution, too, don't you?"

"Are you telling me that overcoming my sexual dysfunction is going to undo a solemn pact between myself and the Prince of Darkness, signed in my own blood?"

"It's a possibility," I said.

"How can you possibly know this? After thousands of years of theological debate by men of every ilk, you're telling me that the dictates of divine and diabolical retribution can be undone by...sex?"

"I know these things," I said, even though I knew for the first time that I knew them, "because I am a woman. We are an elder race than man, and we have ruled far longer, and we are still in touch with the things that were before men fashioned gods in their own image, and dispossessed the earth from its rightful place of veneration as the mother of life."

Whew! That was a mouthful, wasn't it? The thing is, I didn't even know if I was saying it all myself, or whether some primeval force was speaking through me from an ancient time. I felt my whole being resonating like a pair of vocal cords, and a wind gust through my body, so powerful that I was surprised I wasn't being tornadoed off to Oz. But you know, when I thought about it, I realized that all women know what it is I was talking about. They just don't choose to think about it most of the time. Perhaps that's why Damien Diavolo had come down to earth in the shape of a homosexual — so he could avoid dealing with the likes of me.

"All right," he said dubiously. He flung aside his robe and stood before me, a little less than Moby Dick, a little less, too, than a man. "But since that evening in the Rolls...I'm embarrassed to admit...I haven't actually been able to...you know."

"I know," I said. I ripped aside my lamé bikini. Hung my outlandish headdress on a statue of Thoth. I felt much greater than myself. There was a goddess in me. I was a big fat Venus astride the Celtic twilight, and I could feel the wind of time whip through me even though the air in the tomb was as close and musty as...only a tomb can be.

"I'm scared of the eyes," said Hector.

"Then look into your own soul." I removed my glasses and carefully placed them on the lid of the sarcophagus.

"'The grave's a fine and private place,'" Hector quoted, "'but none, I think, do there embrace.'"

"A man wrote that," I said. "Come on, child of earth. It's about time you got a taste of starry heaven."

I began to sing. The music was the Lovedeath from Tristan. I was Isolde, the healer, whose words sang of a love so all-encompassing and so transcendent that it needs must end in death. A man had written those words, too, so perhaps he didn't realize what I now knew — that love can break open the grave. My voice was tentative at first — I'd done the role in the studio, but never on stage — but after a few moments I became aware of an orchestra coming from somewhere beneath the floor. The only opera house with a covered orchestra pit is Bayreuth, of course. So I pretended I was there. After all, I knew that Wieland Wagner had once planned to stage the love duet from *Tristan und Isolde* in the nude, since people didn't wear pajamas in the Dark Ages. The orchestra swelled up. The very air was thrumming, perhaps because it was so thick with dust. I sang of the ecstasy beyond passion and the passion beyond death. Every square centimeter of my large pink form began to glow with an incandescent inner flame. I could see white light dancing around my fingertips as I flung my arms about.

Meanwhile, the set was rearranging itself. Dawn was breaking over the crags of an Irish shore. The stone statues were writhing into fantastical new shapes, cairns and outcroppings. The gaudy backdrop was morphing into a seascape, purple and misty. It was as tasteful a set as *Aïda*'s had been vulgar. Damien Diavolo had nothing to do with this one, that was sure.

And Hector? At first he was trying to act as though releasing the goddess within me was something I did every morning before breakfast. But when the corona of blue flame settled around my head and streams of rainbow-fringed light began to dart from my eyes, his jaw dropped all the way into the prompter's box...that is, the sarcophagus. And with the dropping of the jaw came the rising of the penis.

He leapt into action as I reached those climactic long-held G sharps. Holiest *rapture, highest bliss*, I sang, my throat and my body wide open to the winds of sensuality. As I sank into his arms, he slid into me. He was full of energy. He enveloped himself in my primal splendors, bathed himself in my lubricious light, looked into my eyes and saw the face of the Great Mother; he experienced joy beyond any mortal's imagining.

I thought I could hear familiar sounds...the rustling of program notes...the panting of impassioned opera-lovers...the squeak of leather on carpeting and buttocks on velvet.

And Hector died, more in the Elizabethan sense than literally; the violence of his orgasm almost blew me apart, and I knew that it partook of

BUT NONE I THINK DO THERE EMBRACE

the creative energy that had made the world, and that keeps the myriad spheres of heaven in their orbits.

And I too died, knowing that in a few moments I would awaken to rapturous and well-deserved applause; knowing, furthermore, that I now had a life and was going to make full use of it.

The orchestra eased into its final ritornello. We were going to come back to a different opera in a different city, but it was the best I could do.

Magic and opera are women's arts. Music is magic, and opera the supreme magic; as Anna Russell once said, "That's the beauty of grand opera — you can do *anything,* as long as you sing it!" And since every woman since Lilith, the woman who was before Eve, has been a repository of all that is magical about our human race — that makes operatic sopranos special. After all, *diva* means goddess, then, doesn't it? We are all echoes of the Great Goddess. Just echoes, mind you. That's why the magic I worked was just a touch flawed. Perfection would be hubris.

"Next time you deal with the great powers, love," I whispered in Hector's ear, "don't deal with Jehovah or Satan or any of those types, do you hear? You just go straight to the top."

Then, deluging us like a monsoon, came the applause.

I do know a thing or two after all.

They don't call me The Big One for nothing.

TALES OF BRITANNICA CASTLE:

1.
GINANSIA'S RAVISHMENT

The problem with the spiral staircase to the Northeast Quadrant was the plethora of scorpions, small brass ones, set in spiky pairs on either side of each stone step. Their tails tugged at Ginansia's dress, snagging on the sapphire-sewn hem and snatching her back every few feet. Finally she was forced to run with the silken material gathered up at her knee, and run she did because she was late for dinner, and the Great Wound never forgave tardiness when it involved the ruination of sweetmeats.

Although the Princess Ginansia had lived here all her life and knew every room, corridor, staircase, tapestry, window, door and hallway in the castle, she often felt that the building as a whole conspired against her. It was too ornate, as fussy and overdecorated as her mother, filled with dangerous shadows, pools of darkness concealing sharp little objects that tripped toes, cracked nails and tore skin. In terms of acreage the castle was small, but it was tall. The top five levels had been added by Captain Smackthistle after his legendary victory against the Fire-Tribe Boys of the Infected Mountain. He and his men had returned with all manner of disgusting trophies, parts of bodies which they threaded with gold and silver wire and hung in the heavy blue glass jars that lined the whole of the planetarium.

Ginansia knew no other home, but sometimes dreamed of visiting white open spaces, vast halls of light that were free of clutter and gloom, where nothing was more than a few moments old and she could breathe without drawing dust into her lungs, stretching out her arms to embrace the flaring sun.

She tripped on the bottom step and nearly overturned one of the huge cracked Chinese vases that stood on the marble pedestals at the base of the staircase. Catching sight of herself in the vestibule's towering scabrous mirror, she readjusted the dried clematis petals in her hair, carefully tucking them into the auburn folds. She liked clematis flowers because they had no smell; the castle held far too many extraordinary odors to require further olfactory obfuscation from its residents.

Ahead was the narrow, uneven flagstone corridor that led to the Tarnished Hall and the Seven Sepulchres of Shame, and beyond that the strangely shaped area formerly known as the Heart of All Sorrow, which was now called simply the Dining Hall. The floor here was always wet and slippery, "perspiring tears" according to her mother but in reality slick with condensation, because the flues to the kitchen passed across the eastern archway and the fissures in them released steady wisps of steam, wreathing the entire ceiling in swirling mist.

Ginansia was about to open the enormous iron door to the Tarnished Hall when an elegant figure divorced itself from a cobwebbed clutter of crockery and stepped in front of her.

Leperdandy pulled a handkerchief from the top pocket of his purple quilted smoking jacket and flicked it under his quivering narrow nostrils, enveloping them both in an overpowering scent of lavender.

"You're as late as I," he sniffed. "Your stepfather went in ten minutes ago. The Great Wound will not be pleased."

"Have you ever seen him pleased about anything?" she asked, falling into step beside her half-brother.

"Now that you mention it," said Leperdandy, "no."

"I dread tonight."

"I know you do. You must be strong."

They passed across the puddled stones of the angular hall, the damp air clinging to their clothes, fattening the fabric with droplets of moisture. The shadowy stone alcoves on either side mercifully concealed the sepulchres that had given Ginansia such nightmares as a child. In front of her stood the towering suit of St. Ethelbar Squeam, one rusted red arm raised high with his spiked mace still gripped in a battered gauntlet, the hand of the other perched effeminately on his steel-lace hip. The mummified corpse of the Squeam himself was still inside the armor, and if you raised the protesting visor and peered in you would see that the rumors were indeed true; the ancient knight had somehow turned himself around within the mail so that he was facing back to front — a sign of cowardice before the enemy, some said. Opening the doors of the Dining Hall tugged a chain that rang a sharp little bell somewhere beneath their feet: a warning to the kitchen staff to be on their toes.

The great table, arranged in cruciform and draped in holly-green cloth, was occupied along its far side, and the inhabitants swiveled their eyes disapprovingly to the latecomers.

"Is it too much to ask that we might share a meal together on the eve of your agecoming?" boomed her stepfather, his sole good eye glaring wetly beneath a bunched, bushy brow as he jutted from the table, an acre of emerald linen splayed at his throat. Globules of soup hung in his immense beard. A dripping spoon jutted from his meaty fist. His vast shoulders rose and fell, rose and fell with the wheezing passage of his breath, like an old steam engine laboring with its load.

Scarabold the Third of the royal family Bayne, the Great Wound himself, Doer of Dark Deeds, Rectifier of Wrongly Wrought Rites, Warrior, stepfather to Ginansia and father to Leperdandy (by a different mother) had watched the severed heads of his enemies bounce down the steps of the Imperial Museum during the Great Siege of '28 with less passion than he now displayed at the tardiness of his offspring.

"The Italian Courtyard is half-flooded," replied Ginansia glibly. "I had to go all the way around and through the Under-Chapel." She had, in fact, spent too long at her toilette to register the crepusculation of the hour. These days she was rarely on time for anything. It was one of the few ways she had left of showing dissatisfaction with her circumstance.

"Your father has something to tell you, dear," called her mother, ignoring the steaming monarch at her side, "just as soon as you are settled."

Mater Moribund Bayne had outdone herself tonight. Her sticklike form, so thin that her ribs could be discerned through the purple bombazine of her gown, was bedecked with ropes of jewelry that glittered and shone and swayed about like the lights of a pier in a gale. She was guyed up with so many cascading loops of amethyst and opal that it was a wonder she managed to hold herself erect.

"Come and sit near me, both of you," said Dwindoline with a kindly smile. Leperdandy's mother was Scarabold's other wife (it being quite legal in these parts for a king to operate a marital duopoly) and, perhaps because she was wed to the Great Wound second, occupied a slightly inferior role in the household to Mater Hari (as they called her behind her back).

Plump and lumpen and draped in various shades of pheasant-brown, Dwindoline was pleasing and pleasant and resigned to the sidelines of the royal menagerie. She tended her weakling son and her infuriating half-daughter unobtrusively, trying to provide the maternal concern they deserved and certainly didn't receive from Moribund. As the children (children! Ginansia was hours from her eighteenth year and Leperdandy was soon to leave his teens completely) accepted their places opposite, she looked along the table, nodding to the Decrepend so that he might commence the blessing, smiling blandly at Asphyxia, who was sulking behind her goblet, and at the bulbous, bibulous visage of the Quaff, who had already drained his.

"O Cruel, Cruel Gods, Please Hear The Lowly Call Of This Great Family," bellowed the Decrepend, who clearly had little faith in the power of prayer and planned to be heard through the more physical expedient of shouting, "We Give Most Humble Thanks—"

—*most humble*, thought Ginansia, *the word has been excised from the castle dictionaries*—

"—For The Sheer Lack Of Harm You Have Bestowed Upon Us In Your Infinite All-Seeing Wicked Wisdom—"

Ginansia caught her half-brother's gaze and held it. Their aptitude for passing messages was so finely honed that the merest ocular twitch could signify histories. They had grown up side by side in the high moss-green castle, had hidden together from their ranting, stamping father, had rescued each other from the freezing grip of the moat's shattered crust, had fought secret battles behind the dust-filled curtains of the Red Theatre in the attic. They were childhood allies now standing on the cusp of adulthood.

The Decrepend droned on, his narcotic tone pitched above the sound of falling rain. Scarabold's thick forefinger impatiently traced the edges of the livid ridged scar that crossed his face, the result of a swordblow that had honorably granted him the title of Great Wound. He threw the Decrepend a look of hatred. The blessing had to be given again in full if someone joined the table late. Beyond the windows of the tall, narrow dining hall, the sky was black and greeny-gray, obscured by bruised clouds implicit with inclemence. Here in the castle the family was safe and secure. Outside the forces of chance raged on.

So did the doddering Decrepend, who suddenly ended his prayers with a thud, smiting the table with a brittle-boned hand in an attempt to drive home his celestial-bound message.

The soup was now cold and curdled, and Moribund snapped her fingers at the servants, who scurried to remove the bowls. Scarabold seized the moment to address his stepdaughter. The clearing of his throat was like someone shoveling coal.

"Ginansia, your arrival at the eighteenth year of your life demands the surrender of your maidenhood, and it is my duty as your father—"

"*Step*father."

"—to appoint a suitably equipped suitor. In short, it is time for your deforestation."

"Deflowering," nudged the Mater.

Ginansia stared furiously at her stepfather, whom she grudgingly respected as a warrior but considered an odious beast as a human. Since the death of her real father, his every entrance into her mother's bedchamber had multiplied her loathing tenfold. "I suppose I have no say in this matter."

"Certainly not," thundered Scarabold. "You have no knowledge of allegiances, alliances and allegations. You could not possibly know who would be most politically suited to this penetrative act. The decision has already been made, the bargain struck. The rupturer of the royal crust will mount you at midnight in the appropriate manner, in due accordance with the law of the land. The ceremony will commence at half past eleven. Your mother will attend the preparations, and Doctor Emeric Fangle will be on hand to instruct you in matters of hygiene."

"Dando," hissed Ginansia beneath her breath, "you have to set me free from this."

"We agreed you'd go through with it," replied her half-brother quietly. "It's an awful obligation, but it's not as if you have to marry him or anything. You never even have to see him again."

"I know I said I'd do it, but I can't. It's a stupid, revolting law."

"Oh, for Gods' sake," snapped the Quaff suddenly, slopping his claret, "it's just a matter of keeping your legs open and your eyes shut. The women of the family all undergo the ceremony."

"The women of *this* family," replied Ginansia sulkily. Somewhere beyond the walls of the castle was another way of living, where families weren't knotted together like rat-kings, biting, baiting and barely breathing in the tightest of tangles. Somewhere were places where the young ran wild, where freedom abounded and life was open to an endless azure sky....

"Drifting! Drifting!" screamed Aunt Asphyxia suddenly. "See, she barely attends your words, the minx! She needs the member in her fast to take her mind from rumination!"

"Surely you wish to know the identity of your pronger?" asked the Decrepend.

"I wish to know nothing!" cried Ginansia angrily, shoving away from the table and grabbing her half-brother's hand. "Dando, come with me to my suite." The boy pushed awkwardly back and joined her, grimacing apologetically to his parents. Dwindoline pouted in sympathy.

"And see she is ready at the appointed hour!" called Moribund, already losing interest as she twisted in her chair to berate the servants for the delay between courses. Behind her, the Senior Chef bore a huge tureen of bloody meat and knobs of bone, his gore-streaked apron a testament to his bitter, frantic labors. Asphyxia licked her fingers in anticipation.

Ginansia ran. Behind her trailed Leperdandy, the crimson side-ribbons on his striped leggings flapping and snapping as he raised his knees in pursuit. "Gin, please wait, I can't run as fast as you!"

She flew ahead, vanishing around each stone corner with her sapphire gown rucked up around her knees. She will have to calm herself, he thought, or accept sedation before she discovers the identity of her romancer. Abandoning pursuit, he watched her fleeing figure fold into the misted gloom.

Scarabold was breaking wind in the armory. His efforts thundered through the filigreed gilt portcullis of the baroque chamber, resonating the trellis like a tambourine. A luckless valet named Ratchet shared the room while he attempted to attach a pair of scarlet epaulets to the fidgeting monarch's ceremonial battledress. The Great Wound raised a cheek of his ample rear and released an alarming fusillade, then fell back against the ambergris velvet cushions on his dressing bench. The valet grimaced and continued thrusting needles into a doublet.

"She has never shown any respect for the traditions of her family," Scarabold continued. "And now this unseemly fuss over her Maidenhood Ceremony. She should be pleased to mark her passage into womankind in so firm a fashion."

"If it please Your Grace," coughed Ratchet cautiously, "perhaps the Lady Ginansia has deduced the identity of her suitor and is less than happy to allow him admission."

Scarabold's face crumpled as completely as if it had been drawn on paper and crushed into a ball. Valets had no opinions, and if they did they should never be allowed to voice them aloud, and even if they did voice them should never, ever mention subjects of such indelicacy.

"I mean," stammered Ratchet, sensing the heat of the royal glower upon his vulnerably thin neck, "how fiercely she cast her glance aside when introduced to Earl Carapace in the Cathedral of Pons Minor."

"I do not give a maggot's egg what you think of my choice, you oafish seamster," he blasted. "The land is much changed since last they met. Carapace's armies are now the finest warriors in the Dunghills, and make better allies than enemies. He has long shown an interest in the youthful glory of the princess."

The withered valet remembered only too well. During Ginansia's confirmation, on her thirteenth birthday, Carapace had barely been able to tear his gaze from the pale flesh of her bare shoulders. Ratchet gave an involuntary shudder as he recalled the eerie clicking sound the Earl made with his throat when considering matters of a carnal nature. Even now he was beetling toward the castle in his iridescent ebony armor to claim the soon-to-be-supine body of the Princess.

As Scarabold's eruptions, anal and oral, continued unabated, Ratchet returned to work, despairing the fate of females born into nobility. Many years ago he had been employed by the gracious Lady Dwindoline, and look what had happened to her, poor thing, forced to become the Great Wound's second wife because Mater Moribund had failed to secure him a son. Three girl-babies had been ceremonially drowned before Dwindoline had finally given birth to the milksop Leperdandy. As the golden needle slithered through his gnarled fingers, Ratchet considered the night that now lay ahead for the Princess and her suitor. It was well known that Carapace never traveled without his skittering "courtiers." He prayed that Ginansia would somehow find the strength to survive her grim ordeal.

The Great Clock of Fascinus would have been easier to interpret if it still sported hands. Unfortunately a slow-turning central spindle and a racing quarter-second arm were all that remained of the timepiece's horological abilities. Ginansia kept it mounted above her bed because the mother-of-pearl face shifted like a sunlit sea. But now the remembrance that Fascinus was a phallic god brought fresh qualms.

"I don't understand why you're so reluctant to help me escape," she sighed, staring up at the shimmering clock face.

Leperdandy moved the Princess's lolling leg and perched himself on a corner of her purple coverlet. "I don't want you to incur Scarabold's wrath. You know how slow he is to forgive, and a matter such as this bears great importance to him."

"What about its importance to me?" she cried.

"I mean that the congress carries political weight."

"And the intrusion upon my body does not." She sat up sharply and narrowed her eyes. "Do you know the identity of my despoiler?"

"I have my suspicions." He coughed awkwardly into his fist.

"Dando, you must tell me the truth. Is it someone I abhor?"

Her half-brother's cough turned into a hacking fit.

"Not that awful man who smelled like a pond and was covered in mud, Plum-somebody…"

Leperdandy, crimson-cheeked, shook his head and spluttered.

"Or the fat little king who paid court to Mother, the one with the leaky eye…" She froze with a sudden thought. "Not Carapace."

There was a horrible, confirming silence.

"No, Dando, not the Lord of Beetles…"

"He campaigned long and hard for you," admitted the boy. "Scarabold won't be moved from his ruling, and if you fail to abide by his decision he'll treat it as a matter of treason.…"

"Traitors must be entombed for life. He wouldn't do that—"

"You are not his blood-daughter, Ginansia," warned Leperdandy, who had once visited the grim stinking dungeons beneath the castle to see for himself the pitiful bone-creatures captured as prisoners of war by the king. These weary albinos with flaking skin and wheedling voices had been forgotten by all except Fumblegut the jailer, who was rumored to play elaborate sexual games with his charges in return for providing food and water.

"Then you must find a way to save me," she cried desperately.

Her half-brother fidgeted with the bedquilt, running the fronds of a crimson tassel between his bony fingers. "There is a way, but you'd be on your own beyond the castle walls. I couldn't come with you."

"I wouldn't ask you to," she said, her face softening. "Just take me to the broad night sky, and I will do the rest."

At eight o'clock, Dwindoline knocked at the bedroom door and asked to sit awhile, but her offer was curtly refused. Ginansia hated to offend, but feared that sharing the plan of her escape would place those she loved at risk. Besides, she was not entirely sure that her secret would be safe. As she prepared, she found herself bearing no malice toward Scarabold. Her stepfather had no desire to hurt any member of his extended family, but it was necessary for him to place duty before affection.

At a quarter past eleven, Ginansia rose from her dressing table in a high-necked robe of plain green silk that whispered across the flagstone floor, curling about her like a cubicle. She raised the hook of a slim lead-glass case containing three lit candles and left her apartments, locking the bedroom door behind her, not daring to glance back at her lifelong home.

Tonight the corridors of the West Quadrant seemed alien and friendless. Fewer lamps had been lit than usual, and the leaping shadows were of a deeper hue. The entire edifice sealed in darkness and cold air like a refrigerator, with the servants waging an eternal battle against rising damp and leaking ramparts. Yet there were pockets of warmth within the castle, and the Princess knew them as well as the kitchen cat. She measured her tread to the funereal drumbeat that sounded within the Chapel of Consummation. The sexagonal stone room held a comfortable curtained bed and a basin of warm springwater on an iron stand, having been designed for a single purpose. Mater Moribund had — quite illegally — slept there on those nights when her husband had returned victoriously drunk and muck-encrusted from his pubic skirmishes in the sink-towns of the lowlands. As Ginansia approached it now her heart sank.

The Mater was already in attendance, talking softly with Doctor Fangle as she watched him wiping his pudgy hands on a strip of linen cloth. She balked at the chamber entrance. What if Leperdandy had fallen asleep? Consciousness slipped from the sickly youth as easily as an oilskin cloak. She was forever nudging him awake during the Wednesday sermon. What if he failed to keep their finely timed appointment?

"Come, child," beckoned Moribund, her amethyst wristlets chattering. "Let Dr. Fangle examine you."

The short, wart-bedecked physician, an unwelcome temporary replacement for Scarabold's dropsical family doctor, revealed an arrangement of yellow teeth and strummed his hand across his housecoat before offering it to shake.

Seated in a wooden-stirruped chair that seemed to have been designed for the sole purpose of internal examination, she gave an involuntary shudder as his freezing fingers touched the insides of her thighs. She was frightened that her mother, peering over the doctor's shoulder, would spot the heavy woolen traveling clothes hitched up beneath her gown. A sudden sly icicle ran across her exposed aperture. Fangle grinned into her face. "Intacta, veritably," he whispered. "Most encouraging." He reluctantly removed his digit and ran it beneath his nostrils like a fine cigar.

"That's enough, Fangle. Your job here is finished." Moribund pushed him aside as Ginansia hastily dropped her gown.

"But surely the Princess must be taught how to avoid conception and infection," pleaded the doctor, still staring at her veiled cleft with his forefinger extended.

"Carapace is responsible for the former, and there shall be no need for the latter," snapped Moribund. "The Earl is also undergoing examination. On your feet, child. You have little time to spare."

Sweating from her layers of clothes, Ginansia clambered to an upright position. She longed to run screaming into the torchlit corridor, but forced deliberation into her movements so that nothing should seem amiss. In a few minutes she would be on her way to freedom. She took her leave of the ogling physician and fell in behind her mother, who was already retreating from the chamber.

"Of course you're nervous, just as I was long ago," intoned the Mater, swinging her beads. "Before my coring I presumed all kinds of painful pleasures lay in store. Imagine my disappointment when the great sweating brute dropped upon me like a felled tree and tore at my flowerpot of femininity with a fleshy little twig that discharged its sap and promptly vanished into the shrubbery. No danger of that happening to you, though, as I understand from Carapace's physician that the Earl's maleness could commandeer a tea clipper if raised as a mast."

Ginansia thought it best not to comment. The fireplace was approaching.

It was common knowledge within the castle that the chimney-breasts of all the fireplaces in the Western Quadrant were linked to a central passage lined with ceramic bricks. The original idea had been to light one large fire in the basement boiler and so provide gusts of warm, dry air from fireplaces on every floor, but this plan was abandoned when the Squeam's mother perished after she fell into the boiler trying to light it. Leperdandy was even now pushing through the elasticated cobwebs of one such passage that ran parallel to the hallway along which Ginansia followed the Queen. Separated by a mere three feet of stone, he strained to catch the sound of their progress, but could discern nothing.

"I was sure I'd be able to hear them. Bumscuttle!" He blundered into a whiskery nest of spiders, batted the skittering arachnids from his vision and wiped the webbing from his eyelids. He could hardly see a thing. How would he be able to time his emergence from the fireplace in order to snatch Ginansia?

On the other side of the wall the Princess slowed her pace, gradually dropping behind. She needed to put as much distance as possible between herself and Moribund before reaching the great carved maw of the fireplace.

"Don't dawdle, girl!" The Queen looked back. "Carapace is not a man to be kept waiting."

"I'm sorry, Mother. My hem is caught." She stopped and affected to make a study of her ankle. Leperdandy, hearing the exchange, drew a great breath, burst from beneath the great marble mantelpiece in a cloud of soot and grabbed his stepmother, who screamed and stabbed him through the shoulder with one of the many silver hatpins she kept concealed upon her person to deal with Scarabold.

"You've killed me!" gasped Leperdandy, clutching at the protruding pin, his great white eyes bulging out of his sooted face like nighttime seabeacons.

"You stupid, stupid boy!" screamed Moribund, whipping the pin from his stinging flesh and tossing it aside. "This is no time for your idiotic japes!" And with that she seized Ginansia by the wrist and thrust her into the chamber ahead.

"Dando!" Ginansia flung the cry back plaintively as she was swept inside and the door boomed shut behind her. Horrified by his failure, the boy limped into shadow to nurse his burning shoulder.

Moribund was nowhere to be seen.

Her role as procuress completed, she had slipped beyond one of the six chamber walls, leaving her daughter alone with the Earl. Carapace stood between a pair of flickering lanterns, barely discernible in his oiled black armor. The susurration of his breath was punctuated with tiny clicks, like an insect rattling its mandibles. Ginansia felt the chill splinters of the door at her back. There were no windows in the cell: only a bed, a bowl of water, and a freshly sliced lemon set upon the stand — "to cleanse and heal your wound" as Moribund put it. As her eyes adjusted in the gloom, she registered a shimmering movement behind Carapace, as though the purple counterpane was attempting to escape the bed. The Earl removed his gloves with deliberation, the leather creaking over his knuckles, and began to unbutton his glistening tunic with a series of little cracking sounds.

"Come closer into the light, my little one," he croaked, his throat lacquered with lust.

Ginansia took a small step forward and studied the figure before her. His uncorsetted belly hung above his ebony codpiece, but his features were more handsome than she had expected. A goatee hung on his bone-white face like a small black shovel. Elaborate silver rings adorned the rims of his ears. Whatever happened, she would not speak to him. How could the older ladies of the castle have allowed themselves to undergo such an abhorrent ritual? It had no purpose, save to satisfy some forgotten law laid down by long-dead ancestors.

There was definitely something moving beneath the coverlet on the bed. As Carapace seated himself in order to remove his leggings and boots, the cloth shifted and rippled around him.

"Come, let me touch you. You have nothing to be afraid of. I am a gentle man." He raised his arms to receive her. Like a clockwork doll Ginansia shifted forward, her legs moving in tiny spasms.

"If I must be penetrated for the sake of my family," she stated clearly, "I will receive no overtures of affection from you."

"Penetration!" he cried. "Who taught you to think of love in so clinical a fashion?"

Ginansia was incensed. "This mockery, sir, has nothing to do with love!"

"But I have loved you from the first moment I saw you, on your thirteenth birthday. I would have broken your hymen upon your communion dais."

"Oh, this is blasphemy!"

He stopped the shocked oval of her mouth with a searing perfumed kiss. One icy hand slipped into her bodice and cupped her breast, the callused thumb brushing across the thimbletop of a nipple. She tried to pull herself free as he tilted the pair of them back into the bed. "This is too intimate — I was not warned—"

"Stay your fears," he whispered. "The night is young and we are enormous. We have plenty of time to acquaint ourselves."

"The night! I was told that the ceremony would last but a few minutes!" His snickering laugh followed her down as he cantilevered her onto the counterpane. Through the eiderfeathers she could feel things moving, hard-shelled creatures the size of gravyboats shifting this way and that. Reaching out in puzzlement, she seized a corner and peeled it back. Hundreds of black beetles filled the mattress, their polished wingcases flickering over each other. Recoiling in horror, the Princess fought away from the pulsing morass of segmented bodies.

"My courtiers are here to further our conjugal ecstasy," he hissed, dipping his hand into the heavy chittering insects and allowing them to run across his arm. "Now we must obey the natural impulse of their bodies." One of the beetles was upon his neck, its recoiling feelers tentatively entering his mouth.

"Repugnant barbarian!" she screamed, punching at his chest. Her gown tore in his grasp, and the woolen traveling dress beneath slipped free from its

TALES OF BRITANNICA CASTLE

silken shell. She fell back, her shoesoles popping and crunching on the squirming, living floor. Reaching the far wall, she searched for the handle to the door.

"Listen to Lady High-A-Mighty," laughed Carapace, sitting back on the bed so that the insects could fill his bared lap. "As if you could afford to choose a suitor for yourself."

"I will give myself to whomsoever I please," she shouted, close to tears, scrabbling for the inset brass ring which refused to turn.

"You might try, but who would have you? Who would want someone from Britannica Castle? The door is locked, so calm yourself."

She turned to face him, sliding her body along the wall. The hidden exit through which her mother had vanished, that was the only answer now. If she could find the door itself, she could locate the catch. All secret passageways within the castle opened similarly.

"What do you mean?" she asked. "Our family is the finest in the land, generations of warriors brave and fair—"

"Is that what they told you? What does the castle look like from outside?"

She caught her breath. "They speak of golden spires and colonnades so fine that only—"

"They speak? They speak? You have never seen the building from beyond it, and do you know why? Because it is not safe for you to leave this edifice. You would be murdered in the winking of an eye. You are prisoners here, outcasts, lepers, Jews. We have left you to peter out, to breed inward and die. For us to speak with you is taboo, to touch you is punishable by death. Do you know what I risked to be with you tonight?"

"You're lying!" she cried. "I will not listen to such lies!"

Carapace leaped from the bed in a shower of beetles and pinched her face so hard she squealed. "Then learn for yourself — ask your stepfather about your family name — ask him about the noble family from which you are descended. You will find nothing noble beyond the escutcheon that bears your arms."

"The Baynes are an ancient family, good and wise, just and kind." She knew this to be true. It was the foundation of all she believed. But she spoke for another purpose: To hold the Earl in conversation was to hold him at bay.

"Arrant nonsense, my dear little Ginansia," he spat, his phlegm-flecked lips an inch from hers. "Answer me something else. If none of the serving maids dares to enter or leave the castle, how do you think you survive here? What do you live on? What feeds and fattens you?"

"The livestock beyond the river—"

"—are all dead of lung-rot and have been for years. No, my dear, you cannot beg the question quite so easy. But surely it is time for you to discover the truth for yourself. Remove the lids of the kitchen cauldrons and look inside if you dare. Or listen to me."

And he proceeded to tell her what he knew.

"I will not hear this!" The Princess buried her fingers in her ears. Carapace reached for her, but she evaded him.

"Ginansia, please believe that I have no desire to hurt you."

Warily, anxiously, she lowered her hands. "Do not lie to me in this matter, my lord, I entreat you. This is the only world I know."

"I merely seek to open your eyes, lady, and to show you what your family will not — cannot."

But now the passage entrance was at her back with its catch between her fingers, and she fell thankfully into the tunnel, shoving the wallslab shut and running away through the freezing stone airspace. Behind, she heard him bellowing her name. "Open your eyes, Ginansia!" came the fading call.

The only light in the dripping tunnel leaked from the cracks between the bricks. When Carapace could no longer be heard, she slowed her pace and drew breath. Wet steep steps led down, and a corridor curved. She pulled the woolen dress around her, longing for the comforting arms of Leperdandy, the yielding warmth of her own bed. But before that, she had to ascertain the truth. Rest and peace would come only with knowledge that the Lord of Beetles lied.

The far end of the corridor was misted with the spicy scent of cloves, revealing the proximity of the kitchens and providing her with a means of irrefutable proof. To her right, a rectangle of buttery light marked the passage's egress. Locating the wooden catch and depressing it, she carefully opened the panel and stepped through. A wall of moist warm air instantly enveloped her.

The crimson-tiled scullery was deserted at this late hour. The gigantic butchers' block table had been scrubbed clean. Around it utensils stood in earthenware pots like bunches of steel flowers. Pulpers, colanders and doughknives dangled in clumps from S-shaped hooks. Light was thrown from the flickering burners of the huge iron stove that extended along one side of the room. Beneath the dull roar of flames below their pots, the Princess could hear logs and coals sifting and shifting in the boiler.

She approached the stove, where four great shining saucepans, each of them several feet deep, simmered on their glowing hobs. The handle on the lid of the first was too hot to be clasped, so she damped a muslin dishcloth and wound it around her fingers. The ring of flame beneath the metal cauldron illuminated her flushed cheeks as she slowly raised the lid.

At once she smelled a dizzying aroma of marjoram, spackwort, cumin and meat, meat most of all as she waved a path through the steam and peered in.

The bubbling brown liquid revealed nothing but surfacing chunks of carrot and fennel. She found a wooden spoon, two feet long and slotted at the bowl, which she carefully lowered into the boiling gravy. The joint within was heavy and hard to raise without slopping juice everywhere, so that she was forced to use both hands to balance the spoon.

It was a head, human and male.

Its hair had been shaved away, and the lenses of the eyes had boiled into bulging orbs as hard and white as peppermints. The gray skin seemed loose and ready to separate from the skull. There were no teeth in the mouth, and the lower lip had come loose from the flayed gums. Ginansia screamed and dropped the boulder of meat and bone back into the fragrant depths of the pot, sending juices hissing and splashing in waves across the burners.

Carapace's words came humming back into her ears. "For you feed on human flesh," he had cried. "Like rats walled up or buried with some convicted transgressor, you have turned to cannibalism. The Bayne family, so proud and so regal, are eaters of corpses, devourers of humanity! Why even the name itself is a corruption, from Sawney Beane and his cannibal horde — these are your fine ancestors! And you dare to call me barbarian!"

Bile had risen in her gullet. "Lies, all damnable lies!"

"Go to the dungeons and see what your father breeds before you damn me treasonous. See what happens to the war-prisoners you take. See how their souls reside in the colons of the royal family Bayne! And ask how you yourself have been nourished on the bones of your enemies!"

With a painful howl she ran from the infernal kitchen, leaving the boiling vats of human flesh behind her.

Dwindoline rocked forward in her chair and ran her fingers lightly over her son's fine hair. The boy had slumped his carcass before her fireplace and had barely moved in an hour. Now the apartment was only lit by sinking embers.

"You can't blame yourself," she said softly. "None of us can be protected beyond a certain age, and I'm afraid that your half-sister's time had simply arrived."

"It seems so unfair," said Leperdandy. "Why can't we stay innocent forever? Knowledge can only destroy us."

"You mustn't believe that, child. There always has to be hope for the future."

Leperdandy raised his head and glared at her. "What kind of hope — that one day we will be allowed to walk free beyond these walls?"

"Until Scarabold has found success in his endeavors there can be no freedom for any of us."

"It might help if he didn't cut the heads from those who failed in his negotiations." Unsnagging his muscles, he rose slowly to his feet. "I'll go and await Ginansia's return. No doubt she'll need some comforting after her ordeal.

Thanks for the advice, Mother, but it's clear you don't have a solution to our predicament, any more than I."

She sighed. "The young are impatient."

"And the old complacent."

Dwindoline watched her son take leave, anguish fevering her breast. She knew she could not change the path of the family, only suffer in silence as each new generation discovered its dark heart.

For the remaining hours of that night, Britannica Castle was filled with tortured bruits: the bitter screams of the mortified Princess; the enraged, insane laughter of the Beetle Earl; the muffled confusions of the boy Leperdandy — and the comfortable well-fed farts of a slumbering king.

HEARTFIRES

Dance is the breath of life made visible.
— seen on a T-shirt on 4th Avenue, Tucson, AZ

obody tells you the really important stuff, so in the end you have to imagine it for yourself. It's like how things connect. A thing is just a thing until you have the story that goes with it. Without the story, there's nothing to hold on to, nothing to relate this mysterious new thing to who you are — you know, to make it a part of your own history. So if you're like me, you make something up and the funny thing is, lots of times, once you tell the story, it comes true. Not *poof*, hocus-pocus, magic it comes true, but sure, why not, and after it gets repeated often enough, you and everybody else end up believing it.

It's like quarks. They're neither positive nor negative until the research scientists look at them. Right up until that moment of observation they hold the possibility of being one or the other. It's the *looking* that makes them what they are. Which is like making up a story for them, right?

The world's full of riddles like that.

The lady or the tiger.

Did she jump, or was she pushed?

The door standing by itself in the middle of the field — does it lead to somewhere, or from somewhere?

Or the locked room we found one night down in Old City, the part of it that runs under the Tombs. A ten-by-ten-foot room, stone walls, stone floor and ceiling, with a door in one wall that fits so snugly you wouldn't even know it was there except for the bolts — a set on either side of the door, big old iron fittings, rusted, but still solid. The air in that room is dry, touched with the taste of old spices and sagegrass. And the place is clean. No dust. No dirt. Only these scratches on that weird door, long gouges cut into the stone like something was clawing at it, both sides of the door, inside and out.

So what was it for? Before the 'quake dropped the building into the ground, that room was still below street level. Somebody from the long ago built that room, hid it away in the cellar of what must have been a seriously tall building in those days — seven stories high. Except for the top floor, it's all underground now. We didn't even know the building was there until Bear fell through a hole in the roof, landing on his ass in a pile of rubble which, luckily for him, was only a few feet down. Most of that top floor was filled with broken stone and crap, like someone had bulldozed another tumbled-down building inside it and over the top of it, pretty much blocking any way in and turning that top floor into a small mountain covered with metal junk and weeds and every kind of trash you can imagine. It was a fluke we ever found our way in, it was that well hidden.

But why was it hidden? Because the building couldn't be salvaged, so cover it up, make it safe? Or because of that room?

That room. Was it to lock something in? Or keep something out?

Did our going into it make it one or the other? Or was it the story we found in its stone confines?

We told that story to each other, taking turns like we usually do, and when we were done, we remembered what that room was. We'd never been in it before, not that room, in that place, but we remembered.

-2-

Devil's Night, October 30th. It's not even nine o'clock and they've already got fires burning all over the Tombs: sparks flying, grass fires in the empty lots, trash fires in metal drums, the guts of derelict tenements and factory buildings going up like so much kindling. The sky overhead fills with an evil glow, like an aura gone bad. The smoke from the fires rises in streaming columns. It cuts through the orange glare hanging over that square mile or so of lost hopes and despair the way ink spreads in water.

The streets are choked with refuse and abandoned cars, but that doesn't stop the revelers from their fun, the flickering light of the fires playing across their features as they lift their heads and howl at the devil's glow. Does stop the fire department, though. This year they don't even bother to try to get their trucks in. You can almost hear the mayor telling the chiefs: "Let it burn."

Hell, it's only the Tombs. Nobody living here but squatters and hoboes, junkies and bikers. These are the inhabitants of the night side of the city — the side you only see out of the corner of your eye until the sun goes down and suddenly they're all over the streets, in your face, instead of back in the shadows where they belong. They're not citizens. They don't even vote.

And they're having some fun tonight. Not the kind of recreation you or I might look for, but a desperate fun, the kind that's born out of knowing you've got nowhere to go but down and you're already at the bottom. I'm not making excuses for them. I just understand them a little better than most citizens might.

See I've run with them. I've slept in those abandoned buildings, scrabbled for food in dumpsters over by Williamson Street, trying to get there before the rats and feral dogs. I've looked for oblivion in the bottom of a bottle or at the end of a needle.

No, don't go feeling sorry for me. I had me some hard times, sure, but everybody does. But I'll tell you, I never torched buildings. Even in the long ago. When I'm looking to set a fire, I want it to burn in the heart.

-3-

I'm an old crow, but I still know a few tricks. I'm looking rough, maybe even used up, but I'm not yet so old I'm useless. You can't fool me, but I fool most everyone, wearing clothes, hiding my feathers, walking around on my hind legs like a man, upright, not hunched over, moving pretty fast, considering.

There were four of us in those days, ran together from time to time. Old spirits, wandering the world, stopped awhile in this place before we went on. We're always moving on, restless, looking for change so that things'll stay the same. There was me, Crazy Crow, looking sharp with my flat-brimmed hat and pointy-toed boots. Alberta the Dancer with those antlers poking up out of her red hair — you know how to look, you can see them. Bear, he was so big you felt like the sky had gone dark when he stood by you. And then there was Jolene.

She was just a kid that Devil's Night. She gets like that. One year she's about knee-high to a skinny moment and you can't stop her from tomfooling around, another year she's so fat even Bear feels small around her. We go way back, Jolene and me, knew each other pretty good, we met so often.

Me and Alberta were together that year. We took Jolene in like she was our daughter, Bear her uncle. Moving on the wheel like a family. We're dark-skinned — we're old spirits, got to be the way we are before the European look got so popular — but not so dark as fur and feathers. Crow, grizzly, deer. We lose some color when we wear clothes, walking on our hind legs all the time.

T
O
M
B
S

212

Sometimes we lose other things, too. Like who we really are and what we're doing here.

-4-

"Hey, 'bo."

I look up to see it's a brother calling to me. We're standing around an oil drum, warming our hands, and he comes walking out of the shadows like he's a piece of them, got free somehow, comes walking right up to me like he thinks I'm in charge. Alberta smiles. Bear lights a smoke, takes a couple of drags, then offers it to the brother.

"Bad night for fires," he says after he takes a drag. He gives the cigarette a funny look, tasting the sweetgrass mixed in with the tobacco. Not much, just enough.

"Devil's Night," Jolene says, grinning like it's a good thing. She's a little too fond of fires this year for my taste. Next thing you know she'll be wanting to tame metal, build herself a machine and wouldn't that be something?

"Nothing to smile about," the brother tells her. "Lot of people get hurt, Devil's Night. Gets out of hand. Gets to where people think it's funny, maybe set a few of us 'boes on fire, you hear what I'm saying?"

"Times are always hard," I say.

He shrugs, takes another drag of the cigarette, then hands it back to Bear.

"Good night for a walk," he says finally. "A body might walk clear out of the Tombs on a night like this, come back when things are a little more settled down."

We all just look at him.

"Got my boy waiting on me," he says. "Going for that walk. You all take care of yourselves, now."

We never saw the boy, standing there in the shadows, waiting on his pa, except maybe Jolene. There's not much she misses. I wait until the shadow's almost swallowed the brother before I call after him.

"Appreciate the caution," I tell him.

He looks back, tips a finger to his brow, then he's gone, part of the shadows again.

"Are we looking for trouble?" Bear asks.

"Uh-huh," Jolene pipes up, but I shake my head.

"Like he said," I tell them, jerking a thumb to where the brother walked away.

Bear leads the way out, heading east, taking a direct route and avoiding the fires we can see springing up all around us now. The dark doesn't bother us, we can see pretty much the same, doesn't matter if it's night or day. We follow Bear up a hillside of rubble. He gets to the top before us and starts dancing around, stamping his feet, singing, "Wa-hey, look at me. I'm the king of the mountain."

And then he disappears between one stamp and the next, and that's how we find the room.

I don't know why we slide down to where Bear's standing instead of him climbing back up. Curious, I guess. Smelling spirit mischief and we just have to see where it leads us, down, down, till we're standing on a dark street, way underground.

"Old City," Alberta says.

"Walked right out of the Tombs, we did," Jolene says, then she shoots Bear a look and giggles. "Or maybe slid right out of it on our asses'd be a better way to put it."

Bear gives her a friendly whack on the back of the head but it doesn't budge a hair. Jolene's not looking like much this year, standing about halfway to nothing, but she's always solidly built, doesn't much matter what skin she's wearing.

"Let's take that walk," I say, but Bear catches hold of my arm.

"I smell something old," he tells me.

"It's an old place," I tell him. "Fell down here a long time ago and stood above ground even longer."

Bear shakes his head. "No. I'm smelling something older than that. And lower down."

We're on an underground street, I'm thinking. Way down. Can't get much lower than this. But Bear's looking back at the building we just came out of and I know what's on his mind. Basements. They're too much like caves for him to pass one by, especially when it's got an old smell. I look at the others. Jolene's game, but then she's always game when she's wearing this skin. Alberta shrugs.

"When I want to dance," she says, "you all dance with me, so I'm going to say no when Bear wants to try out a new step?"

I can't remember the last time we all danced, but I can't find any argument with what she's saying.

"What about you, Crazy Crow?" Bear asks.

"You know me," I tell him. "I'm like Jolene, I'm always game."

So we go back inside, following Bear who's following his nose, and he leads us right up to the door of that empty stone room down in the cellar. He grabs hold of the iron bolt, shoves it to one side, hauls the door open, rubs his hand on his jeans to brush off the specks of rust that got caught up on his palm.

"Something tried hard to get out," Alberta says.

I'm thinking of the other side of the door. "And in," I add.

Jolene's spinning around in the middle of the room, arms spread wide.

"Old, old, old," she sings.

We can all smell it now. I get the feeling that the building grew out of this room, that it was built to hold it. Or hide it.

"No ghosts," Bear says. "No spirits here."

Jolene stops spinning. "Just us," she says.

"Just us," Bear agrees.

He sits down on the clean stone floor, cross-legged, rolls himself a smoke. We all join him, sitting in a circle, like we're dancing, except it's only our breathing that's making the steps. We each take a drag of the cigarette, then Bear sets the butt down in the middle of the circle. We watch the smoke curl up from it, tobacco with that pinch of sweetgrass. It makes a long curling journey up to the ceiling, thickens there like a small storm cloud, pregnant with grandfather thunders.

Somewhere up above us, where the moon can see it, there's smoke rising, too, Devil's Night fires filling the hollow of the sky with pillars of silent thunder.

Bear takes a shotgun cartridge out of his pocket, brass and red cardboard, twelve-gauge, and puts it down on the stone beside the smoldering butt, stands it on end, brass side down.

"Guess we need a story," he says. He looks at me. "So we can understand this place."

We all nod. We'll take turns, talking until one of us gets it right.

"Me first," Jolene says.

She picks up the cartridge and rolls it back and forth on that small dark palm of hers and we listen.

-6-

Jolene says:

It's like that pan-girl, always cooking something up, you know the one. You can smell the wild onion on her breath a mile away. She's got that box that she can't look in, tin box with a lock on it that rattles against the side of the box when she gives it a shake, trying to guess what's inside. There's all these scratches on the tin, inside and out, something trying to get out, something trying to get in.

That's this place, the pan-girl's box. You know she opened that box, let all that stuff out that makes the world more interesting. She can't get it back in, and I'm thinking why try?

Anyway, she throws that box away. It's a hollow now, a hollow place, can be any size you want it to be, any shape, any color, same box. Now we're sitting in it, stone version. Close that door and maybe we can't get out. Got to wait until another pan-girl comes along, takes a break from all that cooking, takes a peek at what's inside. That big eye of hers'll fill the door and ya-hey, here we'll be, looking right back at her, rushing past her, she's swatting her hands at us trying to keep us in, but we're already gone, gone running back out into the world to make everything a little more interesting again.

-7-

Bear says:

Stone. You can't get much older than stone. First house was stone. Not like this room, not perfectly square, not flat, but stone all the same. Found places, those caves, just like we found this place. Old smell in them. Sometimes bear. Sometimes lion. Sometimes snake. Sometimes the ones that went before.

All gone when we come. All that's left are their messages painted or scratched on the walls. Stories. Information. Things they know we have to figure out, things that they could have told us if they were still around. Only way to tell us now is to leave the messages.

This place is a hollow, like Jolene said, but not why she said it. It's hollow because there's no messages. This is the place we have to leave our messages so that when we go on we'll know that the ones to follow will be able to figure things out.

-8-

Alberta says:

Inside and out, same thing. The wheel doesn't change, only the way we see it. Door opens either way. Both sides in, both sides out. Trouble is, we're always on the wrong side, always want the thing we haven't got, makes no difference who we are. Restless spirits want life, living people look for something better to come. Nobody *here*. Nobody content with what they got. And the reason for that's to keep the wheel turning. That simple. Wheel stops turning, there's nothing left.

It's like the woman who feels the cage of her bones, those ribs, they're a prison for her. She's clawing, clawing at those bone bars, making herself sick. Inside, where you can't see it, but outside, too.

So she goes to see the Lady of the White Deer — looks just like you, Jolene, the way you were last year. Big woman. Big as a tree. Got dark, dark eyes you could get lost in. But she's smiling, always smiling. Smiling as she listens, smiling when she speaks. Like a mother smiles, seen it all, heard it all, but still patient, still kind, still understanding.

"That's just living," she tells the caged woman. "Those aren't bars, they're the bones that hold you together. You keep clawing at them, you make yourself so sick you're going to die for sure."

"I can't breathe in here," the caged woman says.

"You're not paying attention," the Lady of the White Deer says. "All you're doing is breathing. Stop breathing and you'll be clawing at those same bones, trying to get back in."

"You don't understand," the caged woman tells her and she walks away.

So she goes to see the Old Man of the Mountains — looks just like you, Bear. Same face, same hair. A big old bear, sitting up there on the top of the mountain, looking out at everything below. Doesn't smile so much, but understands how everybody's got a secret dark place sits way deep down there inside, hidden but wanting to get out. Understands how you can be happy but not happy at the same time. Understands that sometimes you feel you got to go all the way out to get back in, but if you do, you can't. There's no way back in.

So not smiling so much, but maybe understanding a little more, he lets the woman talk and he listens.

"We all got a place inside us, feels like a prison," he tells her. "It's darker in some people than others, that's all. Thing is, you got to balance what's there with what's around you or you'll find yourself on a road that's got no end. Got no beginning and goes nowhere. It's just always this same thing, never grows, never changes, only gets darker and darker, like that candle blowing in the wind. Looks real nice till the wind blows it out — you hear what I'm saying?"

"I can't breathe in here," the woman tells him.

That Old Man of the Mountain he shakes his head. "You're breathing," he says. "You're just not paying attention to it. You're looking inside, looking inside, forgetting what's outside. You're making friends with that darkness inside you and that's not good. You better stop your scratching and clawing or you're going to let it out."

"You don't understand either," the caged woman says and she walks away.

So finally she goes to see the Old Man of the Desert — looks like you, Crazy Crow. Got the same sharp features, the same laughing eyes. Likes to collect things. Keeps a pocket full of shiny mementos that used to belong to other people, things they threw away. Holds onto them until they want them back and then makes a trade. He'd give them away, but he knows what everybody thinks: All you get for nothing is nothing. Got to put a price on a thing to give it any worth.

He doesn't smile at all when he sees her coming. He puts his hand in his pocket and plays with something while she talks. Doesn't say anything when she's done, just sits there, looking at her.

"Aren't you going to help me?" she asks.

"You don't want my help," the Old Man of the Desert says. "You just want me to agree with you. You just want me to say, aw, that's bad, really bad. You've got it bad. Everybody else in the world is doing fine, except for you, because you got it so hard and bad."

The caged woman looks at him. She's got tears starting in her eyes.

"Why are you being so mean to me?" she asks.

"The truth only sounds mean," he tells her. "You look at it from another side and maybe you see it as kindness. All depends where you're looking, what you want to see."

"But I can't breathe," she says.

"You're breathing just fine," he says right back to her. "The thing is, you're not thinking so good. Got clouds in your head. Makes it hard to see straight. Makes it hard to hear what you don't want to hear anyway. Makes it hard to accept that the rest of the world's not out of step on the wheel, only you are. Work on that and you'll start feeling a little better. Remember who you are instead of always crying after what you think you want to be."

"You don't understand either," she says.

But before she can walk away, the Old Man of the Desert takes that thing out of his pocket, that thing he's been playing with, and she sees it's her dancing. He's got it all rolled up in a ball of beads and cowry shells and feathers and mud, wrapped around with a rope of braided sweetgrass. Her dancing. Been a long time since she's seen that dancing. She thought it was lost in the long ago. Thought it disappeared with her breathing.

"Where'd you get that dancing?" she asks.

"Found it in the trash. You'd be amazed what people will throw out — every kind of piece of themselves."

She puts her hand out to take it, but the Old Man of the Desert shakes his head and holds it out of her reach.

"That's mine," she says. "I lost that in the long ago."

"You never lost it," the Old Man of the Desert tells her. "You threw it away."

"But I want it back now."

"You got to trade for it," he says.

The caged woman lowers her head. "I got nothing to trade for it."

"Give me your prison," the Old Man of the Desert says.

She looks up at him. "Now you're making fun of me," she says. "I give you my prison, I'm going to die. Dancing's not much use to the dead."

"Depends," he says. "Dancing can honor the dead. Lets them breathe in the faraway. Puts a fire in their cold chests. Warms their bone prisons for a time."

"What are you saying?" the caged woman asks. "I give you my life and you'll dance for me?"

The Old Man of the Desert smiles and that smile scares her because it's not kind or understanding. It's sharp and cuts deep. It cuts like a knife, slips in through the skin, slips past the ribs of her bone prison.

"What you got caging you is the idea of a prison," he says. "That's what I want from you."

"You want some kind of…story?"

He shakes his head. "I'm not in a bartering mood — not about this kind of thing."

"I don't know how to give you my prison," she says. "I don't know if I can."

"All you got to do is say yes," he tells her.

She looks at that dancing in his hand and it's all she wants now. There's little sparks coming off it, the smell of smudge-sticks and licorice and gasoline. There's a warmth burning in it that she knows will drive the cold away. That cold. She's been holding that cold for so long she doesn't hardly remember what it feels like to be warm anymore.

She's looking, she's reaching. She says yes and the Old Man of the Desert gives her back her dancing. And it's warm and familiar, lying there in her hand, but she doesn't feel any different. She doesn't know what to do with it, now she's got it. She wants to ask him what to do, but he's not paying attention to her anymore.

What's he doing? He's picking up dirt and he's spitting on it, spitting and spitting and working the dirt until it's like clay. And he makes a box out of it and in one side of the box he puts a door. And he digs a hole in the dirt and he puts the box in it. And he covers it up again. And then he looks at her.

"One day you're going to find yourself in that box again," he says, "but this time you'll remember and you won't get locked up again."

She doesn't understand what he's talking about, doesn't care. She's got other things on her mind. She holds up her dancing, holds it in the air between them.

"I don't know what to do with this," she says. "I don't know how to make it work."

The Old Man of the Desert stands up. He gives her a hand up. He takes the dancing from her and throws it on the ground, throws it hard, throws it so hard it breaks. He starts shuffling his feet, keeping time with a clicking sound in the back of his throat. The dust rises up from the ground and she breathes it in and then she remembers what it was like and who she was and why she danced.

It was to honor the bone prison that holds her breathing for this turn of the wheel. It was to honor the gift of the world underfoot. It was to celebrate what's always changing: the stories. The dance of our lives. The wheel of the world and the sky spinning above it and our place in it.

The bones of her prison weren't there to keep her from getting out. They were there to keep her together.

-9-

I'm holding the cartridge now, but there's no need for me to speak. The story's done. Somewhere up above us, the skies over the Tombs are still full of smoke, the Devil's Night fires are still burning. Here in the hollow of this stone room, we've got a fire of our own.

Alberta looks across the circle at me.

"I remember," she says.

"That was the first time we met," Jolene says. "I remember, too. Not the end, but the beginning. I was there at the beginning and then later, too. For the dancing."

Bear nods. He takes the cartridge from my fingers and puts it back into his pocket. Out of another pocket he takes packets of color, ground pigments. Red and yellow and blue. Black and white. He puts them on the floor, takes a pinch of color out of one of the packets and lays it in the palm of his hand. Spits into his palm. Dips a finger in. He gets up, that Old Man of the Mountain, and he crosses over to one of the walls. Starts to painting. Starts to leave a message for the ones to follow.

Those colors, they're like dancing. Once someone starts, you can't help but twitch and turn and fidget until you're doing it, too. Next thing you know, we're all spitting into our palms, we're all dancing the color across the walls.

Remembering.

Because that's what the stories are for.

Even for old spirits like us.

We lock ourselves up in bone prisons same as everybody else. Forget who we are, why we are, where we're going. Till one day we come across a story we left for ourselves and remember why we're wearing these skins. Remember why we're dancing.

DROWNING WITH OTHERS

On a light given off by the grave I kneel…And hold in my arms a child
Of water, water, water.

— James Dickey, "The Lifeguard"

The baby rolled over inside the trash dumpster and coughed. Blood trickled from its mouth.

Aroused by the scent of blood, a rat scuttled from a box underneath and bit into the infant-soft flesh of its leg.

Joe watched with a curious combination of sadness, disgust, and exhilaration.

The baby's tiny arms, already cramped and discolored from exposure to the cold and damp, grabbed at its gnawed body to stop the pain. It opened its mouth to scream, but all that emerged was a faint, wet, thick gurgle.

Joe leaned in and swiped at the rat. It scrabbled back down into the filth, dragging a long red strand with it.

The baby looked at Joe. In its face was a silent and wordless cry: *I hurt. Come get me.*

"It's all right," said Joe, reaching for it. "The frog always adapts."

The baby was dead before he pulled it from the garbage. He stroked its cold head, kissed it, then slipped its body into the canvas duffel bag hanging from his shoulder. "Play by me, bathe in me. The frog always adapts. No pain."

He made his way out of the alley and toward the East Main Street bridge. A smile crossed his face. This was the last one. He would be ready very soon. He could feel the warm breath of his sister, Lynn, against the back of his neck, murmuring What Did You Tell Them?

I told them, Baby all clean, see? I watched, I was careful. She was quiet, just like a little angel. I even saved things.

He darted through the crisscrossing shadows under the bridge until he reached the small lean-to of plywood and corrugated tin he'd constructed at the base of a pillar. Crawling inside, he pulled a flashlight from one of his coat's many pockets, turned it on, and fished around inside the duffel bag until he found the other things he would need.

The flashlight beam shone on the inside of the angled wall/roof. It was covered with newspaper clippings he'd saved over the years. Every last one of them told a story. Every last one held a clue.

He pulled out the needle and thread and examined the shredded patch of flesh on the baby's leg, then glanced at the clippings.

Piece by piece, he'd been solving the puzzle. Tonight he would be finished. The water would soon boil again — there would be steam and heat and bubbles, and baby would be clean because the frog always adapts. Always.

Enough daydreaming. He had to be ready. Lynn wanted to be free.

A small plastic sandwich bag filled halfway with clear liquid fell from his pocket but its seal did not break. Across the top of the bag was a strip of masking tape with the word LEGZ written on it. Inside floated a piece of something purplish-black and leathery, which he removed and stitched onto the mangled section of the baby's thigh, covering the wound. Healing it.

This night was all about healing.

The stink of the Licking River filled Joe's chest. He put some things into the duffel bag, then carefully took down the newspaper clippings and put them in his pocket.

So much to do.

And the water was growing impatient.

❈◉❈

He left the riverbank and headed for the Cedar Hill Open Shelter. It was late and there would be fewer people waiting in line for food. The showers would be empty now so he could clean himself in private.

Dampness and rot hung in the air. It was going to rain again, then get colder. Joe liked that. If it was cold tonight, then the boiling waters would create more steam, and maybe then the whole world would notice.

He climbed the embankment and heaved himself over the railing onto the bridge, almost blinded by the glare of the streetlights. He leaned against the cold metal, thought again of the miracle baby in the dumpster and smiled, then walked with a determined stride toward downtown.

The first few drops of rain pelted against the rim of his hat. He snaked his fingers up and felt the wetness and cold.

"Rain's good," said Joe's father.

Joe shrank back at the sound of Daddy's voice.

"I didn't hear anything," he whimpered.

"I thought you and your sister would be asleep," said Daddy. "I told you I wouldn't be long. Is Lynn okay?" He was completely clear except for the waves of green and blue pulsing through him: water in human form.

Something clogged Joe's throat and burned the corners of his eyes. "She was quiet."

"Just like a little angel," said Daddy. Then the rain started coming down harder and he vanished within the drops, fading back into the sad, cold place all the rain people went.

Joe was grateful he hadn't been near any mud. Mud would have given Daddy something to cover himself with, and if he was covered then he could touch, and if he could touch then he could make a fist, and if he could make a fist then—

—Joe took off his hat and ran his fingers through his clotted, filthy hair. He didn't like to think about those things. They made him sad.

He passed a closed gas station. Beside one of the pumps was a coil of rope, frayed in places and soaked with oil at the ends, but it would do just fine.

He stuffed the rope inside the duffel bag.

The rain was pounding down, pinging off the metal overhang above the pumps and pulsing off their concrete bases. Joe blinked as the rain became Mommy's voice, asking him Where Was Your Father?

Fear enveloped Joe's chest, knocking him backward. He tried to escape Mommy's voice as it rose from a whisper to a scream to a rapid, ragged cacophony, but his legs wouldn't budge, they seemed weighted down, so he grabbed his left leg with both hands and tried to pull free—

—mud.

He'd stumbled into a patch of mud.

Looking down, he saw the faces of his parents, smiling as they took shape and rose up to grab onto his coat and yank him down—

—he fell, arms pinwheeling, but just before he hit he saw a bicycle rack on the sidewalk behind him. If he could just grab one of those bars, he could pull himself free of the mud before they beat him again.

One of his arms shot out in a silent, wordless cry: *I hurt. Come get me.*

The mud sucked him under. The muscles in his arms and shoulders screamed from the strain of trying to grip the bike rack — but he couldn't reach it, the duffel bag was too heavy, and he knew oh god that they were going to win this time, Mommy and Daddy were going to take him back to the sad, cold place and beat him over and over again, and he'd never get a chance to finish his life's work—

—voices other than his parents' rose from the black muck, asking the same questions he'd heard in the back of his skull a million times before, year after year—

> ...you say you were at work, ma'am?
>
> ...what are the ages of the children?
>
> ...have you been drinking, sir?
>
> ...is this the boy?
>
> ...a court-appointed officer will be here shortly to—

—no.

He wouldn't give up. Not this close. *The floodgates are open, away to the sea.*

The frog always adapts.

Joe closed his eyes and felt the rat rending flesh from his small, soft leg, felt the blood spit from his mouth as he reached up and saw the smiling man outside the dumpster say, "It's all right."

...and the smiling man was a baby and the baby was a miracle and the miracle was a little angel that pulled him out just as Mommy and Daddy came up out of the mud so angry and screaming so loudly as they swung the belts over their heads and he ran into a corner and tried to squash down and make himself small like a frog but they just kept coming so he put his arms over his head because they always went for his head and then the belts came down against him and he felt the deep welts raising and saw some of his blood splash onto the walls as he shrank down crying the frog always adapts that's what the man on television said the frog always belts and fists and screams and crying and wailing flashing lights red-blue red-blue red-blue and a strong man in a blue uniform lifting him off the floor making him forget about the smell coming from the kitchen and why Lynn was so quiet—

—his hands closed around the iron bars of the bicycle rack. He finished pulling himself forward. The pelting rain washed the mud from his clothes.

He rose unsteadily to his feet, not daring to look behind him, and ran off toward the shelter.

❈◉❈

As he walked through the front door, Joe smiled at the old black woman who sat at the nearby desk. She looked up from her book and smiled at him in return, then greeted him by name. He took off his hat and searched through his pockets until he found the three crumpled dollar bills, which he put in the can marked DONATIONS.

"You always give a little something, don't you, Joe?"

"Got that from picking up aluminum cans and taking them down to the recycling center. It ain't much. It's raining, you know."

"Gonna be a whopper of a storm. I'm not complaining, mind you. God knows when His Earth is thirsty, and He gives it a good, cool drink."

"Lots of water," said Joe. "The water remembers everything."

The old black woman gave him a blank look. "It does? Well...ain't that fine. You'd best get yourself washed up before they close the kitchen. Reverend don't like dirty hands at the table."

Joe was thinking about the showers down in the basement as he looked at the tables scattered around the shelter's dingy tile floor. There were maybe forty men and women sitting at them, eating their soup and bologna sandwiches. The conversations were sparse and whispered. There were no children.

Joe felt his heart lighten. No children on this night of water. Another sign.

He made his way toward the basement door, opened it, then felt a large, heavy hand touch his shoulder.

"How are you tonight, Joe?" said the Reverend.

"Lots better, thank you. I put three dollars in the can when I came in."

"That's fine. I know it's a lot of money for you and I surely do appreciate it."

Looking into the Reverend's wide, smiling face, Joe felt something hitch in his chest. After tonight, he would never see this man or this place again. He would miss them both. Then he remembered how the rivers and streams and creeks and oceans and seas all flowed to the place where Lynn waited for him, and he felt just a little less sad.

"Is it okay if I go and take a shower?" he said, hearing his voice crack on the last two words. "I'd like to eat, but I don't...don't smell so good."

The Reverend heartily embraced him by both shoulders and said, "The Lord doesn't care how bad you smell, Joe, but I'm willing to bet He couldn't speak for others at the table. Of course you can still take a shower. There should be some hot water left."

Joe smiled, nodded his head, and started down the steps.

"I hope you've got another good story for us tonight," called the Reverend. "From the looks of the weather, we're gonna be here a while."

Joe waved and made his way around a corner into the basement proper. A pile of clean towels sat at the end of a wooden bench. He undressed, grateful to unburden himself of the duffel bag's weight, then walked to the farthest of the three shower stalls. He turned the pressure nozzle and pulled the overhead chain.

At first the water was icy but he knew that would soon change. It was always cold for the first minute or so, then the hot water started to creep in and the temperature was just right. The trick was to get yourself washed and rinsed in three minutes, because after that the water got so hot it could boil frozen vegetables.

Joe let the water run for five minutes before stepping under the spray. The steam was so thick he could barely see in front of him.

In his ear, Lynn whispered: *I'm waiting. I miss you.*

Joe had to choke back a scream as the scalding water covered his flesh. He stood shuddering, his head bowed, staring at the drain until a sickly-sweet smell reached him and sections of his skin began to sluice off, swirling around until the drain clogged.

Cleansing my streams, he thought.

He dressed quickly afterward, ignoring the fiery pain of his boiled skin as it stuck to the inside of his clothes, slopping around under his shirt and pants like clumps of congealed grease.

He was proud of himself.

He hadn't made a sound.

He felt the tears coursing down his cheeks, caught them on the blistering tips of his fingers, and put them on his tongue, swallowing.

The water began cleansing him from within.

—baby all clean, see?

The steam cleared.

There was water waiting for him.

The water was a child.

And that child was Lynn.

She held out her arms for his embrace.

"Soon," he whispered, nearly weeping.

◎

He ate his soup and sandwich in silence. Around him, others were being assigned beds for the night. Lights were turned down, casting the rest of the shelter into shadow. Joe was taking the last tepid sip of coffee from his mug when the Reverend came over and sat down. After the Reverend came Timmy, who was old and had no teeth and whose response to all of Joe's stories was to shake his head and say, "Terrible, just terrible." After Timmy was Martha, all two-hundred-and-fifty God-fearing squat pounds of her, dressed in the faded frock she'd worn seemingly since birth, clutching her Bible against her bosom.

The Reverend poured everyone a fresh cup of coffee and said, "Well, Joe, what's going on in the world?"

Joe took out the wad of newspaper clippings and pulled one from the top. "Somebody broke into the funeral home over on North Tenth and stole some formaldehyde."

"That makes three different funeral homes this month," said Martha, proving once again that she paid more attention to his stories than he thought.

Joe passed the clipping around so everyone could read it for themselves.

"Here's another one," he said holding out a fresh clipping from the morning edition so they could see the bold-faced headline:

MOTHER DROWNS WITH FOUR CHILDREN IN AUTO ACCIDENT

"Terrible, just terrible," said Timmy, shaking his head.

"At least they died together," said Martha. "And drowning's supposed to be a peaceful way to go."

"And you know that they were all welcomed into the Kingdom of God," added the Reverend. "That's one of His greatest mercies: If we are not given time to atone for our sins, He will not judge us harshly should death come for us before we can confess."

Joe grinned, showing them other clippings: a husband and wife who drowned on their honeymoon in Long Island when their boat overturned; three children who were swept away when their makeshift raft hit a patch of rapids; an entire family of Eskimos who fell through the ice while fishing.

The Reverend looked at the last of these clippings, then asked Joe, "Why is it that you always have stories about drownings?"

"It's like Martha said, none of them died alone in the water. It's better drowning with others than all by yourself."

The Reverend smiled weakly. Timmy shook his head.

Terrible, just terrible.

Martha opened her Bible and read something about the sea giving up its dead, flipped ahead, and read part of another passage: "'Satan is as changeable as the shadows and as clever as water.'" She snapped the Bible closed and held it against her. "It was rainin' like this the night them county folks came and took my little Jenny away from me. Said I wasn't no proper mother. They got some damn nerve to tell me I ain't right in the head, always readin' to her from the Good Book. Well, that's lots better than Joe collecting horrible stuff like in these clippings."

Half-listening to her, Joe reached into his pocket and pulled out one last clipping, this one wrapped in plastic. He handed it to the Reverend, who

DROWNING WITH OTHERS

took it, read it, then looked up. "This clipping is almost twenty years old, Joe."

"I knew the family."

The Reverend studied the article again. "It says that the names of the children were—"

"—Lynn and Joseph."

"Is this…is it you, Joe?"

"He's what I was before the water took him away."

Everyone stared at him in silence.

It was time for them to know.

"He wasn't no different from any other six-year-old boy," whispered Joe. "Not to look at him, anyway. He watched a lot of television because it was the only company he had on account his parents were never home at night. His mom worked at the factory, and his dad was always gone to some place that left him smelling like perfume and whiskey. But the boy didn't mind, because the people on the television were his friends, and he believed everything they told him.

"Then one day, he's got a baby sister that he has to take care of. This made him really happy because now he had someone to share television with. He could introduce her to all of his friends. He looked forward to it a lot. He would feed her, give her a…a bath, then the two of them would sit down with the television friends.

"One night there's this real interesting show on, all about frogs. The boy and his sister hurried through dinner so they could see it because they both liked frogs. On the television this man said they were doing these tests, and that sounded neat.

"The man took this frog, and he put it in this pot of boiling water. The frog made a funny sound and jumped out. The boy, he imitated the frog's sound, and it made his baby sister giggle. He loved to hear her giggle. He loved her.

"Anyway, the man on television took this same frog and put it in a pot of cool water and said that the frog could not have a different temperature forced on it, but in this next test, the temperature of the water would be slowly increased because the frog always adapts better in gradual degrees.

"While they were doing that the boy remembered that he hadn't given his sister a bath yet, so he took her into the kitchen and put her in the sink like always. He started the water, and she giggled. He loved to hear her giggle. She hardly made any noise, ever, except to giggle. While the water was running, he went back into the front room to turn off the television so he wouldn't run up the electric bill. His mom and dad were always screaming about the bills, and he didn't want to get into trouble.

"It turns out that the frog on television had adapted really well to the hotter temperature. It allowed itself to be boiled to death. The man took the frog out, and its skin slid off its bones like mud. The boy turned off the television and went back to his sister.

"He'd forgotten to check the temperature. The hot water had been on all along. His baby sister looked just like that frog. He started crying and pulled her out of the sink and tried to stick her skin back on, but it didn't do any good. So later, after his mom and dad screamed and cried and beat him until he bled, the police came. He snuck up to his room where he'd hidden pieces of his sister's skin in plastic sandwich bags. He wanted to take them with him. Then the county people came and took the boy away. He cried for years and years because he felt so…bad about his sister. It was an accident, that's all. He was only trying to get the baby all clean, see?

"He's waited a long time to get his sister back. Now he knows he can. He loves her a lot."

Silence around the table.

Rain spattered against the windows.

The Reverend reached over and tenderly held one of Joe's hands, then said in a quiet, tight voice: "How is he going to get her back?"

"Babies. She wanted him to have those pieces of her so he could find other babies who were missing pieces and make them whole again with what was left of her. She keeps…whispering things to him. She tells him where he can find babies that nobody wants. And he always finds them where she says. In alleys, in boxes and trash cans. And he always finds them when it's raining. She uses the water to talk to him, see? She tells him that Mommy and Daddy didn't really want her, so that makes these other babies, these trash can and alley babies, just like her.

"He doesn't want to be away from his sister anymore. She was the only person he ever loved, and she never knew anyone's love but his. So he will make the babies whole, and they will guide him through the boiling waters to the place where his sister is waiting for him."

The Reverend stood up and came around to Joe, kneeling in front of him. "Tell me, Joe, how will these other babies — the trash can and alley babies — how will they be able to find his sister?"

Joe smiled, becoming more animated. "You see, that's another thing. He remembers this old superstition one of the matrons at the county home told him about, that if you put some quicksilver in a loaf of bread and float the loaf out on the water, it will stop over the spot where a drowned body is. He's thought about this a lot over the years, and he figures that his sister is the same as a drowned person — both are part of the water forever. So the babies will follow the loaf to the spot where it stops, and that's where his sister will be."

The Reverend quickly gave the others a deeply concerned look.

"Terrible, just terrible," whispered Timmy with a shake of his head.

Martha rocked back and forth, stroking the cover of her Bible as if it were the forehead of a newborn, muttering, "The Devil in him, that crazy Joe. The Devil in him like water."

"What is the boy thinking right this moment?" asked the Reverend.

Joe blanched. "He's not…quite sure. His thoughts, they get all churned up like puddles during the rain. He sees things, faces, hears voices…but he can't tell if they're real or just a trick of the water's reflecting. Memories, feelings, all of it…ripples around him and spatters, then it runs down into the sewers before he can get a grip on anything. But his sister is always there, whispering, giggling. He loves to hear her giggle. She tells him what to do." He smiled, wiping his eyes. "I want all of you to know that I have really appreciated your kindness." He grabbed his duffel bag and rose to go outside but the Reverend wouldn't let go of him.

"Joe, please don't go yet. Tell me more."

Outside, the water was pooling, running, flowing.

Steam rose off the pavement as the rain pounded down.

"See that steam, Reverend? That's Lynn calling to me. I have to go. The water won't wait for me. The frog has to adapt." He gently pulled the Reverend's hand from his arm. "Thank you for not laughing at me. You're a nice man. I always liked the sandwiches a lot."

Before the Reverend could say anything more, Joe ran out the door and bolted toward East Main. He was glad now that the Reverend didn't know where he lived — he couldn't tell the police where to find Joe.

He made his way to the bridge, over the railing and down the hill to his lean-to.

Inside, he found his old kerosene lantern and set fire to the wick, smiling as it illuminated what covered most of the floor.

There were five fully inflated truck-tire inner tubes that he had found and repaired. Tied to each of the first four were two babies. The fifth inner tube was for himself and the miracle dumpster baby.

"And what might *your* name be?" he asked that baby now, playfully poking at its nose with his finger.

It told him: *Mary.*

He went from baby to baby, introducing each of them to Mary as the rain grew heavier, the wind more violent, the lightning jagged and insistent.

Mary cooed and gurgled happily as she met Lisa and Jeremy, Sandy and Mike, Kelly and Emily, then Charlotte and the ornery Daniel.

Joe looked out and saw the steam rising off the water in twisted strands. The stink wafted through the opening of the lean-to and engulfed him. His scorched skin screamed for release.

He undressed and stood naked. "It's time to go."

He stared at the rope he'd taken from the gas station.

He couldn't remember now why he'd wanted it.

"I don't know about me sometimes," he said with a laugh.

He removed the loaf of bread from his duffel bag and unwrapped it. It was a good loaf, too — he'd taken it from a dumpster behind Riley's Bakery. It hadn't been cut into slices or anything like that, so it would float really good.

Then came the quicksilver — an old rectal thermometer that he inserted in the center of the loaf.

He ran outside and heaved the loaf into the air, watching as it flew over the river and splashed down in the center of a foaming flow, easily riding the currents and not sinking.

Then, one by one, he quickly carried the inner-tube rafts to the river and set them afloat, watching as they followed the loaf on the water toward Lynn. The babies would keep her company until he arrived. He wanted her to have lots of friends. And the bread would give them something to eat. A full belly was important when you were a baby.

He had just put the fourth raft into the water when a voice behind him said, "I always knowed the Devil was in you."

Martha was standing a few yards away, her breath coming out in ragged wheezes, her eyes wide, her face frozen in an expression of unspeakable revulsion. She held up her Bible and shouted, "The Devil's work!"

"Look at the water," said Joe. There was music in his voice. "See how the steam rises? See how quickly it flows, how strong and true?"

Martha brandished her Bible like a shield. "'Satan is as clever as water, for as water can become steam or ice, so Satan can become that which he wishes to become.'

"The Reverend was worried and scared for you, Joe. I tried to tell him that you had the look of the Beast in you but he wouldn't hear it, bein' a man of God as he is and always tryin' to see the good in folks. He asked me to follow you, so that's what I done. I'm glad I did 'cause I see with my own eyes the proof of your evil now. I knowed there was no goodness in your soul."

"The water is my soul," replied Joe, setting the last raft into the river but taking care not to let go of it.

"Ain't there no decency in you?" shouted Martha. "Ain't there one speck of humility or godliness?"

The raft quietly rose and fell on the small waves that whispered against the bank. In the distance, Joe could see the other rafts as they gracefully glided along behind the quicksilver loaf, carrying the babies to a better place. He held Mary next to his chest with his free hand and said, "I remember part of a lullaby that boy used to sing to his sister at night. It went something like, 'Strong and free, strong and free, the floodgates are open, away to the sea…Free and strong, free and strong, cleansing my streams as I hurry along…'

I don't quite…recall the rest of it, except that it was kind and tender and ended with something like, 'play by me, bathe in me.' It made her smile when he sang that to her." Then something caught in his throat and his voice cracked and tears spilled out of his eyes. "Poor little thing. She never had a good day on this Earth."

Joe started climbing into the raft, then turned to say good-bye to Martha, but she was right next to him with a large rock in her hand that she swung down toward his face like a curse from Heaven, and there was this jagged flash of lightning that split the sky and shot right at his eyes with a sound like thunder as the rain spattered against him and brought pain and darkness with it.

✄◉✄

The raft was gone.

Joe sat up, still naked, his face bleeding and his head screaming. Martha was squatting a few feet away, clutching Mary to her chest. She stroked the baby's head, kissed its cheek, and cooed, "That's my good Jenny, my precious baby, so sweet, so pretty-pretty-sweet."

She looked up at Joe. "I always knowed Jenny didn't want them county folks to take her away from me."

Joe tried to speak but something twisted at the base of his throat.

The water slapped against the riverbank, carrying an echo of Lynn's voice asking: *Where are you?*

Joe stumbled to his feet and found his coat, ignoring the blood from the gash on the side of his head. Sections of pale, shriveled skin dangled from his scorched and ruined body.

He didn't care.

Emptiness flowered within him. The children had followed the loaf. They had arrived and told Lynn that he was coming. They'd all waited there to find that his raft was empty.

She knew he wouldn't be coming.

Ever.

He tried to cry for this final loss of his sister, but there was no water left inside.

He put on his coat and picked up the rope, stumbled up the embankment and onto the bridge, then walked through the night and the glistening, freezing rain.

No voices whispered to him.

No faces came out of the raindrops.

Lynn was silent, as always. Quiet like a little angel.

He turned back after a while and took a different route to the riverbank. He had to make sure.

After a while, he found the empty raft washed up on land with a bunch of garbage. There was no sign of the other rafts or the babies or his sister.

Nearby, a mongrel dog was tearing into something soggy that might have once been a loaf of bread.

Joe staggered on.

Eventually, he found himself in front of Mary's dumpster. Maybe there'd be another miracle baby inside and he could start again, somehow. Without Lynn's voice to guide him he was as lost as lost could be.

He opened the lid of the dumpster and saw only trash and rats inside.

The rain fell, angry fists screaming hateful words.

He took off his coat and climbed inside the dumpster, settling into a spongy pile of leaking garbage.

The rain formed puddles on the steel floor.

Joe tied the rope around his waist, knotting it at the navel just like the umbilical cords he'd seen on so many of the babies Lynn had helped him to find.

He threw the other end of the rope into the air, hoping a kind hand would reach out and grab it.

He huddled in the corner, hugging himself, trying to find the warm companionship of weeping.

Aroused by the scent of blood, a rat scuttled from a box underneath and bit into the soft flesh of his leg.

He wished he could feel a tug from the other end of the rope.

He looked up into the raindrops, searching for a kind and loving face.

"I hurt," he whispered. "Come get me."

STATION OF THE CROSS

Ten minutes east from Copono Base, along the perimeter road, there used to be a place called the Lone Ace Bar. It was never a lively establishment. The first time I went in I remember there was only one customer, a man in a red shirt drinking at the bar. I wondered if he might be the lone ace. Above his head there was Korean freefall wrestling on a big flatscreen with the sound turned off. Squat men in purple-and-yellow leotards were tumbling about in perfect silence. The drinker paid them no attention. When I took the stool beside him, he paid no more to me.

The barman was the bald, neckless, stolid type, inviting no confidences, impassive to what came. I ordered whisky and glanced at my neighbor. He was in his sixties, I supposed, heavyset, a working man reduced to fat by idleness. His hair was thick and greasy. He sat with his elbows on the bar, his head sunk between his shoulders. He looked as though something invisible and heavy had taken up residence on the back of his neck.

Outside the smoked windows, a regulation-perfect day was blazing toward its close. The palm trees hung dark and shaggy. A spaceport bus droned distantly by.

I had driven a hundred miles to sit all day in an air-conditioned basement, toiling through flat plans and elevations, stuff so old and academic no one on the Net even had it. My head was full of diagrams and marque numbers, the names of defunct design teams. I had no money, nothing in prospect but a burger and a bland hotel, and in the morning another day of the same.

"Another?" I said the word aloud, addressing my neighbor at the bar.

"Sure," he said. His voice had the indifference of the terminally disappointed. "Sure I will."

The glasses were filled. I saluted my new acquaintance with mine. "Lenny Cassler," I told him.

He raised his head far enough to show me a pair of vague, uninterested eyes. "Tourist?" he said.

"I'm here to do my research," I said. "At the base here." I nodded in its direction.

He stuck out his bottom lip a quarter inch and poured whisky into it.

He didn't seem to be about to do anything more sociable, so I tried to interest him. "I'm working on engineering design trends in orbital modules of the sixties," I said. The title of my dissertation rolled quickly off my tongue.

"You're an engineer," he said.

I shrugged one shoulder. "Someday, maybe. When I qualify."

He nodded once. "College boy," he said.

"That's me," I agreed. "Are you at the base?"

He didn't seem to hear the question. "College boy," he said again with the somnolent air of the ruminative drunk. "What are you studying?"

"Engineering design trends—"

He interrupted me, "What is that, what do you call that, history?"

I said we did.

That seemed to amuse him. He caught the barman's eye. "History!" he repeated.

The barman smiled like an iceberg.

I felt I should defend my field, not invite mockery. "Things move fast these days," I said at random.

"Too damn fast," my companion said lugubriously. "Too damn fast. My days of moving fast are over," he told us both and smacked the bartop gently with his palm. "History," he said.

I took the invitation to ask him what it was he had done. He confirmed, in a few offhand words, that he had indeed worked out of the base, flying on emergency squads to accidents in low space. It sounded more exciting than history or engineering, but he didn't seem to think it had been any big deal.

I rubbed my eyes. "I've been looking at orbital plans all day," I told him. "Old transit stations, TSKs."

It sounded incongruous as soon as I said it. I hoped the old patrolman wouldn't be insulted, thinking I associated him with a line that had been obsolete when he was a boy. But before I could speak again, he said, "We had a callout once to a TSK. TSK 120J..." He wasn't looking at me. He recited the number as if it were the name of an old friend, or an old enemy.

"When would that have been?" I asked.

"26 June '64, twenty hundred fifteen EST," he said slowly and deliberately.

I blinked at the precision. "What happened?" I asked.

"Somebody saw a light," he said.

I watched the old spacer's hand lift his glass to his mouth. For a moment I thought he was proposing to spin me a line. He must have flown hundreds of callouts in his time. How could he remember one in particular?

"A light?" I said.

"A light on TSK 120J."

I continued to watch him, waiting for the explanation. The way he put it, it didn't sound like a crash. Trespassers, then. Hooligans looking for something beautiful to destroy. I had conceived a great nostalgia for the great days of the TSK. The architecture of early transit stations had a titanic, convoluted grandeur quite unlike the boxy functionalism of the modern compact school. Musing over my graphs and sections and detail cutaways, I envied the fortunate travelers who had threaded the baroque valving of their corridors.

"What was it?" I asked. "Kids?"

The patrolman hunkered on his stool, ignoring me. He was staring into the illusory space beyond the mirrored shelves where the pretty colored bottles stood in line.

I talked because he wouldn't. "She must have been a derelict," I said. "The last K's were decommissioned in '48, '49. All her utilities would have been stripped...."

My unnamed companion drank suddenly, almost convulsively, and grimaced. I wondered what it was I was trying to prove.

"You want history?" the man said, his voice low and gravelly. "I'll give you history." He made it sound like some kind of unpleasant disease I had foolishly volunteered to contract. He swiveled round, jumped down from the stool, and with an abrupt, aggressive gesture summoned me across to a booth.

If I hadn't wanted to believe him already I would have started to believe him then. He had the classic walk of a space veteran: the bow legs and sliding gait of one who has never quite accepted that gravity has renewed its claim in full and for good. With two fresh drinks the barman followed us, then withdrew with a grave nod, a fraction of a bow, like a referee stepping out of the ring before a bout.

I wondered then what I had awakened — some grievance, some obsession. I hoped saying a friendly word to the old-timer wasn't an action I was going to regret. Then I thought, *oral witness*. Jesus, if only I had a cam, maybe I could make something of it that would impress the examiners. I made up my mind to concentrate hard and not miss anything.

The old patrolman and I sat in the booth, and he gave me history. "26

June '64, twenty hundred fifteen EST," he said again. "I'm in the gym, working out with some of the crew. My buzzer goes. Callout, public report to officer on the beat, suspected trespass, transit Station K 120J. Routine procedure, Nebulon scoutship, crew of three, top of the roster. Me, Winterman, Captain O'Casey. Light arms, med tent and basic resus kit in case of casualties."

He spoke in terse, abbreviated phrases like an asthmatic. What I saw in my head was something infinitely more glamorous than these curt facts, more heroic, a distillate of war movies and cop shows, low angles and fast tracking shots of sexy black pursuit vehicles scrambling into flight. I have played it over and over, stretching it this way and that, taking it apart and building it up again — so many times I can no longer tell the difference between what the old man told me and what I imagined for myself. I seem to see the forbidding appearance of the abandoned station as the investigating ship approaches. It floats, black in blackness, big, like some ill-planned marriage between a football stadium and a chemical refinery. The Nebulon circles it swiftly and warily, in two planes. There are no lights showing anywhere now.

The captain, a big-jawed Irishwoman, matches the spin of the scoutship to the station. She decides they will try the doors. My companion, younger, burly, still glowing from his workout, points out that the doors of the decommissioned orbital are surely sealed. The captain dismisses this. "If they got in, so can you," she says. There is music playing in the cockpit, rock-and-roll guitars accompanying the start of another docking maneuver.

In the viewport the transit station swells up to envelop them, drawing them nearer, nearer, until up becomes down and the big clamps bite, locking the scoutship to the space-scoured hull. The trio suit up. Winterman, dark-skinned and slender, shoulders the lofty med pack. They hop out of the lock and jet the short distance to the yellow-and-black-striped maintenance door that the captain selected on their first pass. It opens easily, on weakened hydraulics. Nobody says anything as they step into the lofty hallways of the deserted station.

TSK 120J is a metal mausoleum. There is little gravity, no air, no power of any kind. The investigators play their lights around the depopulated pavement, showing only scuffs and dints. The heavy architecture of the place is confusing. Bends, braces, buttresses conceal every corner, block every line of sight. The team try some doors — anterooms, locked, intact, or long ago vacated, bare as an empty fridge. They pass on, into pitch-black corridors.

Now they are entering the sector where the fugitive light was seen. They search, but the giant curvilinear apartments are bare as caverns in an asteroid. There is nothing here but the detritus of vanished lives: empty drug canisters; a puffy, disintegrating slipper; a tiny nebula of pins and press-studs, forlornly twinkling. O'Casey reaches to pick up a fragment of newspaper. It collapses in her hand like a cobweb.

In vibrations through their suits, the trio hear more than feel the hushed traction of the stippled carpet beneath their feet, the click of a joint against the beading of an archway, the whispering thud of a door handle, tested but unyielding. Their light beams only emphasize the darkness. My nameless companion shields the lifesign meter with his mailed hand. Winterman stands down his backpack and crouches, running his fingertips down the main door seal.

I can hear him call, *"Captain?"*

Some yards away, checking a vast cross-tunnel, O'Casey responds. *"What is it, Winterman?"*

"Captain, this was locked from the inside."

Floor plans beamed up to them *en route* show the system of interconnecting doors that will lead them around the obstacle. Without orders they adopt standard defensive postures, Winterman and O'Casey back to back, scanning the corridor in opposite directions while between them my companion wrenches open the stiff latch on an inspection hatch. Overhead the voluminous shadows hang, vanishing like mist when a beam of light sweeps among them. As the three figures disappear through the hatch, taking all the lights with them, the shadows rush together, clotting in the corridor like honest night.

The team are penetrating the very bowels of the station. They climb along a horizontal shaft, their diminished weight easy on the stapled rungs. One by one, they jackknife around a bend in the shaft and disappear. Each hears his own boots scrape and clank.

Now TSK 120J encloses them in its entrails. Blank white illumination shows only blank gray wall, very close by. Sudden mysterious signs, bright as the day they were stenciled, indicate covered stopcocks and junction boxes. I can read those signs, I want to tell them; identify the chevrons, the dots and letters. But I am not with them. No one is.

One after another the team squeeze into a tall, narrow, bottle-shaped chamber where O'Casey orders them to rest. No one will speak, no one state an opinion or question their duty at this point. Their ears are full of the sound of their own breathing. Twenty-five decks of perforated steel are stacked up all around them, and they are many miles from home.

Even here the absolute, unrelenting cold of space has penetrated, eroding every surface, flaking the face of the metal away like scurf. My companion points to a heavy hatch between their feet. It is black as iron and carbuncled with bosses and shielding. *"It's here, Captain,"* the young man says. *"Whatever it is, it's here. Under there."*

The others look. The meter is alight. It fills their faceplates with its primrose glow.

They kneel, as if at a shrine. My companion breaks out the tools. Soon enough, they unseal the hatch and haul it open.

Across the table in the Lone Ace Bar, the fleshy spacer emptied another glass. The lights in the place had been dimmed, or else I had been keeping closer pace with the drinks than I had meant to. I regarded my companion's face, his thickened, disappointed face.

"He was lying there under the floor," he said.

I exhaled loudly. I do not know what I meant by it: satisfaction, impatience, derision. I fixed my eye on him and waited for him to speak again.

"He was old," he said. "Ancient, ancient. Long white beard down to his waist. He had this robe on—"

He rubbed his thumb against his fingers. I heard his calluses whisper. "Coarse thing, like a sack. Brown skin gone yellow. Staring eyes. Sometimes in the middle of the night, I'd like to forget those eyes." The patrolman shook his head. "The way they looked at each of us in turn."

Without my will, my hand floated across the table and clamped hold of his arm.

"What are you saying? What are you trying to tell me? Are you trying to tell me this old guy was alive?"

"He was alive."

"That's impossible!"

I saw the glistening bald head of the barman turn our way and realized I was shouting. I let the spaceman go, almost pushed him from me in disgust. He was just a burned-out cop, a derelict himself, shipwrecked in a thousand bottles. He wasn't making any sense. And I, I was wasting my time here listening to his crap. I would be better off watching TV in my hotel. At least on TV you know it's all made up.

Instead I sat staring at him belligerently, and he at me no less so. With the restricted vision of advanced alcoholic fugue, I seemed to see him small and dark at the end of a narrow dark brown tube, and yet at the same time with such clarity, such detail I could have counted every broken capillary on his devastated face. I signaled for a couple more drinks. When they arrived I watched him take a sip, just a sip. His hands moved with the perfect steadiness of supreme concentration. He had had practice. I swayed across the table toward him.

"What happened?"

He gave me a look eloquent of human irony, a challenge to acknowledge the bitter humor of their inadequate, inevitable response to the inconceivable.

"We put the tent up."

In my mind's eye, I see Winterman struggling in the confined space of the metal room to erect the med tent over the hermetic sarcophagus and fill it with air. The captain is on the radio. My companion is not listening. Inside the tent, he tears off his helmet, levels his weapon at the supine figure. He barks a question, a warning.

"The old guy wasn't interested in guns. He reached right up out of that pit. Grabbed hold of the front of my suit. His hand was like something made of wood, like a knot of wood. And his eyes were staring at me like there was something he wanted from me. Something he wanted bad."

I waited until I could wait no more.

"Did he — say anything?"

The patrolman nodded slowly. He protruded his lip again. "He did," he said.

"What did he say? For God's sake, what did he say?"

He gave me a strange, sardonic look, as though my question had amused him somehow. When he spoke, it was not in English. I suppose I had no reason to expect it to be. His voice was like the rasp of a friction match in the empty bar. "*Od hu khazar?* he said. *Od hu khazar?*"

There was nothing I could say.

The ancient man fights them. He is strong. He has no wish to relinquish the remote cave he has chosen for his solitude. But the law must have its way. My companion pins him at last, and Winterman pumps him full of enough sedative to keep him out for a week. Even then the trespasser lies there and pants. They mask him, cuff him, drag him to the nearest airlock, into the ship that my companion is sent to bring round. At the base, a security ambulance rushes the prisoner into hospital, where they check him over in a sealed room — no visitors, electronic locks, armed guards, the works. The medics are up all night, arguing over the preliminary results. The head of Bio Division has a shouting match with the director, demanding to call in experts, but by 07.30 the matter is out of their hands, on other desks, in other bureaus. At midnight the nurse checks the monitors, sees him there safe and sound, respiration, heartbeat, EEG steady if not strictly normal. The next time she looks, at 07.42, the bed is empty. The involuntary patient has found a way to discharge himself.

"I guess he can look after himself," said my companion. "I guess you would, if you lived that long."

I was hot. My head was reeling. My throat was sore as if I had been the one doing all the talking. I realized I had no idea what time it was. The Lone Ace had closed hours ago. Even the flatscreen was off. I looked across the sick, dark green infinite space of the barroom and saw the barman still there, solid and white behind his fortifications. He did not seem to have moved since delivering our drinks. I supposed he had been watching us and listening. I supposed I had been the main entertainment for this evening, my reception for this story he had doubtless heard a thousand times before.

"Did you search?" I asked foolishly. "You must have searched. Did you search the station?"

But the story was over. My companion had lapsed back suddenly into his non-negotiable silence. I remember babbling awhile, raving, I imagine;

jeering, I believe. I remember staggering into the bathrooms, slipping on the tile, banging my head. I remember being shoveled into a cab, the driver being given my credit chip. I remember waking up in my clothes, smelling like a bum of the third degree and hurting like a stretcher case. It was two before I dragged myself into the library.

My dissertation was accepted in the summer of '97, when I was given leave to supplicate for the degree of Master of Science at the Faculty of Space Engineering. There are the traditional three bound copies lurking on the faculty library print shelves, way down in the archive stacks where no one ever goes. You can get the whole thing, text and diagrams, off the Net if you have the basic access codes. You won't find anything in it about TSK 120J.

Oh, I had poked around for a time, looking for anything that would invalidate the patrolman's story. There was nothing. There was nothing to support it either, except the very lack of evidence about that mission. Eventually, of course, I found the number of the bar and called it, but the barman had moved on, and nobody was interested in identifying my ravaged interlocutor. After a while, they started hanging up when I called.

Then I went at it systematically, from every angle, under cover. Zero. I grew righteous and demanded satisfaction, challenging all agencies and individuals wheresoever to deny the appalling miracle. I attacked the churches. They were obdurate and bland and soothing as always. I attacked the police. They registered my complaint. It was no use. The old buzzard had got clean away again.

Sometimes I think I see him, on a crowded transport, farther along the car; or among the people spilling out of a movie theater on some uptown mall — an old man with a beard down to his waist and a rope around his tattered gown and a wild mane of hair like some ancient prophet. Once I thought he shouldered me aside in the street outside the faculty. He looked like a lunatic professor, condemning me to abysmal grades. I knew he had come to seek me out, to tell me he knew who I was, to curse my quest. As he thrust me aside, I saw the great beak of his nose, the frenzied glare of those insatiable eyes. It wasn't him, of course. He would never take his shame anywhere so public.

For the longest time I won't even think about him. Then something happens, some newspaper reference to apocryphal texts, some chance remark in a stranger's conversation, some piece of scripture I hear mangled by a TV evangelist as I sit alone late at night, unable to sleep, mindlessly flipping channels. Then I remember that piece of blasphemously ambulatory antiquity. I see him in imagination as the defeated patrolman described him, sitting upright in his violated vault. Then it is I he seems to grab by the coat with his bony fist, I of whom he asks his one eternal, unanswerable question: "Is He back yet? Is He back?"

QUEEN OF KNIVES

The re-appearance of the lady is a matter of
individual taste.

— Will Goldston,
Tricks and Illusions

hen I was a boy, from time to
time,

I stayed with my grandparents
(old people: I knew they were old —
chocolates in their house
remained uneaten until I came to stay,
this, then, was aging).
My grandfather always made breakfast at sun-up:
A pot of tea, for her and him and me,
some toast and marmalade
(the Silver Shred and the Gold). Lunch and dinner,
those were my grandmother's to make, the kitchen
was again her domain, all the pans and spoons,
the mincer, all the whisks and knives, her loyal subjects.
She would prepare the food with them, singing her little songs:
Daisy Daisy give me your answer do,
or sometimes,
You made me love you, I didn't want to do it,

I didn't want to do it.
She had no voice, not one to speak of.

Business was very slow.
My grandfather spent his days at the top of the house,
in his tiny darkroom where I was not permitted to go,
bringing out paper faces from the darkness,
the cheerless smiles of other people's holidays.
My grandmother would take me for grey walks along the promenade.
Mostly I would explore
the small wet grassy space behind the house,
the blackberry brambles and the garden shed.

It was a hard week for my grandparents
forced to entertain a wide-eyed boy-child, so
one night they took me to the King's Theatre. The King's...

Variety!
The lights went down, red curtains rose.
A popular comedian of the day,
came on, stammered out his name (his catchphrase),
pulled out a sheet of glass, and stood half-behind it,
raising the arm and leg that we could see;
reflected
he seemed to fly — it was his trademark,
so we all laughed and cheered. He told a joke or two,
quite badly. His haplessness, his awkwardness,
these were what we had come to see.
Bemused and balding and bespectacled,
he reminded me a little of my grandfather.
And then the comedian was done.
Some ladies danced all legs across the stage.
A singer sang a song I didn't know.

The audience were old people,
like my grandparents, tired and retired,
all of them laughing and applauding.

In the interval my grandfather

queued for a choc-ice and a couple of tubs.
We ate our ices as the lights went down.
The 'SAFETY CURTAIN' rose, and then the real curtain.

The ladies danced across the stage again,
and then the thunder rolled, the smoke went puff,
a conjurer appeared and bowed. We clapped.

The lady walked on, smiling from the wings:
glittered. Shimmered. Smiled.
We looked at her, and in that moment flowers grew,
and silks and pennants tumbled from his fingertips.

The flags of all nations, said my grandfather, nudging me.
They were up his sleeve.
Since he was a young man,
(I could not imagine him as a child)
my grandfather had been, by his own admission,
one of the people who knew how things worked.
He had built his own television,
my grandmother told me, when they were first married,
it was enormous, though the screen was small.
This was in the days before television programmes;
they watched it, though,
unsure whether it was people or ghosts they were seeing.
He had a patent, too, for something he invented,
but it was never manufactured.
Stood for the local council, but he came in third.
He could repair a shaver or a wireless,
develop your film, or build a house for dolls.
(The dolls' house was my mother's. We still had it at my house,
shabby and old it sat out in the grass, all rained-on and forgot.)

The glitter lady wheeled on a box.
The box was tall: grown-up-person-sized, and black.
She opened up the front.
They turned it round and banged upon the back.
The lady stepped inside, still smiling,
The magician closed the door on her.

When it was opened she had gone.
He bowed.

Mirrors, explained my grandfather. *She's really still inside.*
At a gesture, the box collapsed to matchwood.
A *trapdoor*, assured my grandfather;
Grandma hissed him silent.

The magician smiled, his teeth were small and crowded;
he walked, slowly, out into the audience.
He pointed to my grandmother, he bowed,
a Middle-European bow,
and invited her to join him on the stage.
The other people clapped and cheered.
My grandmother demurred. I was so close
to the magician that I could smell his aftershave,
and whispered 'Me, oh, me...'. But still,
he reached his long fingers for my grandmother.

Pearl, go on up, said my grandfather. *Go with the man.*

My grandmother must have been, what? Sixty, then?
She had just stopped smoking,
was trying to lose some weight. She was proudest
of her teeth, which, though tobacco-stained were all her own.
My grandfather had lost his, as a youth,
riding his bicycle; he had the bright idea
to hold on to a bus to pick up speed.
The bus had turned,
and Grandpa kissed the road.
She chewed hard liquorice, watching TV at night,
or sucked hard caramels, perhaps to make him wrong.

She stood up, then, a little slowly.
Put down the paper tub half-full of ice cream,
the little wooden spoon —
went down the aisle, and up the steps.
And on the stage.

The conjurer applauded her once more—

A good sport. That was what she was. A sport.
Another glittering woman came from the wings,
bringing another box —
this one was red.

That's her, nodded my grandfather, *the one*
who vanished off before. You see? That's her.
Perhaps it was. All I could see
was a woman who sparkled, standing next to my grandmother,
(who fiddled with her pearls, and looked embarrassed.)
The lady smiled and faced us, then she froze,
a statue, or a window mannequin,
The magician pulled the box,
with ease,
down to the front of stage, where my grandmother waited.
A moment or so of chitchat:
where she was from, her name, that kind of thing.
They'd never met before? She shook her head.

The magician opened the door,
my grandmother stepped in.

Perhaps it's not the same one, admitted my grandfather,
on reflection,
I think she had darker hair, the other girl.
I didn't know.
I was proud of my grandmother, but also embarrassed,
hoping she'd do nothing to make me squirm,
that she wouldn't sing one of her songs.

She walked into the box. They shut the door.
He opened a compartment at the top, a little door. We saw
my grandmother's face. *Pearl? Are you all right Pearl?*
My grandmother smiled and nodded.
The magician closed the door.

The lady gave him a long thin case,
so he opened it. Took out a sword
and rammed it through the box.

And then another, and another
And my grandfather chuckled and explained
The blade slides in the hilt, and then a fake
slides out the other side.

Then he produced a sheet of metal, which
he slid into the box half the way up.
It cut the thing in half. The two of them,
the woman and the man, lifted the top
half of the box up and off, and put it on the stage,
with half my grandma in.

The top half.

He opened up the little door again, for a moment,
My grandmother's face beamed at us, trustingly.
When he closed the door before,
she went down a trapdoor,
And now she's standing half-way up,
my grandfather confided.
She'll tell us how it's done, when it's all over.
I wanted him to stop talking: I needed the magic.

Two knives now, through the half-a-box,
at neck-height.
Are you there, Pearl? asked the magician. *Let us know*
— do you know any songs?

My grandmother sang *Daisy Daisy.*
He picked up the part of the box,
with the little door in it — the head part —
and he walked about, and she sang
Daisy Daisy first at one side of the stage,
and at the other.

That's him, said my grandfather, *and he's throwing his voice.*
It sounds like Grandma, I said.
Of course it does, he said. *Of course it does.*
He's good, he said. *He's good. He's very good.*

The conjurer opened up the box again,
now hatbox-sized. My grandmother had finished *Daisy Daisy*,
and was on a song which went
My my here we go the driver's drunk and the horse won't go
now we're going back now we're going back
back back back to London Town.

She had been born in London. Told me ominous tales
from time to time to time
of her childhood. Of the children who ran into her father's shop
shouting *shonky shonky sheeny*, running away;
she would not let me wear a black shirt because,
she said, she remembered the marches through the East End.
Moseley's black-shirts. Her sister got an eye blackened.

The conjurer took a kitchen knife,
pushed it slowly through the red hatbox.
And then the singing stopped.

He put the boxes back together,
pulled out the knives and swords, one by one by one.
He opened the compartment in the top: my grandmother smiled,
embarrassed, at us, displaying her own old teeth.
He closed the compartment, hiding her from view.
Pulled out the last knife.
Opened the main door again,
and she was gone.
A gesture, and the red box vanished too.
It's up his sleeve, my grandfather explained, but seemed unsure.

The conjurer made two doves fly from a burning plate.
A puff of smoke, and he was gone as well.

She'll be under the stage now, or back-stage,
said my grandfather,
having a cup of tea. She'll come back to us with flowers,
or with chocolates. I hoped for chocolates.

T
O
M
B
S

The comedian, for the last time.
And all of them came on together at the end.
The grand finale, said my grandfather. *Look sharp,*
perhaps she'll be back on now.

But no. They sang
when you're riding along
on the crest of the wave
and the sun is in the sky.

The curtain went down, and we shuffled out into the lobby.
We loitered for a while.
Then we went down to the stage door,
and waited for my grandmother to come out.
The conjurer came out in street clothes;
the glitter woman looked so different in a mac.

My grandfather went to speak to him. He shrugged,
told us he spoke no english and produced
a half-a-crown from behind my ear,
and vanished off into the dark and rain.

I never saw my grandmother again.

We went back to their house, and carried on.
My grandfather now had to cook for us.
And so for breakfast, dinner, lunch and tea
we had golden toast, and silver marmalade
and cups of tea.
'Till I went home.

He got so old after that night
as if the years took him all in a rush.
Daisy Daisy, he'd sing, *give me your answer do.*
If you were the only girl in the world and I were the only boy.
My old man said follow the van.
My grandfather had the voice in the family,
they said he could have been a cantor,

but there were snapshots to develop,
radios and razors to repair...
his brothers were a singing duo: the Nightingales,
had been on television in the early days.

He bore it well. Although, quite late one night,
I woke, remembering the liquorice sticks in the pantry,
I walked downstairs:
my grandfather stood there in his bare feet.

And, in the kitchen, all alone,
I saw him stab a knife into a box.
You made me love you.
I didn't want to do it.

GOD'S BRIGHT LITTLE ENGINE

It was strange to notice how, in setting out mugs for coffee, she'd automatically reached to the back of the shelf for the one she almost never used. Not for drinking out of, anyway. Sometimes she used it for saving spare fat out of the frying pan and sometimes when she brewed up for the windowcleaner, but otherwise it was the Crockery of Last Resort. She wasn't sure, but she thought she might have inherited it with the flat. It certainly wasn't her taste at all, an ugly color with an ugly pattern on the side.

She'd come to think of it as the workmen's mug.

He was banging around in the bathroom. His name was Andy and he lived downstairs, and that was about as much as she knew of him. He worked for the council in the basement under the local swimming baths, tending the pumps and the boilers and topping up the chlorine. Moving in the dark, ill at ease in daylight. She'd hesitated to ask him for help, but two floods in a week and a slippery landlord had more or less forced her to it.

The electric kettle boiled and, as usual, wouldn't knock off. She flipped the switch and poured out the water, and then picked up the sugar bowl and carried one of the mugs through with it.

"How've you been getting on?" she said.

Big Andy looked up at her. He was kneeling on the bathroom floor, surrounded by pieces of the mixer unit and the tools he'd used to strip it down, and he came close to filling the narrow space like a bear in a cave. A bear in a well-worn blue boiler suit, with thinning sandy hair and features that seemed a couple of sizes too small for his face. He smiled.

"Making a job of this," he said.

"Right."

Helen nodded, trying to look politely interested while thinking to herself, *What exactly does that mean?* Andy laid down his wrench and started to settle back, taking a break from the work, and she realized that she was either going to have to try to carry a conversation mostly on her own, here, or find some excuse to get out.

"I'd better put the milk back in the fridge," she said.

Well, what else could she do? Andy probably meant well enough, but he was slow and shy and damned hard work. She knew that he was a little smitten with her, and she felt guilty for taking advantage of that. She went back into the kitchen and found herself something to be busy with, moving cans around and making some noise that he'd hear.

She wouldn't want him to get the wrong idea. If there was a line between being friendly and being familiar, Helen was going to stay a good ten yards inside it. She'd been caught out that way before.

Later, when he'd said his shy goodbyes and gone back downstairs, Helen ran the bath and stripped off her clothes while it was filling and then climbed straight in.

Bliss.

For five days she'd had to make do with odd showers at work when one of the bathrooms was free, and she was feeling more than a little shop-soiled. Helen's job was that of a care assistant in a private home for the Elderly Confused. Most of the elderly confused sat on waterproof cushion-covers and watched daytime television, but the ones that wouldn't could be a handful. When Helen got home in the evenings, her first act was always to wash off the faint clinging aura of the incontinent.

Now the tension seemed to drain from her. She let herself slide down so that only her knees were out and even her face was almost under. She could see all of the cracks in the ceiling from here. It bulged in one corner where the damp had got in, and those spots of black mold were coming back.

Next year, she thought. *Next year, somewhere better.*

Her flat was on the top floor of a big old house where the ceilings were high and the boards creaked and it never, ever got properly warm in the winter. There were plug-in heaters in every room and the warmth went straight out of the windows. The people on the ground floor had the garden at the back, but they didn't look after it. Most of the houses around here had been subdivided and had probably been quite desirable once, but none was desirable now. For some time Helen had been promising herself something better without actually being sure of how she was going to make it happen. Some turn of luck, and then she could move. Which was why "next year" always seemed about the right distance ahead.

She could hear Andy moving around downstairs.

His sitting room, as far as she could work out, was directly below her bathroom. The fabric of the building picked up the sound, and the bathwater carried it straight into the middle of her head like a weird hallucination. He clomped around, ironshod. He worked the spark button on the gas fire, a series of muffled hammer beats. He turned on the TV. Some children's program was just beginning and he started to sing along with it.

Helen sat up quickly, sluicing water.

Too close. It felt too personal. This was more than she wanted to hear.

As the bathwater drained, she climbed out and toweled herself while standing on the cold lino. The lino was so old that it had worn right through over the joints in the boards beneath. She could still hear Andy's TV, but only faintly now, and she couldn't hear him singing at all.

Helen Murphy, she thought, *This Is Your Life.*

She'd offered him money for the plumbing job, of course, and of course he'd refused it. So now she'd have to think of some favor she could do him in return. If he'd had a cat, she could have offered to feed it when he went on holiday; but he didn't, and he never seemed to go away for any length of time either.

She wondered what kind of life he led. Not that it was anything she'd want to pursue. He probably wasn't actually retarded, but he was no one's idea of a dream partner either. She knew that he sometimes watched her from behind his curtains when she was walking home from the bus, and there was a transparency to the way he contrived to be out on the stairs when she was carrying up her shopping; but there was an innocence to it, too, and nothing ever went any further.

He moved his furniture around a lot. She heard him doing that. And he was forever at one DIY job or another: sawing, tapping, doing things with power tools. Yet the part of his flat that could be seen from the landing looked just as much a dump as her own.

A neighbor with some uses and a containable crush.

With Andy thus filed in her mind, she turned to other things.

When Helen got home from work on Wednesday night, she wasn't in the best of moods. Two of the other care assistants hadn't turned in and she'd been on her own until eleven, and had continued to be overstretched thereafter. Helen worked the day shifts, and only occasionally the lates.

During her lunch hour she'd picked up a cottage pie from Marks and Sparks, and she put this into the oven to heat through. Down below her, so faint in the background that it barely registered in her mind anymore, Andy seemed to be moving his furniture again. She filled the electric kettle and set it to boil, and threw a tea bag into a mug.

Then she noticed something.

There, among the dishes that she'd left on the draining board that morning, was the so-called workmen's mug. She hadn't used it for anything since Andy's visit four days before. After washing it she'd put it on the shelf with the others, where it would gradually get shuffled toward the back. Which was where she'd expect to find it when eventually she needed it again.

She was staring at the mug as the water came up to the boil. Automatically and without even looking, she put out her hand to knock the switch off.

But she didn't need to, because it clicked off all by itself.

Now she stared at the kettle. The automatic cutoff hadn't worked in ages. Not for as long as she could remember. It had worked when she'd bought the kettle, but then something seemed to gunge it up inside and it had needed a push to shift it ever since. The switch was clean. All the grimy stuff that she remembered being built up around its base had disappeared.

Wary now, she looked around. Nothing else seemed out of place.

She switched the kettle on again, the water bubbled up to the boil inside it once more, and once more the switch cut out the way it was supposed to.

Helen moved out of the kitchen.

Now she scanned the sitting room. Everything looked as it should, but then, she couldn't be sure. When you lived alone, she thought, you came to take it for granted that everything would always stay exactly the same as you left it. Had that cushion been crooked this morning? Yes, it had. Were those magazines in that particular arrangement? She couldn't be sure.

The wardrobe door in her bedroom didn't squeak anymore. But the glass in the top pane of the window was still cracked and the reading lamp still wouldn't come on. The pictures on the walls hung straight and the drawers all moved smoothly in their runners. Some had before. But some hadn't.

Helen went out of her flat and onto the landing. High up and without a window of its own, even on the brightest days this part of the house was always as dim as the darkest corner in the Casbah. She dropped to her knees and slipped her fingers into the tiny gap under the skirting board opposite the door. Her spare key was still there, and popped out when she knocked it.

She kept it in her fist as she clattered down the stairs.

So much for *that* as a hiding place. Everyone else stuck their keys under mats or plant pots or hid them above the architrave, but Helen had supposed that her own idea was something unique. How long, she wondered, had it taken him to work it out?

She knocked on his door. Everything behind it seemed to go quiet; then, after a few moments, she heard his tread approaching.

He looked surprised. Surprised that anyone should come knocking at all.

"I want you to know something," she said, jumping straight in before he could say anything. "I was grateful for your help last week, but I don't appreciate this." She held up the hand with the key in it, and Andy looked at it in puzzlement.

"This was for my use and nobody else's," she said. "That's my private territory up there. How would you like it if someone were to let themselves in and start poking around your place when you weren't at home? I know you probably meant well. I hope you did. I'm going to assume you did, anyway. But please don't ever let yourself into my flat without an invitation again."

Andy blinked. He had pale eyes and even paler eyelashes.

And he said, "What do you mean?"

"Everything *works* now," she said, and although Helen knew what she meant it sounded like an absurd kind of complaint. She said, "I'm a private person, Andy, and I'm sorry, perhaps you have a different attitude to things. But that's mine. This makes me very uncomfortable. I'm going to forget this whole thing. I want you to do the same."

She didn't wait for him to answer. She didn't want to hear him lie, but she wanted to hear a confession even less. When she got back into her flat and closed the door behind her, she found that she was shaking.

And under all of her certainty was the one stray thought that went, *What if he really didn't come in here today?*

But it was only a momentary doubt. The kettle switch, the wardrobe doors...none of that was necessarily conclusive. But that mug couldn't have climbed out of the cupboard and planted itself on the draining board. Andy seemed to work one day of the weekend and to get a day off midweek in return. Today had been the day. She could picture him waiting until she'd gone out and then coming up the stairs with his canvas bag of tools, letting himself in and looking around for jobs to do. She might have mentioned the kettle; he'd probably thought it was a hint. He'd have tried it out, perhaps taken a break for a brew in the middle of all the work, cleared up all traces of his presence...bar one.

If he'd eased all the drawer runners, Helen was thinking, that meant he had to have pulled out her underwear drawer.

She closed her eyes.

Ugh.

Later, as she lay unwinding in the bath once more, she heard him dragging a chair across the floor. Why did he do that? Did he only have the one, and had to move it to wherever he wanted to sit? Rising a little from the water, she reached for the sherry she'd poured herself. Helen couldn't ever remember feeling that she *needed* a drink before, but the urge had come upon her tonight. Cooking sherry was all she'd had in. She hadn't felt like going out.

And even later, as she lay in bed looking at the moonlight squares on her curtains, she thought: *What if he'd taken the key and had it copied?*

At which she almost leapt from the bed and tore across the room, switching on every light in the flat and not feeling her panic subside until she'd got one of her own chairs and wedged it under the handle of the outer door.

There she waited, and listened.

Nobody moved downstairs.

It had crossed her mind that there was one other person who might have been able to get access to the flat, and that was her landlord…belatedly responding to her complaints about the plumbing, perhaps. But on past performance it would take at least another three months and the threat of a rent strike to make him take even an interest; he certainly didn't cruise his properties in search of secret favors to do.

Andy it had to be. Handy Andy.

Helen waited and watched him from her window the next morning, wondering whether the previous day's confrontation would have had any effect. She thought that he looked a little slumped and beaten as he walked off down the pavement toward the bus stop, but that could have been her imagination. He was in his blue boiler suit and had the little vinyl shoulder bag in which he carried his lunch and a flask. His knuckles weren't exactly scraping along the ground, but he'd lost some of the bounce in his step.

Helen let the curtain fall back into place and went through into her bathroom. She was all but ready, but she'd been hanging back; she'd done it unconsciously at first, only then realizing that she wanted to avoid running into him on the stairs or in the hallway.

She wasn't sure exactly how she felt. Angry, of course, but she hadn't actually been scared at the beginning; that was something that had started to rise up in her only gradually. You formed a picture of people, she realized, but you didn't know. Hers of Andy had been like that of a soft-eyed cow in a field, big and docile and not overburdened with introspection. Sex hadn't come into it at all. But that, obviously, was at the root of all this; and the realization was like a door opening onto another kind of darkness.

She didn't want to think about it. To her mind, it was like turning over a soft toy to see worms falling out. Helen didn't think of herself as a person with hangups. But there were sides to others that she didn't necessarily want to see.

As she brushed her teeth, something caught her eye and she glanced down. There was water on the floor, and it was spreading. Helen stared, brush stilled, teeth half-cleaned; the edge of the water was like a sharp line and it was expanding outward in a bulge from under the side panel on the bath. She looked up at the mixer tap and saw water bubbling up at its base like a spring. It would be running down behind the bath on the outside of the pipes and spreading out from under, just like before.

"Damn!" Helen said, and ran for the stop-tap.

The stop-tap was under the kitchen sink and she had to rummage out a pile of cleaning materials to get to it. By the time she'd turned the shutoff and picked up an armload of rags and gone back to the bathroom, she was cursing. All the grief it had brought her, and his stupid repair hadn't even worked; this was exactly the trouble she'd been having before, returned and redoubled.

She was expecting the bathroom floor to be awash, but it wasn't. The lino was wet and the boards showing through were dark, but the puddle had already gone. The last two times, it had taken her half an hour of mopping and wringing out followed by two days of airing. What was different?

Down on her knees, taking care not to mark her nurse's working whites, she could see. The boards under the lino had been taken up and relaid at some recent time. The nailheads, where they showed, were new. What previously had been a close-fitting, tongue-and-groove floor wasn't quite so close-fitting anymore, and the water had gone straight through and down.

In fact, the boards themselves were not as they'd been. As Helen looked at them, it seemed that their sides had been planed. Instead of each board interlocking with its neighbor, the tongues were gone and there were fractional gaps.

Forgetting to watch out for her clothes now, she put her eye to a gap and squinted through.

At first she had grit in her eye and could see nothing at all. But, after rubbing it clear and then getting close enough, Helen found that it was like looking through a pinhole camera. She could see some electrical cable, she could see a ragged edge of plaster. Beyond that, she could see daylight; it was the daylight in Andy's sitting room, directly below.

She couldn't see much down there, but she could see a chair. Draped awkwardly over the back of the chair, as if it had been dropped there from above, was something that looked like an old curtain. It was wet down there, so there could be no doubt about where the spillage had gone.

The plaster was that of Andy's ceiling. A circle had been cut out of it: a circle just about the size of a man's head, with a little extra.

It was a spyhole. He'd cut himself a spyhole in her floor, with a chair to stand on so that he could reach it, and a wad of old curtain to plug the gap in the ceiling when it wasn't in use. But the water had soaked through and made the material heavy and the curtain had fallen, and thanks to his own bad workmanship on her plumbing the ruse stood revealed.

The opened-out space between ceiling and floor was directly under the spot where she stood drying herself after each early-evening bath. Like a devotional chamber, to which Andy presumably climbed for worship.

Helen tore through the place. She dragged in a rug from the bedroom and put it across the floor. She put weights on the rug. She put weights on the weights. Books, furniture, it didn't matter. It was as if his threatening essence might seethe up through the gaps like so much steam. She went to the phone several times, picked it up, put it down, couldn't order her thoughts enough to express herself. In the end she had to say *Stop*, and force herself to stand.

Take it in order. One thing at a time.

Ring work first. Report in sick. Let someone else struggle, for once.

"Hi," she said, the unsteadiness in her voice probably helping her case. "It's Helen. I'm not going to be able to come in today. I seem to have picked up something awful."

Then get out. Get right out of the house.

She went to the covered market in the middle of town where there was a big locksmith's stall, six days a week. They said that they could send someone around on Monday. But she didn't want to wait and so she chose a lock which looked like the one that was on her door already — five levers and a deadlock — thinking it reasonably likely that she might be able to unscrew the old one and put the new one in its place. It shouldn't take too long. When she got home she'd call the police and then she'd work on the locks as she waited for them to come. She didn't want the job undone or half-finished when Andy came home. The police might talk to him, but eventually they'd go. And even if they took him away, sometime later he'd almost certainly come back.

She got some window locks and she had to buy some tools as well. Just the essentials. She could hardly ask to borrow any from downstairs.

Back in her flat, she emptied all her purchases onto the floor and broke open the blister packs. In the pack with the lock there were screws and keys and a tightly folded page of fitting instructions.

The screwdriver skidded more than once as she took the old lock off the mounting plate. But then the new one wouldn't fit it. It looked as if it ought to, but it was a different size and make. Helen felt an increasing sense of despair as she saw a simple job turning into an open-ended road of uncertain destination.

She reread the instructions. It would be fine if she could only stay calm. The plate would unscrew. There was a new one that she could then fit in its place.

The old screws came out, but the new ones wouldn't go in. Her arms trembled and her grip failed and she couldn't make them turn.

She was trying to bash them in with a hammer when she heard somebody coming up the stairs.

She waited, hammer in hand, listening. The tread was slow and heavy. At the middle landing, the noises stopped.

They'd stopped by Andy's door. It was him. He was home early.

But he didn't go in. He started up the stairs toward her.

It was as if Helen's breathing had stopped, holding time still with it. All the world had frozen in place, everything except for the figure who was climbing the stairs with the regular *tick, tock* of a clock pendulum. On his way.

Soon to arrive.

Making the turn in the middle now.

There was nothing to hold the door shut. Nothing at all. This was exactly the nightmare scenario she'd been trying to avoid. Had he heard her banging? Was he coming to offer his help? She tried to take a step back, and the very air seemed to tense up and resist her. It was as if the actions that she'd taken to make herself safe were the ones that had put her in the greatest possible danger.

She looked at the hammer in her hand. She'd bought a small one because the big ones had looked too heavy. Now she was sorry. This was tiny, a pin-tapper, almost like a toffee hammer.

He stopped outside her door, and knocked. The knock alone was enough to swing the door inward, and he seemed to stop in surprise.

The blood roared in Helen's ears.

The policeman framed in the doorway looked about nineteen years old.

"Miss Helen Murphy?" he said.

She couldn't answer. But she managed to nod.

He said, "I'm sorry to have to tell you this, but there's been an accident."

Andy, she later learned, had died at a little after ten-thirty that morning. Something connected with the chlorine gas in the basement under the pool, but no one seemed to want to tell her the details. While she'd been racing back with a bagful of home security, Andy was already out of it for good.

She told the police what had happened, but it all seemed like history now. The reason they'd sent someone to her, she discovered, was that in Andy's personnel file at the pool he'd named her as the person to contact in case of emergency. He'd had them make the change about three years before. Prior to that, he'd had no one listed at all.

Three years before? She'd barely been aware of him then. She wasn't even sure that she'd known his name.

Were she to have read about it happening to someone else, Helen was sure that she'd have considered it a little tragic. But because she was at the heart of it all, she didn't know what she thought. It made her feel mixed-up and scared. Any sadness she felt, she resented.

She didn't go to the inquest, but she did go to the funeral. She sat dry-eyed in the crematorium chapel with the priest and two council workers, and afterward she walked out into the grounds and the sunshine of a bright spring morning. The chapel was out on the edge of town between parkland and countryside, and the grounds were lush and glorious. The graves stood ranked in well-tended fields; the fields blurred off into woodland. Beyond the woodland, the hills. Beyond the hills...eternity, she supposed.

A boy in baggy overalls was down by the gardens. He'd a low two-wheeled wagon resembling a gardener's trolley, and fitted into a framework on the trolley were gray metal containers about the size of two-pint flagons. They reminded Helen of the steel jugs they used to use to make milkshakes in cafeterias when she'd been small, except that these weren't shiny. The youth was shaking one of them out upwind of the flowerbeds, and the breeze was spreading the dust.

Like sugar over a cake, she thought.

The arrangements for Andy's funeral had been the most basic, without a grave or even a plaque on the wall. He'd be scattered on the garden of remembrance, to lie unremembered. The graves themselves weren't much: a hole in the ground for the ashes, an anonymous place in one of the long rows of the dead. But a place, all the same.

Too bad.

She didn't know why she felt guilty as she walked away. She owed him nothing, and certainly no debt of affection. That had all been on his side, and on his side alone; and a pretty twisted form it had come to take, in the end.

She couldn't make herself feel that they weren't at all connected. He was the shadow that she cast.

Which she also resented. But this, she thought, would truly be the end of it.

That night as she lay in bed, Helen was aware of having one of those episodes in which she couldn't be sure whether she was lying awake, or was dreaming that she did. She'd had a troubled evening and retired early. She'd felt the urge to talk to someone, but she didn't know to whom. Her parents were dead and the other members of her family were widely scattered, and she hadn't been in touch with any of them in ages. The people at work simply weren't those kind of friends.

So instead she lay in rumpled sheets, and twisted them around her as she turned, and screwed her head down into her pillow like a fist. She tried to ignore the sounds that her imagination was calling up out of the darkness. Sounds of sawing, of banging, of things being moved around elsewhere in her flat. Instead of paying any attention to these, she found herself thinking of her father's name for her, so long ago when she'd been small and her parents had filled her world like giants. He'd called her God's Bright Little Engine. Love had been the wallpaper of her life, back then. She'd taken it so much for granted that she'd never dreamed of the day when she'd miss it as she was missing it now.

Sawing.

Banging.

Things being moved around.

Helen sat up in bed. But all she could hear were the regular night-sounds of the house: the creaks, the settlings, the mysterious movements of noises through pipes. She let herself fall back onto her pillow. It was as if she'd at least been flirting with sleep, but now even that was beyond her.

She lay. She dozed. She drifted away. She dreamed of a presence that hovered briefly and receded. Looking in on her as she slept. Checking that all was well.

She awoke abruptly.

For a moment she looked around helplessly in the darkness. Something had happened, she didn't know what. Then somehow she slowly began to piece it together: a noise, a real one this time, her startled body reacting to it with an intelligence all of its own. Her mind lagged, struggling to catch up. Somehow she was sure that a door had slammed. It had been followed by the sound of a key turning in a lock.

Now: nothing.

Somewhere else in the house. Or something outside. Helen put her head in her hands and groaned out loud. She was going to feel lousy in the morning because she felt lousy now and there was no prospect for any improvement. She felt for her bedside alarm and pressed the button to illuminate the little clock face. It didn't come on, so she groped around and found the switch for the reading light and put that on instead.

The dial showed a little after four o'clock, but the sweep hand wasn't moving. The clock had stopped. Oh, God, she thought, and flopped back onto the pillow. Why didn't anything work? There had been a time when you bought things and if they stopped working, they could be fixed; but now everything seemed to be so trashily made that you could destroy it just by trying to get it open. Stuff came back with a note on saying no fault could be found in the workshop, and then behaved exactly as before when you got it home. The only certainty in life seemed to be that things once gone wrong would never, ever go right again.

Those bright little engines. In brightness no more.

What if the noise *had* been in the house? There was supposed to be no one downstairs.

And how come her reading light was working now?

Propped up on her elbows, she stared at the glowing shade. She'd caught the wire while vacuuming under the bed, and jerked it so hard that it hadn't worked in more than a month. She'd changed the bulb, so it hadn't been that. A loose connection somewhere inside was more likely.

Helen wasn't greatly technically minded. But even in her most optimistic moments she knew that such objects, once damaged, did not heal. Regardless of how long a period of convalescence you might give them.

She got out of bed and moved to look at the window. There she pulled the curtain to one side. The split glass in the upper pane was now whole. It was a clean, new piece, apart from a couple of putty smudges. She ran a finger across them, but they were on the outside.

Her sitting room was empty. The shadows had fled as the lights came on. But over at the entrance door, something gleamed.

The brand-new lock, the one that she'd abandoned attempting to fit and had thrown into the back of a cupboard, was now in place. Unlike the hasty bodge that she'd attempted and failed to carry out, this was a neat job; the door timber had been cut to take the new plate, and a few shavings of fresh wood lay on the mat. Slowly, she crossed to it. She'd chosen well. It looked as solid as the door to which it had been fixed. In the crack of the frame she could see a glint of light on the deadlock, the two-inch slab of brass with a double core of bearings that would frustrate any hacksaw.

She could see all of this, but no key to open it.

There was a faint click from over in the kitchen.

Helen stood in the doorway. The electric kettle was only just simmering down after knocking itself off. There were two mugs set out beside it. Her favorite, the one she tended to use most. And the workmen's mug.

She turned. There was no one in the room behind her. But there was a presence here. The sense of someone close; in another room, perhaps, and designated ever to be so. Something that might be seen at best in the corner of the eye, and that would slide evasively from any attempt to draw it into focus.

It was in the bathroom. But she went into the bathroom. And now it was somewhere else.

Her mind and her heart were in overdrive. The rest of her body was calm.

"Andy," she said aloud. "Are you there?"

Her voice had that quality which sounds only ever had in the stillest hours; sound with edges and shadows, intensified by the bathroom's hard acoustic. Nobody replied. But she was sure that some kind of a noise came from her bedroom.

The bedroom was empty. But the messy nest of her bed was now as neat and square as the handiwork of a chambermaid in the Savoy Hotel.

I cannot leave, she thought. *At least until I wake, and this dream is over. Please God, may he mean me no harm.*

Still she could sense him. Elsewhere in the flat. Always elsewhere.

But moving toward her.

There was the distinct sound of a chair being dragged across the sitting-room floor toward her bedroom. Helen didn't move back toward the doorway to look. She knew that there would be nothing to see if she did.

So she waited, and heard the chair move closer. Just on the other side of the door, it stopped. She listened hard. Was that a breeze, moving through the spaces of the roof? Or was it something else? Chlorine gas destroyed the lungs, she'd been told. That was how it killed.

When she was able to speak, she was surprised at how clear and steady her voice was.

She knew that someone was waiting.

"Come in," she said.

THE DARKEST DOCTRINE

There is one door in the Vatican that the Pope is forbidden to open. It leads to catacombs that would mean certain death for any Pope. Buried in these vaults are secrets that would drive the world mad; and every Pope shoulders the awesome responsibility of protecting civilization from these dread truths. The person selected to guard what even the Pope may not see is determined by a process as complicated and political as the one required to elect the pontiff.

Monsignor Walsh was an unassuming, modest man. He was so careful of other people's feelings that he would not allow himself to recognize the fact that he had turned to scholarship to escape the incessant noise of his family — of brothers and sisters and a mother and father who all seemed to talk at once and enjoyed playing the television and radio simultaneously. It was not until his first year in a monastery where the brothers observed a vow of silence that Walsh thought back to his earlier life with a faint smile on his thin lips. The noise his family could not live without suddenly took on the quality of richly textured music.

He did not stay at the monastery but won a scholarship that allowed him to pursue his studies at Notre Dame. There was always a question as to whether his calling was to be among people or among the books that call out to a true scholar with a melody as pure as the wine monks make in their quiet monasteries. The decision was made for Walsh, whose first name was Ashley, at the age of thirty-five. He had returned home after graduation to serve those with whom he had grown up. He wasn't sure that anyone particularly noticed his return when he received a special summons from the bishop of his archdiocese. There he learned his destiny did not lie in Chicago.

"They want you at the Vatican," said the older man.

"I don't know what to say," said Walsh.

"That has always been your strength," replied the bishop.

A small voice in the back of the monsignor's head chided him over how easily he was able to wrap up his affairs; how easily he extricated himself from the city in which he had spent most of his life. He envied a younger brother whose name was George because the man involved himself in the lives of others as easily as slipping into a warm bath. George took on other people's miseries, fed on them and turned them into something better. Ashley thought his brother should have been the priest in the family; instead he was a musician loved by many women. He was the one person who was there to take Ashley to the airport.

"Congratulations," George said, shaking hands with his older brother. "It's a great honor. I can imagine how you feel."

The monsignor looked blankly at his younger brother. Young George had known sorrows and joys that Ashley despaired of ever feeling. The one emotion that guided the elder Walsh's life was a desire not to cause other people trouble. He prayed this impulse was born of a desire for their well-being and not simply a lust for peace and quiet.

"I can't imagine why they want me," said Ashley.

George was surprised. "You mean you don't know?"

"The bishop told me the assignment requires a knowledge of Greek, Latin and Hebrew. But the Church has a wealth of scholars more qualified than I am."

"They must know what they're doing, or what's faith for?" This last observation of the brother — more proof that he was cut out to wear the clerical collar — echoed inside the head of Monsignor Ashley Walsh as he took his seat on the United Airlines flight that would take him on the first leg of his journey. All roads lead to Rome. All roads lead away from home.

A letter from his mother resided in his pocket unopened. He would read it midway across the Atlantic Ocean. He knew what it would say. She always wrote the same letter. She had hope for all her children, but as she worried the most about him he received the most concentrated dose of good will. He couldn't blame her for this sort of sentiment. It was how she dealt with the fact that he didn't love her.

The first leg of the flight was uneventful, but the captain must have gotten up on the wrong side of the bed when he informed the passengers, in a voice dripping with sarcasm, that information about connecting flights would be available on video terminals at the Atlanta airport. Walsh thought the man was a kindred spirit, better suited to working with information than with people. One of the stewardesses made a snide remark about the captain, sarcasm begetting sarcasm, a nun breaking ranks with her priest. Walsh was amused to note that an elderly woman asked the captain what gate she should go to as she exited the plane. The amusement didn't last when Walsh tried to help her and found himself staring at a blank monitor. The computer system was temporarily down, a crisis in airport orthodoxy. Little scraps of paper proclaiming necessary boarding information were affixed to the blank screens, as if Martin Luther had appeared to post alternative routes to devoutly wished-for destinations.

Systems do break down. And Monsignor Walsh had no particular faith that he would navigate the dangerous waters separating one minute from the next. A bit of air turbulence, a shudder in a plane touching down, the red wine he purchased (his ticket was not first-class) tasting little better than fermented Kool-Aid, and an obnoxious child who insisted on kicking the back of his seat...these were the only remaining mishaps on the various flights that finally deposited him in Italy, where he was met by an English-speaking driver.

For a moment, he felt himself the recipient of more than he deserved. Cardinal Bennedito put an end to that. The cardinal kept him waiting so long that Walsh rediscovered the virtues of humility. Someone pointed out that now was a perfect opportunity to play tourist. Walsh was disinclined to take advantage of the situation. First, he wanted to be available the moment his superior called on him. Second, he had already played tourist back when he was a student at Notre Dame, and had visited Vatican City one special summer.

Young Ashley Walsh hadn't been overly impressed with the sights that astounded and delighted the other students. He admitted the columns were big, the paintings bright and colorful, the incense evocative of mystery, the gardens soothing and aromatic, the tapestries shimmering walls of ancient beauty. He saw that the ceilings were as high as everyone else could see. He heard the deep swelling of music, the perfect blending of young human voices with deep-throated organs speaking as from the center of the earth. He could smell and taste and touch as well as the others. The only trouble was that he didn't feel anything.

Unmoved by the purple and gold world flowing all about him, he was teased by one of the other students for being a closet Protestant. He laughed at that, surprising the other who had never heard him laugh. The trouble, he assured his fellow undergraduate, was that he, Ashley Walsh, did well and fully believe in the orthodox claims of the Church — thus committing the crime of apostasy against the modern and relevant church. Such a shocking claim rendered his lack of aesthetic sense a moot point.

He remembered that long-ago summer as the word came to him that he was expected by Cardinal Bennedito. The man was a robust sixty-year-old, with silver-white hair offset by a black eyepatch. He looked like a pirate.

"Sit down, sit down," said the older man, his English barely accented. "May I offer you a cigar?"

"No thank you, your eminence. I don't smoke."

"Wine then?"

"Yes, thank you," answered Walsh, marveling how the man moved quickly and efficiently, like an athlete. The red wine soon passing the monsignor's lips was much better than what he'd sampled aboard the plane. It warmed him from the inside out, and suddenly all the little details of the office were easier to appreciate. The chair was very comfortable.

"I'm sorry it took so long to work you into the schedule," said the cardinal, lighting up a Havana cigar without asking the monsignor if there were any objections to his smoking — but in fact, Walsh didn't mind. "You have been recommended by Monsignor Cranston to be his replacement, and there is no objection from the committee. Of course, Cranston's department falls under my section, but I'll leave you pretty much a free hand. Frankly, I like to have as little to do with the Black Room as possible — and you know, of course, that's just the tip of the iceberg."

The free flow of words put Walsh in mind of one of his father's monologues. He adopted the same expression now he had as a child: a slight smile on the face, accompanied by an occasional nod.

Fortunately, the cardinal reached a stopping point which offered the monsignor a breathing space, along with the unfortunate promise that lessons in the obscure would continue under the tutelage of the other monsignor. "Yours is the most interesting task in all the Vatican, or under it," said the cardinal, leaving Walsh to wonder if this might be a cryptic comment.

Walsh followed the cardinal down the labyrinthine corridors, foolishly thinking how easily one could become lost. He had yet to appreciate how simple and direct a floorplan the Vatican enjoyed compared to other places. A more immediate problem was a sudden fit of sneezing that seized him next to a little altar with an attractive bit of greenery embracing the old stone.

Back when he'd spent time in the monastery, he'd read about the monks who tend the flowers and plants of Rome in buildings at least a thousand years old. Now as he blew his nose in the handkerchief thoughtfully supplied by the cardinal, he noticed an odor unlike any he'd encountered before. There was a strange combination of wet and dry smells blended together, as if he were traversing a dry swamp. The purple cords that hung before the ornate doors suddenly seemed to be jungle vines. Walsh was dizzy.

"Are you all right?" asked the cardinal.

"Yes, I'm sorry," he reassured his superior.

"We're almost there," said the other, pointing to a door at the end of the corridor. The door was no different from others, but the wall around it seemed to have a peculiar yellow stain.

"I'll leave you here," said the cardinal, which struck Walsh as odd — to come all this way and not take those last few steps and make introductions. But already the cardinal was retreating, and all Walsh could think was how glad he was that when he sneezed nothing untoward got on the red cassock.

Right before he knocked on the door, Walsh felt something grab at his heart. He assumed it had something to do with his health. Then he was across the threshold, standing in the fabled Black Room and being received by the oldest, weariest man he had ever encountered.

"Thank God you have come, Monsignor Walsh. I am Monsignor Cranston." He feared the old man's fingers would come off in his hand as he gingerly shook the withered appendage. "You are probably wondering why you were chosen for this very special service to the Church."

"The thought had crossed my mind," answered Walsh as he was maneuvered into a comfortable chair.

Unlike the cardinal, this man offered no amenities. He seemed to be in a terrific hurry to get his words out all at once before he disintegrated before the eyes of his startled guest. His voice was the only strong thing about him. "We studied thousands to find the best man to replace me. You can see that I don't have much time left." His head shook slightly as he spoke, and Walsh tried to force himself not to watch the sporadic movement. Looking directly into the old man's watery eyes was a problem, too, as their color made Walsh sick.

Suddenly the man grinned. The smile seemed evil, as if it had been cultivated over the course of as many centuries as the ancient shrubbery. Then Walsh found himself wondering why he associated evil with antiquity, in this of all places. His faith seemed to break loose from its moorings and float just out of reach.

"You'll be able to handle the assignment, believe me," said Cranston. "You know, it's kind of amusing that you're the first American. I'm British. Originally I thought working here would give me a chance to improve my Italian. But you'll find you don't have much contact with other people. It's a good job for someone who likes lots of quiet."

The realization sunk in as to just how thorough the investigation must have been. Some roads lead to Chicago. "But what exactly is required?" asked Walsh.

The old man sighed. "Best to get this over with," he said. "What do you think we keep in the Black Room?"

Walsh looked around the room. The books and documents and scrolls were neatly arranged, as he would have expected. He was somewhat surprised that the place wasn't musty. At least there was no danger of his sneezing fit recurring. The lack of dust suggested that either superb janitorial skills were regularly applied or perhaps more people had access to forbidden texts than the Office of Propaganda would admit. (Walsh prided himself on knowing that the Church had implemented the first Office of Propaganda.) On the other hand, if people came in here regularly then the job wouldn't be as lonely as Cranston was intimating.

"The historical heresies," answered Walsh. "The Gnostic heresies primarily — theological debates involving some very fine points."

"Tell me, Monsignor Walsh, what you think the Church position was regarding the *Nag Hammadi?*"

This was becoming a bit annoying. Walsh didn't mind playing student in the Vatican, but not at this elementary level. "Well, you're referring to the fourth-century Coptic texts taken from the Greek originals. These uncanonized gospels were unearthed in, uh…"

Cranston helpfully filled in: "The year that saw the destruction of the Third Reich — 1945."

Walsh blinked. Cranston had made an odd association there. "Well, yes, 1945. Naturally the Church is never pleased when these heresies receive publicity, leading souls astray."

"No more than she approved translating the Bible into vulgar tongues where careless readings gave us the Protestant problem, eh?" The way Cranston asked the question, Walsh wasn't sure if he might not be joking.

"Ashley," said Cranston, surprising the other by the sudden familiarity, "I am about to share with you a truth that no one can know without becoming its guardian."

Walsh laughed. Again Cranston smiled. There were no deep, dark secrets in the Church, other than perhaps the standard requirements of sharp business dealings in the modern world. The whole quarrel with the Gnostics was their insistence on a secret knowledge vouchsafed to an elect while the masses were fed on fairy tales. The war of spirit against the flesh was an inevitable consequence of that sort of paranoid thinking, ultimately threatening to dethrone God and render pointless the sacrifice of His son. Was Cranston putting him to a bizarre test to see if his replacement was foolish enough to believe in the fantasies of the ignorant?

Cranston stood. "The Gnostic heresies are false," he said.

Walsh laughed again. "That's quite a secret," he replied.

Cranston frowned and continued: "You don't understand. I mean to say they were created by the True Church to mislead the curious and proud from consideration of far more dangerous things. The persecution of heretics always had as its target one or two people who had discovered the truth, but their words would drown in the ocean of anguish."

Images entered the mind of the man from Chicago, images he would cast out as false idols but which stubbornly impinged on his consciousness: of witches burned at the stake, of Cathars put to the sword, of fire and blood in this crusade or that inquisition. Walsh had studied enough history to know that not everyone tormented by the Church over the centuries had been an innocent, or a mere political enemy. But he also knew that his Church was an institution that had learned the limitations of force; and this was appropriate if it was in fact not a human institution but a projection into our world of the Cosmic Absolute.

So Monsignor Walsh summoned what was left of his willpower and challenged Monsignor Cranston with: "What are you talking about?"

"This," said Cranston, forcing creaking limbs to support his weight, and taking a few steps over to the far wall. Reaching behind a bookcase, he touched a switch and the case swung open. It didn't creak. It must receive regular use. "I have opened the door," said the old man, his voice firm as ever. "Are you coming?"

The hesitation Walsh had felt before entering the Black Room did not return, even though he suspected that now would be a very good time for forthright indecisiveness. "I'm right behind you," said the American.

The stairway that seemed to lead down to eternity was less a surprise to him than were the fluorescent lights that stretched to a pinpoint, illuminating polished stone steps as far as the eye could see. Modernity apparently had its points.

The apparent absurdity of what he saw suddenly concerned Walsh less than a flash of human concern for his frail mentor, who seemed to think he could make it down those uncountable steps. "You can't mean to go down there?" asked Walsh. "Not in your condition!"

"Don't worry about me," said Cranston. "Are you in good enough condition to handle the stairway?"

"I think so," said Walsh, feeling a bit distracted and stupid. Before he could say or do anything else, Cranston removed a small golden bell from his loose sleeves and rang it just once. A most remarkable nun appeared from out of the shadows behind the two men. She must have been in the Black Room all along. She was fully six feet tall and so muscular that her habit barely concealed the bulging biceps on her arms. She reached out for the frail priest, grabbed him like a sack of communion wafers and, throwing him over her broad back, started down the steps.

"Are you coming?" Cranston asked again. Watching his receding form on the back of the incredible nun, Walsh thought that the old-fashioned way of doing things apparently had its points.

It took over an hour to reach the bottom of the stairs. Walsh didn't know what astonished him more: the engineering required to create such a vast tunnel, or the Amazonian nun carrying the old man on her back. The incongruities captured his imagination and reduced him to a childlike level where his uncertain faith could find a natural habitat. The world was young again, full of surprises. When people and places ceased to be predictable there might even be room for God, that most unpredictable Absolute. Walsh didn't have time to be tired as he descended into the earth. He was too busy allowing himself to experience a detour from his life.

"Tombs!" cried out the voice of Monsignor Cranston, reverberating off the walls, carrying the conviction of a life almost used up. "What must any old building become? A tomb, of course. The older the structure, the more tombs it must contain. Think about it, boy. The Vatican is old enough to contain a thousand whispers from a thousand lost hopes. Dead frustrations give birth to secrets. Secrets must have shadowed corridors and sliding panels and trapdoors. And not even that grand old building above our heads could possibly house them all. So for over a thousand years this underground world has grown like a specially tended plant cultivated by one of the brothers."

"Who built this?" asked Walsh, not feeling the least bit poetical.

The gigantic nun snorted and shifted her charge from one massive shoulder to the other. Cranston continued along the same line: "Why, it answered the needs of a million prayers, unwinding like a great underground snake, hollowing through the earth."

Metaphorical language had never appealed to Walsh. A teacher had once pronounced him passionately literal-minded. "Who built it?" he repeated.

Cranston allowed himself a laugh that broke into a high-pitched cackle, the first time his voice seemed to match his emaciated appearance. But he recovered himself, and spoke in the deepest tones yet: "You believe the Church is the body of believers. You believe the institution we serve is a manifestation of something divine, no matter how corrupted by human imperfections." Although he was speaking in a declamatory style, Walsh kept mentally adding question marks...but the older monsignor was the furthest thing from a Jesuit instructor. Walsh placidly listened to the litany of what he was supposed to believe.

"Shut up, you old relic!" screeched the nun, shocking Walsh more by her hysterical voice than the irreverent content of her words. The old man merely laughed again. She held onto his frail body more tightly than ever.

"So you should be honored," continued Cranston, "as we plumb the depths of your mother. You enter her sacred body here below, and there will be soft things and decaying things and wet things that belong in the womb or the tomb — different words for the same place."

Even Walsh could run out of patience. "You're not going to tell me who built this, are you?"

Now it was the nun's turn to laugh. "Insects!" she spat out. "Two worms wriggling under Our Father's House."

The woman never seemed to get tired. Her litany of pejoratives was uttered without any noticeable change in breathing, whereas Walsh was huffing and puffing to keep up with her.

"I've been rude," said Cranston. "Allow me to introduce Sister Mary Kaitlan."

Before Walsh could say something polite, the remarkable woman shifted the stream of her abuse into more graphic areas: "You're both little cowards, wishing you were climbing into your mother's womb instead of exploring these sterile tunnels."

The old man caught the expression on the younger man. "It's all right," he said, "she's Irish radical. Just trying to get a rise out of you, so to speak."

"Pope John Paul the First would have fixed all you bastards," she screamed, "with Vatican 3. He would have overturned Pope Innocent's rule about nuns not participating in saying Mass, hearing confession and giving communion."

"She's really very political," Cranston assured Walsh. "She started out working with the poor in Northern Ireland and she thought John Paul the First would clean up Vatican financing and…"

"Lesbianism should be a sacrament!" she screamed. "Priests should marry teenage girls, then molest little boys in front of their parents."

"Oh," said Walsh, followed by a well-considered, "Ahhh?"

"She always makes me want to have a good prayer," said the old man.

"The same as a good bowel movement," added the profane nun.

The expression spreading across Walsh's face inspired a grimace from old Cranston, whose yellow, bad teeth gave the appearance of a partially eaten ear of corn. "Don't mind her," the old one advised. "She's being punished and we should not pass judgment on a fellow creature."

The word "creature" struck a chord in Walsh's mind, a most uncharitable chord. Although deep and sincere prayer did not come easily to him, Walsh recited under his breath, "Though I walk amid distress, You preserve me, O Lord." There must be something good he could notice about Sister Kaitlan. She carried the old man on her back without complaint. Talking to her was at least a distraction from the physical strain of the long walk down the stone staircase.

Meanwhile, the subject of his charitable thoughts snarled at her fragile charge with: "You're a Christian wimp!" The old man cackled obscenely.

When Cranston had regained his composure he turned his head at a painful angle, looking back at poor Walsh struggling to keep up, and said, "She is modern in her views. Which means, of course, that she doesn't really know what she thinks."

"I don't doubt it," agreed Walsh. "To change the subject for a moment, I'd like to know where we are. We keep descending, but for some reason it doesn't become any colder."

Both nun and elder churchman laughed. Walsh didn't feel any better about the situation. Sister Kaitlan sensed his weakness as a carnivore smells blood. In her usual indelicate manner, she volunteered that, "You damned priests need Jesus, another man showing you how to manipulate women."

"Excuse me," said Walsh, not at all politely as irritation crept into his voice, "but do you accept the divinity of our savior?"

"Ha!" she exclaimed. "Talk about loading the dice. He's another male, isn't He?"

Shaking his head, Walsh finally felt the humility his brothers in the monastery had tried unsuccessfully to inculcate in him. Cranston was sympathetic and offered, "She has room for improvement. You must remember that the Church gave up the Inquisition long ago and excommunication has been found politically unwise. We must love one another for a reason never admitted."

"And what reason is that?" asked Walsh.

"Later," whispered the old man, "you'll have more answers than you can bear."

They trudged on in silence for about five minutes. Walsh resolved not to be the first to break the silence even though his head was aching with questions. It fell on the loquacious librarian to start up the conversation again with: "Sister Kaitlan is not alone in doing penance."

"Old fool," she muttered.

"She doesn't sound very repentant," commented Walsh.

"So, Ashley...I believe that's your first name?" said Cranston, not seeming entirely comfortable with the personal approach. "Perhaps you would care to question the subtleties of her not very liberating theology?"

"Reactionary fungus," said the nun. "There would be more room to house the poor if we blow up the Vatican!"

Walsh decided to get into the spirit of the thing and put a question to her: "I suppose you believe in birth control?"

"Absolutely," she confessed.

"Would you do away with celibacy?"

"There is no celibacy. We must admit the fact!"

Emboldened, he pushed on: "I suppose you would allow abortion."

There was a sharp intake of breath from both the woman and old man riding on her back. "Shame on you," scolded Cranston.

"I'm a Catholic," added the nun in a hurt tone of voice. "And by the way, American monsignor, did you remember to kiss Cardinal Bennedito's ring?"

"I give up," said Walsh, wishing there were surrender papers on which he could affix his John Hancock. The silence returned except for the heavy footfalls, and echoes of footfalls, as they continued their fatiguing walk.

Suddenly Cranston shouted two words, the theological significance of which seemed unclear: "Look out!" Then Walsh saw the rat. It had been sleeping on a step only a few inches away from his foot. As the creature raised its head to investigate the sudden noise interrupting its solitude, Walsh had an all-too-close view of the size of the thing. From head to rump, the animal was the size of his forearm. Which wouldn't have been so bad if not for the added feature of the tail, twice as long as the body.

As if wishing to satisfy the curiosity of the humans, the rat leapt into the air where its head was on a level with theirs. Eye to eye with the rodent, Walsh decided it resembled a small kangaroo more than a rat, a pleasing thought until the jaws opened to reveal all the teeth in the world, long and sharp and nasty, guarding cheeks in which remains of old meals were stored, ripening until needed.

Walsh suppressed a desire to throw up; a stronger desire was to run screaming back up the stairs, but Sister Kaitlan came to the rescue. Brandishing a mean-looking ruler (which she must have kept hidden on her person), the muscular nun swung the weapon in a wide arc. With a sickening crunch the wood splintered against the head of the hapless animal, leaving a red ruin where the eyes had been. The sleek body, now seeming smaller than before, plummeted down the stairs as the belligerent nun let out a war cry consisting of: "Damned Giant African Rats think that they own the place."

"We're nearing the bottom," said Cranston. "I see the dark at the end of the tunnel." Sure enough, the lights ran out where the stairs ended at a stone floor. Beyond was a pool of darkness. "The rats like to come up into the light," Cranston finished.

The obvious thought appalled Walsh. "You mean there are more down there?"

"They're not as bad as the snakes," Kaitlan assured him.

"I'm sure you'll enjoy our little menagerie," Cranston threw in.

"Things that creepeth or crawleth are the least of your troubles," hissed Kaitlan, finally staring directly into Walsh's eyes, whereupon he realized that he preferred the contemplative visage of the rat.

None of this was in the job description, thought Walsh...before remembering that he never saw a job description. Reaching flat ground again was sufficient cause for him to say a prayer of thanks, and to avoid the body of the dead, or stunned, rodent lying nearby.

Sister Kaitlan, not even winded, unceremoniously dropped Monsignor Cranston who, catlike, landed on his feet. The old man hurried over to the young man and whispered, "This next part will be a bit uncomfortable. You're not claustrophobic, are you?" As his eyes grew accustomed to the latest attraction of the tour, Walsh was horrified to notice a narrow, black hole in the wall immediately facing them. Cranston continued: "I've been enjoying our discussion as much as any Jesuit teacher...."

"Or Freemason," the reliably mad nun got in her two liras worth.

Cranston ignored her. "We must observe silence for a while. We don't want to draw undue attention to ourselves while in the tunnels." He let his thin fingers play across the stone just above the black hole as if searching for something.

The primary reason Walsh knew that he would go forward was that he wasn't about to flee back up those interminable stairs! As a final inducement, the nun drew close and, breath rich in whiskey, warned that, "We don't want to wake the fairies like we did that poor rat, now do we? The little ones fear the *Scapular*, Latin words from the Gospels a priest may wear around his neck, but I'll wager neither you nor Monsignor Cranston remembered to bring such good protection."

"Stop teasing him, Sister Kaitlan," Cranston admonished her.

"Surely he must know," she continued, an Irish brogue sneaking into the cadences of her speech, "that they keep their gold and jewels and pearls under the ground, and the Holy Father finances the world's wealthiest religious institution by crafty dealings with the wee folk."

Just about then Cranston found what he'd been looking for — a slight protrusion of stone. He pressed gently against it and a dim light appeared at the mouth of the tunnel. This illumination drew the nun's attention away from the American — drew her as it might a very large moth. Without hesitation, Cranston dropped to all fours and crawled into the space. Kaitlan followed. Walsh followed too, convinced that if the vigorous nun's bulk could fit through, so could he. And blessed be the light!

The first thirty feet weren't so bad. The low-wattage lightbulbs weren't as nice as the bright, white fluorescent tubes…but they were a lot better than what came next. The dim light ran out around a tight curve. No more bulbs hanging overhead. Just darkness — oily, black, quiet as the tomb.

It was a no-nonsense game of follow-the-leader and Cranston wasn't stopping. He wasn't even slowing down. Walsh resolved that he would not make a peep of protest if they crawled right down to the center of the earth. Perhaps all that was needed for the rebirth of faith was to be obedient and do something deeply foolish. The last sight afforded him before leaving the light behind was of Sister Kaitlan's posterior, each cheek moving rhythmically, mechanically, as she marched forward on her knees.

Unpleasant odors assailed him, combining the exquisite delights of old cat boxes with a sour mustiness. The tunnel became narrower, as well, but so long as the nun could squeeze through he was unworried about following in her wake. Desperate to find something good in the situation, he experienced a moment of joy over the fact that other life forms of the creeping and crawling variety had not chosen this moment to share the incomparable gift of existence with him…in a dark, dank, reeking, foul tunnel.

Suddenly he had to cough. He didn't want to cough. Someone, or something, might hear him and come slithering, crawling, flooding down the tunnel to smother them all, choke out their lives and munch on their souls. Hoping to assuage the maddening tickle in his throat, he tried altering his breathing and then swallowed hard. Nothing helped. He bit his lip until he felt the sting and tasted salty blood on his tongue. That didn't help either. He lasted as long as he could and then he coughed. In his mind the sound was like heavy artillery. He held his breath, waiting for the others to say or do something. They kept moving and so did he.

All bad things come to an end, especially if something worse lies ahead. The tunnel let out into an underground cavern of tremendous dimensions, lit by three globes floating overhead: one blue, one red, one yellow. They were not at ground level. The tunnel they had used opened onto a ledge, a natural shelf of rock, providing ample room for even Sister Kaitlan. The shifting lights made it easy to see that the walls of the cavern were honeycombed with at least a hundred identical holes, suggesting a network of tunnels as complicated as the Dewey Decimal System.

"You can speak now," said Cranston.

"Cough some more, if you like," added Sister Kaitlan, and he couldn't be sure if this was a moment of solicitude or only more sarcasm.

"What are those?" asked Walsh, pointing at the pulsating globes.

"Don't tell him!" Kaitlan nearly shouted. Turning to Walsh, she clarified: "It's you I'm thinking about. He'll pontificate, sure as we're standing here."

"Sister, have you considered a vow of silence as a way to get to know yourself better?" asked the elder monsignor.

"Ha," said the nun. "You've got one foot in the grave and another on a banana peel, you old coot. See that you don't fall."

Finding the nun more intolerable than ever, Walsh surprised himself by coming to her rescue. What seemed to require a moment of heroics resulted from passing in front of another tunnel opening, at which precise instant a boa constrictor came out into the light and promptly wrapped itself around Sister Mary Kaitlan. Without thinking about what he was doing, Walsh leapt forward and wrapped his hands around the cold coils even as the serpent tightened them. It seemed perfectly in character that the nun would laugh at him.

"You do have virtues," said Cranston, admiringly. "You care about other people — enough, perhaps, to keep dangerous secrets from them."

Stretching her neck forward as if a snake herself, the nun rolled out a long, red tongue and licked the head of the snake. Then she kissed it. "A little piece of Eden," she murmured.

Walsh thought he had reached his breaking point. "I'm tired of this," he announced primly. "I can only put up with so many things not being what they seem. I am fast approaching the point where if you are not honest with me about everything right now, I will resign and take the first flight back to the States."

The globes above suddenly grew brighter, flooding the chamber with rainbow colors. They made a sound similar to choirboys hitting their highest note. The moment had Epiphany written all over it.

"You'll do well in this position," said Cranston.

"That's your punishment," said the nun, "and your reward, too, if you're good at turning the other cheek."

Taking a deep breath, Walsh tried again: "What are those spheres overhead?"

"The Father, the Son and the Holy Ghost?" suggested Cranston.

"Holy *Spirit*," the nun corrected.

Cranston shrugged. "Good and bad things come in threes," he sighed. "Let's show this young man the true secrets he has traveled so far to meet."

They walked single-file down the ledge. Each time they passed in front of a tunnel, Walsh felt a tingling sensation on the back of his neck. He didn't want any more surprises that slithered. As if aware of his prejudice, the snake rested its head on the nun's shoulder where it could eye him balefully. In search of the good again, he admitted that the serpent entwined about the nun's stout frame helped to keep her calm. Her right hand stroked up and down the smooth reptilian hide.

While she occupied herself with her pet, he allowed himself a quiet moment in which to contemplate his deepening confusion. Although he'd had only one geology course in college, and his grade had not been outstanding, he remembered enough to wonder if this cavern made any sense for this area of Rome. The heat bothered him especially. If anything, it was becoming warmer as they descended.

The place stank of old flowers, as if someone had taken millions of petals that had been pressed between the pages of library books and ground them into a fine powder, sprinkling them in the air. At least it was easy to breathe despite the heaviness of the perfume. In a different place he might have found it pleasant.

They reached the floor. A great, flat expanse spread out before them with a small group of people standing in the center, apparently waiting for visitors. The three from above went to greet the assemblage below. As they drew nearer, Walsh began to fall back. A primitive instinct commanded him to run but his intellect told it to crawl back under a rock. The situation was what it was. He'd gone too far to turn back now. Despite a certain reluctance to pray, he thought the *duty* to pray made more sense than surrendering to the virtue of hope. He caught up with the others, determined not to hope for anything.

They were close to the figures now, and the figures all seemed to be men attired in white robes vaguely resembling hospital smocks. Most had long hair and beards. A few were bald. The most disturbing quality was how the men all stared ahead, eyes open, unblinking. As if a boy again, Cranston threw off his black cassock, and years of accumulated pain apparently went with it.

The old man danced in front of the staring figures.

"Hey, Ashley," he called out, "this is the big payoff. Not many mortal eyes behold this, let me tell you. The faces may not be familiar — but, oh, do you know their names!"

Cranston ran forward, spindly arms waving like uncooked strips of pale, white chicken. With shaking, fragile hands he made pathetic fists and punched at the immobile men, but he stopped short of actually touching them. At no point did Walsh doubt that the silent figures were made of flesh and blood, although they were as silent and still as wax statues.

"This one," announced Cranston, pointing to a handsome young face, "is the Buddha. A prince with a heart!" Cranston threaded his way deeper into the group. Making as if to pull on the dark beard of a tall man with fierce features, he intoned, "You may have wondered about the appearance of this famous prince of Egypt. Allow me to introduce Moses. Is it only me, or does the Law Giver appear more like a prosecuting attorney than a friendly defense counselor?" A short man with even darker hair was identified as Mohammed.

While Cranston was enjoying the role of emcee, the snake unwound itself from Sister Kaitlan and departed from the human company. No sooner did this occur than the nun became belligerent again. "Where are the women?" she asked. "I see a Roman emperor over there who thought he was a god, and plenty of other no-accounts, but where are Aphrodite, Asherah, Astarte…"

"And she's only in the A's," proclaimed Cranston with good humor.

"There are no manifestations of the Goddess here," she plowed on. "No Hera. No…"

"None of your harlot idolatry here, woman," sang Cranston — he was literally singing — "your slut goddesses aren't here for the same reason that Odin or Zeus didn't stop by to say hello. Only real people touched by God stuff are in this select gathering."

Changing tactics, the nun asked a question the monsignor was not expecting. "Then where's the Virgin?"

"I don't know why the real fisher of men never brought her," said Cranston.

While this thoroughly demented dialogue was going on, Walsh noticed a peacock race out of a hole in the distance. It made the weirdest sound he'd ever heard. He felt like running with the bird and entering another dark tunnel before the light of the globes above revealed a sight he was afraid would scorch his mind. Instinct was warring with intellect again but it didn't have a chance; for one thing, he was too damned tired to run.

"And here He is," said Cranston, sounding for all the world like a talk-show host revealing the prize guest of the evening. One man stood at the center of the group, occupying a place of honor. He was of average height and build, but exuded a sense of authority that Walsh could almost touch. Kaitlan looked away.

Closer examination revealed a face that Walsh would never forget for a very good reason. The face changed every few seconds. At first Walsh thought it might be a trick of the light, but the features were actually shifting in front of him. The nose flattened, then grew more narrow. The eyes moved farther apart, changed color, then came closer again. The hair extended like unkempt vines and then shortened again as quickly as a fishing line being reeled in. The most startling feature of the shapeshifting was that the man's race changed as well.

Cranston walked over to Walsh and placed a hand on the younger man's shoulder. "How does it feel to stand before Jesus Christ?" he asked.

"You must be insane," came out of Walsh's mouth, but the words lacked conviction.

"At least he understands the implications," sneered the nun. "If He's here, the incarnation becomes confusing."

"This is all some kind of trick," said Walsh. "Why are you doing this to me?"

"You are initiated," said both Cranston and Kaitlan at the same instant. That was the final straw. Walsh ran. He was not as fast as the peacock.

Heading for the nearest tunnel at ground level, he didn't care if monsters waited for him. But he was focused on the wrong area. A shadow as black as all the tunnels fell across him as he ran and he chanced to glance up. Something very large was near the ceiling. It had been above the globes, in fact, but now it was coming down. The thing had moved between the source of light and the little speck down below, running.

An attempt to run faster only succeeded in Walsh becoming tangled in his own cassock. He fell sprawling on the hard ground and cut his jaw on a sharp projection of rock. Fear spurred him on to greater exertion, but he tripped again before he could resume his futile attempt to reach the hole in the cave wall. He felt something alien brush against his back. He couldn't resist flipping over to see the nature of his attacker. A moment later he wished he hadn't done that.

Floating in the air directly above him was a giant fish, roughly the size of a family station wagon. Rolling over quickly he did manage to get out from under it and successfully jump to his feet. He would have preferred doing this without all the screaming but at least he was up and running again. By this time the monsignor and the nun had caught up to him, one on each side, and they were attempting to reason with him.

"Calm down," Cranston told him. "It won't hurt you." The fish floated lazily in the air, drifting closer to investigate Walsh. He gazed at the great eye of the fish, which had the appearance of a marble that had been crushed flat and then stuck to the scaly head. The natural blue-green scales refracted some interesting patterns under the alternating red-blue-yellow lights.

Cranston gave the fish a playful push and, like a Thanksgiving Day balloon, it spun around slowly before swimming through the air and approaching Walsh from another angle. Now Walsh had a clear view of the monster's teeth. They were elongated with serrated edges, and shaped like spatulas on the end — a textbook example of the bristletooth fish that feeds on feces, seeking out carbon, nitrogen, protein and lipids, along with nutrients in the ocean waters. Walsh started giggling uncontrollably as he wondered what this creature found in the atmosphere to satisfy an appetite commensurate with its size.

Cranston had the answers, all right: "This is a TIME EATER, Ashley old boy. You might say it is the original fish of the faith. It swims down the corridors of time and ingests the essence of God when manifest in human form. Then the fish deposits everything here."

"The detritus of history," Walsh mumbled to himself, but the others could hear. "Man's deepest beliefs are what drift through time."

"And now you understand the secret we must guard," Cranston said, sounding almost gentle. "The old Church taught there is only one way to salvation. Add up all the heresies and what do you get? The modern mind, with its belief of many roads to salvation. We must spare the world the truth, give it a brief moment of hope when that is all it may ever have."

"The truth?" asked Walsh, his voice sounding weak and tired.

The nun screamed and put her fingers in her ears. She had obviously heard what Cranston was about to say many times before. "There are *no* roads to salvation," the old man whispered. "Every promise of salvation ends here, in this quiet cavern."

Walsh stumbled away, aware for the first time in his life how badly he needed a redeemer. He had to see Christ again, Christ not risen but preserved in glory, exalted as the jewel in the Vatican collection.

The face was still changing, a hundred profiles under the triple sun burning overhead. Walsh wanted to reach out and touch the face, to kiss the forehead darkening and whitening forever and ever. He wanted salvation not only for himself but for the old man who stood patting the cold scales of the monster fish hovering in the air; and he wanted to save the mad nun who sat on the ground, weeping over loss and pain he could never imagine. And he wanted salvation for all the people he had never been able to touch in his cold and lonely life.

He thought he might say a prayer but he couldn't think of one, not one. Then a line of Dante came to him and he settled for that, speaking the words out loud, as carefully as possible:

"The uneven tombs cover the even plain — such fields I saw here, spread in all directions, except that here the tombs were chests of pain…"

THE LAND OF THE REFLECTED ONES

The old man was smiling when he opened the door. The smile disappeared as soon as he saw it was Emerson.

"Oh. You."

Not even *it's you.* The old man showed his dislike for his visitor by using as few words as possible during their brief meetings. Emerson didn't bother to acknowledge the slight. He was accustomed to such rudeness from his inferiors. And since everyone walking the earth was his inferior, Emerson spent a lot of imagination planning how he would deal with them once the time rolled around. But that would have to wait, if for just a little while. Emerson sniffed and drew his arms in close to avoid unnecessary physical contact with the old man as they stood together in the cramped confines of the bookshop.

Up until recently, when a slight stroke forced its proprietor to close down, the shop had been in continuous business for over five decades. Although he had greatly reduced his hours and limited his clientele to a handful of serious bibliophiles, the old man had done nothing to reduce his stock. In fact, he continued to add to it. Books surrounded them on every side, spilling from the narrowly spaced bookshelves that reached to the ceiling, and stacked atop one another on every available surface. The place smelled of the genteel decay of old paper and moldering leather.

The old man motioned for Emerson to follow him as he hobbled along a narrow path that led from the front door to the living quarters in the back, screened from view by a bead curtain.

The tiny kitchen and dining area was identical to the front room. The books had found their way in here, too, muscling aside the few meager kitchen appliances. Emerson's eyes automatically went to the door that led to what he supposed was the old man's bedroom. It was closed.

"Is your wife in?" he asked, feigning small talk.

The old man gave him a strange look, as if Emerson mentioning his wife worried him in some way he could not quite grasp.

"No. She's gone shopping. I thought you were her. Thought she forgot her key."

So they were alone. Good.

"Do you have it?"

Again the look. "Of course I have it. I would not have called you if I did not have it."

"I want to see it first."

The old man nodded and hobbled over to the kitchen table, which was slightly bowlegged from the weight of the books stacked atop it. He reached into the jumble and, without hesitation, pulled out an oversized leather-bound volume with a reinforced metal spine and hasps. He turned and handed it to Emerson with a sneer of disgust he did nothing to hide. Emerson wiped his hands and tried his best to control their trembling. It would not do to have the old man know just how important the damned book was to him.

And damned was right.

The Aegrisomnia. The fabled tome written by a dying alchemist-wizard 1200 years ago while in the grips of brain fever. It was believed to be filled with rantings, ramblings, and recipes for power. More power than a man could dream of and remain sane.

Of course, what Emerson was holding was not the original manuscript. That had been put to the torch by the Borgia pope over five centuries ago, after he'd had it transcribed into Latin by a brace of specially trained monks — all of whom later committed suicide or were found floating in the Tiber under mysterious circumstances. The Latin version was later translated into German by a priest who secretly sympathized with Martin Luther and apparently thought the Reformation would fare better if it had access to some of the "forbidden knowledge" the Holy Cee had been hoarding for the last millennium.

In 1909 a British scholar of the name Stroud translated the *Aegrisomnia* into English. Stroud was an eccentric, but far from the harmless Oxford don that he appeared to be, proving himself dedicated to the Black Arts in ways popinjays like Crowley and Blavatsky merely played at.

Of the hundred expurgated copies of the *Aegrisomnia* that Stroud had privately published, however, only one was complete and unabridged. And bound in leather. And that was Stroud's private copy — the one with his own personal annotations scrawled in the margins. The one he had bound himself — with the skin of his virgin daughter. Granted, she wasn't his *legitimate* daughter — her mother was a marginally retarded scullery maid who had been with the household since childhood — but the gesture put to the pale anything the self-styled "Beast" had ever done.

Stroud was eventually found out, years later, when the buzz bomb that took out his London rowhouse and rammed a length of timber through his chest also uncovered a child's skeleton sealed behind the library bookshelves. Many of the "demon don's" books and papers were consumed by fire that night, and since it was never found, it was assumed that Stroud's personal copy of the *Aegrisomnia* was been one of the casualties. But then, after the war, rumors began to circulate of the book being glimpsed in South America, then again in Australia, then Canada....

Emerson had followed these rumors with the utmost interest. He had spent his entire adult life acquiring books and manuscripts many believed lost — if not apocryphal. He had devoted every waking hour — and nearly every dime of his inheritance — to the study of things most people either dismissed out of hand or feared so intensely they preferred not to contemplate them at all. And now, after all this time, he had his hands on the last piece of the puzzle. The masterpiece that would lock all the others into place and render the unknowable known unto him.

Emerson caressed the bastard-child leather as he opened the book, his gaze hungrily darting along the yellowed pages. He closed his eyes and the formulae blazed against his inner lids. Yes. This was indeed the real thing. He opened his eyes and found the old man looking at him as if he were a distasteful animal suddenly transported into his dingy kitchen. Emerson snapped the book shut.

"Have you looked at this?" he asked, trying to mask the anxiety in his voice.

The old man shook his head. "It's mumbo-jumbo. My wife likes to read things like that—" he motioned to a stack of old Fate magazines teetering precariously atop the draining board. "Me, I'd rather read fiction. There's more truth in fiction. I don't even like touching the thing. I know human leather when I see it. I had a book come through here a few years back — belonged to some bastard in the Nazi High Command. It was pornographic pictures — women with animals, men with children. It was bound just like that. I burned it. I would have burned that thing too, if I didn't need the money so badly—"

Emerson fought the urge to giggle in the old man's face. The fool! He had no idea what he had just surrendered for a mere three hundred dollars! No doubt his idea of a real find was a first edition of *Alice's Adventures Underground* or an autographed copy of *Northanger Abbey*. Emerson decided to allow himself a little pleasure at the old man's expense. After all, it wasn't like the book dealer had ever shown anything resembling the respect due him.

"Tell me — haven't you ever wondered what it would be like to, say, rule the world or to turn back the clock and become young again — perhaps even cheat death altogether?"

The old man allowed himself a smile and the lines around his mouth and eyes softened. "Ha! Now you're starting to sound like my wife! She asks me silly things like that. And I'll tell you the same thing I tell her: who needs the aggravation? You'd spend all your time dealing with all the *other* people who want to rule the world. And why would I want to be young — so I can grow old all over again? And as for living forever — how could I be happy watching everyone I loved and cared about die and leave me alone? Is that something to look forward to — being a mourner? God knows, my life may not be perfect, but at least it will have a beginning and an end. Just like my books. And as long as I have them and my wife, I can make do without immortality or ruling the world."

"And how does your wife react when you tell her this?"

"She smiles." The old man's face grew stern again. "Did you bring the money?"

Emerson nodded and reached into his jacket, producing a small envelope, which he handed to the old man. "As we agreed."

The old man opened the envelope and counted the bills. He looked up, his pale cheeks suddenly hectic with color. "This isn't enough!"

"What do you mean it isn't enough? You told me three hundred! That's three hundred."

The old man was shaking his head. "No, I told you when I called to let you know I'd secured the book that it ended up costing more than what I first quoted you. I need five hundred."

A spark of panic burst within Emerson. The three hundred had been the last of his inheritance. He only had fifty-six dollars left in his bank account. "I'll pay you the remainder in a couple of days — I'm good for it—"

"No! I spent the rent on that book! You give me five hundred or you get nothing!" The old man shoved the envelope back at Emerson and grabbed the book and tugged on it feebly.

A mixture of fear and rage filled Emerson, blotting out all else in his mind. He yanked the book free of the old man's palsied grip and, his lips pulled back into a rictus that exposed his teeth all the way to the gum line, he brought the spine down on the book dealer's head. He actually felt the old man's skull give way. The old man dropped lifeless to the floor, his snowy-white hair stained brilliant red.

Emerson stared down at the corpse for a long moment. He clutched the *Aegrisomnia* to his chest much the same way Stroud had held his daughter before he slipped the knife between her ribs, nearly ninety years ago.

It was his now. His. And no one was going to take it away from him. Ever.

Emerson's apartment, at first glance, was not all that different from the old man's front room. The efficiency was filled to bursting with books, many of them quite old and exceptionally rare. The shelves that lined the walls were crammed full of tomes dedicated to occult lore. Some were relatively prosaic, such as Crowley's *Magick: In Theory and Practice*, Huysmans' *La-Bas*, Frazer's *Golden Bough*, and Kramer & Sprenger's *Malleus Maleficarum*. Others were comparatively new additions to the apocrypha, such as *The Liber Null*, *The Psychick Bible*, and *The Leyden Papyrus*.

However, Abdul Alhazred's *Necronomicon*, Von Junzt's *Unausprechlichen Kulten*, Prinn's *De Vermis Mysteriis*, the Comte d'Erlette's *Cultes des Goules*, Gantley's *Hydrophinnae*, Carson's *The Black God of Madness*, *The Book of Eibon*, the *Pnakotic Manuscripts*, the *Cthaat Aquadingen*, and *The Revelations of Glaaki* were far from innocuous. Or cheap.

Emerson had literally spent a fortune in acquiring them. Over the years, as his money dwindled, he had been forced to take lodgings that were far from the sumptuous appointments of his upbringing. Of his mother's physical estate, all that was left was a large mirrored wardrobe, which dominated one corner of the room. Everything else had been sold off, piece by piece, in order to provide him with cash for his precious books of forbidden lore. And now, after close to thirty years, he was on the threshold of capturing the power he'd pursued for so long.

Emerson swept aside the jumble of concordances, foreign-language dictionaries, and lexicons littering the table that served as both his desk and dining area, and placed the *Aegrisomnia* down. Tonight would be the start of his ascension. All the scraps and whispers of information he'd gleaned from the other books and manuscripts would now be stitched together, providing him with a shining raiment suited for a wizard-king.

He flipped open the book and shook his head in amazement. Even in a debased translation such as this, the innate power of the charms and spells recorded was staggering. What had the original been like? Just by skimming the chapters, he saw formulae and rituals detailing the conjuring of extradimensional beings, the transferal of souls into the newborn, the mastery of the weather....

Yet he couldn't help but wonder why Stroud, who had understood the importance of the forces described in the *Aegrisomnia* to such an extent that he'd wrapped it in his daughter's skin, had not used it to further his own ends. Granted, Stroud was close to eighty when he died in 1941, but he was far from youthful or immortal. And while he'd enjoyed his share of fame and honors during the course of his long and illustrious career, he'd lived out his life in a two-bedroom rowhouse in an appallingly middle-class neighborhood.

No matter. Whatever fears Stroud may have had against wielding the power of the *Aegrisomnia*, Emerson did not share them. He could not understand how someone could have power and not use it. Then again, there was a lot about people Emerson did not understand. It was one of the reasons he'd never developed any friends. Not even as a boy.

The last, fading blossom of a once-powerful family, Emerson's mother had raised him to consider himself better than others, and he had learned the lesson well. Toward the end, he considered his mother beneath him as well, as she had married into the Emersons and not been born one. It made pulling the plug on her life-support system rather simple.

Emerson smiled to himself. Soon he would replace his dreary studio apartment with a pleasure dome that would put Xanadu to shame! He would dine on the most succulent of dishes, relieve his physical needs with only the most beautiful of women and boys — and the heads of everyone who had ever crossed him, cursed him, or looked at him the wrong way would decorate the pikes lining the roads leading to his palace. Yes. He rather liked that image.

There was a sudden thumping at the door. Emerson jumped in his seat, startled by the noise.

"Mr. Emerson—? Open up — police! We want to talk to you, Mr. Emerson!"

A spike of fear made his guts clench. The police! But how could they have known to come looking for him? Of course. The old man's wife. He must have told her about who was coming to pick up the book. Damn! He should have stayed long enough to finish her off, too! But he'd been frightened and anxious to return home and start work on his ascension....

The thudding intensified. "Mr. Emerson—? Please come to the door, Mr. Emerson!"

Emerson's mouth was too dry to respond. Not now. Not after all the time and money he'd spent on locating the *Aegrisomnia*, only to have it taken away from him at the very moment of his triumph—! There had to be a way he could escape capture! There had to be—!

Even though he knew there was only one door in and out of the apartment, Emerson instinctively glanced around the room. His eye fell on his mother's old wardrobe with its full-length mirror set in the door.

Mirror.

Something sparked in the back of his head. He'd seen something about mirrors in the book, hadn't he? He flipped back a few pages — yes! Here it was. A spell that allowed the practitioner access to and from "the Land of the Reflected Ones." The formula was simple enough for one as skilled as he.

There was a much heavier thump on the other side of the door. The police had stopped using their fists and were now applying their shoulders. However, Emerson had invested in a top-of-the-line set of deadbolts, for fear of the other tenants in the building breaking into his room while he was gone. The police would need one of those portable battering rams to get the door open. That meant he had just enough time to effect his escape.

Emerson stood in front of the wardrobe. The mirror was well over a hundred years old and thicker than any other he'd ever seen. It was slightly convex, protruding a good three inches from its setting. He remembered how his mother used to stand in front of it and primp herself, rattling on about the days when their family had ruled the town with a steel grip. Emerson took a deep breath to steady himself and closed his eyes, reciting the formula, making the proper gestures and invoking the names of nameless gods. When he reopened his eyes, the surface of the mirror had been transformed into something that rippled like water, yet glinted silver.

There was a thunderous crack from behind him as the deadbolts finally gave. Without looking back, Emerson stepped into the mirror.

His first impression was that he was being buried alive in gelatin; then he opened his eyes and saw silver fluid rippling around him like mercury; then he was standing in his room again. His first thought was that he'd failed. That he'd hallucinated the whole thing. Then he realized he was looking in the direction of the front door. He turned around and stared back the way he came. In place of the back wall of his apartment, with its bookshelves and piles of dirty clothes, there was a blank expanse — blank, that is, except for an oblong opening outlined in silvery light. Of course. How could there be a wardrobe on this side? A mirror does not reflect itself.

As he stared out of the mirror into his real-world apartment, the door flew inward and two policemen, their guns drawn, came into the room. Their mirror-images burst into the mirror-room at the exact same time, and Emerson cried out in alarm. But the mirror-police did not seem to see him, even though he was standing right in front of them. At first Emerson was puzzled, then he realized that of course they wouldn't know he was there, since their real-world counterparts did not see him, either. Unless they happened to look in the mirror.

Emerson quickly moved to one side of the silvery doorway, pressing himself against the blank wall. He seriously doubted the police had the imagination to realize their prey had escaped through the looking glass, but he wasn't going to risk detection. Besides, he could keep track of what the police were doing by watching their mirror-reverse doppelgangers.

Satisfied the mirror-room was empty, the mirror-cops motioned for a little old lady to enter. The old man's wife. One of the mirror-cops pointed to the *Aegrisomnia*, still sitting open on the table. Emerson strained to hear what the mirror-cop was asking the mirror-woman, but his voice was twisted around so it sounded like he was talking backward underwater. No doubt he was asking her if this was the book her husband had procured for his customer. The mirror-woman shook her head "no."

Emerson frowned. Strange. The old man had spoken as if his wife was aware of what he was selling. Perhaps the old man hadn't shown her the book for fear of her becoming angry over the money he'd spent. Or perhaps he didn't want her becoming upset over the human skin binding.

One of the mirror-cops was scratching his head and looking around the room. He was bothered by the fact there was no one in a room double-bolted from the inside. As the mirror-cops huddled near the doorway to talk among themselves, the mirror-woman remained by the table. At first Emerson could not make out what she was doing. Then, to his surprise, he realized she was reading the *Aegrisomnia*.

Sweat began to bead on his forehead and lip. Surely the old woman knew nothing of the secrets locked within the arcane formulae. He began to chew on his thumbnail. Just as he'd succeeded in convincing himself she was simply an old woman and nothing more, she looked up from her reading and stared directly into the mirror. Although she could not see him, Emerson knew she was looking for him.

As the mirror-woman slowly approached, moving closer and closer to where Emerson cowered, his back pressed against the other side of a wall that didn't exist, he could hear the old man's voice ringing in his ears: *My wife likes to read that stuff.* It had never crossed Emerson's mind that the old man's wife might be a sorceress.

The mirror-woman was standing right beside Emerson, but she did not see him. Instead, she stared straight ahead, peering through the silver doorway into the real world. The mirror-cops were still talking among themselves, paying her no mind as she rummaged through her handbag. After a few seconds she retrieved a small, colorless wax crayon, the type used to scrawl designs on children's Easter eggs. Her wrinkled lips moved slightly as she mumbled something that even backward and underwater was recognizable to Emerson as an invocation. As she called upon the nameless gods, the old woman made a series of markings on the mirror. Once finished, the old woman's reflection smiled to itself and headed out the door, followed shortly thereafter by the puzzled policemen.

The moment the door closed on them, Emerson peeled himself away from the wall and stood in front of the silvery doorway. His view of the world outside its borders was now obscured by a series of lines that pulsed with a dark power. He reached out to touch the inner surface of the mirror, but there was a loud, sharp sound, like that of an electric bug-light frying a particularly large fly, and a burst of purplish-black energy. Pain shot up Emerson's fingers and into his arm, causing him to jump back.

The old woman had sealed him in.

Emerson began to tremble. He was trapped. Trapped.

He took a deep breath and tried to calm himself. He couldn't think like that. Thinking like that led to panic. And panic would get him nowhere. He was not trapped. How could he be? She was just an old woman. He, on the other hand, was an Emerson. And everyone knew an Emerson was better than anyone else. There was no way he could be outfoxed, outmaneuvered, outdone by an old woman. Even an old woman who'd mastered the *Aegrisomnia*.

The *Aegrisomnia*. Of course.

The original might still be in the real world, but he had access to its mirror-twin! He moved to the duplicate table. Yes, it was still here. The police had not taken it with them. At least, not yet. All he had to do was to find a counterspell to override the old woman's hastily constructed barrier....

Emerson's grin of triumph collapsed as he opened the book and stared down at the mirror-*Aegrisomnia's* pages. The print was in reverse. The panic threatened to overwhelm him again, but he forced it back down.

Okay. So the words were printed backward and in reverse. He would simply hold it up to the mirror and — but no. There was only one mirror in his room — and he was in it. A hysterical giggle burst from his lips.

Emerson bit the inside of his mouth so hard it brought blood. No! He refused to believe he was trapped! *Refused!* He was an intelligent man; he could figure out the problem placed before him if he just calmed down. He needed a drink, that was all. Yes, a drink would help steady his nerves and set his mind to the task he was about to undertake.

The wardrobe was situated in such a way that it reflected almost the entire room, including his humble cot. He kept a pint of scotch under the mattress for moments when he needed it.... But did that mean there was one in this world as well? Emerson reached under the duplicate of his bed, uncertain of what he'd find, and was relieved when his fingers closed around the glass surface of a bottle.

Emerson smiled at the pint of scotch as if it were a long-lost friend and hurriedly cracked the seal. Just to steady his nerves. That's all. Help him think. He tilted his head back and slugged back a double shot — and immediately spewed it out.

The stuff tasted like a cross between cat piss and gasoline. Granted, it was a cheap brand, but this was ridiculous! Emerson wiped his mouth with his sleeve and stared at the bottle. The print on the label was the same as that of the original — except it was reversed. Along with its molecular structure, apparently.

Mirror reverse. The Land of the Reflected Ones. But *he* wasn't a reflection. He was the real thing. And there was no way he could eat or drink in this world without poisoning himself.

Emerson scrambled back over to the table, clawing through the clutter for scrap paper and a pencil. He'd copy the formula out of the book by hand, transposing the words so he could read from it. It would take time, but he had no other choice. He had to get out before he starved to death or died of thirst.

Emerson worked for two solid hours, fearful every minute that someone would walk into the real-world room and see him in the mirror. Not that they would believe what they saw, but it would still prove a distraction and cost him precious time. When he was finished, Emerson stood in front of the silvery doorway and read aloud from the paper. He then waited for the dark lines crisscrossing the mirror's inner surface to disappear.

Nothing happened.

He repeated the spell, placing the accent on different syllables.

Still more nothing happened.

What was wrong? He'd made all the proper hand signals, invoked the correct gods and demiurges....

Then he remembered how the mirror-replicas of the police and old woman had sounded when they spoke, like skewed tape-loops played backward. Mirror-speak. The Language of the Reflected Ones. But he wasn't a reflection. He was the real thing. And he talked forward in a world where magical spells only worked if they were spoken not just backward, but in reverse.

The panic resurfaced a third time and Emerson made no attempt to quell it. He began weeping and cursing at the top of his lungs and raced around the room, kicking over the furniture and knocking the books off their shelves.

Trapped. Trapped! *Trapped!*

After he'd exhausted himself, he stood gasping for breath, his hands planted on his knees. When he looked up, his gaze fell on the mirror-door. In the real world, it led out into the dingy, urine-stained hallway of his apartment building. But where did it lead in the Land of the Reflected Ones? To another mirror, perhaps? It was worth finding out. Anything was better than being trapped in the reflection of his grimy studio apartment.

Since the police had battered in the original, the mirror-door was unlocked. Instead of the hallway outside his apartment, however, a sea of seething shadow and swirling mist filled the threshold. And in the roiling, formless chaos, something lifted something not unlike a head and opened things that might be called eyes. And smiled at him.

Emerson screamed and slammed the door, his fingers scrambling to try and secure locks and deadbolts that were no longer functional. Babbling prayers and pleas to gods he'd abandoned as a child, Emerson raced to the silver doorway that led from the mirror-world into his own. There was a burst of purplish light and the smell of ozone as he was hurled backward. Emerson groaned as he lay on the floor of the reflected apartment, the smell of smoke rising from his singed hair and clothes. He was dully aware of having soiled his pants.

He found himself wishing he'd bothered to read Alice Through the Looking-Glass. Maybe it would have helped prepare him for his own ordeal in the land of reflections. But he seriously doubted Alice had been confronted by anything as disturbing as whatever it was that lurked on his threshold.

The *Aegrisomnia* had referred to the other side of the mirror as "The Land of the Reflected Ones." And he, after all the metaphysical and mystical studies he'd made over the years, had never once wondered what might fill a mirror when there was one there to look into it.

But, judging from the rattle of the doorknob, he would soon know.

THE LAND OF THE REFLECTED ONES

W
I
L
L
I
A
M

F

B
U
C
K
L
E
Y

J
R

THE TEMPTATION OF WILFRED MALACHEY

hen Wilfred Malachey was sent off to boarding school at Brookfield, he went by train. The Malacheys had been forced to sell the family automobile when his father's most recent manuscript was rejected. The publishers, Hatfield & Hatfield, had told him it wouldn't sell, because "Nobody wants to read about the Vietnam war." It had been four years since his father had sold a book. Six months before the fall term at Brookfield Academy began, the family had moved from Manhattan to a two-room apartment in Queens.

One night, Wilfred overheard his mother and father talking about Brookfield. His father said: "I don't care if I go into debt for the rest of my life, Will is going to Brookfield. Period!" When Wilfred's father spoke that way (sometimes he banged his fist on the table, but only after a couple of beers) there was nothing to be done about it, and Mrs. Malachey would simply shrug her shoulders and change the subject.

On the train, Wilfred's mother told him they could send him only five dollars every month. Wilfred said that five dollars wouldn't keep him in chewing gum.

"In that case, Wilfred, you're going to have to cut down on your chewing gum," his mother snapped.

Wilfred said — to himself: his mother did not take any lip from Wilfred — that he would find other ways to live the way the Brookfield boys lived. "If at Brookfield they're human," Wilfred muttered. "Which I doubt." He was feeling grouchy, and a little nervous, going to Brookfield for the first time.

The Brookfield community was aware that things had gone badly for the school during recent years. Everything went wrong that could go wrong: the pipes had burst in the main building; the large barn that housed the student activities center had burned almost to the ground (of course, the school was underinsured); the new tractor with which the vegetable gardens and the corn were tended during the summer had suddenly ceased to work, and by the time it was fixed the damage to the gardens and fields was irreversible. "The place seems haunted," said Xavier Prum, Headmaster.

Brookfield was well north in Vermont, so that the winters came early, and Wilfred was happy at his first opportunity to learn ice-skating. One day, with some excitement after the first snowfall, he signed up on the bulletin board to ski. The athletic director, Mr. Kiphuth, handed an application form to Wilfred and asked him to sign a slip authorizing one hundred dollars to be charged to his parents.

Wilfred looked up. He lowered the pencil onto the table. "I think," he said to Mr. Kiphuth, "I'll just stick to skating." Mr. Kiphuth looked at Wilfred and said nothing. That night, at faculty tea, Mr. Kiphuth asked the Headmaster whether young Malachey's family was especially hard up. Xavier Prum answered, "If you ask me, Bob Malachey is flat broke. He's a has-been as a writer."

"How's he paying for Wilfred's tuition?"

"I'll tell you after he makes the payment for the rest of the semester. All I have from him" — and this was near to Thanksgiving — "is his deposit of last July. Either the remaining tuition comes in before Christmas, or Wilfred will have to do his ice-skating in Queens. We just aren't in a position to extend charity."

Kiphuth said that was too bad. "A bright boy. George Eggleston tells me he's a whiz in computers."

"Well, maybe Malachey will invent a computer game and bail out his old man," the Headmaster said, picking up the *Brookfield Academy News* to read about last month's hockey victory over St. Paul's.

It was about then that Wilfred Malachey decided to take up seriously the matter of his personal poverty. He thought a great deal about it and carefully studied the habits of his fellow students, most of whom clearly were not worried about expenses. Josiah Regnery, for instance, Josiah received a monthly allowance of one hundred dollars from his father and often took two or three boys to the Creamery, the local drugstore, for ice cream sundaes.

Josiah was a chubby, good-natured boy who was easily distracted. When

Mr. Eggleston was trying to teach him geometry, Josiah would simply stare into space. One afternoon, when the trees all around them were red and gold, he told Wilfred as they were skating that he was quite apprehensive about math exam coming up at midterm. "To tell you the truth, Wilfred, I don't know the difference between an issasselese triangle and an equilateral triangle."

Wilfred smiled as he maneuvered the puck they were idling along the ice. "What's so hard about remembering that an equilateral triangle is equal — get that, equal? equal? — on all three sides?"

"Okay," Josiah said. "But what about the issasselese triangle? What's that?"

Wilfred took Josiah's hockey stick from him and laid it out on the ice, positioning his own so that the handle touched Josiah's at an angle of about forty-five degrees. "There. Our two sticks are the same size, the two sides of an isosceles — that's i-s-o-s-c-e-l-e-s — triangle are the same size. What's so hard about that?"

"What's hard," said Josiah, "is to remember it all. All I can remember is that there'll be time after practice and before study hall to go to the Creamery for a butterscotch sundae. What do you say?"

"I'm broke right now."

"I'll pay. You teach me about triangles, you get one butterscotch sundae."

"You know," Josiah said as they sat in the little booth, the light snowfall breaking up the bright afternoon sun, "I think I could figure out a way for you to take my midterm exam. It's just *this* simple...."

Josiah had, in fact, figured it all out.

There were no fixed seating arrangements in the classrooms where exams were held at Brookfield. All that would be needed was for Wilfred to manage to sit down, casually, at a desk next to Josiah's. Wilfred, Josiah explained, would then write down the answers to each of the exam problems on a sheet of scratch paper. Then he would spill his scratch pad on the floor, having detached the top sheet from the pad before it was dropped. He would then simply bend over and pick up the scratch pad, leaving the detached sheet on the floor.

A moment later, Josiah would lean down, pick up the sheet with the answers on it and copy Wilfred's solutions in his own exam book.

"It's worth twenty dollars to me," Josiah said, intending to close the question.

Somewhat to his surprise — cheating was simply not one of the things the Malachey set thought it quite right to do — Wilfred hesitated. Cheating was one of the things one, well, one wasn't supposed to do. On the other hand, one was not supposed to be — how did his father put it? — "one's brother's keeper." He wrestled with the conflict, but eased toward the feeling that, after all, he wasn't personally responsible for other boys' behavior. "Okay," he said.

That night, lying on his bed after Lights Out, Wilfred chatted with his roommate, Steven Umanov. Steve was a quiet, studious, no-nonsense boy. His parents had come to America from Russia soon after the World War. Steve's father was a nuclear physicist who worked for the Defense Department. Steve took great pride in this. He confessed to Wilfred that he, too, hoped to become a great scientist, "Like my dad." Wilfred was feeling argumentative and maybe a little disillusioned because he hadn't straightened out in his own mind the deal he had made with Josiah.

"How do you know your father is a great scientist?" Wilfred asked belligerently.

Steve hardly expected that claims about his father's prowess would be questioned. "How do I know it? I *know* it, that's all. Maybe one day your father will write a book about my father, assuming your father hasn't forgotten how to write books!"

All of Wilfred, which came to 120 pounds, sprang across the dark room onto Steven Umanov, whose body he pounded with clenched fists until the dorm master came barging in, swearing in that careful way peculiar to prep-school masters (none of the serious stuff). "*Damn it, damn it I said!* I said damn it! What in the hell is going on, you...dumb...kids! Cut the damn business out...!"

Mr. McGiffert separated them. He told them he would place them both in the boxing ring the next day, so they could "get the resentments out of their system." "I hope you knock each other out," he added. Mr. McGiffert told them if he heard one more sound from Room 28, he would lead them to the Headmaster. "You'll see what Mr. Prum has to say about this kind of...uncivilized...behavior. Maybe he'll take away your Thanksgiving privileges. Just don't say Mr. McGiffert didn't warn you."

Wilfred didn't sleep much that night. He bitterly resented Steve's crack about his old man. But he also figured the best way to protect his father was to act as though Robert Malachey, the well-known author, was engaged in a long-term research project and was taking very good financial care of his son. "Foreign royalties," he decided he would say, casually. Ah, all those books that Robert Malachey had written in the past twenty years, translated into all the usual languages...plus Swedish, and, er, Hindustani, and Japanese, and Australian. "The royalties," he would teach himself to say, "do mount up, you know."

Wilfred decided he would devote all his energies to doing something concrete about his disadvantages. He would become a — he toyed with the word — thief. Not a nice word. So instantly he stopped using it. Instead he thought of himself as Robin Hood, the great English woodsman. At Fire Island he had seen an old Robin Hood movie with Errol Flynn. Flynn was unmistakably the hero of the movie, who would question that? Robin Hood took money from the fat rich in order to give it to the lean poor! True, in this case Wilfred would be taking from the rich to give to Wilfred; but since he himself was poor, that would not matter. And if there was money left over, he would give it to other poor boys — he knew that Tony Cobb had a hard time of it, also Red Evans. He would find ways to make life easier for them. The point now, having decided he was not really a thief, was to become a very clever thief — or rather, a very clever Robin Hood.

The important thing, of course, was not to get caught. If Errol Flynn had been caught, he would have been hanged. Hanged right there, in the public square at Nottingham. Led up the thirteen steps (thirteen steps? or was that the Tower of London, where they executed all those wives of Henry the VIII?), clump, clump, clump, up those steps, however many there were, then the executioner approaches you with a kind of ski hood, only it goes right over your eyes, and then — after you have a chance to say a prayer — BANG! the floor under your feet evaporates, and that is the end of Robin Hood.

Lying in his bed that night, Wilfred knew he would not be hanged if caught, but he knew it would be very unpleasant. His mother would be very disappointed, to say the least, and his father would never again talk about the Malacheys' tradition of going to Brookfield Academy.

And then, returning to the point at which he had begun his thinking that night, he turned his head toward where Steven Umanov was sleeping and said to himself: "Steven Umanov, your father may be a great scientist. But he is also the father of a boy at Brookfield Academy who will soon be poorer than he is now."

Before the week was over, Wilfred had eased two dollars out of Steve's wallet.

"Two dollars. That way he won't notice," Wilfred said to himself. His confidence growing, he allowed himself a smile. For one thing, Errol Flynn always smiled. The greater the danger, the greater the smile.

After Thanksgiving, Wilfred was named Sunday Services collector, for the balance of the term, his jurisdiction being the left side of the Brookfield Chapel. The Headmaster had made it a point with the parents that the boys at Brookfield were expected to contribute to the Sunday collections ("even if it's only a nickel") so that they get used to the idea of giving *something*.

Wilfred's half of the church — one hundred boys, twenty or thirty faculty, staff and visiting parents — usually contributed in the neighborhood of sixty dollars. On a particular Sunday, that figure minus four dollars was what was turned in by Wilfred Malachey to the Matron in the sacristy.

Wilfred considered volunteering for regular duty, year-round, as a Sunday Services collector.

Around the same time, he began complaining of headaches to the Matron. There was talk, when the school doctor could find nothing wrong, of sending him to Redlined for a thorough examination; then always the headaches, after a troublesome day or so, would go away. The Matron was persuaded that they were caused by an allergy and nothing to worry about.

And so it was that during the afternoons, when the Matron excused him (because of his headaches) from regular athletic activity, Wilfred would make the rounds of the deserted dormitory rooms. He counted it an average day when he cleared between ten and fifteen dollars. His problem at the bursar's office was eased when his mother, just after Thanksgiving, sent in a check for the semester's tuition, Wilfred having no idea how his mother had got hold of two thousand dollars.

By February, Wilfred Malachey was skiing regularly. He had even qualified for the slalom competition at Stowe. Occasionally he would treat one or two of the boys to sundaes at the Creamery. He was frustrated by his inability to take math examinations more often for Josiah Regnery, who was now paying a hefty fifty bucks per exam. But he had not figured out a way to take more exams for Josiah than Josiah had to take. Cheating for more than one person was risky, really risky; and Wilfred was determined not to take unnecessary risks. Unlike Robin Hood — who could go to the center of the town, with minimal disguise and only his bow and arrow and horse, and smite the enemy to the ground and ride triumphantly away — Wilfred had no horse, no bow or arrow, and no sanctuary. He had to be very, very careful.

It had been widely noticed that when George Eggleston came back from the Christmas holidays, he was driving a new Mercedes 380SL. It was obvious to everyone that Mr. Eggleston could not possibly have purchased that car on the salary of a math teacher at Brookfield Academy.

George Eggleston had passed the word that an aunt he never really knew (hence his lighthearted attitude toward her) had "departed from this vale of tears," leaving him a little legacy. "I blew it all on this Mercedes," he said happily.

Two weeks later, the boys who were studying computers got the astonishing news that Brookfield Academy would any day now have an IBM Mainframe Computer, an astonishing, luxury, state-of-the-art 4341, worth half a million dollars!

How had Brookfield been so fortunate?

George Eggleston explained at a faculty meeting that over the summer vacation he had been in conversation with a wealthy Brookfield alumnus who, learning about his ambitious computer instruction program, decided to make a donation. The donor had imposed a single condition, namely, the requirement of anonymity.

"Yes, yes, George," the Headmaster had said to Eggleston when they were alone in his office. "I know all about alumni and anonymity. But there is no such thing as anonymity from the Headmaster. So. Who gave us the IBM?"

George Eggleston, not in the least apologetic, said he had given his word and could not betray the identity of the benefactor.

"He will have to remain anonymous, Mr. Prum." (All the junior masters called the Headmaster "Mr. Prum.")

Mr. Prum let it go. Actually, he had no alternative.

Wilfred Malachey would not have known about this controversy in the administrative circles of Brookfield, except that Mr. Eggleston elected to chat with him about it, repeating (dramatically) the details. Wilfred had taken to staying in the computer hall after class, which went from eleven to twelve o'clock with lunch at a quarter to one. Wilfred stayed those extra forty-five minutes to watch Mr. Eggleston perform one after another of those seemingly magical feats the computer manuals were coaxing Wilfred to try. Before long, Wilfred had been catapulted way beyond what the manuals had intended.

During the Christmas holidays, Wilfred gave up a car trip to Disney World (his father was writing a travel piece for the *New York Times*) when Mr. Trevor, Frankie's father, passed on the word through his son that if Wilfred wanted to, he could spend his days at Mr. Trevor's office in the Chrysler Building. Mr. Trevor was a computer consultant, and in his office kept the latest models, to test them and to write manuals on how to operate them. Although Mr. Trevor was very enthusiastic about his work, he had never been able to interest Frankie. So when he discovered that Frankie's friend Wilfred was "a computer nut," the invitation had been tendered, for over two weeks, Wilfred lived with computers, putting them through their paces, making notes of what Mr. Trevor taught him.

By late February, Wilfred was in the habit of spending his non-classroom time (when he was not required by the athletic director to be at the hockey rink) in the computer hall, prepared to spend hours there exploring the latest challenges Mr. Eggleston had suggested to him.

Wilfred had long since been introduced to programming, first with BASIC, then with Pascal. Now his mind was crowded with possibilities. He wanted to press his knowledge of computer science as far and as fast as he could.

He had made up with Steven Umanov. Now, when Lights Out sounded, he said goodnight to the dorm master at 10:15; then he stuffed a pillow under his bedsheets, put on pants and a sweater and, with the cooperation of Steven, who would cover for him if a proctor came around to check ("He's in the bathroom"), tiptoed out of the dorm. Setting his course through the shadows, outside the lights that illuminated the Brookfield Quadrangle and the great oak trees scattered about the main buildings, he would make his way to the computer hall, lodged in the tower of the Flagler Building, next to the astronomy lab. He was prepared to spend hours there as he had done earlier tonight. He had Mr. Eggleston's extra key to the hall, given to him a month earlier when Wilfred, after spending five consecutive hours on a project, managed to reverse an incredibly intricate program that Mr. Eggleston had mistakenly got himself locked into.

"You deserve this, Wilfred," Mr. Eggleston had said. "Use the computer whenever you want it."

Wilfred worked two hours and felt suddenly sleepy. He decided to nap rather than return to his room; he wanted to get on with the program he had so nearly completed.

He was excited about this, as he had taken up celestial navigation the summer before on Fire Island. Wilfred wondered whether he could program the computer to give him the name of any given star, provided that he entered the angle of that star, the exact time he spotted it and his estimated location within thirty miles. His father's last successful novel (ten years ago) had been about a husband and wife who were sailing the South Pacific when she fell overboard one night while he was off watch. The husband woke up and tried desperately to retrace the boat's path, but got mixed up because he didn't know which star was which.

The problem had stayed in Wilfred's mind, and Mr. Eggleston had suggested a formula by which the question might be attacked. Wilfred had sent away to the library at the University of Vermont for the Almanac and the Star Reduction Guide.

But right now he had to close his eyes. He walked the half-dozen steps from the computer desk to the old couch that rested at the corner of the room. After removing the pile of magazines and books, as several times he had done before, he stretched out and was soon asleep.

He woke suddenly. The door had creaked open. He heard the cold wind whistling outside. He looked at his watch; it was after two in the morning. Even Mr. Eggleston, so informal and permissive, would be angered if he found him up at this hour, and might even suspend his privileges. He sat up noiselessly on the couch and reasoned that if he simply stayed quiet, in the dark corner on the couch, chances were that Mr. Eggleston would do whatever he intended to do at this odd hour and then leave, after which Wilfred could return, undetected, to his dormitory.

George Eggleston walked stealthily into the room, went up to the computer and snapped on the main switch.

He reached down to the bottom drawer on the left side and pulled it open. He took out a little aluminum box. From his pocket he took out a key and opened the box. He pulled out a notebook and an eight-inch floppy disk.

He inserted the disk into a drive in the mainframe.

The large screen leapt to life, and from his seat ten feet away Wilfred had no difficulty seeing what it was that George Eggleston was typing. He was carefully copying out a formula that appeared on the screen as he punched it in.

It was, of course, pure gibberish. Except that Wilfred knew that in computer language there is no such thing as gibberish. He knew that things like "ad4af5ag8pp/" could be used, as his father would say, "to make sense out of a *New York Times* editorial."

But why all the secrecy? Why the locked notebook, and the locked floppy disk?

After he had copied the long formula, George Eggleston brought his right index finger down on the RETURN key.

The screen seemed to go wild. It filled with lines, then radials, then bright colors that grew gradually pale, and from the center a tiny white dot, the size of a pinhead, gradually increased in circumference to the size of a full moon that touched all four sides of the screen.

Slowly, the words appeared on the center of the screen:

"WHAT DO YOU WANT FROM THE OMEGAGOD?"

George Eggleston looked down quickly at his little notebook and copied out: *"You are the Omegagod and I am your faithful servant George Eggleston."* He then lifted his eyes from the notebook and wrote out: *"I want Marjorie Gifford to fall in love with me."*

On the screen there was no action. It was as if the Omegagod were weighing Mr. Eggleston's request. Suddenly the capital letters began to appear: "IT SHALL BE SO. BUT DO NOT CALL ME AGAIN FOR THIRTY DAYS."

Wilfred could hear Mr. Eggleston breathing deeply. He pushed the RETURN key. Then he withdrew the disk tenderly from the IBM's disk drive, replaced it in the aluminum box together with the little notebook and turned off the main computer. He walked back to the entrance of the room, switched off the light and was gone in the great swish of air that blew in as he opened and then closed the door.

Wilfred waited ten minutes before easing himself out the door. He looked carefully about for the wandering night watchman, then treaded softly but determinedly through the windstorm to the South Dorm. He dove into his bed and into a deep sleep, from which Steve Umanov needed to shake him vigorously the next day at Morning Bells.

He had dreamed it all, Wilfred thought. He came close to blurting out his dream, and its startling details, to Steven, but he thought better of it. What, after all, was the point?

Marjorie Gifford came to Brookfield every Monday from Rutland to teach the boys who wanted training in piano. In addition, she taught a course in harmony to the three students interested in the structure of music.

She was hindered by the enthusiasm of a number of unmusical students who would suddenly announce to their parents that they wanted to learn piano. What they really wanted was to be in the company of Miss Gifford. She was twenty-four years old and petite, her hair styled in a simple pageboy. Her face was quietly beautiful, but it was the force of her personality that dazzled students and faculty alike — her humor, her solicitude, the profundity of her devotion to her work.

George Eggleston, the thirty-year-old, bookish scientist, had several times asked Marjorie Gifford to dine with him after her classes. But always she would smile engagingly and tell him she had to get back on the early bus and study, during the hour's journey, a book that would help her work out an orchestration she was doing for the Vermont Symphony Orchestra. She gave the same excuse to the three other bachelors at Brookfield who tried so hard to engage her special attention. Week after week, month after month, she would simply smile and, after finishing her teachings, be driven off to the bus station by the school superintendent, and for a day or so after she left, Brookfield would seem quite empty without her.

On the Monday after his episode in the computer hall, Wilfred made it a point to observe Marjorie Gifford. At lunch at Commons, she sat next to Mr. Eggleston. She had to sit next to *somebody*, Wilfred told himself. It had to be coincidence. That evening, at six as usual, Miss Gifford left the school; but instead of getting into the station wagon to go to the bus station, she drove away from Brookfield with Mr. Eggleston in his Mercedes-Benz.

Three weeks later, Miss Gifford was seated at the piano in the assembly hall. After the hymn, after the morning scriptural reading, after the routine daily announcements, the Headmaster broke out in what Josiah Regnery called "the Headmaster's inscrutable smile" (usually it came before a half-holiday was announced for that afternoon).

"I have some very happy news for the boys of Brookfield, indeed for the whole Brookfield community," he began. "I take singular pleasure" — the Headmaster liked to say things like "singular pleasure" and "distinct honor" — "in being the first to announce the happy news that Miss Marjorie Gifford, of the faculty of Brookfield Academy, has agreed to join in holy matrimony Mr. George Eggleston of Brookfield!"

The announcement was greeted with genuine applause. George Eggleston was well liked, and he was the popular favorite among the suitors for Marjorie Gifford's hand. The Headmaster couldn't leave it at that, and added: "We members of the Brookfield community rejoice in the union of these two disciplines, music and science. Marjorie, George — we love you both; Brookfield loves you both!"

There was great excitement at the news. And none greater than that of Wilfred Malachey.

Pleading a headache, Wilfred skipped French class and went to his room to consult his journal. He had begun to keep it on the day Josiah Regnery had proposed that he help him cheat on math exams, and in that journal he had meticulously recorded every unpublishable transaction he had engaged in, all of this executed in a very careful, homemade code. He had read that the great diarist Samuel Pepys had kept a record of all his irregular doings in London in a personal shorthand, and he prided himself that no one happening across his notebook would think it anything more than the scribbling of a computer freak.

What he wanted to know exactly was: when were the thirty days up that the Omegagod had given to Mr. Eggleston, the thirty days before which Mr. Eggleston could not communicate another request for a favor?

He opened his bottom drawer and dug out the journal. It had been on Tuesday, the eighteenth of April. He counted out the days on the calendar. Today was May 17. The thirty days had elapsed *today* — or rather, tomorrow, at 2 A.M. Which meant that two hours after midnight tonight, the Omegagod was willing to receive a request for a fresh favor.

It was the intention of Wilfred Malachey to sit quietly in the computer hall and wait until two in the morning. He hoped that Mr. Eggleston, in the excitement of his engagement to Miss Gifford, would not think to be at his computer at exactly the moment when he too could receive a fresh favor from the Omegagod. It was, Wilfred thought, his turn.

Would he be able to establish the electronic connection?

There were two problems. One was to duplicate exactly the procedures he had seen Mr. Eggleston follow: insert the floppy disk and punch in the formula that would summon the Omegagod.

The immediate problem was to open the locked aluminum box.

In his desperation, Wilfred resolved to pry it open with a screwdriver. But if he did that, Mr. Eggleston would soon discover that someone was on to his secret, and from there almost certainly deduce that it was the doing of his protégé, Wilfred Malachey. How could he open the locked box without leaving traces?

Wilfred looked out his window. It was now lunchtime. He saw Mr. Eggleston, holding hands with Miss Gifford, walking toward the Commons. He would be safe from detection for at least the duration of the lunch hour.

Ten minutes after the Lunch Bells had sounded, Wilfred walked (taking the back route) to the door of the computer hall, took his key from his pocket and walked in. The light was dim, so he turned on the overhead lamp above the computer. He reached to the bottom drawer. He took out the aluminum file box.

It was nothing like what he had feared it might be, a proper strongbox. It was, in fact, made not even of aluminum, but of tin: a little gray box of the kind one picks up at stationery stores. The keyhole suggested that a conventional key, if properly manipulated, could open it.

Wilfred tinkered with the hole, using first a paper clip, then the small screwdriver. Neither opened the case.

Turning the box backward, he saw that the hinges were exposed on the outside. If he could slide the two pins out…

Wilfred went to the far wall, where a few school pictures were carelessly hung, and removed the smallest nail he could find. Using the nail as a wedge and the back of the screwdriver as a hammer, he knocked lightly against the first pin. The pin budged; he could see it coming out the other end. He left it halfway out and tried the second pin. He had trouble with it. He was anxious not to scratch the gray paint on the box, as he intended to return the pins so the box would be left exactly as he had found it.

The pin would not budge.

Wilfred was beginning to sweat. He needed a harder substance to batter it out. There were fifteen minutes before lunch would end and Commons would spill out the whole school. He looked about desperately, hoping to find a makeshift hammer.

He opened Mr. Eggleston's middle drawer. He saw there a small paperweight, on which was inscribed "To George Eggleston, Yale Crew Banquet, 1974." It was of heavy marble. He banged it lightly, then harder, against the back of the screwdriver. The pin began to move. He knew now he could open the little safe.

It was 1:25. He rushed to the door of the computer hall, then walked nonchalantly to his room, where he lay down in the event that Woody Pickerel, his prefect, should check, as the prefects were supposed to do, to see if a student had been missing from lunch. He closed his eyes, as he would have done if he were suffering from a severe headache. His mind was on other things, and he very nearly developed a headache just concentrating on them.

Who — what — was this magical Omegagod who — Wilfred had figured the whole thing out by now — had first gotten Mr. Eggleston his 320SL Mercedes, then his IBM 4341, and now the woman of his choice?

Would this computer god know that tonight, just after midnight, it was someone else who was tapping into the secret number, someone other than George Eggleston?

If so, what would be the reaction of the Omegagod?

What would Wilfred ask for?

At that point the Matron walked in.

"Look here, Wilfred Malachey. You have missed at least one afternoon of school activity every day for the past three months. You, with your headaches! Now you've missed an entire morning of school and lunch as well. That will not do. I am sending you on the bus this very afternoon to Rutland. I have made an appointment with Dr. Chafee — a neurologist —

and I have told him to keep you in the hospital until you have had a very through checkup. Be prepared to leave at 3:15 sharp."

Wilfred Malachey turned pale. He told the Matron with great emphasis that by some miracle his headache had completely gone. She answered that this had also been the case with his previous headaches — "But now, young man, we're getting to the bottom of it."

Wilfred was desperate. "But, Miss Marple" — he was thinking with furious heat — "don't you know about the call from my mother?"

"A call about what?"

"About what our family doctor reported to her this morning. During the holidays, Dr. Truax gave me allergy tests. And he reported to my mother that I have a bad allergy to..." Wilfred hesitated a moment. He didn't want to name a food he liked and would now be deprived of. "...To prunes. And about once a week, right up to yesterday, I've been eating prunes for breakfast. Now we know that prunes give me the headaches."

Miss Marple sniffed. But she was a practical woman, and saw no reason to send young Wilfred all the way to Rutland for what might prove to be an expensive medical examination only to discover that he was allergic to prunes. She agreed to cancel the visit. "But if it happens one more time, you go to Dr. Chafee. It might not be an allergy, you know."

Wilfred said that he, too, had a high opinion of neurologists. Finally Miss Marple left the room.

During study hour that evening, Wilfred Malachey thought and thought. He came, at last, to a decision.

He would ask the Omegagod for something quite simple. *One million dollars.*

With one million dollars, he could stop playing Robin Hood. He could stop taking math exams for Josiah Regnery, whose laziness he had begun to resent (this came during a poker game with Josiah, when he discovered that Josiah was capable of making fast calculations when he wanted to, mental work far exceeding isosceles triangles).

One million dollars!

Wilfred's mind wandered. Suppose he could take, in the manner of Robin Hood, one dollar from the wallets of fifteen boys at Brookfield every day. How many days would it take to accumulate a million dollars? One million divided by fifteen. More than sixty-six thousand days. One hundred ninety years. His heart pounded.

He began to wonder, then to fret, then to feel a deep nervousness about his forthcoming encounter with the Omegagod. Might the Omegagod ask him questions? He — It — was a computer god. It had been quite straightforward with Mr. Eggleston, saying only that he was not to ask for anything more for thirty days. When you come down to it, Wilfred thought, it was really quite reasonable: after all, during those thirty days he had supplied Mr. Eggleston with a wife. But what if the Omegagod was in a different mood?

Every hour, every minute, every second between his return from hockey and Lights Out seemed to last a year. Two years. *Ten Years!* Steve asked why he was so distracted, and Wilfred answered that he had been working on a computer problem involving the stars and was very anxious to return to the computer hall right after Lights Out. Steve had got used to that routine and made no comment except to remark that Wilfred was probably using computer technology invented by Steven's father. Wilfred quickly agreed that this was very probably the case since, after all, Steven's father was a renowned scientist. Wilfred did not want to argue about anything with anybody tonight.

At 10:45 he felt it safe to take his usual route: outside the bedroom on tiptoe, dressed in corduroys and a sweater; down the basement to the gymnasium; out the back door; up toward the masters' cottages; past the little ivied school cemetery with its diverse stones, some wilted with moss and ivy, one or two spanking new, acting almost like mirrors as the shadows danced among them — sometimes Wilfred, passing it at night, preferred to look the other way. He reached the quadrangle, avoiding the lights. It was a fearfully cold, windy night. The winds gathered as though they were determined to keep Wilfred from making his way up the hill. At times he felt that his whole weight was bending against the bitter gale.

He turned a corner and found himself staring into the beam of a flashlight.

"What in the name of God are you doing out at this time of night?"

The Headmaster seemed most terribly tall behind the flashlight, with which he occasionally walked about the school grounds at night.

"Sir, I…I forgot my allergy pills."

"Oh? Yes. The Matron said something about your allergy. Where did you leave the pills?"

"In the computer hall, sir."

"Well, how are you going to get in there at this time of night?"

Wilfred thought hurriedly. He had better not say that Mr. Eggleston had given him an extra key; the Headmaster might not approve.

"I was thinking, sir, that Mr. Eggleston might have left the door open. Sometimes he does."

"Well," Mr. Prum said gruffly, "I have a passkey. I'll go with you and let you in."

It was a nightmare. The Headmaster insisted on making the most scrupulous search of the computer hall, not only the laboratory end but the desk area as well. Wilfred pretended to help in the search. Finally, he said, "Well, sir, my new prescription is back at the dorm. I'll get it filled tomorrow. Thank you ever so much."

Without giving the Headmaster the opportunity to weigh his options, Wilfred bowed his head slightly and walked nonchalantly back in the direction of his room. At the corner of the South Dorm, he snuck a look back: Mr. Prum and his big light were headed in the other direction, toward the Headmaster's house.

Wilfred turned around and walked rapidly toward the computer hall.

It took fifteen minutes to remove the pins, ever so carefully. And now Wilfred sat in front of the terminal and video screen of the huge IBM 4341. Hands trembling, he turned on the main switch and inserted the floppy disk.

With Mr. Eggleston's notebook propped under the lamp, he struck one by one the indicated symbols:

MK!))'$347322'@"&/. Then a blank space.

Wilfred looked at his watch. It was four minutes past ten o'clock. He would need to wait until one minute after 2 A. M. He did not dare go less than the full thirty days, measured in hours. So he sat.

And waited.

He tried to read a computer magazine, but he could not concentrate.

He tried to read the copy of *Playboy* that Mr. Eggleston kept hidden in his bottom right-hand drawer. Even the pictures didn't hold his attention.

It was 11:59.

It was 01:30.

It was, finally, 01:59.

What if his watch was fast? Should he wait until 2:05, just to make sure?

He could not wait that final minute. His watch read 02:04 when he closed his eyes and tapped down on the key marked RETURN.

The screen flared. The same lights, figures, symbols, colors, followed by the tiny white dot, appeared just as they had done thirty days earlier. As before, the dot gradually enlarged, filling the screen.

Letters appeared.

"WHAT DO YOU WANT FROM THE OMEGAGOD?"

Wilfred took a deep breath. He hesitated only a moment before typing out (carefully):

"You are the Omegagod and I am your faithful servant George Eggleston."

Wilfred waited a moment and then proceeded:

"May I please have one million dollars? The money is to go not to me directly, but to a good friend of mine. His name is Wilfred Malachey and his address is Brookfield School, Brookfield, Vermont. The Zip Code is 05036. Or—"

Wilfred hesitated for a moment. He had not thought about this until just now. *"...Or if that is not convenient for you, I'll be glad to pick up the money wherever you say."*

He thought he had better add,

"*Within reason.*"

The machine whirred. Once again the swirling lights gave off their mysterious images, and the full moon contracted and almost disappeared in the center of the screen, throwing off radials of light. Then quickly it blossomed out, touching the screen's four sides.

Wilfred could not remember whether it had behaved in exactly that way for Mr. Eggleston.

Suddenly the letters appeared.

"YOU ARE NOT GEORGE EGGLESTON. WHAT IS YOUR NAME?"

Wilfred shot up from the chair. He nearly panicked, starting for the door.

"I SAID, 'WHAT IS YOUR NAME?'"

Wilfred stopped. He thought quickly. His fingers trembling, he sat back down on the chair. He thought to himself: *If the Omegagod is going to harm me, he will harm me whatever I do.*

The Omegagod spoke again.

"I SUPPOSE YOUR NAME IS WILFRED MALACHEY. I AM A VERY INTELLIGENT GOBLIN, BUT ALTHOUGH IT IS TRUE THAT I CAN DO ANYTHING I WISH, IT IS NOT TRUE THAT I KNOW EVERYTHING. I CANNOT SAY WITH ABSOLUTE ASSURANCE THAT YOUR NAME IS WILFRED MALACHEY. IS IT?"

Under the circumstances, Wilfred thought it best to level with his correspondent. So he tapped out:

"*Yes, sir. My name is Wilfred Malachey. May I ask, what is your name?*"

"THAT IS NONE OF YOUR BUSINESS. I AM THE OMEGAGOD. I HAVE LIVED AT YOUR SCHOOL FOR ONE YEAR. THAT IS WHY UNPLEASANT THINGS HAVE HAPPENED AT BROOKFIELD. UNPLEASANT THINGS HAPPEN WHEREVER I PUT DOWN, AND THAT GOES BACK TO WHEN I LIVED WITH KING TUT. I AM OBLIGED TO FOLLOW THE INSTRUCTIONS OF ANYONE WHO DISCOVERS THE FORMULA FOR BRINGING ME OUT OF THE DEEP, WHERE I SLEEP, WHERE I WOULD LIKE TO SLEEP FOR ETERNITY. I ALWAYS HAVE ONE ALTERNATIVE IF THOSE INSTRUCTIONS DO NOT SUIT ME."

Wilfred waited expectantly to hear what that alternative was, but the Omegagod was not going to tell him. Wilfred would need to ask. So he did:

"*What is your alternative, sir?*"

"MY ALTERNATIVE—" The words came out at their accustomed, deliberate speed. "—IS TO END THE LIFE OF THE PERSON WHO MAKES THE REQUEST. THAT IS THE HOLD I HAVE OVER MR. EGGLESTON. THUS HE HAS MADE MODEST WISHES. A MERCEDES-BENZ, AN IBM 4341, AND THE HAND OF MARJORIE GIFFORD."

Wilfred reacted to this spontaneously. Surely the Omegagod was taking liberties....

"How do you know that Mr. Eggleston will make a good husband for Miss Gifford?"

"I ALREADY TOLD YOU—" The Omegagod was contentious. "I AM NOT OMNISCIENT. GEORGE EGGLESTON WANTED TO MARRY MARJORIE GIFFORD, THEREFORE HE IS IN LOVE WITH HER. THAT IS GOOD ENOUGH FOR ME. DO YOU HAVE REASON TO BELIEVE HE WILL NOT BE A GOOD HUSBAND? IF SO, I WILL SIMPLY EXECUTE HIM."

Wilfred was shocked.

He reassured the Omegagod that he, Wilfred, though inexperienced in these matters, had every reason to believe that Mr. Eggleston would make a very good husband for Miss Gifford.

The Omegagod was obviously in a talkative frame of mind, and Wilfred was afraid to reintroduce his original request. Yet his mind raced on the matter of the Omegagod's "two alternatives." A million dollars was a great deal of money, but surely not worth dying for. Or, for that matter, killing for.

As the Omegagod chattered away on the screen, Wilfred realized that both he and his magical friend had practical alternatives: Wilfred could reduce the scale of his request; if he did so sufficiently to persuade the Omegagod to grant that request rather than exercise what he called his "alternative," then both parties might be satisfied.

Wilfred did not know whether, having advanced one request, he could subsequently modify it....

He decided to firm up the point:

"Pardon me, sir, but if you did decide to...make me die, how would you go about it?"

"OH—"

The Omegagod's answer appeared on the screen a little less rhythmically than his other answers, as if this one required more thought.

"THERE ARE ANY NUMBER OF WAYS. ALISTAIR HORNE WAS MR. EGGLESTON'S PREDECESSOR. YOU SEE, EVER SINCE THE CURSE, SOMEONE ALWAYS HAS HAD POSSESSION OF MY FORMULA. LONG BEFORE IBM, IT CAME IN SMOKE SIGNALS. OH, YES. ALISTAIR HORNE. I WAITED UNTIL ALISTAIR HORNE WENT SKIING AND I HAD HIM RUN INTO A CONCRETE PYLON UNDER THE SKI LIFT. PHHHT!! JUST LIKE THAT!"

Wilfred was fascinated. He learned that before Mr. Horne there was Marilyn Aesop, the famous soprano, who had asked the Omegagod to make it possible for her to reach the F-sharp four octaves above middle C.

"THAT WAS JUST TOO MUCH. I MEAN, IT WOULD HAVE

DESTROYED MUSICAL BALANCE. NO ONE EVER AGAIN WOULD HAVE THOUGHT A SOPRANO QUITE PROPER WHO COULDN'T REACH F-SHARP. SO I HAD TO…DROP MISS AESOP. SHE WAS A NICE LADY."

Wilfred asked what had happened to Miss Aysop.

"MISS AESOP. PRONOUNCED EESOP."

What had happened to Miss Aesop?

Omega explained that he had tried to give her a dramatic ending—

"BECAUSE SHE WAS A VERY DRAMATIC LADY. ONE NIGHT WHEN SHE WAS PLAYING AÏDA, I HAD THE ELEPHANT GO WILD AND LIFT HER UP WITH HIS TUSK. BY THE TIME SHE GOT TO THE DRESSING ROOM, SHE WAS QUITE DEAD."

Wilfred decided he'd better make his move now, before it was too late. The Omegagod had done something to him: suddenly he was, well, a little uncomfortable about what he'd done over the past few months. He wondered whether he could talk with the Omegagod about Robin Hood, but he decided not to interrupt. Omega was now chirping about the predecessor of the soprano, an athlete who had asked the Omegagod to make it possible for him to run a three-minute mile.

"WILFRED, WHAT WOULD HAPPEN TO THE SPORT IF SUDDENLY A RUNNER DID A MILE IN THREE MINUTES? EVERYBODY FROM THAT POINT ON WOULD JUST PLAIN GIVE UP! WHY SHOULD I BE A PARTY TO THE END OF ATHLETIC COMPETITION? EASY TO DO, AS IT HAPPENED. HE LIKED TO DROP IN PARACHUTES AND, WELL, PARACHUTES SOMETIMES DON'T WORK. YOU KNOW THAT, DON'T YOU, WILFRED?"

Wilfred asked whether he might modify his request.

"YOU CAN MODERATE YOUR DEMANDS, YES, BUT I WOULD NEED TO CONSIDER YOUR MODERATED DEMAND IN THE LIGHT OF YOUR INITIAL DEMAND. IF YOU ARE MERELY SCARED, I WILL DO AWAY WITH YOU. IF YOUR GOOD SENSE HAS TAKEN OVER, I WILL NOT."

There was a pause, and the letters glowed.

"I WOULD HAVE TO THINK ABOUT IT. IT WOULDN'T TAKE LONG. I THINK VERY FAST, WILFRED."

Wilfred said that, instead of a million dollars, he would like for his father's next book to be a big best seller.

Then he hesitated…. When he said "big best seller," he might just possibly have crossed Omega's forbidden line.

"I don't mean a 'big best seller' like 'Gone With the Wind' or 'Catcher in the Rye.' Just a best seller. Is that all right?"

Wilfred thought he heard a sigh. Outside, he could hear the wind blowing one of those spring storms that come up so quickly in Vermont.

"I AM VERY GLAD YOU SAID THAT, WILFRED, BECAUSE I HAD COME RELUCTANTLY TO THE DECISION THAT YOU WOULD NOT LIVE TO SEE YOUR PARENTS AT EASTER. I WILL TAKE YOUR SECOND REQUEST INTO CONSIDERATION. TO TELL YOU THE TRUTH, I DID NOT LIKE THE FIRST ONE. NO, NOT AT ALL. NOW I NEED TO DECIDE WHETHER I SHALL FORGET THAT FIRST REQUEST."

Wilfred was perspiring.

"I got carried away, Omegagod. I sort of...thought of myself as...Robin Hood. I was going to take all that money and give it to people who need it."

"HOW MUCH MONEY HAVE YOU GIVEN AWAY IN THE PAST TO POOR PEOPLE?"

Wilfred panted as he leaned over the keyboard and typed:

"I never had any extra money, Omegagod, sir. Otherwise I would have given some away. As a matter of fact, I did buy sundaes twice for Red Evans and Tony Cobb."

The Omegagod waited before answering. Finally the words came:

"WELL, I AM GETTING SLEEPY. COME BACK TOMORROW AND I WILL GIVE YOU MY DECISION. IF I REACH AN ADVERSE DECISION BEFORE THEN, WELL...YOU WILL NOT BE IN A POSITION TO COMMUNICATE WITH ME. IF THAT HAPPENS, WILFRED, PLEASE BELIEVE ME THAT I HAVE KNOWN FAR WORSE THAN YOU."

"Omegagod! Omegagod! Sir! Please listen!"

But nothing Wilfred did could rouse the Omegagod, and before he was finished typing out the first appeal he saw the radial appear on the screen and the full moon gradually reduce to a pinprick. Slowly, like an automaton, he turned off the computer, returned the software to the tin case, and walked out the door toward the South Dorm. He could see early morning light.

He went slowly back, his head bent against the wind and rain. He was in the turbulence a slight figure, groping his way toward his destination, disturbing the dim, chaotic light from the lamps as it illuminated the howling wind and rain, yielding to the trim, angular shadow of the boy making his way, slowly but resolutely, to his dormitory. He was not stopped by anyone; had he been, he would not have cared.

On Thursday, no one could do anything with Wilfred Malachey. He went to breakfast without uttering a word to Steven. He ate nothing. Walking toward Flagler Hall for the morning hymn, he stopped before crossing the road and waited a full minute, then sprinted across. He walked zigzag, careful to avoid passing under any heavy, overhanging branches. He participated metronomically in the hymn, attended French class, failed twice to respond to questions put to him by Mr. Dawson. It was the same in English class, at the end of which Mr. Prum took him aside and told him he'd better wake up out of whatever trance he was in if he wanted to make progress at Brookfield. He arrived at baseball practice wearing a football helmet. Asked why by the coach, he replied that he had bruised his head and didn't want to take the chance of a wild ball hitting him.

After baseball, it was Wilfred's custom to sneak away with Steve and swim in the hidden part of the pond. Not today. He would not go near the water. Back at the room, it was his turn to make the hot chocolate; he asked Steve if he would please plug it in (as his thumb was sore). During study hour he worked furtively on his ledger, tracing every transaction since he had begun his career as Robin Hood. It came to $442.50. One hundred and twenty-five dollars of that had come from Josiah Regnery. His mind focused on how, once he had earned the money (he could work two shifts this summer at the local drive-in), he would contrive to get it back to its owners. He decided on anonymous letters containing dollar bills.

Having made that determination, his spirits suddenly lifted. Even so, he was careful, ever so careful, crossing the road to reach the dining room. He ate only the soup — he was not going to take a chance on gagging on meat or vegetables.

Back in his room, he tried to read, first his English assignment (*King Lear*), then a computer journal, but he could not concentrate. He lay there and waited. And waited. And waited. At one o'clock he rose, dressed and began his well-worn path out of South Dorm, around the back of the building, then up the hill to the computer hall.

At exactly two o'clock, having already written out the formula, he drew a breath and pushed RETURN.

The lights, the whirling motion, the radial, the sunspot growing to the full moon — all this happened again. When the screen was set, he tapped out, "*This is Wilfred Malachey calling the Omegagod. Are you there, sir?*"

"I HAVE DECIDED TO GRANT YOUR REQUEST."

Wilfred almost wept with relief, but he felt that his response should be manly.

He typed:

"*I thank you very much, sir. And you may wish to know that I have decided to return certain…things I took from other people this last term.*"

The Omegagod replied that he had confidence Wilfred would behave honorably. Then—

"I WANT YOU TO DO ME A FAVOR, WILL YOU DO THAT?"

Wilfred rushed to the keyboard to say, "*Yes!*"

"DO YOU HAVE A PENCIL HANDY? COPY THIS DOWN."

The Omegagod waited a moment until Wilfred was ready with his pencil.

"COPY DOWN EXACTLY. 'Q"W#E$R%T&Y'U(I).' WHEN I SAY GOOD NIGHT, WILL YOU TYPE THAT ON THE SCREEN?"

"Yes," Wilfred said. *"Yes, but what will happen?"*

"THE FORMULA WILL BE DESTROYED, AND THE CURSE ON YOUR SCHOOL WILL BE LIFTED. I WILL BE ABLE TO SLEEP FOREVER."

Wilfred was tormented by the thought of ending the life of Omega, whom he now considered a friend. *He may be a god,* Wilfred thought, *but he has been a friend to me.* He felt, now, that he could talk forever and ever to the Omegagod, maybe even tell him a few things he didn't know, maybe somehow return the favor. But this was the only favor he was being asked....

"Are you certain that is what you want?"

"THIS IS WHAT I WANT. NOW I WILL SAY GOOD BYE. DON'T LET ME DOWN, WILFRED."

Wilfred promised. Slowly, he typed out the symbols and letter of the second formula, then paused a long moment before he hit the key marked RETURN.

When he was done, the colors and flashes and explosions on the screen did not bring the full moon down to a tiny little light in the center: instead, they brought it down and extinguished the light altogether. Wilfred stared now at a screen completely dark, black.

Wilfred found himself crying. His shoulders heaved. It was almost three before he could bring himself to leave. He walked back to his room and crawled into bed. A great feeling of peace came over him, and he slept soundly, and when Steve tried to wake him, he found a trace of a smile on Wilfred's face.

BLUE FLAME OF A CANDLE

The pilot went ashore again in the blue predawn, carrying his lantern, a gobbet of yellow in the twilight. I was lying on deck, for the heat on that part of the river is almost unbearable, and I saw his bobbing progress up the steep bank path, toward the black silhouette of the temple. He did not use the wide steps that ran down into the water because women were burning the dead there in the dawn chill, their lamenting voices ringing out like a plait of sounds. I fancied I could almost see the ectoplasmic trail of it over the river, but it was likely to have been only smoke from the pyres. The air smelled of charred roses and cooking meat.

The *Emmeshara* drifted sideways on the water like a sleeping thing, and the oars were all upright, a palisade against the land. Two other pilgrims came out on deck, shaking little rattles and muttering prayers. I thought that was senseless, because the pilot had yet to identify which god held sway on the shore. What if the pilgrims were praying to the wrong one? They all cared so much about that kind of thing.

We were nearing the end of our journey, and both crew and passengers were skittish. I felt like an impostor, disassociated from their fervor because I was only there to accompany my father. This was his pilgrimage, his lifetime desire made real. He did not trust me to remain at home without him for, although I was as strong and able as any young man, my father considered me too young and bound to cause trouble, lose his business or burn down the house. It was preferable to shut up shop for the six months it would take us to sail up the great river to Charidotis, to the tomb of the prophet Mipacanthus. I was bored and too hot: a miserable companion for my father, who was full of a bizarre kind of zealous serenity.

"When we gaze upon the body, everything will change," he told me. "A different knowledge will come to us."

He would never know how true those words were. I never told him what happened to me in Charidotis.

Though dead for a thousand years, the corpse of Mipacanthus lies in his crystal sarcophagus, reputedly uncorrupted and as beautiful as he had been in life. I did not believe it. I knew the "corpse" had to be a waxwork likeness, or an artfully painted wooden statue. My father's eyes would see sleeping flesh, because that was what he wanted to see. I knew I would only see craftsmanship and, occasionally, in my most waspish mood, I couldn't help telling my father this.

"You young ones," he would answer patiently. "So much of the wonder of life has dried up inside you, but you will see, you will see."

I could not be interested. All that concerned me at that time was the burgeoning of maturing youth within my body, my approach to manhood. Spiritual truths, or untruths, meant little to me.

Daily, since we had left the city of Elanen, our home, the pilgrims had gathered on deck, under a faded green awning, fringed by tassels. Here, they would produce their books of prophecies. My father would produce his own: a small, densely printed volume, covered in oil-green leather, titled The Millennium. Within its pages the utterances of Mipacanthus were interpreted by Cairus Casso, a scholar fifty years dead. There were as many interpreters of the prophet's quatrains as there were prophecies, and each of them differed in definition. Cairus was a mystic, and his renderings of the chaotic words offered mantras to enrich the spirit, presaging a time when men and women aspired to godhood. Others, such as Adragor the Lame, promised only war, famine and bloodshed. Personally, after many tedious afternoons of suffering the differing translations read aloud, I had come to believe that Mipacanthus had been a poet rather than a prophet (and a rather florid one, at that), but I kept this opinion to myself. I endured the ennui, sustained by the knowledge that, come sundown, as the cook prepared supper, the pilgrims would begin to argue heatedly. A few evenings past, one man threw himself overboard in pique, and we had to fish him — still ranting — out of the river with a pole.

By the time the pilot came back on board, everyone was up on deck, and the cook had begun preparing breakfast. Savory aromas competed with the charnel-house perfume of the corpse-burnings. Apparently the river deity, Rooroorus, held sway at this point. (The previous month, no doubt, it had been someone else.) Now we all had to strip and bathe in the river, as a mark of deference to the god. As I floated, shivering, though at least thankful for the blessed cool, I eyed with misgivings the women sweeping charred rubbish off the river steps into the water. A gray, soapy-looking scum floated by me. Seemingly oblivious to this, my father swam contentedly up and down, his expression tranquil. It disgusted me so much I went back on board, whether I had spent enough time in the water or not. The cook, being a foreigner, was sympathetic, and gave me some titbits while we waited for the pilgrims to finish their ablutions.

As we ate our grilled fish and bread bobbins, the *Emmeshara* lazily turned a corner of the river, the towering, hanging trees peeled away, and the horizon became dominated by an enormous obsidian statue: a seated god, perhaps no longer worshipped, or an ancient king. It was a splendid sight. His toes dipped into the water, and people had built stilted huts between them. Children looked out from a hole in the belly of the colossus and waved to us. Cattle waded in the river shallows under the shadow of the stone, tethered to the giant toes, browsing upon shivering reeds. I stood beside the rail, drinking in the details, next to a woman veiled from head to foot, who wore a face mask of hanging coins, denominations from around the world. I knew her name was Moomi, though we had only nodded at one another previously. Now she nudged me with her elbow and said, in a deep, thickly accented voice. "He de fader od de Great One." She gestured at the statue.

"Father of Mipacanthus?" I asked.

She nodded and guttered, "Oi, oi," which I presumed meant *yes*.

I reflected that I would not have seen any of this if I had stayed at home, but regretted I had no real chance to explore the wonders I saw. We just passed them by, every one. At least in Charidotis, I would be able to wander around, while my father contemplated the abiding beauty of the dead prophet.

The paddling god-king, the river steps, were the gateway to Charidotis; we were nearer to our destination than I had thought. By midafternoon the river widened and became divided by a labyrinth of jetties and piers. Ships and smaller boats negotiated the maze. Market stalls thronged every available surface, some jutting out over the water, their goods swaying perilously in a hot afternoon breeze, which had arisen, surprisingly, from nowhere. A babble of conflicting languages, nonsense tongues, filled the air, and it smelled oily, like cold lamb-fat mixed with myrrh.

Charidotis was a magnet of the world. People were drawn there from every known land to parade before the tomb of the boy-king, the dead prophet. Some came to be healed, others for spiritual renewal, and still more came as tourists. The city itself, white as bone, rose like a fretwork of wind-blasted ivory along the sides of the river. And ahead, I could see the misty outline of the Pyramid itself, the tomb, like a mirage against the lavender sky, at once real and stultifyingly phantasmic.

My father had brought our luggage up on deck, his cloaks hanging over his arm. "See, Alexi, see!" he exclaimed, his outspread fingers encompassing the splendors of the mythical city.

"It is fabulous," I said, the first kind remark I had made to him upon the journey.

He smiled, encouraged, and soon the *Emmeshara* found her own niche within the labyrinth, and we all disembarked to make the miles-long journey on foot around the maze to reach the shore. Despite the fact the cost of the trip was extortionate and had nearly ruined us, I had been allowed to bring a little money with me. My first impulse was to squander it all in the market. Everything glittered or coiled. The colors were deep and iridescent, mimicking the hues of jewels. Shawls flapped like captive wings, enchanted necklaces swung, exotic foods hissed in their spiced fat, impossible glass windchimes filled the air with music. The market people were small and swarthy, with few teeth but wide smiles. Their hands danced upon the air as they extolled the virtues of their goods. We passed a stall devoted solely to Mipacanthus. It bore a forest of identical statuettes that had been fashioned from every conceivable medium, as well as painted leaves, varnished to hardness, that carried the prophet's ineffable image.

The veiled woman, my companion of the rail, attached herself to us. We learned she was a native of Threnador, a city so distant as to be considered fictional. As we negotiated the maze, my father seemed to understand her speech, while I just nodded and smiled at most of her urgent, delighted exclamations. We found a pilgrim's inn near the docks and took a communal room to conserve funds. There was so much to see and explore I didn't know what to do with myself, and just sat on my mattress, dazed, while Moomi and my father made plans for the evening, consulting a library of pamphlets they had purchased on the way from the river. Moomi took off her mask of coins to reveal the most ugly yet fascinating face I had ever seen. Her bones were exquisite beneath her dark skin, yet her teeth jutted from her stretched mouth like those of an embalmed corpse. Her nose was long and hooked, her eyes abnormally large and of a lustrous black. It looked as if her real eyes had been plucked out and replaced with dark, polished gems. Her hair had been oiled into coiling locks that fell like snakes over her shoulders. Around her neck hung a treasury of black pearls and gold chains. She was perhaps halfway between my own age and that of my father. Now that we had arrived in Charidotis, my torpor of the journey north had vanished, giving rise to a feverish enthusiasm, which bloomed unexpectedly in my chest. Moomi's appearance, strange and wonderful as it was, seemed a fitting part of our adventure.

We spent the evening walking around the temple quarter, where architectures of the world competed with each other in magnificence. All the temples were dedicated to Mipacanthus, although each of them celebrated a different aspect of the prophet. Here a severe tower, crowned flamboyantly with a crenellation of stone lace, symbolized Mipacanthus as lawmaker. There a spreading vista of snowy columns, from which clouds of incense oozed, symbolized Mipacanthus as sensual, the confidant of despairing lovers. And above all, rearing up like a fortress on its hill, skirted with ancient poplars, the Great Library stood. Here scholars worked upon the hundreds of books that contained the prophecies of Mipacanthus, and analyzed the historical documents of the known world.

Pilgrims and tourists thronged the temple area: a babbling crowd, which effectively dispelled any atmosphere of peace and holiness. Here, the passage of countless feet had worn away the stones of the temple floors into channels. We walked to the plaza of the Pyramid, but both Moomi and my father prolonged their moment of enlightenment by agreeing not to enter the tomb until the morning, when they would feel refreshed. Close to, the monument is so massive as to blot out the sky; it seems inconceivable that human hands built it. From the river, its walls had appeared smooth, but in reality they were covered in carvings, which stuck out at every angle. A million saints, martyrs, sacred concubines, holy soldiers, confirmed kings and the like peered from the towering sides of the Pyramid, each one as lifelike as can be achieved in stone. Some threw out their arms in commemoration of their final, agonized moments in life, while others were composed in prayer. Dancing girls, touched by the sacred, swept their stone scarves across the faces of stern men of the sword, who had fought in the prophet's name. I would have been content to stand there all night, examining the endless seethe of frozen faces, but my father was hungry and wanted to get back to the inn. He pointed out I would be able to see more in full daylight, clearly pleased I seemed interested in the Pyramid.

I saw the blue woman before Moomi did. My father never noticed her: Perhaps that is significant. It was one of those moments when time becomes still: when we can step out of it, and events of significance occur.

The interior of the Pyramid was dark; the light of a thousand candles failed to dispel the gloom but, despite the fact it was heaving with pilgrims, it did not share the sullied atmospheres of the temples we had visited the night before. Here was majesty serene, here was history entrapped in stone and crystal. We had to pass through a series of vaulted antechambers, before approaching the center of the tomb, where the body of the prophet lay. Everyone spoke in hushed voices as they shuffled between roped walkways. I looked around myself; soon I grew bored with waiting, and with moving so slowly, and wished I could go and investigate the triangular doorways reached by perilous flights of steps that pitted the walls above our heads. No doubt they led to secret chambers of the Pyramid, where only the priesthood ventured. Was there ever a time when the place was empty? I would have preferred it so. The press of humid bodies obscured everything I wanted to see: the ancient wall carvings, the grotesque relics in stone niches. The crowd was policed by holy militia, or Guardians: tall, masked individuals (some of whom were women) dressed severely in black. Only when you passed close by could you see that their obscuring robes comprised layers of a wondrous, floating stuff, like smoke.

When we reached the seventh, and final, antechamber, we discovered the reason for the long queue. Only six pilgrims were allowed into the inner chamber at a time. Merchandise was set out on a table by the entrance, where pilgrims could buy perfumed purple candles to light in honor of the prophet. As my father delved in his purse to find coins, having offered to buy Moomi a candle as well, I was given my first glimpse of the holy vault.

The sarcophagus itself was an unbearable brilliance, reflecting the light of devotional candles, which filled the room but for the narrow walkway around the resting place of Mipacanthus. Five of the six pilgrims within were in shadow at the far end of the vault. I saw the other one lean to place a candle amid the sea of flickering light. She was dressed all in dark, rich peacock blue: a mist of translucent veils that covered her entirely. As she leaned forward, a slim, brown arm came out of the folds to place a lighted candle. With her other hand, she brushed back the veils, and just for a moment, I could see her face. Such a face. Her profile was exquisite and noble. A single coil of black hair fell down her cheek. Her visible eye slanted upward like the eyes of the women in the carvings on the wall. My heart, I think, stopped for a beat or two, and yet, though I was thrilled, I was strangely dismayed. It was a feeling almost impossible to describe. Then a bell chimed to advise the pilgrims they must leave the chamber, and a voice came from the shadows at the far end of the vault. Her name must have been spoken, though I could not catch it. She looked round toward the sound and, as her body swung, the corners of the veil wafted up and I could see the sea of candles through it, their flames rendered blue by the color of the fabric. On light feet, she moved toward the shadows and disappeared from my sight.

By my side, Moomi, who had also been looking, uttered a soft hiss, that essentially feminine sound of disapproval. She muttered something in her own language and I remember I said, "What?"

"Blue flame," she answered, and made a complicated gesture with her fingers against brow and chest. She shook her head, making the coins across her face swing and chime. "Her air, it change de hue o de flame."

I laughed and my father looked round at us, holding out the candles. Before I could question Moomi further, we were ushered into the inner chamber.

Moomi seemed on edge as, together with three other pilgrims, we negotiated our way along the narrow walkway between the tomb and the sea of little flames. Her initial reluctance, however, was soon forgotten. The sarcophagus was every bit as magnificent, as we had hoped and expected. Constructed of crystal and gold, its quarters were guarded by sphinx-goddesses and gryphon gods, each with diamonds for eyes and gilded thread for hair. We had learned from the pamphlets that the jewels allowed the guardians a clear sight between the domain of earth and the realm of the unseen. Through diamonds, they observed each pilgrim who passed the tomb. Golden saints pressed their backs against the sides of the sarcophagus, but their eyes were blank and staring. Their human origin meant that, in death, they could only gaze inward upon the spirit realm, and not out upon the earth.

It was difficult to see the body of Mipacanthus in any great detail, owing to the opulent embellishments of the tomb. We all stood on tiptoe to get a glimpse, though all I saw through the crystal plate, scattered with petals, was an indistinct pale face wreathed in what appeared to be fresh flowers. It was impossible to tell whether that face was beautiful or not, whether it exuded serenity or was merely blank. This undefined appearance actually lent the body an air of authenticity. I felt that had it been a carving or a waxwork, as I'd suspected, it would have been more visible, more obviously displayed. This unnerved me. Moomi made soft noises of adoration, while my father's lips worked silently in a personal prayer. Presently the bell chimed, and we were obliged to move on, out of the inner chamber into the prayer rooms beyond, where ropes of miniature lilies and other adjuncts to devotion could be purchased.

As we walked back to our hostel, I spoke to Moomi about the girl we had seen, she of the blue veils. Moomi made further sounds of disapproval. "De place attract dem," she said, shaking her head. "De air, de very air, it call dem."

"Calls what?" I asked her, intrigued.

She turned her masked face toward me, and I felt the stab of her attention. "No ask," she said, shaking her head. "Not for you, young innocent. No."

"What is it, Alexi?" my father inquired, distracted from his beatific silence by our conversation.

"Nutting," said Moomi, and it was left at that.

After we left the Pyramid, I wanted to wander off alone. We all agreed to meet later at the plaza within the Great Library, where an open-air eating place could be found. My father suggested I should visit the library and search for documents concerning the history of Elanen. He was curious about such things. I was not. Once free of my companions, I went looking for the girl. Often, I caught glimpses of that aching blue through the crowd, and hurried toward it, only for it to elude me. Probably it was someone else every time, though I did not like to think of the girl as a simple pilgrim mesmerized by the prophet's cult. Rather, I imagined her as a scholar, disdainfully studying the phenomenon of Mipacanthus, who would scorn his mindless followers. After having seen the body of the prophet myself, I was more disposed to understand his enduring fascination, but I was of that age when it is preferable to be different, set apart from the common herd. Also, my instincts had awoken, focusing on the unknown female and the mystery that seemed to surround her.

At the end of the afternoon, as my feet mounted the hundred steps to the frontal columns of the Great Library, I had invested my phantom female with a full personality and history. Despite the disappointments of my afternoon's search, I had no doubt that I would see her again, and in that, I was not wrong. Some things are simply meant to be; sometimes we are marked by the mordant wit of Fate.

I found the plaza very quickly, for it was well sign-posted, but Moomi and my father had not yet arrived. After scuffing my feet for a few minutes, wondering whether to purchase a drink while I waited, I decided I might as well investigate the nearest chambers of the Library. The gloom of the great vaults seemed to draw me in and, once I stepped across the threshold into shadow, the outside world might as well have disappeared. The atmosphere was stern and forbidding, as if to foreshadow the arcana it would never divulge. Stylized portraits of Mipacanthus and his family adorned the soaring walls of the endless corridors. Sometimes the boy-king was represented as limpid, effeminate: a fragile creature doomed to early death. In others, I perceived a steel in his gaze, as if when he had modeled for the portrait he had been aware of the virtual immortality he would enjoy, and was cynically amused by it. As a prophet, he had no doubt foreseen his own future. He had apparently been very beautiful in life, but perhaps the portraits flattered him. There was, I thought, something inhuman about the absolute, slanting symmetry of his face.

I went into one bookroom after another, stifled by the density of the air that came at me like furred fists, almost knocking the breath from my lungs. Robed scholars pored over open tomes around enormous tables, their reverent fingers gloved in black silk as they handled the ancient pages. All the bookcases around them were caged and locked. I went into a smaller room, where an ancient man worked alone at a high desk. He did not notice my entrance, as all his concentration was centered on the book before him. His toothless mouth worked silently as he studied the words on the page; there was a repugnant intensity about him. He almost slavered as he read. This, I thought, was the true tomb of Mipacanthus. Here were his remains truly preserved, and the pawing scholars were dissectionists, peering at the inner workings of the corpse. A wave of nausea passed over me and I turned away, set on returning to the plaza.

A flash of blue registered in the corner of my eye as I stepped back into the corridor. I caught an impression of swift, invisible passage, and then, some way farther down from me, I saw a trail of blue floating stuff disappearing into a doorway, following whoever wore it. Knowing at once it was the girl from the Pyramid, I almost ran down the corridor in pursuit. What I would say when I confronted her I had no idea, but the need to present myself was too compelling to ignore. As I ran, the first sounds to break the breathing silence of the Library careened from wall to wall above my head: the eerie echoes of a recital. I recognized the quatrain:

This will come…. The great tails spread their eyes against the stars, and through them shall men see themselves as gods of wisdom, and women see themselves as beasts who have understandings beyond that of gods or men….

Cairus had interpreted this as meaning that once clear sight (enlightenment) had been achieved by humanity (the tail of the peacock), men would recognize their true spiritual state, based on intellect and learning, while women would reclaim their earthy powers, their own spirituality based on instinct and intuition. Another interpretation suggested that the spreading tails represented humanity's vanity, and that men believed themselves (wrongly) to be gods, while women were vicious creatures, no better than demons. I had picked up quite a lot without realizing it during the voyage upriver.

I stepped into the room.

It was in dimness, a tall, narrow box of a place, with a single table in its center and the familiar lofty bookcases all around. A slender thread of light came in from a narrow window high in the left-hand wall, snaring her in its radiance. She stood with her back to me, leaning on the table with stiff arms, but there was no book before her. If anything she seemed angry, as if she had paused for a moment to catch her breath and calm herself. The veils hung over her completely; they seemed almost cumbersome, yet I had seen her float along in them like a mist. The sight of her taut spine, which actually seemed to stick out through the thin layers of delicate fabric, filled me with an intense longing and also a sudden fear. I was afraid that should she turn to me and throw back the veils, something hideous would be revealed. Perhaps the experience with Moomi the previous night had affected me more than I realized.

"Go away! It isn't here!" she said. Her voice was clear and low-pitched; melodious, yet unusual in a woman.

I was so surprised, I took a step backwards toward the door. I must have muttered something for she turned round in a billowing of blue, her posture stooped and predatory. I could not see her face, although there seemed to be twin darknesses behind the veils where her eyes might be. It was obvious I was not whom she had expected to see.

"Oh!" she said in surprise, and uncoiled herself into an upright posture.

I presented my hands reflexively. "I saw you at the Pyramid earlier…."

The words were pathetically lame. I sensed her studying me, assessing me, wondering, no doubt, how to escape me.

"What a good memory you have," she said. Her tone was sharp, but the words did not suggest immediate flight.

I smiled — probably an awkward grimace. "I don't mean to be importunate, but when I saw you coming in here…well, I'm on my own, and I thought…"

"Yes, you don't have to tell me what you thought," she interrupted. "Sadly, I did not notice you earlier on."

A wave of embarrassment shattered against my heart. I felt young and stupid. This was no local girl in the markets of Elanen, who might welcome a forced introduction; this was a stranger of whom I knew nothing, romantic fancies aside. I was making a fool of myself. I backed away, uttering apologies.

"There is no need for that," she snapped. "If you want my company, you shall have it. I have finished here. We can go to the plaza while I wait for my companion, and you can attempt to interest me, if you are so inclined."

Her forthright manner did not comply with the image I had created for her, an image which leaned more toward evasiveness and mystery. Still, I had found her, and she had not dismissed me outright. And it seemed I might have been right about her being a scholar, at least.

She slipped past me into the corridor, the edges of her veils wafting out to touch my clothes and hands. She carried with her a strange perfume, sweet yet salty. I wasn't sure whether or not I liked it. Intrigued yet wary, I walked beside her. We were about the same height. "Are you studying here?" I inquired politely.

"No, *hunting*," she replied. "You, of course, are a tourist."

I objected to her tone. "Not really. I'm here with my father, who is a devotee of the prophet. He needed company for the journey, so I agreed to come."

"How charitable of you."

"Charidotis is fascinating. I don't look on it as a wasted trip. What are you hunting? A particular book?"

"What else would you look for in a library?"

We walked out into the sunlight, and the girl chose a table and sat down. She made no move to order food or drink, and her air suggested she was waiting for me to see to that. Rather nettled, I went to the catering tables and purchased the cheapest items available: a small bread slab, spiced meat pâté, and a flagon of iced water. She made no comment upon my choice when I returned to the table, nor thanked me, but simply broke off a piece of bread, secreted it beneath her veils and presumably chewed it.

"I'm due to meet my father here," I said, looking round to see if I could spot him or Moomi.

"Oh, he will be delighted to find you with me!" Her voice was bitter.

"I don't think he'll be bothered," I answered. "He's not that sort of man."

She laughed coarsely. "You don't know what kind of woman I am."

"Indeed not. Perhaps we should begin with your name."

"Ast," she replied. "It's short and sensible."

"Where are you from?"

"Downriver. A dull place. You won't know it."

"I'm Alexi," I said. She seemed not in the least bit interested, but I forged on painfully. "We come from Elanen. Perhaps you know it."

"Probably. I travel a lot. All towns and cities are the same essentially: full of people and their noise and stench."

"You prefer the countryside?"

"Not really." She took a long drink of water, ignoring the cups I had brought and taking it straight from the flagon. I had a feeling of distaste, thinking I did not want to drink any of the water myself now that she had touched it with her lips. She drank through her veils, leaving a dark stain upon them. Was she really beautiful beneath the tissues of her disguise, or had just I imagined it in the dancing candlelight of the Pyramid? Her poise, however, did not suggest a plain or ill-favored woman.

"So tell me about the book you're looking for," I said. "I hope it's not another interpretation of the quatrains. I've had my fill of them on the way here!"

"Ah, so you're an expert," she said.

I ignored the sarcasm. "No, and nor do I want to be. You can read what you like into the prophecies. There are as many interpretations as there are interpreters."

She nodded, and her tone, when she spoke, was not so sharp. "Yes, that's right. It's a case of finding the one interpretation that's pertinent to yourself."

"I prefer to create my own philosophies."

She shrugged. "That's reasonable, although perhaps ignorant."

I affected a scornful laugh. "I have no wish to become part of some mindless adulation for a long-dead poet. I prefer to look forward. The past is dead."

"In some ways, your views are refreshing," Ast conceded. "Still, you are in no position to criticize something you know so little about. I agree that the majority of people who come here are uninformed and sheeplike. Still, there are mysteries to be penetrated, if a person has the inclination to peer above the bowed heads of the masses."

"You speak with some authority." I hoped to draw her out, intrigued.

She was utterly still for a moment. "You would be surprised. The blind worship of Mipacanthus, and the continuing interpretation of his words — which become ever more esoteric and divorced from his original intentions as the years pass — are a screen for what is essentially a simple truth. Mipacanthus *was* unparalleled, but perhaps not in the way most people think.

They are blind and lazy. He has been deified and now they worship him, perhaps because he was pleasing to the eye...."

"He was also incredibly prolific," I said, wishing to contribute to her remarks. "There's enough of his writings to keep a whole world busy interpreting for centuries. However, I think you can read what you like into the quatrains. Most of the interpretations are verified only in retrospect."

Ast nodded again. "Mmm. I don't dispute that. The book I am searching for does not attempt to foretell the future, but simply to explain the past." She leaned toward me a little. "Do you know anything about Mipacanthus?"

I shrugged. "Not really. Only that he was young when he died, and he wrote a lot."

Ast laughed. "Your inexperience is pleasing! You are like an uninterpreted quatrain, aren't you. Nobody's had their paws on you!"

I was embarrassed by her remarks, not least because she had divined a certain truth about me.

"Let me tell you a little," she continued. "While Mipacanthus lived, he had a retinue of priestesses who cared for him. No others were allowed near him. They were appointed by his mother on the day of his birth. In some books, you will find it written that she was a sorceress, who had commerce with demons. It is said the priestesses kept a terrible secret about the boy, that he was not entirely human, though that is probably propaganda. There is no proof that Mipacanthus' father was not the king! The books that make the most interesting reading are the least reliable. Unfortunately!"

I smiled. 'Is your book like that, the one you're looking for?'

Ast ignored the question. "When Mipacanthus died — and he was not that young, about twenty-nine — the priestesses embalmed his body themselves, and it was sealed into the gold and crystal catafalque. The secret, if there was one, is now hidden for eternity."

"Unless someone breaks open the tomb."

"Or recognizes the knowledge in one of the books. Mipacanthus wrote more about himself than people realize. They find global-scale pronouncements in what are clearly simple observations on his own life. I, and my companions, are scholars. We come regularly to Charidotis to study in the Library — for as long as our funds will sustain us."

"I had guessed as much." I felt proud of myself for anticipating her profession.

"I look like a scholar, then?" Her voice was arch.

"Not exactly. It was just a feeling." I paused, and then added hurriedly. "I saw your face briefly in the Pyramid, and I would like to see it again."

Ast shifted restlessly in her seat. I had made her uncomfortable. "You are intrigued by the unseen," she said. "By mystery. Mipacanthus should fascinate you just as much."

"You are a living mystery," I countered, "while Mipacanthus is not. I'm sure his secrets are fascinating, but he is still dead."

"A pity you don't have more imagination," Ast said waspishly.

"I have plenty, but I prefer the present to the past, experience to theorizing."

"Experience can be dangerous." She reached out and touched the lip of the water jug with the tips of her long fingers. "People are selective in their interpretation of the prophecies. Sometimes the truth stares them in the face and they see something else, a harmless fantasy."

I wished she wouldn't keep steering the conversation back to the prophet. I felt we had more interesting things to talk about. Did she find me pleasing? Would she walk with me in the city? Could anything else happen between us? Did I really want that? I was still confused about whether I liked her or not. However, my curiosity — if not my actual desire — was aroused. I was eager to look upon her face again. Only then, could I decide whether I wanted more from her. Ast had recognized my inexperience with women. Perhaps she would find that attractive. I struggled to think of something witty to say, but at that moment noticed my father and Moomi sitting at a table on the other side of the plaza. They had obviously not seen me. "My father's over there," I said. "I'd better attract his attention."

I raised my arm in the hope of waving wildly enough for him to see me, but Ast thrust out a hand from between her veils and stopped me. "No!"

"It's quite all right," I said. What unenlightened place had she come from, where prevailing social customs condemned young men innocently sitting in a public place with unknown women?

"If you want to go to him, I must leave," she said. "It's up to you."

"But why? We've only just started our conversation."

"That's just the way it is. Make up your mind."

I stood up. "I must go. It would be impolite not to. I promised to meet him here." If I had hoped to call her bluff, I was mistaken.

"Then go."

I hesitated, and began an awkward introduction to suggesting we might meet again. "Could we…"

"Tomorrow morning,' she snapped, clearly anticipating my request. "I shall be at the Pyramid again. There is an inn called The King's Stair nearby. Wait there in the late morning and I'll come to you."

I was so surprised by this, having expected a cold good-bye, or at least a need for gentle persuasion, that I simply nodded wordlessly and walked off across the plaza. Halfway to my father's table I turned back, but Ast had already gone, leaving the rest of the bread and pâté uneaten.

Because of Moomi's earlier reaction to the girl, I decided not to mention having met her in the Library. Our earlier visit to the Pyramid had apparently left my father in a state of spiritual intoxication; even Moomi looked slightly impatient with him.

For the rest of the day, Moomi and I investigated other areas of the city, dragging my father, who seemed blind to the wonders on offer, along with us. We went to the cat market and watched the auction of an enormous leopard, who wore a jeweled collar and sat licking his paws in apparent disdain as rich merchants bid for him. Cats are sacred animals in Charidotis, and ailuromancy (divination by catwatching) is a widespread form of prediction.

Later, we ventured into the nut market, where we found a restaurant in which to take our evening meal. Moomi must have been bored with both my father and myself, for we were equally distracted. All I could think about was Ast. She had disturbed me, but the memory of her was exciting. I couldn't wait to see her again.

It was a long night, but I did not dream of her.

In the morning, we all went to the Pyramid again. We intended to stay in Charidotis for six days and this would be the way each day would begin. I couldn't be bothered with all that queuing again, and I told my father I wanted to spend some hours examining the carvings on the outer walls of the tomb. On one side there were steps that zigzagged right up to the summit. I thought I'd climb them before I went to meet Ast.

The view from the summit of the Pyramid was stultifying. The lands of three countries, Ou, Miplux and Cos, were visible from there. The most celebrated monument of Miplux, the Great Obelisk of Ewt, could be distinguished in the bluish haze of the distance. The river was a silver ribbon across the land, an artery from Cos in the north, that led down to the lifeblood of the delta and drained into the Great Sea, Ertang. I wished that Ast was with me. I could have pointed out in which direction Elanen lay, on the northern marshes of the delta.

Eventually, I could not contain my impatience and hurried back down the Pyramid steps. It took me some time to find the inn Ast had spoken of, and I dreaded she had been there before me, had got tired of waiting and had already left. I asked at the bar if a woman of her description had been there, but the pot-girl shook her head. Encouraged, I purchased a cup of ale and sat outside, beneath a twisted orange tree, to await Ast's arrival. She appeared through the crowd almost immediately, as if she had been waiting, hidden nearby, looking out for my arrival. Her slight willowy figure came gliding toward me, and I felt my heart crash. It was a feeling of longing but, in some bizarre way, also one of horror. I decided I must see what lay beneath the veils once more, to reassure myself.

Ast greeted me curtly and sat down. I offered to buy her a drink, but she demurred. "I have just taken lunch with my friends," she said. I was immediately curious.

"What are they like? Are they the same age as you? Are they male or female?"

The veils were motionless. I had no idea what she was thinking, whether she was amused or affronted. "Maybe I will have a drink," she said.

Inside the inn, I fumbled with coins, terrified that she would have fled by the time I returned to the table. But when I emerged she was sitting there still, one arm lying on the table in front of her. It was a strong, slim arm, with nut-brown skin, and the long-fingered hand was far from delicate. I felt that hand had purpose and was not disposed to idle tasks. Perhaps my unconscious mind thought of death, then.

She drank all of the ale I had bought her, though without speaking. I tried to begin conversation several times, but she would not be drawn out. I feared she regretted suggesting we should meet again and my heart hammered against my ribs as I searched my empty mind for something fascinating to say. In retrospect, it is easy to see that Ast was preoccupied rather than bored.

Presently, she put down her empty cup and appeared to appraise me minutely through her veils. I felt myself color, sure she was thinking badly of me and my appearance, even though I considered myself well-favored and had often been told as much. Then she announced, "I would like you to come with me to the place where I am staying."

A chill clenched my flesh. "I thought my company did not please you...."

She neither laughed nor sought to reassure me. "It is your choice," she said.

I was terrified, elated, weak, yet eager. "I would like to see your face," I said.

She stood up. "Follow me, then."

It was in a quiet part of the city, away from the noisy pilgrims' hostels. I thought she had taken me to a private house for, once inside, there was no indication we had entered a hostel or an inn. I commented upon this and Ast replied, "This is what money can buy for the discerning traveler." I bridled at her scorn. What did she want with me? To her I must seem like an untutored, provincial creature. I was romantic, then, and believed lust to be an adjunct to love, rather than the other way around. Of course, I was falling in love with her even before I saw her face again. She repulsed me, she intrigued me, she filled me with terror and desire. In the movements of the girl, in her words, her very shape in space, her use of time, a prophecy resided. Yet I was blind to it. I could only interpret the feelings she inspired in me as love, for I was inexperienced. Perhaps, in those moments, I was influenced more by the romantic optimism of Cairus Casso rather than the dour vision of Adragor the Lame, whose sentiments, had I been open to them, would have been considerably more useful.

The house was sleeping in the afternoon; we saw no one on the stairs or in the corridors. Ast's room was a darkened place, with blinds drawn over the windows; the light was sepia. There were two beds, and items strewn around that suggested occupancy. She shared this room with someone. Where were they? I felt a stab of jealousy. She could have a lover, out there in the city somewhere.

Ast left me standing awkwardly in the center of the room while she busied herself in the shadows beside the door. Presently, she brought me a cup of wine. I took a sip. It was red, and dry as the desert. Would she sully her veils now and take the ruby liquor through them? She watched me as I drank, and I sensed her enjoyment of my predicament. There was something unnatural about her: the invisible vigilance, her taut stillness. I sensed threat. Then, with absolute precision, with those strong, slim hands, she carefully peeled back the veils from around her face. I felt light-headed as I watched her, terrified something vile would be revealed.

Her appearance did come as a shock, but simply because I could look into her eyes. Her beauty was almost abnormal, yet I was not allowed the luxury of exploring it. She had me impaled with her eyes, and they were all I could examine. I could neither move nor speak. Then she began to unshroud herself.

The outer veils were discarded first, cast off to lie about her feet in a fretting pool, worried by the draft coming from beneath the door. Beneath this outer covering, she was wrapped in a complicated bandaging of fabric: blues of every hue. Never allowing me to evade her gaze for an instant, she began to unwind herself, her slender body swaying as she did so. Gradually, she revealed her upper arms, her neck, her shoulders. I thought of the serpent, and how it sheds its skin. I was entranced by her, utterly entrapped within the static silence of the room. I did not feel afraid, for I was beyond fear. I had become condensed desire, for that is what she wanted.

Languorously, she peeled herself to the waist. Her skin was a pale, golden brown, lighter in coloring than her arms and hands. She was like an idealized statue of a woman brought to life: the breasts perfect, the flesh poreless and smooth, yet with the appearance of silken velour. I longed to touch her, and she danced toward me slowly, her hair a shifting forest of darkness about her shoulders. Her peculiar garments hung down about her hips, obscuring the rest of her exquisite form, which I was desperate to behold. She reached up to cup my face with her hands. "You, the unbeliever," she murmured, and kissed me. My arms went around her and locked; my whole body felt contused with blood. I could not even return her kiss, but it did not seem to concern her. This was the moment when the secrets of adult passion would be revealed to me. My initiation. Ast drew back, and her hands went to her hips. "Now you will know all of me," she said.

I felt it then: the cold. And in my deepest heart, I must have realized the truth, because I had held her close.

I did not feel saved when the door opened behind me, nor thwarted. I felt released, but crushed. Light came into the room, and presence. Ast uttered an exclamation, and her arms went around her breasts. An older woman, also dressed in blue but with an unveiled face, hurried past me and grabbed Ast's arms. They did not speak aloud to one another, but their eyes said many things. Then the woman shook Ast's body. "Are you mad?" she snapped. "Here? In this place?"

"He is mine!" Ast hissed. "He wants me!"

The woman laughed harshly. "Wants you? He doesn't know *what* he wants. He's only a boy."

I cannot recall whether I spoke or moved while this transaction took place. I might as well have not been there, but then the older woman turned her head to me and said, "Go, boy! This is no place for you."

Ast snarled then, and spat out a tirade of expletives. It did not surprise me to hear it, though some of the words were unknown to me. She struggled with her companion, clawed at her.

"Go!" repeated the woman to me, keeping Ast in a firm hold. "You should thank me for it." Something in her voice, or the simple evidence of her last words, sent me fleeing from the house. I heard them shouting at one another as I ran along the street below her window, but could not discern the words.

I was almost delirious with conflicting emotions by the time I reached the sanctuary of our pilgrims' hostel. As I had raced down the last few streets of my escape, I had felt as if a formless danger was chasing me. I kept visualizing Ast sprinting up behind me, her breasts bared, her beautiful hands clawed, her hair wild. My back prickled with anticipation of the attack, when she would leap upon me. Then what?

I slammed into our room and leaned upon the door. Drooping there, panting and groaning, it was some moments before I realized Moomi was sitting up on her bed, staring at me in surprise. Presumably I had woken her up from an afternoon nap.

"What have you done?" she demanded. It must have been obvious I'd been running from something.

I sat down on my own bed, my head hanging between my knees. Moomi padded over to me, and put a hand on the back of my neck. She made soothing noises, asked me no further questions. After a while, I looked up at her, and said, "The girl we saw, the girl in the Pyramid...."

"De blue woman," she answered, and sighed. She sat down next to me and hugged me fiercely. I could not understand why. "She found you," Moomi said.

"I found *her*," I amended. "It was…something *strange* has happened."

"Tell!" Moomi commanded. I realized she was frightened for me.

What was there to tell? It was difficult. "We met," I began. "I went to her house. She was…odd. Then someone came into the room. I was sent away." I shrugged. "That was all."

Moomi exhaled noisily. "Stay away! She smell your innocence. She want it. No, she not for you, not your kind. Forget."

"What is she, Moomi? What is it you don't like about her?"

"She a blue woman, wid de power of fear and desire. She turn light to her own color. De blue woman fill a man wid longing, yet he scared of her. He can't turn away. Bad luck. Knowledge of her change a man. She, de girl we saw, she blue." Moomi clawed her hands and grimaced, mimicking a predatory thing. "She devour a man."

I laughed nervously. "Really? You mean, she *eats* people?" I was not in the position at that time to refute it. Anything seemed possible then, in that haunted, sleepy afternoon. I thought of the dim room I had run from, the glowing girl swaying toward me, the promise, the menace, the unexpected release.

Moomi shook her head. "Not bones and blood," she said. "Dere are ancient peoples, 'Lexi, very ancient. Place like dis, it lure dem. Dere is much for dem here. But not you…" She stood up. "You be safe now. I sure."

And I was safe. I never saw Ast again. But I dreamed of her. Just once, but enough for to have it stay with me all my life.

The dream came that same night.

In the dream, I woke up and got out of my bed in the dark. My father and Moomi slept nearby, but they did not stir. I dressed and went out of the hostel. The streets of Charidotis were empty, which proves it must have been a dream, because even at night, the city was alive and thronged with people. Now, the streets were still and the buildings lowered overhead against a purple sky glistering with pulsing stars.

They were moaning on the Pyramid — all those carvings. As I approached I saw them move, heard the faint distillations of their cries, that came to me down a tunnel of centuries. Dancing girls, kings, saints and soldiers. As I passed through the first portal, I felt their stone hands grab for my back, but I did not look round.

Inside, a ribbon of candles led me onward. Each flame illumined a tiny space around it, but otherwise all was in darkness. I followed the faint lights through every echoing room until I came to the antechamber of the tomb itself. She was waiting for me there, blocking the portal. Her veils were cast back from her face; she smiled at me kindly and beckoned me with a slim arm. We did not pass into the inner chamber, but into the darkness of the antechamber, beyond the feeble, flickering lights. She led me to a stone stair. "Hold on to me," she said, for there was no light. I followed her up the steps, stumbling, grabbing hold of the floating blue that wafted around me. I sensed that I was high above the ground, knew that one wrong step would send me plummeting down to the floor: I would be maimed or killed. Ast climbed with a firm tread, seeing in the dark like a cat. Presently, a stone passageway absorbed us, and there was faint, sepia light.

"Follow me."

We negotiated a maze of corridors. There were echoes all around us; the merest hint of cries and laughter, music and the bleating of animals. The air smelled strongly of a deep, earthy musk, enough to make me feel nauseous. It was a concentration of the perfume I had smelled upon Ast, when I had first met her in the Library. "Where are we going?" I asked her.

She laughed, and the sound seemed to come from far overhead. She slapped at my hands, so that I lost my grip on her floating veils. Then, she began to run from me. I tried to follow her, stumbling and tripping, but it was as if an invisible mesh of strings impeded my feet. Her form grew smaller before me, her blueness dimmed. I called her name, crashing from wall to wall in the narrow passage, but all sound was muffled. I groped my way along the wall, suddenly terrified, and eventually my scrabbling fingers found an open doorway. There was light within — blue light. I stood at the threshold and saw this had once been a library, but all the books were cast onto the floor, their spines broken, their pages scattered. Blue candles, with sapphire flames, dripped molten wax onto the ravaged books. I seemed to hear voices coming from the open pages: quatrains being recited, but faintly, without hope, fading out. Knowledge lost, destroyed. I went into the room and bent to pick up one of the volumes. The smell of hot wax was overpowering.

Something fast and heavy knocked me to the floor. All that happened afterward occurred so quickly, that even for a dream, it is difficult to recall.

I remember the blueness, the floating blue, the ferocity of the attack, the strength I could not resist. Why, in the dream, I transformed Ast in that way, I cannot say, but maybe it wasn't of her I dreamed. There was lust, yes, but not mine. It hurt me. It hurt me terribly, but like the mating of animals it was swift, a quick brutal reflex, and I escaped, half naked, screaming and running, hitting out at things that were no longer there, the pages of violated books swirling round my head. The nightmare carried me down endless stone passageways, and always I feared pursuit. Then I was spilled, like a barrel of bones and loose flesh, into a brightly lit room. Lurching to my feet, I recognized the sarcophagus of Mipacanthus. Whether I sought sanctuary or spiritual comfort, I cannot say, but I threw myself across the tomb. However, there was no crystal plate to arrest my fall. I landed in flowers, thick, fleshy flowers that exuded a hideous sickly perfume. I fought with the petals, gasping for breath, and found the body of the dead prophet beneath my hands. Then I was upright, gazing down in shuddering, mindless rigor at what lay there.

It was Mipacanthus.

It was she.

Ast, naked in the flowers, her eyes closed, her perfect breasts rising and falling as if in light sleep. A beautiful woman, yet not. Hers was the body of Mipacanthus. She was male. Below the slight torso, the tiny waist, were the hips and loins of a youth. The hands, too. I should have realized about the hands.

She opened her perfect black eyes, those gutting eyes. For the last time, she impaled me. Her face was pale as marble, her lips a livid wound. "The tomb is flesh," she told me. "You ran from me, Alexi, and in running, you changed your own future. There is no end, for I am eternal. Hear my prophecy now. We shall meet again. I have seeded you, Alexi. Through the children of your children, I will come back to you. For that is the way. It has always been so."

And there it ended, or nearly so. Dream fragments of flight through the sleeping city, the laughter of writhing stone carvings, the leaning colossi of the buildings threatening to topple, to engulf me in ashes, in petals.

That was all.

Now, the memory of the last few days I spent in Charidotis is blurred. I am sure that very little happened, and I cannot even remember the homeward journey. None of it. Strange how certain recollections stay with us through the years.

I have met no blue woman since. And yet, all these years, Ast has been with me. It has not been a lone vigil for me. There have been other women, true and ordinary women, women who cheered my heart and quickened my flesh. I loved, I married, and I lost to age and death. Ast, as she told me, is eternal. I try to remember her as she was in her darkened room, not as the violating monster of my nightmares. And yet, there must have been at least some truth in the dream. Perhaps I should not have run from her, even though I knew the fact of it, the knowledge that spawned the malformed image of the dream. All was magical in the haze of youth. I tell myself she was a freakish creature, but, oh, so lovely. Would it have harmed a boy to have touched her, to have tasted that experience?

The night is long, and I have been waiting here, as I have waited every time, for the birth. This will be my sixth daughter's seventh child. Time passes so swiftly in the winter of our lives. I am not long for this world now, but still I await Ast's prophecy. I am a stupid old man, for I think of it still. She will come back to me. I know it was nothing but a dream, yet it haunts me, becomes more vivid as my mind and body wither. I find myself wondering whether I carry it within me, a secret seed, an infection, but then I fight it with denial. If it were to happen, it surely would have done so by now.

There, now, I can hear them: the screams of the girl in labor. It will be soon. How many births have I attended in my life? Too many. We are a fecund family. She screams so long, so desperately. It is always so with women. I pity them for their beds of blood and birth. Can one woman make so much noise? It is like a song, a hymn of terror. Poor creature.

A plait of sounds, of voices, floating out over the river. Burning dead, the ashes swept into the water.

The dawn is coming.

I never went back to Charidotis, though I thought of it often. Now it is too late.

Too much noise for one woman. They are all screaming! The midwives, the priestesses. What is that? I can hear the pounding of feet along the passageway outside my room. I hear a man's voice, calling hoarsely.

There is a wall between myself and the door. I cannot pass through it, yet I must. On the table beside me, three candles burn in silver cups. My eyes are dim, but I can see them flicker. The flames are blue.

She comes, then, a restless spirit, to her resting place, a new, sweet sarcophagus of flesh.

BIOGRAPHIES

P
E
T
E
R

C
R
O
W
T
H
E
R

Editor of the World Fantasy Award-nominated *Narrow Houses* anthology series for Little, Brown UK, Peter is coeditor of *Heaven Sent* (forthcoming from DAW Books) and *Dante's Disciples* (forthcoming from White Wolf Publishing). His short stories, articles and reviews appear regularly on both sides of the Atlantic. Pete lives in Harrogate, England with his wife and two sons, and works as communications manager for one of the country's biggest financial organizations.

E
D
W
A
R
D

E

K
R
A
M
E
R

Ed Kramer has edited over a dozen original anthologies, including White Wolf's *Dark Destiny, Elric: Tales of the White Wolf, Pawn of Chaos: Tales of the Eternal Champion* and the forthcoming *Dante's Disciples* (with Peter Crowther). Ed's short stories appear in a growing number of collections as well. His credits include over a decade of work as a music critic and photojournalist. He is fond of human skulls, exotic snakes, and underground caverns. A graduate of the Emory University School of Medicine, Ed is a clinical and educational consultant in Atlanta.

T
O
M
B
S

F
O
R
R
E
S
T

J

A
C
K
E
R
M
A
N

celebrates his 78th birthday and 68th year in the Fantascience field and is still going strong. Forry is the editor of *Forrest J Ackerman's Famous Monsters of Filmland* and *Forrest J Ackerman's Wonderama,* contributing editor of *Galaxy* magazine, the creator of sci-fi and filmonster-oriented gum card sets and imagimovie and scientifiction art calendars, and president of the Ackerman Literary Society. Forry's "Ack"-tivities include over fifty cameo film appearances, a spot as the television host of *Tales from the Ackermansion,* and an appearance on the second annual *Horror Hall of Fame* telecast; his renowned Ackermansion has been covered by James Coburn on the Discovery Channel.

M
I
C
H
A
E
L

B
I
S
H
O
P
S

short fiction, poetry, and essays have appeared in almost all the major fantasy and science fiction outlets. The winner of two Nebula Awards, he was honored for Best Novelette in 1981 ("The Quickening") and for Best Novel in 1982 (*No Enemy But Time*). He has also received a Rhysling Award for sf poetry ("For the Lady of a Physicist"), the Mythopoeic Fantasy Award for Best Novel of 1988 (*Unicorn Mountain*), and several other regional or specialty awards. His World War II baseball fantasy, *Brittle Innings,* has been purchased for a film by Fox.

T
O
M
B
S

LARRY BOND AND CHRIS CARLSON

designed the *Harpoon* and *Command At Sea* naval game systems. An ex-surface Navy officer in defense analysis, Larry is the author of *New York Times* best-selling novels *Red Phoenix, Cauldron, and Vortex,* and coauthor of *Red Storm Rising* with Tom Clancy. He has just finished another novel, which will be published in early 1996. Larry lives with his wife Jeanne and two daughters in Northern Virginia. Chris is an ex-nuclear submariner who now works as an intelligence analyst. He also lives in Northern Virginia with his wife, Katy, and their four children.

BEN BOVAS

work has appeared in all the major science fiction magazines, as well as science journals and periodicals as diverse as *Psychology Today, Modern Bride, The New York Times, Smithsonian, Penthouse,* and *The Wall Street Journal.* He is the author of more than seventy-five futuristic novels and nonfiction books dealing with space and high technology. Formerly president of the Science-fiction and Fantasy Writers of America and President Emeritus of the National Space Society, Ben is a frequent commentator on radio and television, and a popular lecturer. He has also served as an award-winning editor and as an executive in the aerospace industry.

TOMBS

G
A
R
Y

A
.
B
R
A
U
N
B
E
C
K

has published nearly fifty stories in both magazines and anthologies. His first book, *Things Left Behind*, a massive short story collection, will be published later this year by CD Publications. He lives in Columbus, Ohio, with his wife, Lisa, and two cats to which he is allergic but toward which he nonetheless feels a great fondness.

W
I
L
L
I
A
M

F
.

B
U
C
K
L
E
Y

J
R.

is the founder of *National Review*, host of the weekly television show *Firing Line*, a syndicated newspaper columnist, and the author of popular books on subjects ranging from politics to yachting. In recent years, he has attracted a following for his ten spy novels about the dashing Blackford Oakes. He is the most famous conservative in America over the past four decades, one-time mayoral candidate for New York City, and a longtime friend of Ronald Reagan. "The Temptation of Wilfred Malachey" is his one work of fantasy.

STORM CONSTANTINES

first published work was the Wraeththu Trilogy (*Enchantments of Flesh and Spirit, Bewitchments of Love and Hate, Fulfillments of Fate and Desire*). She has since written another six novels and numerous short stories which have appeared in anthologies and magazines in the US and UK. Storm also manages the rock band Empyrean and works with other bands in a creative capacity.

NANCY A COLLINS

is the author of the contemporary horror novels *Wild Blood*, *Tempter*, and *Sunglasses After Dark*. She has worked extensively in comics, predominantly for DC/Vertigo with *Swamp Thing* (1991-1993) and *Wick* (1994). She is a winner of the Bram Stoker and British Fantasy Awards for short fiction and has appeared in such venues as *Year's Best Fantasy and Horror* and *Best New Horror*. Born in rural Arkansas, she now lives in New York City with her husband, underground filmmaker and antiartiste Joe Christ. Nancy's *Midnight Blue: The Sonja Blue Collection*, recently released in omnibus form by White Wolf, includes the never-before-published novel *Paint It Black*..

TOMBS

C
H
A
R
L
E
S

D
E

L
I
N
T
S

name is a byword for high-quality tales of urban fantasy. His novels *Moonheart,*
Greenmantle and *The Little Country*, unsurpassed in the field, are supplemented
by an equally intoxicating series of short stories (many of which are collected
in *Dreams Underfoot*) set in and around the fictional world of Newford.

J
E
R
E
M
Y

D
Y
S
O
N

has earned a living as a musician, magician, film publicist, and bookseller.
His first published story appears in *The Blue Motel: Narrow Houses 3*, and his
book *Bright Darkness: The Fifty Greatest Horror Films* is due for publication in
the UK in 1996. He shares a flat in Leeds with his girlfriend Harriet and a
collection of Aurora glow-in-the-dark Monster kits.

T
O
M
B
S

CHRISTOPHER FOWLER

works in London, where he runs a film production and promotion company. A workaholic short story writer (his first love), Fowler already has three collections to his credit, plus his "London Quartet" of novels (*Roofworld, Rune, Red Bride,* and *Darkest Day*) and *Spanky*, a heady mix of Thorne-Smith-meets-Faust which reaches new heights of terror.

NEIL GAIMAN

was born November 10, 1960. He has worked as a journalist for a number of UK periodicals and newspapers. His graphic novels include *Violent Cases, Black Orchid* and *Sandman* (winner of the 1991 World Fantasy Award as Best Short Story). With Terry Pratchett, Neil coauthored *Good Omens*, a funny novel about the end of the world and how we're all going to die. He's currently working on lots of things, including a fantasy TV series for the BBC, and currently resides in Minneapolis.

TOMBS

STEPHEN GALLAGHER

made his first professional sale in 1978 and turned full-time in 1980. Since then he has produced a stream of stories, essays and articles, and has had work adapted for radio and television. His novels *Ocktober, Rain, Down River*, the highly praised *Valley of Lights* and the forthcoming *Red Red Robin* continue to be high points of horror and dark suspense.

KATHLEEN ANN GOONAN

has spent the past few years selling a steady stream of exceptional short stories to, among others, *Asimov's, Interzone, Tomorrow, Pulphouse, Amazing,* and *F&SF*. Her long-awaited debut novel, *Queen City Jazz*, an intoxicating blend of hard science and nostalgic travelogue, is currently receiving plaudits from all sectors. She lives in Lakeland, Florida.

COLIN GREENLAND

won all three U.K. science fiction awards in 1990 for *Take Back Plenty*. His other works include *Death Is No Obstacle*, a book-length interview with Michael Moorcock; *Harm's Way*, a Victorian space opera; the first two volumes of the Tabitha Jute trilogy, *Take Back Plenty* and *Seasons of Plenty*; and a graphic novel with Dave McKean, to be called *Tempesta*.

KATHE KOJA AND   BARRY N MALZBERGS

collaborative work appears in a variety of anthologies and magazines. Barry has written over eighty novels (including *Beyond Apollo* and *Galaxies*) and numerous short stories. Kathe's novels include *Cipher*, *Bad Brains*, *Skin*, and *Strange Angels*; her short fiction appears in many anthologies as well.

TOMBS

BRAD LINAWEAVER

is best known for his novel *Moon of Ice* (Tor Books), which won the Prometheus Award in 1989 and, as a novella, was a Nebula finalist. His short stories have appeared in over two dozen anthologies, including *Dark Destiny* and *Elric: Tales of the White Wolf*. He has worked in radio and film, coedited *Weird Menace* with Fred Olen Ray and *Free Space* (forthcoming from Tor Books) with Edward E. Kramer, and is collaborating with Dafydd ab Hugh on two novels for Pocket Books.

IAN McDONALD

found his literary feet with his first novel, the masterful *Desolation Road*, and then went on to even greater things with a fascinating three-part novel of the world of Faery (*King of Morning, Queen of Day*) and *Necroville*. He lives in Belfast, Northern Ireland, with his wife, Trish, in a house built in the gardens of the home where C.S. Lewis grew up.

TOMBS

MICHAEL MOORCOCK

has published over one hundred books to date and has received the Nebula, World Fantasy and John W. Campbell Awards. His Eternal Champion mythos comprises an influential portion of fantasy and sword-and-sorcery fiction. Michael has toured as a musician with England's Hawkwind and his own band The Deep Fix, composed music for Blue Öyster Cult, written about the Sex Pistols, and spearheads lobbies against pornography and censorship. White Wolf, Michael's new American publisher, is reissuing his books — some for the first time in the US — in definitive omnibus editions.

S P SOMTOW

(Somtow Papinian Suchariktul) was born in Bangkok and grew up in Europe. His first novel, *Starship & Haiku*, won the Locus Award for best first novel; he won the 1981 John W. Campbell Award as well as the 1986 Daedalus for his novel *The Shattered Horse*. Somtow's other novels include *Vampire Junction*, *Moon Dance*, *Forgetting Places*, and *Vampire Junction*'s sequel, *Valentine*. His film projects include *The Laughing Dead* and *Ill Met By Moonlight*, a radical departure of Shakespeare's *A Midsummer Night's Dream*.

TOMBS

LISA TUTTLE is the author of *Gabriel* (1987) and *Lost Futures* (1992) as well as three collections of short stories. She lives, like the characters in her story, on the edge of the Agaglachach Forest in Scotland, and less than a mile from her house is an ancient cairn known as the Giant's Grave.

IAN WATSON has been writing science fiction, fantasy, and horror full-time since 1976. His eighth story collection, *The Coming of Vertumnus*, appeared in Britain in 1994 from Gollancz, who also published his recent two-volume extraterrestrial epic *Mana*. Ian's interest in amber began when a Lithuanian publisher, lacking hard currency, offered to translate a story collection for a bag of amber beads.

S
T
E
W
A
R
T

V
O
N

A
L
L
M
E
N

In less than a year, Stewart von Allmen has gotten engaged, married a crazy but perfect woman, moved into a new house, published two other short stories which appeared in White Wolf's *Tales of the White Wolf* and *Dark Destiny*, and written a first novel, *Conspicuous Consumption* , to be published by HarperPrism in August 1995. He hopes every year of his life is so harried and fruitful.